Lantern
of
the Wicked

Lantern
of
the Wicked

Charles Clement

FLETCHER & CO.
PUBLISHERS
Every book is a journey

Fletcher & Co. Publishers
www.fletcherpublishers.com

ISBN-10: 0-6154-8425-5
ISBN-13: 978-0-615-48425-9
Library of Congress Catalog Number 2011929493

Fletcher & Co. Publishers LLC
www.fletcherpublishers.com

Interior design & typesetting: Michael Aytchman
Cover design: Karl Jerome.
Photo: street view at night in Shanghai, courtesy of the Library of Congress, LC-USZ62-80214.

Publisher's Cataloging-in-Publication Data

Clement, Charles.
    Lantern of the Wicked / Charles Clement
    p. cm.
    ISBN 978-0-615-48425-9
1. Shanghai (China)—Fiction. 2. Shanghai (China)—History–20th century—Fiction. 3. China—History—1928-1937—Fiction. 4. Detective and mystery stories. 5. Historical Fiction. I. Title

PS3553.L3931 L3 2011
[Fic]   2011929493

First Edition
Printed in the United States of America

To Ming...

About the Author

CHARLES CLEMENT
is a former foreign correspondent in Asia who enjoyed many memorable
adventures in Shanghai—including several lively evenings in the
Seamen's Club, a long-faded remnant of The Shanghai Club that only
boasts but a small section of the once noteworthy Long Bar.

Contents

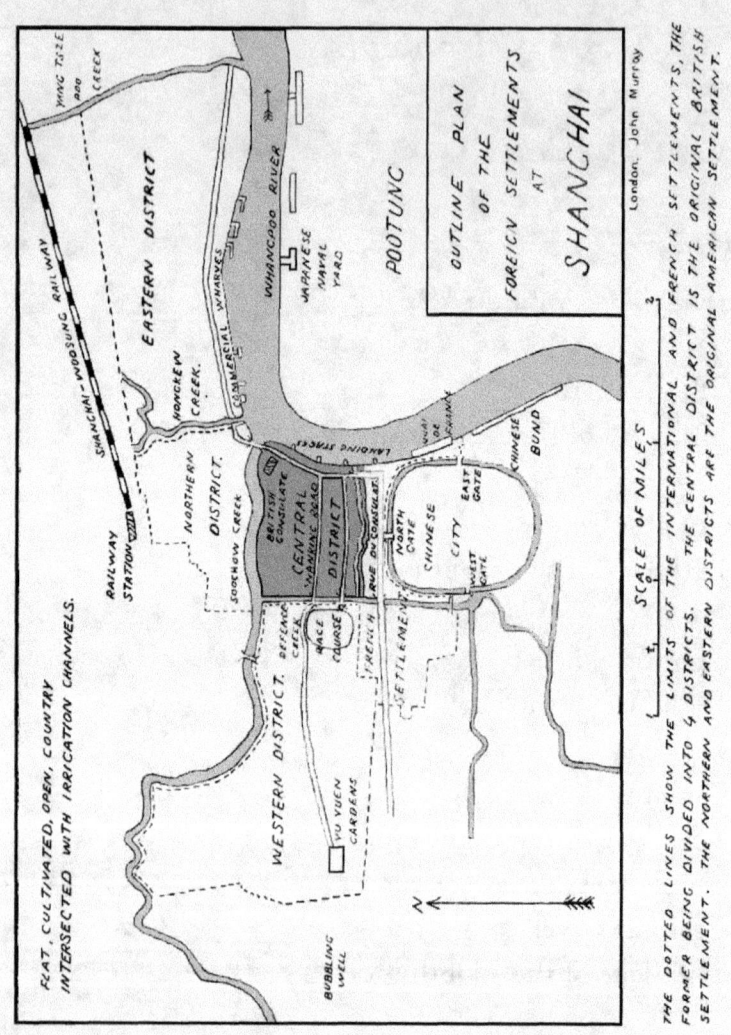

Foreign Settlements in Shanghai, courtesy of the University of Texas Libraries, The University of Texas at Austin [Colonel A. M. Murray, *Imperial Outposts, from a Strategical and Commercial Aspect, with Special Reference to the Japanese Alliance,* (London: John Murray, 1907)].

Note to the Reader

The people you are about to meet are characters who live in 1929 in a world recreated from facts about Shanghai—from the streets they traveled, to the ingredients used in an elixir of immortality, the burial waters found beneath funeral piers, and the White Russian newspapers they read. Also included are details about Chinese mythology and Taoism.

As a former newspaper reporter in Asia, I traveled to Shanghai numerous times and heard many tales from those who lived there long ago. While the photographs in no way represent any characters within this tale, they are intended solely to be windows to the past. My aim through historical research combined with fiction is to take you back in time so you can experience life as it was back then in the decadent and appalling Pearl of the Orient.

24 Hours in a
Chinese Duodenary Time Cycle

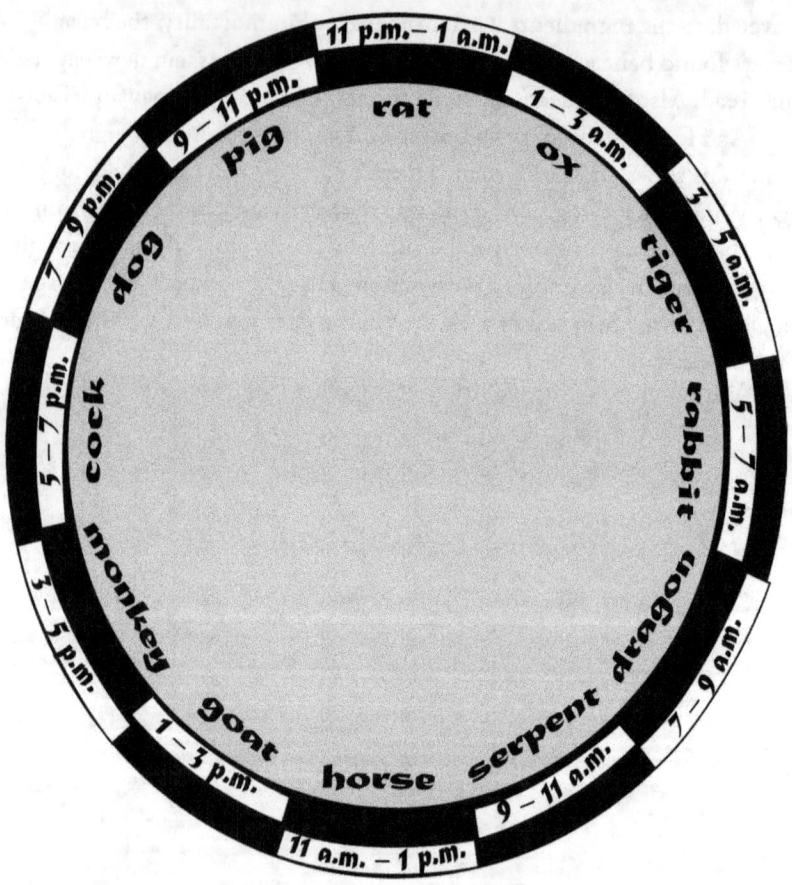

An ancient Chinese manner of tracking time in two-hour cycles, each assigned to the cosmic animal who influences that particular time period.

Prologue: Shanghai – Autumn 1929

An invisible battle of spirits waged above this great Chinese seaport where 180 million souls fought for their salvation. Lust, anger, pride, covetousness, gluttony, sloth, and envy were so pronounced among the people of Shanghai that it seemed as if mankind was abandoned unto itself. The stench of death clouded the air. Evils abounded through gambling, prostitution, opium addiction, slavery, greed, drunkenness, licentiousness, and murder. Most everyone living here along the Whangpoo River was enslaved to pleasure.

They eagerly awaited the Mid-Autumn Moon Festival in honor of T'ai Yin Hsing Chŭ, the beautiful Goddess of the Moon, also known as Chang E. Her fame dated back to Emperor Yao's reign in 2000 B.C.

According to legend, Chang-E was drawn one day to a soft light emitting from a sweetly scented pill of immortality, which her husband, the miraculous archer Hou Yi, had hidden in their house. Chang-E swallowed the forbidden pill. Realizing she could fly and fearing her husband, she soared out of the window. Her husband discovered her treachery and chased her across the sky while shooting magic arrows at her. Once safe on the Moon, Chang-E, out of breath, spat out the pill, which transformed into a jade rabbit. At that instant, Chang-E turned into a three-legged toad—and has lived on the Moon ever since. From his palace on the Sun, her husband continues to fire magic flaming arrows at her on the 15th of every month.

The clock was ticking. Every 120 minutes ushered in another hour in Chinese duodenary time. Soon Chang E would appear for the Mid-Autumn Moon Festival upon the arrival of the Eighth Moon. To win her favor, Shanghai's rich and poor alike planned to worship the Moon Goddess to make nocturnal offerings to her under the glow of the full moon.

Few, however, realized that in Heaven and on Earth, the cup of justice overflowed.

The Shanghai Club (left) and the Canadian Pacific Ocean Services Ltd. building.

CHAPTER ONE

12th Day of the Eighth Moon

Beyond the Old Walled City in central Shanghai, London-born Roddy Erskine trotted next to an older man along an outdoor corridor of the Shanghai Municipal Police Station, headquarters of Special Branch, the most elite of the city's plentiful multinational law enforcement operations in both the French Concession and the International Settlement. Only a handful of detectives lingered. In starched white or beige linen suits, they blended with columns studding the Neo-Greco building at 185 Foochow Road. Some smoked cigarettes on the wide veranda. Some stood beneath the shade under Chinese parasol trees. Most cooled themselves off with their hats, or palm-leaf fans. A late afternoon breeze drifted over from the Whangpoo River and transported a foul odor permeating even the best sections of Shanghai.

"Righto!" Roddy Erskine blurted.

"What are you blathering about?" grunted Chief Inspector Haymes.

"Nothing, sir. Nothing at all. I was thinking aloud. Sorry." Roddy blushed. "Guv, I've heard that American chap is box clever. No matter though, you can count on me to do my part. Of that, you can be sure! It'll be just as you've planned."

Chief Inspector Haymes grumbled.

Descending stairs, they made their way across a parking lot to a black Duesenberg sedan. Haymes walked in silence. His opal-blue eyes turned to the pavement. Gray streaks cut through his thick black hair. The "old Bulldog" was legendary among both Shanghai's rubber heels and crooks. Criminals feared his intuition. Detectives marveled at his ability to solve seemingly impossible cases. Bored by triad crimes, he preferred espionage, and this one case would do nicely. He liked keeping tabs on the Japanese because he didn't trust their military in China's important coastal ports. How would he manage, though, being forced to take on young Erskine? What did the Consul General know about General Togawa, the Black Eel from Osaka? Why, this lad was fresh-off-the-boat, family connections or not! Haymes motioned to a plainclothes police driver, leaning against the Duesenberg, with one leg hoisted rakishly on the running board. The

The so-called "king" of a beggar's guild in Loong Wah near Shanghai.

driver jumped to open the doors. Roddy slid in beside the Inspector. The driver, jumping behind the wheel, tilted the brim of his white straw fedora until it rested on the back on his head. "Evening, sir. Where to?"

"Nanking Road. The Saints & Sinners Club."

The Duesenberg swung around the parking lot and crawled past an iron gate. Sikh police officers from the Punjab stepped aside, allowing it to pass. Their Webley revolvers, in polished leather holsters, were slung over khaki uniforms. They clicked the heels of their riding boots, raised hands to their red turbans, and saluted.

Soon the sedan skimmed along the International Settlement's broad boulevards shielded from the sun by poplar and sycamore trees. Twin, postcard-sized Union Jack flags rippled from hood mounts. As much part of the landscape as the stone lions guarding entrances to the estates of European and American *taipan* millionaires, beggars staked their turf on shaded sidewalks bordered by high brick walls topped with broken glass. As the Duesenberg passed, they leaned forward on their ragged mats and newspapers to shake empty tins of Three Castle Brand cigarettes at the passing car.

Roddy turned from the window. His freckled hands smoothed back tufts of his ginger-colored hair. "Guv, I'd like to learn the native language to get along better."

"Rubbish. If you learn to talk like them, you'll learn to think like them. We'll have none of that, lad. None of that!"

Frowning, Roddy settled into the leather upholstery. Somehow, he'd find a chance to prove himself.

Shards of afternoon light slipped through latticed windows in the bedchamber and beamed triangles on Pockmarked Fang. His narrow back slithered against the wide, square back of a red-lacquered throne carved with swirling clouds and five-clawed dragons. Skeletal fingers trembled inside the left sleeve of his Mandarin gown. Nail protectors of golden mesh scratched the blue silk inside the horseshoe-shaped cuff. His fingertips clicked against an ivory back-scratcher, curving round its handle. Emerging from the sleeve, the back-scratcher crashed against the throne.

"*Yen tsiang!*"

One-eyed Wong exhaled with relief. His fat belly contracted

underneath his long pink gown. Master wants a smoking pistol. Yes, several puffs of black earth from the smoking pistol will prepare him for the bad news. He'll be in better spirits when he learns we haven't captured Eggplant Ho of the Red Gang. Adjusting a Tommy gun slung round his shoulder, he turned to a lacquered table and grabbed an opium pipe.

"Kwai—kwai!"

"Of course, Master," said One-eyed Wong, lighting the pipe with a bamboo stick from a smoldering urn.

Pockmarked Fang shifted impatiently. It was 3 o'clock. He scowled as the opium took effect—tears formed, and his nose dripped. Like other opium ghosts, he slept by day, awoke in the afternoon, and came to life at night. He winced at the sunlight, cradled his shaved head in one hand, grasped the pipe in the other, and sucked in the smoke. Soon, his pulse slowed. Black satin slippers dropped from his feet onto a platform supporting the throne. A sweet, oily film covered his tongue. Skin tightened on his small oval face, cratered with scars from black smallpox contracted in childhood. Relaxing his grip on the pipe, he giggled at the burning sensation in his throat. His topaz-colored eyes clouded. He gazed at white wisps of smoke writhing to the ceiling. Closing his eyes, he felt himself floating upwards.

When the sallow hoods of his eyelids lifted, he dreamt he was enveloped in a Five-Colored Cloud known for its black, red, azure, white, and yellow fluffs. A magic cloud-sweeper fly whisk appeared in his right palm at the same time as a white celestial stork materialized at his side. Parting the skirt of his gown, Pockmarked Fang mounted the stork's back. He tapped it with the whisk's auburn monkey hairs. Immediately, the stork soared through the sky to the Three Heavens, or San Ch'ing, where the Three Pure Ones reign.

Ascending beyond the Third Heaven, he scanned its pillars, towers, and pavilions of white jade emanating from the clouds. The T'ai Ch'ing was governed by Shen Pao, Ruler of the Treasure of the Spirits and Educator of the Emperors.

Rising upwards to the second air forming the Shang Ch'ing, Pockmarked Fang dug his heels into the stork's sides, causing its wings to flap slower. The stork lowered its neck and headed for the Second Heaven. Pockmarked Fang grinned at the thought of meeting Ling-pao T'ien-tsun, Sovereign of the Symmetry between the Yin and Yang. Perhaps the

Illustrious Guardian of Sacred Books would permit him to learn the secrets of immortality. However, just as the stork neared the jasper gates of the Shang Ch'ing, a dark silhouette of a man on a black unicorn emerged from the Five-Colored Cloud. The shadowy figure on the unicorn darted across his path before bolting across the sky.

Pockmarked Fang nearly toppled off the stork. Narrowing his eyes, he clutched the stork's neck. "That son of a turtle!" Repeatedly digging his knees against the stork's saddle feathers, he cracked the magic fly whisk against the bird's head, urging it to pursue the man riding the *ch'i-lin*. The two men raced through the heavens with the shadowy figure on the unicorn in the lead. Both disappeared in and out of clouds. Nearing five red pillars towering before the boundaries of heaven, the man yanked the unicorn's gilt bit. Then, the dark figure spiraled upwards towards the air forming the First Heaven and vanished into a purple mist.

Seething, Pockmarked Fang charged after him and emerged from the purple mist at the Yü Ch'ing. Bringing the stork to a halt, he looked about and found himself alone. Turning his back to the red pillars, he frowned. Perhaps he should forget about the man on the unicorn and proceed to the Jade Mountain of the Yü Ch'ing, where the Jade Emperor, Yü Huang, presided as Supreme Origin of All Truth. Surely he would receive immortality and his name would be inscribed on the Register of 800 Taoist Divinities.

The stork seemed to read his mind. Wings outstretched, it flapped effortlessly, cutting a swath through the clouds to the Jade Mountain, which jutted from a mist-like jagged gemstone. The bird slowly climbed to a shimmering wall surrounding the Golden Door Palace on the mountaintop. Clusters of turrets, arches, and pavilions gleamed in amber sunlight. Pockmarked Fang dismounted outside a massive gate of reflective glass topped with peacock-feathered tiles. He hesitated. Suddenly, he heard a melodic tinkling similar to a musical pocket watch. The gate swung open.

No longer reluctant, Pockmarked Fang strode inside to a field containing Three-Colored Lotus Flowers, which paid homage to eternity. Blue petals indicated heaven, red denoted the sun, and white signified the moon. He plucked a flower. An incredibly sweet aroma exploded from the blossom. He let the fragrance fill his nostrils. Without warning, the hair rose on the back of his neck. He dropped the flower and spun around.

A band of four men with traditional Chinese instruments.

Seated behind him on the black unicorn was the same warrior who had caused Pockmarked Fang to lose face outside the Second Heaven. The man wore a suit of fish-scale armor joined with iron strips. A red tassel, affixed with a falcon feather, jutted from the top of the bronze fox-headed helmet concealing his face.

Pockmarked Fang glowered and spat.

The man jumped off. As he did, the skirt of his armor showed three copper symbols: one depicted two beasts resting back-to-back, signifying judgment; the other bore an axe portraying decisiveness; and the last showed algae, which represented cleanliness. The man slowly removed his fox-head helmet. It was Lei Tsu, God of Lightning and Great Ancestor of Thunder! His eyes sparkled wildly and blue-gray skin shone on his bald head. Pockmarked Fang gaped at a flashing third eye in forehead of Lei Tsu, the mighty Prince of the Laws Ruling Rain and Clouds. Stepping back, he frantically waved his arms. "Save life—save life! Oh, mighty Voice of Thunder, Celestial Regulator of the Universe, save life!"

The Celestial and Highly Honored Ruler of the Nine Orbits of the Heavens cocked his head sideways. A ray of light burst from his third eye. It cast a two-foot-long beam as Lei Tsu reached for a panther-skin bag slung around his saddle horn.

Pockmarked Fang, wailing at the sight of the magical pouch, kowtowed. He felt a sharp pain in his head. Yowling, he opened his eyes and found himself in Shanghai sprawled on the floor in his bedchamber. Blood trickled across his cheek.

One-eyed Wong rushed over. "Shall I send for medicine, Master?"

"No, prepare the Dragon-Tiger Elixir!" He scowled at the bad omen from Lei Tsu and screamed, "Music!"

Behind a gauze curtain across the room, musicians clashed gongs. Fiddles, mandolins, and lutes screeched the opening of a Monkey King ballad from the Peking opera, *"Havoc in Heaven."* Sandalwood incense spewed from two incense burners on pillars carved with jade dragons. Smoke swirled out from openings between the dragons' twisting bodies.

One-eyed Wong busied himself at a rosewood tea table. Pinching powder and shriveled flakes from a bronze tray, his pudgy fingers dropped bits of chrysanthemum petals, tree fungus, pomegranate seeds, ground pearls, wild peaches, and bat skin into a jade mortar. He retrieved a

Removing silk from reels for drying.

rhinoceros-horn scabbard from inside his sleeve. With a knife, he scraped pieces of rind from a *fuh-shao* orange, prized because its five stumps grew like fingers on Buddha's hand. After the orange rind, he added a splash of fermented rice wine called *shao-hsing chiu*. He mashed the mixture with a jade pestle and poured it into a bronze teapot's spout. A gold chain prevented would-be poisoners from tampering with the teapot's lid, which was clamped firmly in place.

Yawning, Pockmarked Fang slid the ivory backscratcher down the back of his gown. The top of his right ear had been bitten off during his youth hustling along Shanghai's opium wharves. One-eyed Wong handed over the teapot. Pockmarked Fang extended both hands. He admired the decorative turquoise bats for luck and *shou* characters for longevity adorning his three-inch-long nail protectors. Raising the spout to his quivering lips, he downed the Dragon-Tiger Elixir of Immortality.

"To my Master's long-eyebrowed longevity!" exclaimed One-eyed Wong. "May you live 1,000 years!"

Fiddles screeched as the ballad described how the Dragon King told the Emperor of Heaven about the Monkey King's theft of a rare metal. Pockmarked Fang belched. His mind turned to the insults he unknowingly had heaped on the Voice of Thunder. He wondered how to avoid retribution. Moments later, a thin smile appeared on his pitted face.

"Go buy 100 coffins, for the poor and take them to the funeral piers!"

Pockmarked Fang snickered with delight at his plan to earn transcendent merit. Glancing at the afternoon sun through the lattice window slats of his bedchamber, he thought such benevolence would make amends. Immortality remained within reach!

Jack "Ace" Jordan stopped chewing his chewing gum, adjusted his goggles and looked out the open cockpit's glass windscreen. His aeroplane sliced through clear azure sky at 400 feet. Its approaching drone incited muffled curses from peasants, tending mulberry trees in fields below, who kicked up dust while racing for thatched huts where infant silkworms, white and as fine as hair, slumbered in darkness. Hatched five days earlier, these infants had begun turning yellowish. According to superstition, loud noises interfered with their ability to produce silk.

Terraced fields.

The plane rose higher to prevent undue anxiety below. Ace was glad to see peasants along the Yangtze River's lower reaches who still cultivated mulberry trees and spun silk instead of growing opium poppies as peasants in most other provinces. Inside the cockpit, the wet compass bobbed in its white kerosene stabilizer, marking a northwesterly course to Shanghai some 20 minutes away. Ace stretched his neck muscles. Periodically, a farmer or water buffalo glanced up from muddy rice paddies forming checkerboard patterns between dry ground, wild sugarcane, or long grass.

Heat from the Autumn Tiger weather persisted after this unusually hot summer. Lugging ahead in the same northerly direction, a battered locomotive on the Hu-Han-Ying line sent puffs of black smoke and white steam from its engine. Seeing the white steam curling upwards over the dry earth, Ace's mind journeyed back, as it had so many times before, to June 13, 1917 when 14 German Gothas dropped bombs in their first daylight raid on London. Three weeks later, his dreams of military glory became reality when on July 3 he flew as a squadron leader in the new American Expeditionary Forces' first mission over France.

Shanghai approached. A few miles ahead appeared rolling hills surrounding the Dragon Flower Pagoda in Lunghwa. Its seven octagonal stories ascended gracefully from a Buddhist courtyard lined with cassia and plum trees. Ten minutes to go until landing at Hungjao Aerodrome.

Idina Soames *née* Erskine reclined against white satin pillows on a white brocaded divan. Gripping a cocktail in one hand, she clicked her fingernails against the crystal glass and studied Number Two Boy lighting pearl-like lanterns of white silk gauze from a wide moon doorway overlooking a veranda. He moved noiselessly from one lantern to the next, placing glowing candles inside. Sired at The Nine Orbits on Yates Road—a southwestern slice of the International Settlement that Americans nicknamed "Pants Alley" and the English called "Street of a Thousand Nighties"—Number Two Boy had been sold as an upstairs servant six months earlier to the Soames household. At that awkward age before manhood, his most prominent feature was a large Adam's apple protruding above the collar of his long black *p'ao-tzu* silk gown.

Idina lifted the glass to her red lips. She gulped murky liquor that matched her gray-green eyes. Across the room near her dressing table, a jeweled boudoir clock stood next to a vase of white chrysanthemums on a carved mahogany table. Her fingertips resumed the drum roll against the glass. The clock chimed.

"Boy, fetch me another absinthe cocktail," she slurred, tossing her head back. A curly, platinum strand from her bobbed mane fell across her forehead.

"Yes, *T'ai-t'ai.*"

"Kindly tell Number One Boy he put in *much, too much* water. The next one must have a dash more of bitters."

"Certainly, *T'ai-t'ai.*"

The door closed. Glass in hand, Idina teetered to the moon doorway and looked into the distance beyond a grass tennis court. From the villa's second floor, she searched the distance beyond the back wall. Open, rotting wooden coffins jutted from ancient burial mounds along the causeway of an abandoned canal. Concrete runways of the Hungjao Aerodrome cut through barren fields.

"Idina?" a man's voice called out. "Darling?"

"Yeow!" She spun around, dropping the cocktail glass, which shattered against the parquet floor.

"Maxwell!" Idina's red lips twisted. "You idiot!"

A partially bald, bespectacled man in a dove-gray suit entered her bedroom. He adjusted a polka-dot tie around the wing-tip collar of his white shirt. His build was slight. Despite custom-made, doeskin spats with two-inch heels, Maxwell stood a few inches shorter than Idina. He grimaced, puckering his small, full lips together as if he'd sucked a lemon. Hesitating, he held out a satin pouch embroidered with white cranes symbolizing longevity.

"Frightfully sorry, dear. Do forgive me," he pleaded, waving the pouch at her. "Here, darling, a little something for you. Fruit from my little partnership with the Japanese."

Idina's eyes darted to the object, while the corners of her mouth rose. She snatched the pouch and heaped herself down on the divan. Opening the pouch, she turned it upside-down and a 36-inch strand of pearls cascaded onto her lap. Each pearl was the size of a peony bud.

"Oh—my word!" Each syllable rose an octave. "Why Maxwell, I'm thrilled beyond belief." She stroked the necklace against her cheek.

Rubbing his hands together, Maxwell beamed. "So glad you approve, darling."

"I've never seen anything like these pearls. Their size is so extraordinary, so very immense!" she slurred. "Wherever did you get them?"

"Manchuria, actually." Maxwell cleared his throat. "They're called Dong-chow pearls."

Pushing a pair of round, gold-rimmed spectacles up the bridge of his nose, he began pacing.

"No doubt you're aware it would've been utterly impossible to obtain them 20 years ago during the Ch'ing Dynasty. Large pearls like those you hold were prized adornments for court necklaces, hairpins, and the like. As a matter of fact, it was forbidden under pain of death for anyone except the royal family to own Dong-chow pearls," he gloated. "Of course, my dear, times have changed for the better in China. I daresay that goes for us, too—thanks to the Black Eel!"

Number Two Boy rapped softly on the door before he entered. Looking downcast, he carried an absinthe cocktail on a silver tray. Ice tinkled against the glass.

"Boy, set my cocktail over there." Idina waved her hand at the carved mahogany table across the room. A mischievous smile emerged on her face. Turning a playful grin first at Number Two Boy and then at Maxwell, she purred, "Darling, shall I try the necklace on?"

"That'd be lovely, my dear." Maxwell dabbed his brow with a handkerchief.

Idina unsteadily arose and started to untie the sash around her dressing gown.

Number Two Boy's tray clanged to the floor.

"Idina! Have you lost hold of your senses?" Maxwell rushed and shook her by the shoulders. "Boy, leave this room at once! Madame is unwell."

The youth's black silk robe swished as he raced out.

"I will not have this, Idina! The Black Eel will not stand for any hint of scandal. We can't afford to have word of this get out. We must get rid of that boy straight away."

Nanking Road in Shanghai.

Idina sauntered to the mahogany table, kicking the fallen tray from her path. "Don't be absurd! Who cares about those beastly servants?"

"Idina, one day you'll go too far!" Maxwell jabbed his finger at her. "Too far, even for me—you mark my words. Now stop drinking that blasted concoction!"

She faced him. "Say? You're a fine one putting on airs. I bet those pearls are paste. You haven't been to Manchuria for some time. No one has. Why just the other day, the Consul General's wife said people are still evacuating from Mukden and Dairen. She says warlord Young Marshal Chang, the Reds, and the Japanese are causing all the trouble. Do tell, are those pearls phony like you?"

Ignoring her, Maxwell remained silent as he looked out at the sunset from the veranda. His thoughts were on the Japanese.

Staring out the car window, Roddy Erskine and Chief Inspector Haymes sat in silence. Nightfall encroached. The Duesenberg turned left on Nanking Road into an onslaught of automobiles, pedicabs, streetcars, rickshaws, and bicycles all jockeying for position. Nanking Road, called Dao Ma Lu (Big Horse Road) by the Shanghainese, cut through the heart of the city's shopping and nightclub districts. The busiest reputable establishment was Canton Department Store, popular for its imported Russian furs, French lingerie, Victrola gramophones, American wireless radios, Baby Ruth candy bars, and Lucky Strike cigarettes. The sedan traveled west past the Golf Club in the Recreation Ground opposite the Foreign Y.M.C.A.

From nowhere, a Chinese man in his 20s, clad in a gray Mandarin gown, rushed blindly into the street. He clutched a bundle of newspapers close to his chest. The sedan jolted as its tires screeched to a stop. *Thump!* The man's black skullcap flew off as he bounced onto the sedan's hood, flew backwards, and slammed into a hawker's booth. Bamboo, newspapers, and Moon Festival rabbit lanterns scattered.

Roddy, Haymes, and the driver looked out of their windows. Curious Shanghainese swarmed around the Duesenberg and the body on the sidewalk. A whistle shrilled as a band of nationalist Kuo-min Tang officers, who had apparently been chasing the youth, burst onto the scene.

Protesters amid a crowd.

"Oh, blast it!" the driver exclaimed. "That 'Young John Chinaman' has gone off and dented our motorcar!"

"Never mind the flipping car!" Haymes answered. "Let's not hang about all day. Go clear it up and be quick about it."

The driver climbed out of the sedan and approached the Kuo-min Tang officers. Large safety pins held insignia patches, attesting to rank, fastened onto the cotton sleeves of their dark indigo uniforms. They spoke briefly. Then the senior KMT officer blew his whistle, while the soldiers beat back onlookers with truncheons allowing Special Branch to leave.

Taking up the wheel again, the driver spoke excitedly. "Another Red spy. This one was hiding out as a librarian. The KMT Blue Shirts were onto him, though. They caught him before he could hand out that Red newspaper."

"The *Shanghai Pao?*" Roddy asked. "I thought we'd seen the last of that! You'd think the Reds would've gotten the message after the Blue Shirts raided the King Tong Printing Press a fortnight ago."

The driver replied, "Especially since the Blue Shirts beheaded the owner and his workers. My cook saw it all—said some of the heads were stuck on spikes and left in the Old Walled City's square, their heads went into birdcages hung up on tree branches. Why, one bloke's head still had its spectacles on. Can you believe that?"

Chief Inspector Haymes reached over and swatted the driver's straw fedora. "Get on with it, man!" He turned to Roddy. "Laddie, in case you haven't realized it by now, the Reds have infiltrated every layer of Shanghainese society. But Special Branch doesn't trifle with what the KMT do with their own. Is that clear?"

"Yes, sir, very clear, sir."

"There's one more thing we may as well clear up straight away. Like it or not, I'm being forced to accept your hand in this case for two reasons. First off, your brother-in-law Maxwell Soames is a valued member of our community and esteemed by the Consul General. Secondly, you've got an inside track at the Asian Aviation Corps, where we believe a spy is operating. However, if you muck up this espionage case, you'll find yourself setting off for Mongolia on a camel!"

Roddy flushed to the roots of his ginger-colored hair and looked at his wristwatch.

No trace of the suspect yet. The Duesenberg remained parked outside a two-story, gray stone building.

"Shall we give it a miss until tomorrow, sir?" Roddy asked, yawning and stretching his legs.

"No. It can't wait. I would've preferred having a nice, quiet little chat with him out here instead of inside that Club, but he's late."

"You can say that again mate," the driver blurted.

"As I was about to say," said Haymes, glowering at the driver, "as much as I detest these Yanks and their blasted club, I've a mind for a whiskey and soda. Come along, Erskine, let's wait inside."

Before they lifted the door handles, the driver turned to them. "Are you sure, Guv? Those Yanks don't take kindly to Special Branch bluebottles nosing around in their pubs. Remember when Detective Ashcroft came here."

"Nonsense! They wouldn't dare chuck me out."

"I'm game if you are, sir," Roddy opened the door. "I've always wanted to have a look inside. It's got quite a sordid reputation you know?"

They took their place in line among young men and women. Roddy felt self-conscious about wearing his daytime linen suit, but Haymes waited without a care. Above the entrance, a red neon sign cast scarlet hues on the people below. It beckoned:

Come Early, Stay Late!
The Saints & Sinners Club

The emblem on the doorman's red, double-breasted silk uniform was an embroidered, elliptic gold halo encircling a black pitchfork's prongs. Tipping his gold cap, trimmed with a wide black band, he frowned in disapproval at Special Branch as he opened white entrance doors oval-shaped like the moon and painted with a mist of ethereal clouds. Haymes strode in first. His shoes sunk into a wall-to-wall red carpet decorated with a halo and pitchfork motif. Strategically placed, soft gold lights illuminated the foyer with its mirrored walls, potted palm trees, chrome ashtrays, and glass tabletops as the two men checked in their hats.

Roddy admired a cigarette girl, wearing a skin-tight, backless, metallic gold gown. A Clara Bow look-alike, she leaned against the wall next to the entrance of a large dining room and tapped her toes in time with saucy trombone bursts issuing from around the corner. Most men wore formal black tailcoats and pants, while the women slunk around in long, clinging evening dresses.

The maître d, Bunny Vance, immediately noticed Special Branch. His fingers swept through brown hair that shone with brilliantine, and he began twisting one edge of his pencil-thin moustache while watching the Chief Inspector and his protégé shoulder their way towards him.

"My, my, my," Bunny said. "If it ain't the old Bulldog in the flesh— Chief Inspector Haymes. A real treat to see you boys here. We don't get many stuffed shirts, excuse me, English gents at our jazz parlor. Are you dining tonight, muscling in to nab Mr. Big, or did you come to see for yourself how us Yanks keep a joint jumping?"

Haymes turned to Roddy. "Quite a disappointing impersonation of a speakeasy thug. Not sinister or nasty enough. Perhaps the young wretch has finished play-acting and will show us to a table."

"My pleasure," Bunny quipped, grabbing two menus and marching into the dining room. Fanning away wafts of cigarette smoke with the menus, he led them to a center table facing a bandshell where a drummer pounded out a solo.

"Here, take a load off your dogs." He slapped the menus on the table. "Take your pick of the eats."

After showing Haymes to a chrome chair, Bunny looked over the junior detective. Shaking his head in disapproval and clicking his tongue, he pointed to a chair for Roddy, whose face flushed.

"Two whiskey and sodas. Make them Irish. We'll give it a miss on your so-called eats," said Haymes, scooping up the menus and jabbing them into Bunny's stomach.

Bunny grabbed the menus and bent down to the Chief Inspector's ear. "Listen, you. We don't want no monkey business around here. You don't have no pals here, see? So, watch your step."

Chief Inspector Haymes seized Bunny's moustache and pulled it close enough for a kiss before releasing it.

Bunny winced. His spine stiffened and he straightened his lapels. Rubbing the corner of his moustache, he tucked the menus under one arm and did an about-face before gliding over to a Chinese waiter, interrupting the latter's flirting session with the Clara Bow cigarette girl.

The detectives sat quietly in contrast to clattering plates, outbursts of laughter, and a monotonous drone of conversations. They scanned the crowd. People packed the tables that curved around the dance floor. On the other side, the white bandshell was adorned with moon and cloud cut-outs. Several minutes passed before a Chinese waiter brought the drinks. Lights dimmed. Twelve Black musicians gripped their instruments. Red cigarette tips glowed in semi-darkness. Conversations muted.

A spotlight blared on a grinning emcee, who strutted to a microphone in front of the bandshell. His white coat and tails glowed under the harsh glaring light.

"Folks, have we've got a real treat in store for you tonight!" The emcee waved his left hand at the jazz band. "Straight from Harlem. Let me introduce to you: Sweets Floyd and His Blue Troubadours!"

The band ripped open with saucy instrumental jazz number.

Haymes winced at the music, but kept his eyes on the crowd.

Roddy sipped his drink and toyed with a cloth napkin. His foot tapped to the rhythm. "Guv, I realize it's a bit dark in here, but I don't see him anywhere. Maybe he won't show up at all."

Haymes watched couples dancing the Charleston while searching the faces of the men. "He'll be here. It's only a matter of time. Watch the bartender over in the corner. That's Chicago Charlie, a two-bit peddler of opium pills. Sells them to hotels for room service. He and our man are great chums."

At the bar, Chicago leaned over the counter and talked to a party of three men and a woman seated in chrome chairs. He had a beaked nose, a thin frame, and wiry blond hair slicked back with a center part. Fetching three liquor bottles from a middle row along a back wall, he began to make an Angel Face cocktail of apricot brandy, gin, and Calvados. He poured one-third of a jigger from each bottle into a silver cocktail shaker. His body shimmied in time with the music. Bouncing the shaker against his hipbone, he blended the mixture in the shaker before stopping to strain the liquid into a cocktail glass.

The emcee took to the microphone again.

"Now, for the next number! One of my favorites. A real foot-stomper called, *'You're the Cat's Pajamas.'*"

The bandmaster waved his baton, and a Black tenor from Harlem launched into a melody in cut time.

The Chief Inspector cleared his throat. "This is it, Erskine. He's finally come round. Look to the back—on the right. He's behind the bandshell now. Most likely going to meet his friend at the bar."

A horn section piped in as the tenor's voice rose to a higher pitch. Ignoring the music, Haymes began to grin in heightened anticipation. The lights snapped on, and the audience applauded wildly. Some yelled, "Get hot, get hot!"

"Call a waiter, lad," said Chief Inspector Haymes, politely clapping. "We'll order ourselves another drink, and while we're at it, we shall buy one for our Mr. Jack Jordan, or, Ace, as he's known."

"Righto, Guv!" Roddy waved to a waiter clearing dinner plates at the next table.

The waiter's sandy-colored hair, dark Chinese eyes, wide nose, and full lips spoke of his mixed heritage. He sauntered over.

"Yeah?" the Eurasian waiter asked, in an American accent. "What can I do for yuh?"

Roddy pointed toward the bar. "Do you see that tall chap with dark hair standing behind the bar with his back to us? He's wearing a black waistcoat and trousers."

The waiter perused the bar and shrugged his shoulders. "No such luck. I can't make him out. Now, what'll it be? Do yuh want some more hooch?"

"Two whiskey sodas. Now kindly turn your attention back to the bar, please." Roddy pointed again. "Now, that tall chap over there..."

"Cripes," the waiter answered. "Just look around, will yuh? This joint is full of dark-haired fellas in monkey suits."

"The gentleman we're referring to is a tall, black-haired man standing in the middle," Chief Inspector Haymes bellowed. "To the left of that young woman with a red-flowered corsage on her shoulder. Please be good enough to fetch our drinks and, while you're at it, go buy one for our man over there. Put it on our check. Now, be off with you."

The waiter glared and made a beeline for the bar, where he tapped

Jack Jordan on the shoulder. Ace turned, spoke to the waiter, and nodded. His eyes traveled across the room to Roddy and Chief Inspector Haymes. Roddy waved. Ace started to walk to the two detectives when Bunny Vance strode through the crowd and blocked his path, refusing to budge.

"Say, what gives, Ace? On the level, are you in a jam? Why is the heat on? Why do you have the coppers on your neck?"

"Hey pal, what's the big idea? What are you squawking about?" Ace patted Bunny on the shoulder and laughed. "Keep your shirt on."

"There's something going on, pal. Something big by the looks of it!" Bunny cast a furtive glance at the detectives. "You know as well as I do that those two monkeys don't belong here!"

"So what? Ease up, old pal. Maybe they're having a night on the town," Ace chuckled. "Besides, I know the redheaded kid. He's square. I work for his brother-in-law. The other one stumps me, though. I've never seen him before. Anyway, they just bought me a drink."

Bunny moved in close. Ace detected the smell of his brilliantine perfumed hair.

"Honest to goodness Ace! Are you nuts? That old mug is a real big noise. Why, he's the granddaddy of all the flatfoots in Special Branch."

Ace peered over Bunny's shoulder. "You don't say?"

Bunny Vance whispered. "Ever hear of Malloy? The bird who ran Kwei-Lee Shipbuilding? Why, the old stinker Haymes put the kibosh on him for snooping for the Japanese. You know what happened next? Malloy got lead poisoning from a Kuo-min Tang firing squad."

"I could care less about political jamborees," Ace replied. "They're a first-class sedative."

"Wise up, will you?"

Ace brushed him aside.

Indignantly, Bunny called out, "Don't say I didn't warn you!"

Ace started off toward the two men. He edged his way around waiters carrying plates of pork chops, scrambled eggs, and corned beef sandwiches. When Ace arrived at their table, Roddy rose and extended his hand.

"Hello kid, how's tricks?"

"Good evening Ace. Glad to see you again. I'd like you to meet my colleague."

"How do you do. I'm Haymes. Chief Inspector Haymes."

They shook hands. Haymes noticed a jagged scar across Ace's left cheek and recalled Ace's record as a war hero, former captain and squadron leader of the U.S. Air Service, who scored 25 victories and received the Croix de Guerre. Now the top aviator at Asian Aviation Corps. And a spy, to boot!

"Join us, won't you?" Roddy motioned to an empty chrome chair.

"Don't mind if I do." Ace sat down and balanced his weight tilting the chair backwards. Roddy leaned over the table. No one spoke.

Ace and Haymes eyed each other as the Eurasian waiter appeared with the drinks.

"Here's your poison." The highballs slid in front of the detectives. Their empty glasses were removed to a tray. "A Douglas Fairbanks over here." The waiter placed a pinkish cocktail in front of Ace. "Anything else, boys? How 'bout some lamb chops?"

They all shook their heads and sipped their drinks. Tasting a mixture of apricot brandy, French vermouth, and dry gin, Ace raised his eyes over the top of his glass and studied the older man.

Roddy reached for a silver cigarette case inside his jacket pocket. "How goes it at the aerodrome? My sister Idina tells me she's hardly seen you lately."

He removed a cigarette and thumped the butt against the flat case. "Has Maxwell been keeping you busy? I hear you've been flying inland, Hangchow, if I'm not mistaken."

"Yep, that's a fact."

The Chief Inspector's empty glass landed on the table with a thud. He crossed his arms over his chest. "Hangchow. Kindly tell us all about Hangchow, Mr. Jordan."

Ace took a long swallow. Light from a candle on the table bounced off his gold pinkie ring; its diamond studs formed the shape of an albatross against a black onyx setting. Ace carefully placed the glass down. "If you boys want information about Hangchow, you're going to be disappointed. I don't know much. The flight's not bad. It's 150 miles south on the Ch'ien-t'ang River. Built in the old Ming style. Probably hasn't changed much since Marco Polo, but I wouldn't know. I refuel there and usually grab a bite of cat-ear noodle soup—triangle noodles, shrimp, chicken, ham, and scallops. It's their specialty. A real pip, too!"

Haymes rolled his eyes. "Enough trivia, Mr. Jordan. Tell us what you've been doing there."

American goods for sale.

"Why get sore at me? I don't know what you're fishing for. I'm making an honest living. Today, I flew a bit off course. Just outside Hangchow. I went over the 43-foot-tall Laughing Buddha, the carving in the limestone hill at a place called The Peak that Flew from Afar. It's near the Temple of the Soul's Retreat. I wanted to see it for myself. What's it to you?"

Roddy stabbed his cigarette into a chrome ashtray. "Very interesting discourse, Ace."

Haymes cracked his knuckles.

"My pleasure." Ace reached for the Douglas Fairbanks and gulped it down. After chewing the ice, he set the glass down. "Now if you boys don't mind, I've got to scram. Thanks for the hooch."

"Not so fast, Mr. Jordan. You forgot to tell us about the photographs."

Ace frowned. "You boys must be cuckoo. I haven't the foggiest idea what you're yammering about."

"Mr. Jordan, let us, as you Americans say, get down to brass tacks. Lately, our Nationalist friends in the Nanking government have been troubled by saboteurs. It's their artillery, you see. After arriving in Hangchow for shipment up the Grand Canal into the interior, the Kuomin Tang's artillery is being waylaid."

"Now, hold on a minute." Ace looked at them both. "I'm not playing possum. I don't know anything, and I haven't seen anything. Get it?"

"No, I don't get it. And, I won't get it, Mr. Jordan, until you cooperate."

"That's right, mate." Roddy nodded. "You'd better do as he tells you."

Chief Inspector Haymes looked at his fingernails. "As you might imagine, details about the arms' shipments have been hush-hush. The Reds, however, have shown extraordinary intuition. They seem to know precisely when to strike and precisely when the shipments arrive from abroad."

"You boys must think you're plenty smart, but you've got it all wrong. I'm not mixed up in any of that." Ace jumped to his feet. "So put away your brass knuckles!"

"Be seated!" Chief Inspector Haymes ordered.

Chatter ceased from tables nearby. Bunny Vance swooped down.

"I knew you two would pull some monkey business here. I warned you flatfoots already. Another peep out of you and you're finished here. Get it? If you mugs have any troubles to settle, you'd better settle them somewhere else or I'm liable to take a poke at you!"

Ace pulled Bunny aside. "Simmer down, pal. They'll play nice. You've got my word."

"Alright then, if you say so, Ace."

Bunny looked at the detectives. "Like I told those mugs before, we don't go looking for trouble, see? But we don't run away from it neither."

"Humph," the Chief Inspector grunted.

Ace waved his hand toward the table. "See Bunny, they'll call it quits. Why, just look at them—ever seen such Nice Nellies before? So powder. We were just finishing up. Isn't that right, boys?"

"Yes, quite right." Roddy cleared his throat. "We'll be on our way in a moment."

"What a dope!" Bunny shook his head in disgust at Ace before striding away.

The Chief Inspector waited until they were alone. "No need to leave just yet, Mr. Jordan. I've got a deal for you, and it's in your best interest to hear me out."

"Alright, let's have it." Ace folded his arms. "I'll hear you out, but I'm not saying I'll play ball with you. Get me?"

"Very well. We at Special Branch believed the Reds were responsible for the missing artillery, but it seems we were wrong. A few days ago, one of our gunboats captured a shipment bound for Manchuria. We found a Japanese crew masquerading as Reds. We also found aerial photographs taken from over Hangchow."

"Yeah? So what?"

"Mr. Jordan, I needn't remind you that the Chinese view taking aerial photographs for spying purposes as punishable by death."

"What? A spy?" The color drained from Ace's face. "What kind of a yellow-bellied rat do you take me for?"

Roddy lit up another cigarette and blew smoke over Ace's head. "This is quite a serious matter. Don't think you can get away with it because you're an American and subject to your laws in the U.S. court here," warned Roddy. "We at Special Branch can arrange for your extradition into Chinese jurisdiction if you're charged with espionage. You wouldn't stand a snowball's chance in hell should that happen."

"Listen here you mugs." Ace flushed with anger, "don't try to hang that rap on me. I don't get mixed up in politics or spying. I'm no sucker!"

"No need to lose your temper, Mr. Jordan." Leaning forward, Haymes spoke calmly. "For the moment, let's forget about the extradition. Here's the deal. I want information about Colonel Togawa. I want to get my hands on that Black Eel. Tell us what he's got up his sleeve this time. We'll take care of the rest."

Ace began to laugh. "I've got to hand it to you, boys. You've got all the angles figured out. Now try this one on for size. Sure, I've been taking pictures, but you've got it all wrong. You'd better talk to Maxwell Soames, who has been sending me to Hangchow. Apparently, one of his pals wants pictures of the terrain there because he's thinking of building a rail spur. Maybe Maxwell's pal isn't on the up and up, but I couldn't give a hoot."

Roddy pounded the table. "How dare you mention my brother-in-law in this sordid affair!"

"You'd better get a grip on yourself, kid," Ace snickered. "Or else, Bunny's liable to give you the boot."

"Think it over, Mr. Jordan," Haymes said. "We'll pay far more than the Japanese. I'm not after you. It's the Black Eel who interests me."

Just then, a spotlight shone on the emcee. "Hope you're ready for the next number, folks. I sure am! Here it is. A pretty little number called *'Sunshine Melody.'*"

The sound of a lilting piano filled the dining room. Whining violins followed as couples took to the dance floor. "This has been a real scream boys," Ace said nonchalantly, planning to get away amidst the commotion. "But, if it's all the same to you, I'll be on my way."

"Very well, then. However, I must have your answer by midday tomorrow," Haymes replied. "Think it over very carefully. Someone in your position can be extremely useful to us, and we can pay you quite handsomely."

Rising from the chair, Ace stooped down to the two men. "Fat chance. I'm no sneak thief. I don't snatch nickels from babies, and I don't rat either." He spun around and headed toward the front door.

People surged to the dance floor. In the bandshell, the tenor began to sway and croon. Horns hummed while couples danced and held each other closely as Ace walked past the foyer. He saw a strawberry blonde in a long, black sequined gown with a rhinestone halter strap. She walked in front of a young man and stopped. Then, spinning on her heels, she slapped the young man across his face. He pulled his hand back.

Ace caught the her by the elbow as she hurried to the exit.

"Any trouble, Miss?"

Startled, she swung around. Her brown eyes challenged Ace. "Buzz off, you louse!"

"Get a hold of yourself, sister. I saw what happened. I'm only trying to find out if you need any help, that's all."

The strawberry blonde exhaled. "I'm alright, but I'll feel better when I get out of this joint. A certain man over there just gave me a bad case of the jitters."

"I know that feeling well. Something similar just happened to me." Ace glanced over his shoulder. "If you don't mind, Miss, I'll walk you out."

"That's okay by me."

"After you."

The strawberry blonde tossed her head back as they passed the hatcheck near the entrance.

After scooting through the moon doors, they squeezed past the line outside The Saints & Sinner's Club. Night had arrived. Neon signs in blue, red, and yellow glowered down from surrounding buildings. Street traffic hummed along adjacent Nanking Road. Chinese prostitutes made catcalls at passing men. Revealing thigh-high slits in their satin *cheong-sams*, the prostitutes sat alongside bodyguard pimps inside pedicabs and rickshaws parked on both sides of the wide road.

After Ace had walked a few steps along the street, the strawberry blonde stopped and faced him. "Well, mister, thanks for the escort."

Ace moved in closer. "They call me Ace Jordan. And, who might you be?"

"Helen Hanlon," she answered. "Now, if it's all the same to you, I'll be on my way."

She started to step away, but Ace followed. "Say, Miss Hanlon, I've never seen you around before. Do you live in Shanghai, or are you visiting from the States?"

"I'm a reporter at the *North China Daily News*. That means I live here. Okay?" She stopped at the curb and lifted her hand to hail a rickshaw.

Ace reached out, catching her hand. "Don't go just yet. I'll give you a lift. My car is right around the corner. I promise I won't get fresh." She gave him a sideways look.

"Okay. You don't look like the type who needs a muzzle. Maybe we should get acquainted. Who knows? Someday you might give me a story for my newspaper. A girl needs all the help she can get, especially in Shanghai."

"Oh, I don't think so." Ace laughed. "I'm a pilot. An ordinary Joe. I've lived in China for a few years. Every now and then, I move from place to place, but I don't know much about anything except aeroplanes and flying."

They walked in silence crossing in front of The Grand Moving Picture Palace at 216 Nanking Road. A wall poster, touting the latest talking picture from America, depicted Clara Bow waving.

Helen and Ace stepped away to avoid a queue outside the box office.

"So, what's your line of work?" she asked. "Do you transport cargo?"

Before he could answer, he was interrupted by the squeal of tires. They turned toward the sound. A convertible black Dodge touring car sped past the movie palace and skidded to a stop next door at the Valentino Club. Shanghainese bodyguards stood on the Dodge's running boards and pointed their Tommy guns outward. One of them opened a door for a thin Chinese man, with a shaved head and jagged ear, who parted his long blue gown and climbed onto the sidewalk.

"Wow!" Helen said. "Let's see what's up." She picked up the hem of her gown and dashed off to the Valentino Club. Its blue lettering twinkled:

THE VALENTINO CLUB PRESENTS:
MADAME PUSKIN & HER WHITE RUSSIAN NYMPHETS
*** TAXI DANCING *** DANCE TICKETS $75 A BOOK

Men standing outside the club moved aside, leaving a wide berth for the arrival of the Green Gang. The man in blue, Pockmarked Fang, stood outside. One-eyed Wong pushed aside a Tommy gun dangling from his shoulder and disappeared into a glass revolving door at the entrance.

"Hey, move over!" Helen elbowed her way through the onlookers.

Ace followed. "See anything?" he whispered. "What gives?"

Without turning around, she answered. "Pockmarked Fang is here. He's trouble with a capital 'T.' This dive must belong to the Red Gang."

Maybe the club's been holding out on Fang's protection money."

Taller than the others, Ace edged over to the curb and surveyed the scene. Bodyguards formed a line along the sidewalk, their Tommy guns pointing toward the street. One of them kicked a White Russian beggar trying to crawl up the gutter. The beggar's bottle of vodka crashed to the street and shattered.

No one noticed a long, navy-blue Buick blending into the night with its headlights out. The Buick crawled forward until it was a few car lengths behind the parked Dodge.

Ace pulled out a stick of chewing gum from his jacket pocket. He unwrapped the gum and popped it into his mouth. Turning away to toss the wrapper onto the street, he saw the Buick creeping nearer. He felt a kick in the stomach as he looked from the Buick to Pockmarked Fang, who stood with his back to the street.

"Hey!" Ace yelled. "Down! Everybody get down! It's a hit!"

The bodyguards, whirling toward Ace, turned their backs to the street. The Buick lurched forward. At the sound of burning rubber, they spun back around. Gunfire crackled. People scrambled in all directions. Helen screamed. Pockmarked Fang yawned.

"Get down, you dope!" Ace yelled to him. "Get down or you'll get shot!"

Ace ran over and tackled Pockmarked Fang. They fell to the sidewalk. Three bodyguards toppled over. Holes ripped into one of the Buick's sides. Bullets kicked up concrete from the sidewalk. Ace crawled, dragging the old Chinese man inside a space between the revolving door's panels and pushed the door until they were safely inside. Glass shattered above their heads. Then the gunfire stopped. Ace pressed his hands against the floor and rose. His right palm was sticky with blood. His eyes moved to Pockmarked Fang. Scarlet ooze spread from the shoulder of the blue silk gown. Ace bent to examine the bullet wound.

Casting a cold stare at Ace, Pockmarked Fang muttered, "Devil from over the ocean!"

In the distance, gunfire exploded in a short burst followed by horn blaring with the weight of the Buick's dead driver.

Shouting in Shanghai dialect, One-eyed Wong rushed out of a dimly lit hallway inside the club. Finding his master on the floor, he shoved Ace aside. "Aiyah!"

One-eyed Wong lifted Pockmarked Fang's body and carried him outside like a baby. By then, White Russian girls in skimpy cocktail dresses were fleeing the ballroom.

Ace took a deep breath. He started to dust off his black evening jacket when he remembered Helen and ran outside. A policeman blew a whistle. One-eyed Wong barked orders to the bodyguards, tossing their dead into the back of the open touring car. Helen jumped from the throng out onto the sidewalk. "Ace, are you okay?"

"Yeah." With his left hand, he pushed his hair back. "Let's scram."

A bewildered look crossed her face. "Are you nuts? This is a story of a lifetime. And it's all mine!"

"Suit yourself." Ace shrugged his shoulders. "I'm going home to get some shuteye."

With that, he left Helen behind and pushed through the onlookers until he reached a clearing at the curb. He weaved through bicycles, pedicabs, and cars until he crossed the street. Ignoring beckoning rickshaw drivers, Ace kept to the sidewalk. Although his car was parked a few yards ahead, he decided a stroll to his hotel some 20 minutes away. He needed to calm down after that shoot-out and figure a way out of that jam with Special Branch.

Ace looked up into the dark sky. The moon floated above, showering its white rays below.

Busy waterway traffic on Soochow Creek near Garden Bridge.

CHAPTER TWO

13th Day of the Eighth Moon

T he drop chain of a whirring metal ceiling fan swayed above a four-poster bed where Ace slept in the Cathay Hotel. Every so often, he sighed. A claret-colored bedspread of flossy goose velvet lay crumpled on the wooden floor near the foot of the bed. Humid and hot, the air in his suite seemed heavy. The hotel's cooling, heating, and ventilation systems—promoted as the latest hallmark of civilization to arrive in Shanghai—performed miserably. Worse yet, the hotel remained several weeks from its official opening despite the passage of nearly two years since ground broke on East Nanking Road.

The Cathay Hotel, with its 10 floors, was the tallest building to dominate Shanghai's commercial district along the Bund. British water-works inspectors strolled on the floors below through many of the 230 private suites and rooms, where plumbers installed silver faucets in red marble bathrooms. The general manager barked orders from the top floor. Dozens of Chinese in starched white uniforms responded by rushing from a dining room into the Tower Nightclub. Inside its 300-person-capacity ballroom, the Chinese staff hung silk lanterns, polished bronze Buddhas, and arranged carved dragons for the Moon Festival.

Sterilized water, from a three-mile-long pipeline linked to Bubbling Well Springs, flowed into the Cathay Hotel. Called the Sea's Eye by the Shanghainese, the springs were much hallowed. Water there arose from marsh formations, and noxious carbonic-acid gas spumed around a grand pavilion. The ancients believed frogs living at Bubbling Well Springs had become so impressed after reading Buddhist sutras that they commemorated the event by erecting the pavilion and inscribing above the main doorway: *The Fountain That Bubbles Toward Heaven.*

The naturally sterilized water from Bubbling Well Springs prompted Ace to take a long-term lease and endure inconveniences at the hotel. Despite being adventurous, he always tried to maintain the highest sanitation standards, especially in China. Four weeks earlier, he moved into Suite 444 from temporary quarters at the aerodrome's bungalow. His new job at Asia Aviation offered security, hence the more permanent residence.

In regard to the suite's security, Shanghainese hotel maids held a different opinion. Nothing could entice them to live in Suite 444. A single digit four was bad enough, but a triple four meant disaster because the Chinese character for the number differed only in its pronunciation from the word for death.

Ace rolled on his right side. A sledgehammer noise pounded a drainpipe along the terrace. Subconsciously hearing the hammering and whirring ceiling fan, Ace dug his fingers into his pillow. His was back in World War I leading Squadron No. 219 on a combat mission into France. He sat in the cockpit of a lone De Havilland affixed with four 25-pound bombs for a ground attack. Looking out the port side beyond the trailing edge, he watched the biplane's shadow speed across grassy hills some 6,500 below in the Baussant region of the Toul sector. The German border loomed ahead. His heart began to beat faster. His hands tingled. Each time before combat, he wondered whether his life would end that day.

Ack-ack-ack-ack-ack!

Fiery orange flashes raced past. Bullets bore holes into the canvas covering the D.H.-5's port-side wings. Ace looked up. A black German cross leaped from greenish, lozenge camouflage on the starboard side of a single-seater Albatross D III. Adrenaline surged through his veins. He made a quick zoom, skirting from the line of fire. Suddenly, a second D.H.-5 from Squadron 215 appeared. It moved into a dogfight position behind the Albatross scout. Ace circled the aeroplane and dove just as the second D.H.-5 opened fire. *Ack-ack-ack!*

In astonishment, he saw a dark object plummet from the sky. It hit the engine cowling of his aeroplane, flew up, and clipped the left side of his head. He watched it plunge to the ground. Catching his breath, he turned to his bloodied windscreen and recoiled in horror as a German aviator dropped from the sky. The body fell to the ground faster than the Albatross D III, which descended with one set of wings in a flat, spiral glide. Ace shuddered. He untied a white silk scarf around his neck and wiped the blood from his head before releasing the scarf into the air. It fluttered away. On the ground below, a burst of dirt in the shape of a mushroom cap rose from the place where the Albatross scout slammed into the hillside.

Ace jolted from his sleep into a sitting position. His gray eyes widened. Perspiration covered his face and hands as he cringed at the jackhammer noise. The Great War was over. Workmen were responsible for those sounds, not the enemy. He rose from the four-poster bed and straightened his blue and white checkered pajamas.

Walking unsteadily into the bathroom, he stared into the mirror. With trembling hands, he splashed cold water on his face until he felt refreshed. He smoothed the black hair from his face. Reaching for a cigarette from a pack of cigarettes on a linen shelf, he lit up, and exhaled a long stream of smoke. Boy, that Helen Hanlon, what a looker! She seemed to have brains, too. Not just another dizzy dame. Ace put on a robe and shuffled into the sitting room. He lifted a telephone receiver from its cradle and dialed. "Hello? Room service? This is Suite 444. Send over some coffee right away. *Chop-chop!* No, I don't want it white—no cream, only black. Better make it a pot. Thanks."

He hung up and went out on the terrace. A hurly-burly of sounds greeted his ears—shrilling ship sirens, barking boat dogs, clanking anchor chains, sputtering *sampan* motors, whistling petty officers, and chanting dockyard coolies. His room overlooked the Bund, a wide paved walkway curving eight miles along the banks of the Whangpoo River. A large white vessel, glimmering in the sunlight, was moored midstream in rocking waters. A dozen men stood on the deck of the white steamer owned by the *Holland-East Asia Line.* Ace heard a nervous cough and saw a Chinese roomboy peeking through the doorway. A monkey cap, held firmly in place with a chin strap, sat at an angle on the boy's head. "Excuse, sir."

"It's okay. Come on in."

The boy brought over a portable tray table covered with Irish linen, a silver coffee pot, a delicate *fên-ting* porcelain cup and saucer, and a silver vase crowned with a cassia flower. Not all the petals on the cinnamon flower had unfurled.

"Wait here a second, kid." Ace strode into the suite and rummaged on top of a nightstand littered with cigarettes, nightclub matchbooks, a wrinkled handkerchief, a diamond-studded gold pinkie ring, some Mexican dollars, and a wad of crisp 20 gold-unit bills from the Central Bank of China. He grabbed a handful of copper Chinese coins and returned to the terrace. "Here's your *cumsha*, kid." The boy bowed and left. Ace poured black coffee into the porcelain cup. He walked to the balustrade and leaned against it. He lifted the cup to his lips, blew at the steam, and sipped the bitter liquid while searching for something to see

A busy section of the Bund in Shanghai.

interesting on the promenade along the Bund. His eyes settled on a walkway next to Nanking Road Jetty where two unlikely characters conversed. A slim, young Chinese man in a long gown knelt next to a legless beggar. Leather straps held the beggar's torso upright on a small bamboo platform with tiny rusted wheels. A shock of black hair dusted with uneven white streaks made the old beggar resemble a grizzled porcupine. That's odd, Ace thought. Beggars aren't allowed on the Bund. Why is that young man talking so attentively to him instead of running that beggar off? The beggar nodded twice in affirmation.

Ace looked for clues about the young Chinese man. Was he an aristocrat, a merchant, a college student, a Communist, or gangster? The young man had a wide face, high cheekbones, and hair greased back above a widow's peak. White cotton stockings and black cloth shoes showed under his brown gown, a traditional garb giving no hint about his occupation. The youth stood up. The beggar tucked a shallow basket under one arm, grabbed a wooden dumbbell in each hand, and laboriously dragged himself away. The wooden dumbbells clanked against the pavement. Swerving amid people's feet, the beggar disappeared into the crowd, while the young Chinese man slowly walked toward the Cathay Hotel. As he drew closer, Ace noticed a long strand of amber beads and jade amulets around his neck. That necklace—so he's a Red Pole enforcer, a Green Gang's martial arts expert. I wonder what is doing here? What's his racket?

The youth came closer. The fingers of his right hand writhed around two steel balls as he exercised tendons in his hand. Reaching the Cathay Hotel, he stopped next to a large camphor tree directly across from Ace's suite. His head lifted to the 4th floor. Their eyes met.

A telephone rang inside the suite. Ace bolted through the French doors and grabbed the phone. "Hi yuh, flyboy," a voice whined. "It's me, Chicago Charlie."

"Hang on a minute." Without waiting for a reply, Ace dropped the handset and hurried to the balcony. The young gangster remained looking up at Ace's balcony. In the distance, a Japanese gunboat cruised the waters. Sending white clouds from two smokestacks, the *S.S. Nippon* sailed in front of Britain's prized gunboat, the *S.S. War Diadem*. Ace returned to the phone. "Alright, Chicago. Let's have it."

"Say, did I wake yuh or somethin'? Why are yuh talkin' to me like

A British warship alongside the waterfront in Shanghai.

that? I ain't no Jake flake! It's me, Chicago. We're pals. Remember?"

"Stop that yapping, will you? Either shoot or wrap up!"

"Gee, Ace, don't get sore before yuh hear me out. I'm callin' about last night. I got my hands on this here scandal sheet, see. I wuz lookin' for the Funny Section. Yuh know, tryin' to find 'Little Orphan Annie' like I always do. Yuh should get a load of that dog of hers, Sandy. Why, it's a real scream today..."

"Chicago, I don't give a hoot about the funnies. Listen up, now. I've got some business, and I've got itchy feet. Get me?"

"Oh, keep your shirt on, Ace. I'll come to the point. This here front page says yuh wuz a real boy wonder last night. If yuh ask me, I'd say you're sittin' mighty pretty with old Pockmarked Fang. Now, I got an angle all figured out..."

"Sorry to gum up your parade, but I'm not interested. Look Chicago, I've got to scram. There's some mug I've got to see—a mug who's trying to make a monkey out of me." Ace hung up the telephone. He didn't mind taking the rap if there was a good reason, but this business with the photographs, the Japanese, and Special Branch was different. He wasn't going to take the fall for anyone. Maxwell Soames had better have a good reason for wanting those aerial photos taken.

Roddy Erskine dipped a piece of sausage into syrup floating around a stack of griddle cakes at the Soames estate. "Maxwell, old chap, we'd better clear out soon. We don't want to keep Genghis Khan waiting."

"Right you are," answered Maxwell, sipping Earl Grey tea. He dabbed each corner of his small, full lips with a napkin. "First, I must have a look at this morning's *North China Daily News*. No doubt Roddy, you'll soon learn that a well-bred gentleman must keep abreast of important goings on by reading this newspaper at the outset of each day. This is how you'll succeed in Shanghai whether in you're business or politics."

Idina rolled her gray-green eyes. "Skip it, darling. Let's get on with breakfast, shall we?" She pushed back her dressing gown's ostrich feather sleeves and reached for marmalade. The only sound in the room was a knife scraping against a piece of toast.

Idina began to seethe. She flicked the knife back and forth in fast strokes. "Maxwell, the big shot! Roddy, the horseman! What a load of tosh! Imagine the lunacy of the Blue Lantern Hunt in this infernal country." Slamming her knife down on the table, she crunched toast while speaking. "Grown men tramping about on beastly Chinese ponies through bamboo groves and tea fields—sloshing through the marshes. All in pursuit of lanterns hidden there by some idiotic Hunt Master. Oh my, what a daring sport! What brave men to go off hunting for lanterns made of paper. It's simply ludicrous, I tell you!"

Maxwell and Roddy exchanged glances. Clearing his throat again, Maxwell placed his teacup on a saucer and jingled a cut-glass servant's bell.

Ling, a Chinese butler with a wide face and hooded eyes, walked quietly into the room. Unlike the other servants who wore Chinese uniforms, Ling dressed like his English counterparts. "Yes, *Hsien-sheng?*"

"Has Number One Boy finished ironing my newspaper yet?"

"Yes, *Hsien-sheng.*"

"Very well then, I wish to see it immediately."

"Certainly." Ling bowed and left.

Idina looked at her younger brother, and her face softened.

"Honestly, Roddy, I become all chewed up every time you go out on one of those blasted Shanghai Race Club hunts." She turned to sneer at her husband, who was quietly refilling his teacup. "As for our Maxwell, well, he's clever enough. He can take care of himself in more ways than one, if you ask me, but I really worry about you, Roddy."

Roddy leaned over and placed his hand protectively on her arm. "Silly goose, pull yourself together. Don't bother about me at all. You've got nothing to fear. Why, my groom is the best *mafoo* in Shanghai. He keeps my pony in tip-top shape. Besides, I myself have been training Genghis Khan. You really should see that animal. What a magnificent pony, too! He's unbelievably clever and has incredible fortitude. Why Idina, I daresay I'll make him into a first-rate jumper by the time the Shanghai Derby rolls around for New Year's. Just you wait and see!"

Idina pulled away. "Those *tarpans*, or whatever you fools call those Tartar and Mongol ponies, they give me the horrors. They're completely wild totally unpredictable beasts. I'm surprised no one has been killed by one of them yet. Haven't you any sense at all?" She fought back tears.

"Roddy, I need you. Don't you see? That's why Maxwell used his influence in London to get you posted here. I don't know what I'd do if anything happened to you."

Ling placed the newspaper on a silver tray before Maxwell.

"Old sport," said Roddy, looking helplessly at his brother-in-law, "please do make her understand."

Maxwell grunted. His beady eyes peered through round gold-rimmed spectacles at the front of the *North China Daily News*. "Well, well, look here. If it isn't that fool of an American. One of these days that Ace is going to get hold of the wrong end of the stick."

Roddy looked puzzled. "Don't tell me there's a write up about that aviator fellow?"

"Yes, of sorts," Maxwell answered. "Listen to this headline: 'Thanks to Yank, Opium Czar Escapes Death—Again.'"

Perking up, Idina tossed her napkin on the table. "Go on, do. This sounds intriguing."

Maxwell pulled the newspaper closer under his nose and read aloud.

"After a daring ambush last night on Nanking Road, Pockmarked Fang, the notorious head of the Green Gang, narrowly escaped the clutches of death amid a volley of gunfire. In an act of heroism, Mr. Jack 'Ace' Jordan, an American aviator, ignored blazing machine guns to save the Opium Czar from certain death. This reporter witnessed the surprise attack by gangsters, most likely members of the rival Red Gang. This was the fourth public assassination attempt on Pockmarked Fang within the last month. International Settlement Police refused to discuss last night's ambush. However, informed sources say Pockmarked Fang is behind an International Settlement Police crackdown on Red Gang pongs controlling the waterfront. Both gangs have been at war since the Red Gang began to muscle in on the Opium Czar's lucrative narcotics trade in the French Concession. There will be no formal investigation of the attack—even though it occurred in the International Settlement. Police say the matter is under the jurisdiction of the Shanghai Native Government and the Chinese Provisional Court because it concerned a Shanghainese."

Maxwell folded the newspaper on the tray. Roddy clicked his tongue. "That Ace fellow sure does get about."

"Repeat that. What?" Idina cocked her platinum bob to one side. "Roddy, dear, whatever do you mean?"

"Did I say something? Never mind. Take no notice, my dear." Roddy said nervously glancing about.

"What are you talking about?" she persisted. "Brother dear, I can tell you're holding back. Please don't. You know I can be trusted."

Leaning over the table, he whispered, "Special Branch is trying to get to the bottom of something. It concerns Ace. But you mustn't breathe a word to anyone. It's all rather hush-hush, if you get my drift."

Half listening, Maxwell pushed the spectacles up the bridge of his nose. He licked his small lips until they glistened like the top of his balding head.

"Come again? Did you say Ace? Surely, you can tell us something more. It's all in the family here. After all, you can trust us!"

"Alright, if you both don't repeat a word. I'll tell you this, yes, indeed. Chief Inspector Haymes and I had a chat, shall we say, with Ace at The Saints & Sinners Club."

Idina scrunched her face. "The what?"

"Sorry," he chuckled. "Of course, you wouldn't know of such a place. It's not bad, though, if you don't mind associating with Yanks."

Maxwell tapped Roddy on the shoulder.

"Please do go on. I'm most interested. After all, I've taken Ace under my wing, so to speak. Idina and I've always treated him like a member of our little family since he joined my Asian Aviation Corp."

"Yes, indeed," Roddy answered. "But please understand I cannot elaborate any further except to say it didn't go very well for Ace at the club. He left with some American woman. Quite a pretty little thing, she was, too."

Idina's eyes smoldered with jealousy. She gritted her teeth and rose.

"Well, gentlemen, this has been a cheerful morning. I must be off. I know you'll both be leaving soon."

Tossing her head back, she turned to Roddy.

"You know I don't like you dashing about on those monstrous ponies, but if there's nothing I can do to dissuade you from going on that Blue Lantern Hunt, it's your funeral. Don't say I didn't warn you!" She stomped out the room.

Ace's yellow Rolls-Royce Phantom 1 Ascot raced along the Street of One Hundred Blossoms. The convertible's whitewall tires, accentuated by black fenders and running boards, expelled pebbles from the unpaved road. Here in the Western suburb of Hungjao, far from the action in Shanghai, traffic was light. Occasional bicycles and rickety donkey carts driven by peasant farmers traveled along the wide street. The late morning sun beat down on the donkeys, whose tongues protruded as they dutifully plodded along without encouragement from a whip.

All the peasants carted watermelons for the Mid-Autumn Moon Festival. Melons would be hollowed, with the top edges sliced like curved petals before the outer skin was carved to the rind. In this manner, the Lotus-Petal Watermelons resembled the flower's green-outlined, white petals. In the center, a candle would be placed to complete the lotus, one of eight Buddhist symbols for good luck. The Chinese would decorate gardens with Lotus-Petal Watermelons in homage to the Moon Goddess. Shanghai would radiate under candles and lanterns, while people frolicked outdoors with lanterns in moonlit picnics and parties along sidewalks, in parks, or atop boat decks.

Turning his mind to the noonday heat, Ace freed one hand from the mahogany steering wheel and dug into his pants pocket for a handkerchief. He dabbed his forehead and tilted back the brim of his Panama hat. Alternating his hands while driving, he loosened his suspenders and rolled up his shirt sleeves. At length, the Rolls-Royce Phantom approached a six-foot-high stone wall bordered inside by parasol trees whose clusters of greenish-white flowers burst from maple-like leaves. Turning right, the Phantom screeched to a stop in front of double black-iron gates. Its horn blared. A fat Chinese watchman with a white crewcut stepped from behind a brick guardhouse. Cupping his hands to his mouth, Ace called out, "Lao Liang. Open the gates, will you? It's me."

Lao Liang spat on the ground, unfastened the gates, and stepped aside.

Weeding the lawn of a rich foreign house in Shanghai.

The Rolls-Royce drove past and snaked up an *S*-shaped driveway through the grounds of the Soames estate. Rosebushes dotted gardens on the right. On the opposite side, dozens of grass-cutters squatted in the middle of a rolling lawn. The women resembled a flock of crows that had descended upon a green plain. All wore black Mandarin-collared jackets and wide pants. Their knife blades reflected sunlight each time they hacked at the grass, while their voices chanted a melancholy ode of a farmer. Written between 332-295 B.C. by the famous Ch'ü Yüan, it's name was "Dissipation of Sorrows," and it told the sad take of a worker's labors. Ace drove the Phantom up to the two-story, red brick villa and slammed on its brakes.

Something along the lawn caught his eye. A teen-aged youth in a servant's long black gown sat with his head slumped forward. A 20-pound wooden collar, fashioned to rest on the shoulders without chafing the neck, hung around Number Two Boy's neck. Bound by a jute cord, the boy's limp hands were attached to one corner of the wooden *cangue* to prevent him from falling down.

"For crying out loud!" Ace lurched the convertible forward until it jolted to a stop under a brown brick *porte-cochère* in front of the villa. He jumped out and ran up a walkway to the front door. He pounded the door with the nose ring of a griffin doorknocker. A bolt slid back, and the door cracked, revealing a pair of dull eyes.

"Open the door, Ling! I've come to see Mr. Soames."

The eyes of the butler stared back. "*Hsien-sheng* not home." The door started to close, but Ace threw his weight against it. Ling did the same. The door wavered a few inches as both men pushed against it. "Ling, you'd better cut it out and let me in."

"Master not home." Ling cried. "Go away—go away!"

Heels danced up the walkway behind Ace. A woman's husky voice called out playfully. "Why, if it isn't that first-class stinker, Mr. Jordan. How *do* you do?"

The door slammed shut as Ace stepped back and faced Idina. With smiling red lips, she posed like a graceful mannequin in a pajama-style pantsuit of white georgette. She held a basket of freshly cut large, white Macartney roses. Her penciled eyebrows darted up. "Why, Ace, what's the trouble? I saw you motor up, and I came right over only to find you being troublesome with Ling. What exactly do you think you're doing?"

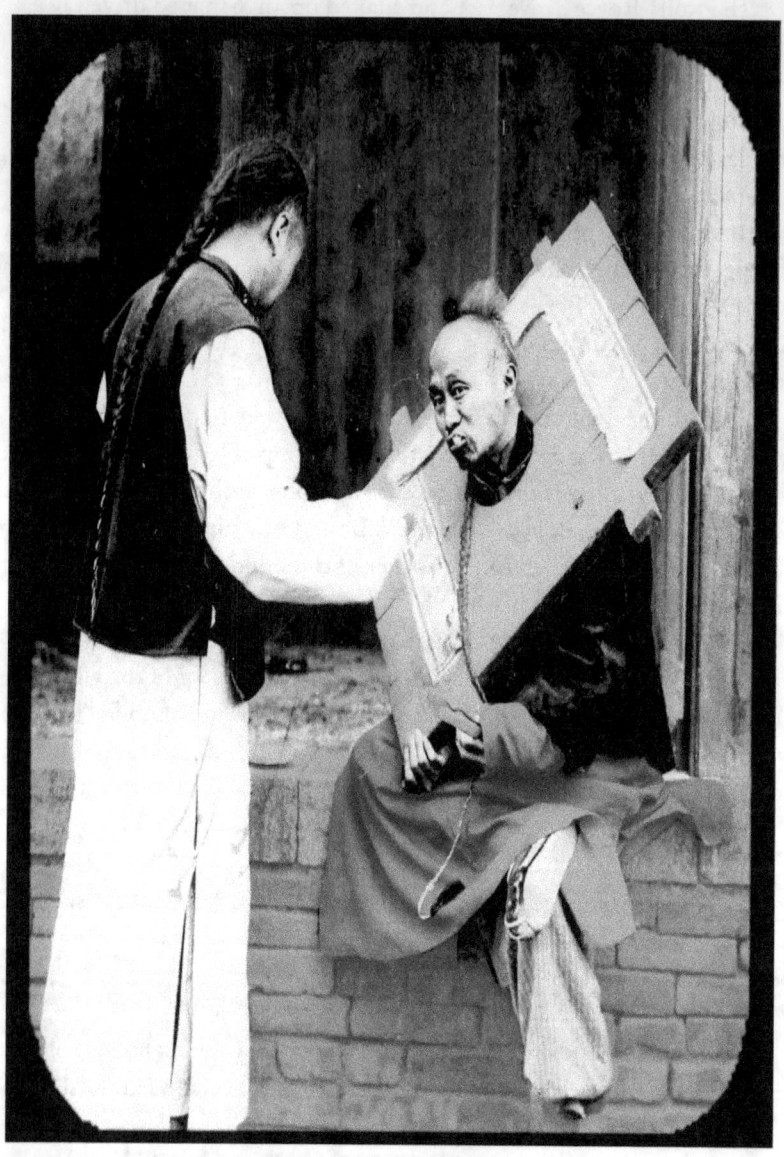

Feeding a prisoner in a cangue.

"Where's Maxwell?"

She stepped closer. The sweet fragrance from the roses followed. "I missed you terribly last night. I hoped you'd stop by to say hello before leaving the aerodrome, but you didn't. And I felt painfully lonely."

Moving closer, she curled her fingertips around his suspenders. "Maxwell is truly a poisonous bore. You understand what I'm driving at, don't you?" She tugged the suspender. "I feel half silly whenever I'm near you. Do you object to that?"

"Yes, I do!" Ace stepped backward. "Idina, I've got something important to talk over with Maxwell. Is *your husband* here or not?" She yanked back the suspender and released it with a snap.

"Nice trick, Idina." He flushed. "Learn anything else in charm school?"

"Ace, darling, did you know Maxwell and I were speaking of you only this morning? Actually, it was dear Roddy who brought up your name."

He moved out of her reach. "Either you tell me where I can find Maxwell, or I scram. Get it?"

She chuckled, throwing her head back. "Don't be such a bore, darling. Actually, you do look a little liverish in this heat. Won't you come into the sitting room? I'll have Ling fetch Maxwell. Then, we'll all have a nice little natter."

"Okey-dokey," Ace answered tersely. "Say, wait a minute, Idina. What gives out there on the football field?"

"What on earth are you talking about?"

"That kid out there in the wooden collar."

"Oh, yes, the *chokey*." She brushed past Ace. "That's Number Two Boy."

He grabbed her arm. "Well, what did he do? Pinch the family silver or something?"

"These servants are hopeless, absolutely hopeless," she answered impatiently. "I've had some frightful trouble lately. If you only had an inkling of what I must put up with, you wouldn't pester me about him."

Ace gripped her elbow. "What are you going to do with that kid? How long are you going to keep him like that?"

She smiled slyly, moving her face closer to his.

"Let's not bother about him. He won't be there for long—perhaps an hour or so. I haven't decided yet. I may ring the lads at Ward Road Gaol, or sell him at the Chinese Market in the Old Walled City."

He released her. "I'll take the kid off your hands. How much do you want?"

"Why, Ace! If you could only see your face." Idina giggled. "I do believe you're really serious. Well, I never!"

"I'm dead serious."

Her brows furrowed. "You do realize I wouldn't even entertain the thought of doing such a thing for anyone else but you."

"How much, Idina?"

"Hmmm." She smacked her lips. "Actually, I've had my eye on a delicious sable wrap at The Siberian Fur Store. It's very costly, though."

"Consider it yours. It'll be delivered first thing tomorrow."

"That would be positively delightful." She grinned. "Ling will ensure the *chokey* is taken off Number Two Boy, who will await you in your motorcar."

"Alright, whatever you say."

"Won't you please come inside, now?" She waved her right her foot towards the doorway.

"Ling will show you to the sitting room. I must change into something cooler, otherwise, I'll surely get a frightful case of prickly heat. It's simply stifling out here."

"And Maxwell?"

"Yes, dreary old Maxwell." She rolled her eyes. "He'll be along shortly."

Maxwell walked a few paces behind Roddy in a wooded field at the end of Bubbling Well Road, the site of the Blue Lantern Hunt in the far western outreaches of the International Settlement. Both men were outfitted for the occasion in ecru jackets, tan jodhpurs, and black riding boots.

"Let's be as quick as we can, old chap!" Roddy shouted. "It's early yet, and I want to ride Genghis Khan before the race starts."

However, Maxwell continued his leisurely gait past two European men in riding costumes. Surrounded by the sweet aroma of clove tobacco, the pair chatted and puffed on *cheroots* under the shade of a Chinese cork tree.

Roddy walked briskly past the cork trees into a clearing where white-washed stables and a tack room stood. "What's keeping you, old sport?" he shouted. "Come along, I want to show you my new saddle." He disappeared through the doorway, returning with his arms tucked around a golden Manchu saddle with an angular-shaped skirt that curved upward. "Isn't it magnificent?" Trying to get a better grip, Roddy wriggled his right arm underneath the saddlebow, which jutted in an upside-down "Y."

Maxwell looked on.

"It's made entirely of gilt iron," Roddy explained excitedly. "A masterpiece of craftsmanship! Just look at the engravings. Wait until you see the yellow satin saddlecloth. It's embroidered with gold and silver thread, and even trimmed in mink, too. Rather takes your breath away, doesn't it?"

Maxwell adjusted his spectacles for a closer look. His fingertips traced the outline of handsome engraved dragons inlaid with ruby eyes and jade bodies. "It certainly is grand, in a cheap tawdry way."

Placing the saddle on the ground, Roddy rubbed his hands together. "I saw it in a pawnshop window. It belonged to a Manchu imperial clansman called a Yellow Girdle. Nowadays the old Manchu is a ruined souser pawning his belongings for liquor."

Maxwell removed his spectacles, pulled out a handkerchief, and polished the lenses. Without looking up, he spoke in a matter-of-fact voice. "Roddy, about our conversation this morning. The more I think of it, the more troubled I am about that American chap."

"What do you mean? I don't follow."

"My dear boy, I don't understand what to make of it all, really I don't, but alas, I have to ask."

"Ask?" Roddy nervously ran his fingers through his ginger-colored hair.

"Yes, I simply must know for Idina's sake, you understand. She is so fond of Ace, you know. Do tell, is he a dangerous fellow?"

Roddy looked to the ground. "Maxwell, you're making things difficult for me."

"I'm afraid I must impose on you. It's my sense of duty, nothing more." Maxwell blocked his path. "You needn't worry—I swear I'll never betray you. No one will ever know about this. However, I simply must act on Idina's behalf. Tell me, what were you questioning that aviator chap about last night?"

Roddy thought of his sister and hesitated. "Very well, then. I don't want any harm to come to Idina, but you mustn't tell a soul. I suppose it'll all come to an end in a day or so, anyway. We're closing in on Ace, you see.

We strongly suspect he's been spying for Colonel Togawa, also known as the Black Eel, who commands Japanese forces in Manchuria, you know."

"My, my, you don't say? So that American fellow is a traitor, is he? I never would've guessed him the sort to stoop so low! Yes, I can appreciate why this case is so important to Special Branch."

Roddy puffed his chest. "There's more besides. I've been put in charge of gathering evidence about Ace at the aerodrome. You see, the people at your company will talk more freely to me than to an outsider."

Maxwell's eyes narrowed. He mustn't panic. He had to act. Time was of the essence. Roddy mustn't ask anything of anyone at Asian Aviation. Special Branch will have to be stopped in its tracks—immediately.

"Mind you, Maxwell," Roddy added, as he picked up his Manchu saddle, "this is top secret. I haven't told you anything."

"You needn't worry. No harm done." Maxwell tugged at a gold chain in his vest pocket and looked at his watch. "Roddy, old boy, don't you think it's about time you went for a ride on that Manchu saddle of yours to warm up before the race begins? If it's all the same with you, I'd rather have a word with that useless *mafoo* of mine. He's more frightened of my *tarpan* than that silly pony is afraid of him."

"Very well, old sport," Roddy answered. "I'll see you later when the race commences at the starting line."

Half an hour later, the Blue Lantern Hunt was ready. Near the starting line in a wide clearing between the woods, two dozen men rode up on stocky, short-necked ponies who kicked up dust in their wake. The Mongol *tarpans* were dun-colored compared to black-and-white Tibetan *tangun* ponies. Chinese menservants, wearing long, dark-blue satin gowns and matching skullcaps with knotted knobs, poured white chalk across the starting line. The Hunt Master, attired in indigo clothing, rode a pony bearing the Shanghai Race Club's official scarlet reins and brown leather saddle. In the distance, varnished Peking blue paper lanterns swayed from the broad branches of mulberry trees. Each year, the Blue Lantern Hunt launched the Shanghai Race Club's new season. For the next six months, club members lived only for horse racing—to the dismay of their wives, girlfriends, and mistresses.

Setting aside the chalk, the Chinese menservants scurried to the sidelines and picked up brass cymbals and miniature nine-toned gongs. Four medics, distinguished by armbands with red crosses, mounted their ponies in readiness, while contestants maneuvered their unruly beasts into formation at the starting line. The ponies whinnied and bucked.

Roddy took center spot. In search of Maxwell, his eyes traveled to the woods as he tried to control Genghis Khan. Finally Maxwell and his *tarpan* joined the starting line.

The Hunt Master blew a trumpet. The Chinese menservants, taking their cue, raised the handles of their nine-toned brass gongs, which were suspended within a square wooden frame and arranged in rows of three. Wooden mallets crashed against the metal, the harsh sound reverberating the start of the Hunt. Riders gripped their saddles. Ponies straightened their necks and lunged. As usual, the ponies galloped every which way. Despite their best efforts to stay mounted, some riders fell off. Veering to the left, one piebald Tibetan *tangun* jerked his neck around and bit a rider's leg. Another contestant flew off in mid-air.

Roddy yanked the reins as Genghis Khan pounded across the dirt toward the blue lanterns that lay hidden among tree branches along the eight-mile course. He was determined to be the first to "hunt" each lantern and reach the finish line. Genghis Khan skirted around trees, dodged burial mounds rising from marshlands, and trampled over arched stone bridges. They were out front by a good distance when suddenly the lanterns led to a dead-end at a wide creek.

At a standstill on the creek bank, Roddy threw his hands in the air. Blast it! Perhaps that lantern hanging from a limb across the creek was to test riding across the water. Of course they could reach the other side! He dug his heels into the pony, but Genghis Khan refused to budge. "Get going, you brute!"

The pony stubbornly shook his thick brown mane.

"*Aiyah!*" a Chinese man hollered.

Roddy turned toward the strange voice. A peasant youth sat on his haunches inside a slipper-shaped, flat-bottom boat floating down the creek.

"*Yang keui-tzu!*" The peasant waved a chicken-feather fan at the barbarian on the pony.

"Oh, shut up, you half-naked moron!" shouted Roddy, shaking his fist at the bronzed peasant, who was clad only in faded, brown cotton pants rolled up at the calf. Reeling with laughter, the peasant squatted near the pointed bow inside the skiff.

"You dirty, filthy heathen! Why don't you mind your own business?"

A bridge over Soochow canal.

"*Yang keui-tzu!*" This was the peasant's first journey to Shanghai from his inland village of Kiating Fu. He planned to make a handsome profit selling his insect wax cargo—50 catties molded into brittle, colorless, odorless cakes. In the past, the peasant had sold his crop of insect eggs to porters, who relayed the egg cones in six days to hatcheries. This season, however, he wanted more money. So, he waited for the insects to hatch, molt, and secrete wax on his ash trees. Then, he furiously scraped tree branches encrusted with the scale insects' wax secretions. Next, the wax was placed in boiling water where it floated to the surface to be molded into cakes hardened in cold water. Shanghai residents depended on great quantities of insect-wax cakes for coating medicinal pills or glossing expensive paper, fine furniture, cloth, and jade. Now at the outskirts of Shanghai, the peasant eagerly awaited its surprises. This first glimpse of a devil from over the sea fulfilled his expectations about ugly barbarians.

Just as the skiff passed Roddy on horseback, the peasant grabbed a green cylindrical object and jumped to his feet.

Roddy dug the toes of his boots into the stirrups, grabbed the saddlebow, and stood over the saddle.

At the same time, the peasant hurled the teacup across the water. It struck Roddy between the eyes. He fell headfirst into the creek. The pony whinnied and reared. Laughing uncontrollably, the peasant snatched a pair of gray wooden oars and paddled away quickly.

Witnessing the assault while hidden among mulberry trees, Maxwell's heart leapt. This chance encounter with the peasant would fit better in his plan to kill Roddy before the latter learned anything at the aerodrome. Maxwell dismounted and waded into the water near Roddy, who was dazed with blood trickling down his face. He tried to stand, but the soles of his leather boots slipped on slick rocks beneath the water. He fell sideways. His arms groped about in the muddy water.

"Roddy, old boy, I'm over here. It's Maxwell." He nervously licked his lips and moved in. "Stay right there. Don't move, old boy, you look as though you're badly injured."

A few minutes later, Maxwell quickly mounted his pony and sent it cantering with a slap on the rump. All he must do now was return the blue lanterns to their rightful places on the branches. He chuckled. Earlier he hadn't known exactly how to silence Roddy—only that it must be done during the Blue Lantern Hunt. What a very tidy business it had been. His spirits soared. With Roddy gone, Special Branch couldn't connect him or Idina to the Black Eel. Their secret was safe.

The Hour of the Goat
1-3 PM

Ace didn't care for Idina's sitting room. Slouching cross-legged in a chair, he scowled at the floral chintz upholstery and Chinese peel furniture of jasmine-yellow rattan interwoven with slender grasses. A tall glass of lithia mineral water with melting ice cubes remained untouched. He snatched his Panama hat from his knee and stepped to a window overlooking the estate's front lawn. Only five more minutes. If Maxwell didn't appear by then, he'd start a room-by-room search.

The sitting room's massive double doors groaned open.

Idina appeared in a stunning white, *Canton crêpe* dress with three-quarter-length sleeves and a short hemline. Layers of sheer ruffles surrounded her neckline. A white silk scarf, as transparent as moth wings, rippled from her fingertips as she breezed into the room. "Nothing like a good scrub. I feel marvelous—absolutely tip-top. It's so nice to be alone here with you." As she sailed past, he inhaled flowery perfume.

"Honestly, I don't know what makes dames like you so darn dizzy. Now stop with the baloney. Where's Maxwell?"

She sauntered to a Gramophone, picked up a 78-r.p.m. record from a rack and placed it on the turntable. "Didn't I tell you? How silly of me." She shrugged her shoulders and giggled. "Why, Maxwell isn't at home. He and Roddy went on that Blue Lantern Hunt with all those beastly ponies. I give you my word of honor, though, Maxwell will turn up later today."

"So, you're a liar now, too. I shouldn't have expected honesty from you." Ace put on the Panama hat, cocking the brim over his left eye. "For now, it looks like you're one up on me—for now! If it's all the same to you, I'm going to scram."

"Oh Ace, please don't be cross with me. Oh, do sit down," Idina pleaded, pointing to a rattan chair. "Please! There is something I simply must clear up with you straight away. Then, you can decide whether you want to clear out or not."

She seemed so desperate that Ace almost felt sorry for her. She might have turned out differently if she'd stayed in England. Life in Shanghai often became impossible for Western women. He'd seen it happen before—far too often. "Alright, I'll stay for a minute. I guess I'm a soft touch. Go ahead, say whatever it is you've got to say. I'm all ears. Make it snappy, though, I've got to clear up something with Maxwell."

"Very well then." She smiled prettily. "There is something I want you to listen to. It'll take only a moment. Afterwards, you can do whatever you want to do." She whirled around to the Gramophone and cranked its handle. The needle traveled over the record. Playful trombones interjected with trumpets in a thin metallic tune. Drumsticks twice struck a cymbal. Idina turned to Ace. A dreamy expression crept over her face. She swayed in time with the music as if dancing with an unseen partner as a tenor in a high-pitch began to warble. Waving her long white scarf, Idina twirled to the window where Ace stood. He ducked around her, hurried to the Gramophone, and snatched the needle. The music stopped with a loud scratch.

"Look here, Idina! I don't know what's gotten into that fool head of yours, but I can pretty well guess. If it's what I'm thinking, here's your answer. 'No!' It's out of the question!"

Idina froze. "What on earth do you hope to gain by leading me up the garden path?" Her gray-green eyes flashed and her lips twisted.

"What? You must be nuts! Me? Leading you up the garden path? That's a good one—a real laugh. Why, I've never been interested in you—never. Not in a million years and not for all the tea in China!"

"Surely, Ace, this must be a joke of some sort." She coiled the scarf around her wrist. "I can assure you I don't find it amusing in the least."

"Look Idina, you're a swell kid." Ace lowered his voice. "But let's get two things straight. First, I don't go for married dames. Second, even if you weren't married, you're not my type. It's as simple as that, no offense."

"Unless you fancy someone else, I can be your type. I can be quite pleasing, you know!" Idina began to pace. "Unless, of course, you're mixed up with that American woman. Yes, I know all about her. Roddy saw you with her last night."

"Hold on right there." Ace grabbed her by the shoulders. "Can't you get it through your head? This has nothing to do with Helen, or anyone else. Do you hear? I'm not interested in you. I've never been, and I never will be. Get it?"

"Helen, you say?" Idina snickered. "What a quaint name."

He shook his head. "I give up! Of all the screwy dames in the world, I've got to come across you!"

Idina watched him leave through the massive double doors. She remained in front of the window, unwrapped the scarf from around her wrist, and started to hum. A telephone trilled. She hurried and lifted the handset.

"Yes." She threw her head back and rolled her eyes. "Of course, this is Madame Soames. Who else would it be?" She toyed with the telephone cord. "I beg your pardon! What did you say about my brother?"

Idina fainted and crashed to the floor alongside the handset.

Outside the Soames mansion, Ace jumped into his Phantom convertible. Number Two Boy was curled up on the passenger seat. The engine whirred. Ace gripped the wooden steering wheel and sped out the wrought-iron front gates. He turned onto the Street of One Hundred Blossoms.

"Boy, oh, boy, kid, I'm sure glad to get out of this joint, but I bet you're even gladder." He glanced at the youth, who didn't move or speak. Maneuvering the convertible around a donkey cart, he parked the Phantom on the shoulder of a dusty road bordering the southern part of Hungjao Golf Links.

"Hey, kid, you don't look so swell." Ace opened a mahogany-paneled glove box. "I've got something in here that'll give you a little pep. You look like you could use some, too." He held out a silver flask. Number Two Boy lifted his head and grimaced in pain. The top of his black silk gown was ripped. Unscrewing the cap, Ace lifted the flask to the boy's mouth. "Here, take a snort of this."

Number Two Boy hesitated.

"Come on. It won't kill you. It's Dutch gin."

Number Two Boy opened his mouth. The gin trickled down his face. He coughed, but continued to drink.

"That's a boy, just a little more." Ace pulled away the flask, capped it, and returned it to the glove box. He watched the kid blink a few times before shutting his eyes. Ace leaned back in the black leather seat. The road looked clear except for a taupe-colored Packard Eight sedan cruising past. Ace should have paid attention to it. If he had, he would have seen One-eyed Wong inside. Instead, Ace glanced at his wristwatch and wondered how long it would take to drive to the end of Bubbling Well Road. Surely, the Blue Lantern Hunt would be coming to an end soon.

At the edge of the creek bank, Chief Inspector Haymes folded his arms across his chest. He stood next to the Hunt Master, who removed a handkerchief from his indigo blazer and dabbed his forehead. Neither spoke. Their eyes focused on the Chinese Municipal Council River Police, three Shanghainese men in baggy gray uniforms hopped aboard a motorized *sampan*. Literally meaning three planks, the boat was less than five feet wide. A Chinese Nationalist government flag drooped from its mast. Two of the River Police ducked under the mat roof and disappeared inside the cabin. The other roused the motor. Watching the *sampan* scud away toward Shanghai, the Hunt Master turned to Haymes.

"Do you think the Water Police will be able to find that wretched scoundrel?"

"Doubtful," Chief Inspector Haymes grunted. He felt very tired and very old. The midday sun beat against his thick, dark hair streaked with gray. He scratched the stubble on his face. The skin on his flabby cheeks felt dry and leathery despite the intense humidity.

"Abominable business," the Hunt Master lamented, still wiping his perspiration. "If that murderous Chinese man isn't apprehended, not one single word of this can get out! No sense putting ideas into the heads of these natives. There's 500 of them for every one of us. We've simply got to keep quiet about this nasty business."

"Quite right," Haymes agreed. "Special Branch are well aware of our tenuous hold on the native population."

"Chief Inspector, we'd best clear out of this dreadful place. Nothing doing here anymore."

"Yes, you're right."

Both men slowly walked away. The Hunt Master shoved his handkerchief into a jacket pocket. Chief Inspector Haymes broke the silence. "By the way, there's something puzzling me. Why would young Roddy, I mean Erskine, venture over to this creek? None of the other riders lost their way."

"How do you mean? I don't follow."

"This creek is a good distance from the Hunt's main course.

A Manchu horseman.

If Maxwell Soames hadn't noticed Erskine had gone missing and saw the Chinese sail away, we might never have known what happened."

"I assure you I haven't the faintest idea how Erskine came to the creek, or how he got so far off course. The lad was a marvelous horseman—a natural, truly the best in the Club. Perhaps that *tarpan* was up to some mischief, stung by a bee or some such. Everyone knows those wretched ponies can be exceedingly temperamental."

"Yes, I see," the Chief Inspector answered. "I'll just have a word with Soames. Everyone else is free to leave."

At the starting line an assortment of uniformed men waited: plainclothes Special Branch detectives in white-linen suits, blue-uniformed constables from the Bubbling Well Police Station, and riders in jodhpurs. Also milling about in uniforms were *mafoo* grooms, menservants, and chauffeurs. Everyone stopped talking and looked over to Bubbling Well Road where chauffeurs lingered around luxury American and British automobiles. All eyes watched an approaching ambulance from Lester Hospital.

Maxwell, choking back tears, sat slumped on a log along the road. When the ambulance parked a few feet away, he blew his nose loudly into a handkerchief. As the body was placed inside, a deep voice boomed, "Send the ambulance along now. It's done what it came for. There's no point keeping it here any longer." Maxwell turned toward the gravel-like voice. A heavy-set man in his 50s approached. He wore a rumpled gray suit, unlike the neat white ones of the other Special Branch detectives. He tapped Maxwell on the shoulder.

"Mr. Soames, I believe?"

"Yes?" Maxwell removed his spectacles to dab at his eyes.

"Mr. Soames, I'd like to extend my deepest sympathies to you. I'm Chief Inspector Haymes of Special Branch."

"Oh, I see." Maxwell sniffled and cleared his throat. "Yes, Roddy spoke of you."

"Did he now?" the Chief Inspector's voice rose slightly. He sat on the log next to Maxwell. "I realize this has been a dreadful shock, but there are some questions I must ask of you, if you'll excuse me."

"Must you, Chief Inspector? Is it absolutely necessary?"

Haymes waited for the ambulance to drive off before answering.

"Yes, Soames, I must. It's a matter of procedure. Routine inquiries. There will be an inquest, you see."

"Oh, really?" Maxwell held up his spectacles and frowned at the smudged lenses. "Very well then, I must do my duty. Yes, of course, ask me anything you like."

"Would you be so good as to describe, in detail, exactly how you came upon the deceased?"

Maxwell methodically cleaned the lenses with a handkerchief. "I had a wager with him. We'd bet on Roddy's new Manchu saddle. If he were to win the Blue Lantern Hunt, I'd buy him a new pony. If I won, he'd give me the saddle."

"A wager?" Haymes shifted his legs uncomfortably on the log.

"Yes, young Roddy was very sporting fellow, you know. An extremely fine horseman, too. Anyhow, he was in the lead. I was some distance behind him in second place. After I'd gone quite a ways, I noticed there weren't any tracks in front of me." Stopping abruptly, he sniffled loudly.

"Do go on," Haymes urged.

"Very well," said Maxwell, placing the spectacles on his nose. "I began to wonder if anything was amiss. I went back to the place where I last saw the tracks and followed the hoof prints. They led me to the creek." His words flowed quicker. "As I rode closer to the creek, I heard shouting and a most terrible row taking place. I drew closer. I saw that half-naked native sailing away in a boat. He was laughing, mind you! And, poor Roddy, he was dead, drowned—murdered by that monster!"

Haymes sympathetically patted Maxwell on the back.

"Really, Chief Inspector, there's nothing more I can say. I've been waiting here for some time now. I simply must go home to Idina, my wife. She's Roddy's sister, you know. She must be completely in shambles."

"Alright, Soames, that's fine. Thank you for your cooperation at this most difficult time. I'm quite satisfied with this investigation, as it is." Haymes lumbered to his feet and dusted off his trousers. "This shocking tragedy very well may be a lesson to us all. Shanghai is changing, and not for the better, I'm afraid. Many thanks, Soames. Good-day."

"Goodbye," replied Maxwell, rising to his feet. He watched Haymes amble back to the clearing. When he was certain the old man wouldn't return, Maxwell hastened to Bubbling Well Road to find his motorcar, a white Auburn sedan with chocolate-brown accents. Spotting it down the road, he kept his eyes downcast and his arms close to his sides while darting around the cars parked along the road. He wanted to avoid everyone. Most of the riders still dawdled along the road. Within a few yards of his auto, Maxwell heard a horn blare from a pale-yellow Rolls-Royce Phantom Ascot speeding towards him.

"Oh, blast!" he shouted, walking hurriedly up the road. He stopped. Whitewall tires slid on gravel. Footsteps hit the ground behind him. Maxwell didn't need to turn around to know what it meant. He dashed to his Auburn sedan where his chauffeur, Orloff, sat behind the wheel.

Catching sight of Maxwell rushing over, Orloff craned his head out the window and tilted the brim of his blue chauffeur's cap. He scratched at his jaw-length blond hair.

"Hey, Maxwell!" yelled Ace, gaining ground. "Hold it right there!"

Bolting to the white sedan's passenger door, Maxwell groped for the handle. His fingers slipped off the shiny chrome as he tried to open it. "Let me in, you White Russian idiot!" Orloff sat there gaping.

A hand clamped around Maxwell's forearm. His body was yanked around and slammed against the sedan. Trying to catch his breath, Ace towered over Maxwell. "What's the idea? Trying to pull a fast one on me, you little weasel?"

"Unhand me immediately!"

"You'd better stop yapping at me plenty fast, weasel. What gives with those pictures you had me take over Hangchow? It's time to spill it if you know what's good for you. I don't take kindly to double-crossers."

Ace squeezed the arm harder, pulling Maxwell to his face.

"Unhand me at once, I say!" Maxwell winced. "I know all about your notorious goings-on! And I know someone from Special Branch who is most interested in what I have to say, so, you'd best turn me loose. I have the upper hand!"

"Why, you dirty little rat!" Ace stepped backwards. "You think the game is all sewn up, don't you? But I'm wise to you, do you hear? I'm going to find out whatever it is you're up to. That's a promise! You're not going to make a chump out of me. Get it? I'll run along now, but I'll be back so you'd better watch over your shoulder."

"How dare you threaten me, you impudent rogue," Maxwell retorted.

Ace clenched his fists and jumped into his convertible. Where should he begin? With Hangchow? That could take some time. The Brits? No, he'd best stay clear of them. Colonel Togawa? That was too tough, especially now that their new warship was moored in the harbor. Nothing added up. Ace looked at his watch. He'd lay low for a little while until The Saints & Sinners Club opened. By then, he'd better have a plan.

Pockmarked Fang awakened from his slumber. He nestled his shaven head onto soft pillows of golden *yüeh-hwa-twan* moonlight satin lining panels of his lacquered opium bed. He stretched his arms. Gilded mesh protecting his fingernails scratched against satin pillows. He smacked his lips. His mouth tasted acrid like *yin-shi*, the bitter residue that stuck to opium pipe bowls. His topaz eyes fixed on the oval, rouged face of White Orchid, a frail 12-year-old girl, the newest of his 20 *ch'ieh* concubines. She stood alongside his opium bed. He had bought the girl from her father, who blamed her for causing his wife's death in childbirth. Her father's hatred for the girl extended so far as to his using in her milk name the word "white"—an unlucky color symbolizing grief and death. Since joining the gangster's household, White Orchid and the other *ch'ieh* wives had their own living quarters. However, the first wife, *ch'i*, ranked as the most important. According to custom, Pockmarked Fang dominated the household as the sun, while the *ch'i* held her own as the moon, and the remaining *ch'ieh* wives orbited in their proper positions as stars.

Dismissing his superstitious nature, Pockmarked Fang ignored White Orchid's bad name. He was smitten by her round face, which reminded him of a *fei t'ao* peach, the fruit of immortality. She applied a poultice of herbs, made of powdered mugwort and Chinese gall from insect bile, to his gunshot wound.

"Master?" she whispered, arching her eyebrows, blackened with a charred stick to accentuate their crescent-moon shape. "The alchemist left a potion black pepper for your fever. You must drink it before taking the Elixir of Longevity."

"Very well, but be quick about it," he replied. "Then prepare my opium pipe." She set about her work. Pockmarked Fang paid no attention. Instead, his mind reviewed the latest attempt on his life. Gazing at the walls in the smoking room of his summerhouse, his eyes rested on two bamboo-paper scrolls hanging on the East Wall. One scroll, flanking a six-paneled screen inlaid with mother-of-pearl, seemed appropriate to his situation. Its elegant crimson brush strokes predicted:

> *To treasure an evil man is like caring for a tiger;*
> *If you fail to feed him enough, he will swallow you up;*
> *Or, similar to raising a hawk;*
> *He will stand beside you if he is starving,*
> *And, then, he'll fly off when he eats his fill.*

His wound stung the skin where the bullet had grazed his withered body, yellowed like old parchment from years of smoking opium. White Orchid raised the miniature golden teapot spout to his lips. He gulped the potion. She dabbed his mouth with a warm cotton hand towel when he finished. Hoisting himself upright and swinging his legs over the four-foot-high bed platform, Pockmarked Fang thought Eggplant Ho, so nicknamed because of his head's elongated shape. They'd been childhood friends, street urchins living by their wits in Shanghai. As teens, they had joined the Three Harmonies Society and rose through the triad's ranks until forming their own Red and Green gangs to divide the city's spoils. Now, they were rival gang lords. Eggplant Ho was trying to take over opium trafficking in the French Concession, but Pockmarked Fang remained determined to retain his title as Shanghai's Opium Czar. Pockmarked Fang smiled. One-eyed Wong had better capture Eggplant Ho, get the American barbarian, and bring both of them over. If not, the "Death by 1,000" punishment awaited. He glanced at the other scroll on the East Wall. Its irregular, cursive, black grass-hand characters proclaimed:

> *"Ivory is not found in a rat's mouth."*

Pondering ways to torture a person through their teeth, he looked out a wide lattice window patterned with wooden left-handed swastikas symbolizing long life and the number 10,000. The window opened onto to a courtyard garden. Long shadows cast by eaves curving from slate-colored roof tiles announced the approach of darkness.

Ace watched Number Two Boy devour a bowl of rice sprinkled with slivers of red-glazed pork, bamboo shoots, tree fungus, and spinach. "You don't have to stay with me, kid. You're free to go anywhere you please."

Number Two Boy held the bowl below his chin. A pair of chopsticks shoveled the contents rapidly into his mouth. An Adam's apple traveled up and down his throat as he swallowed.

"Do you understand what I'm trying to say? You're free!"

The kid paused, looked at Ace, and took a swig of gunpowder tea. His tongue ran over his front teeth and dislodged a piece of a leaf.

Deciding to try Pidgin English, Ace continued: "Speak-ee Eng-ee-lish?" Then, jumping to his feet in frustration, he yelled, "Look, whatever your name is, I don't care what you did. It's true I bought you, but that doesn't mean anything to me, not a thing. I had to get you out of that joint. Get it? The door's over there. You can scram when you're done filling your face. I'll even give you some of my clothes and enough dough to go wherever you like."

The boy refilled his teacup.

"Gee whiz!" Ace shook his head. "Why am I even trying to explain anything to you? You probably don't understand a single word I've been saying."

"You may call me Babe," the boy answered, sipping the tea and observing Ace over the rim of the teacup.

"What did you say?"

"You heard me."

Ace sat on the settee and ran his fingers through his black hair. "I must be dreaming. First, you let me go on like a clown and never say a word. Then, you say to call you Babe. What's with the name?"

Number Two Boy replied haughtily, "I bet you wouldn't say that to Babe Ruth."

"Well, if that don't beat all!" Ace laughed and threw his hands up. "Alright, I quit. Suppose you do the talking now. I'm all out of air. Come on, tell me how a kid like you knows anything about Babe Ruth. I'm all ears."

The boy set the rice bowl on his lap, stretched back in his chair, and crossed his hands behind his head. "I don't know my father. My mother's clan is from Soochow. She works in a brothel on Yates Road. I grew up there. I was sold before the Lunar New Year to pay off the brothel's debts."

"Go on, kid. You're doing fine so far." Ace polished his gold ring against his leg.

"American sailors who went to the brothel were very kind. One sailor, Hank, liked me a lot. He bought me treats and taught me to speak English. He's from New York. His family is rich, but he disgraced them. He ran away to become a sailor. He's a Yankee's fan. He called me Babe. You may do the same."

"Did Maxwell Soames know anything about this?" Ace looked puzzled. "Were you in trouble because of your past?"

"Not at all. Surely you must know that in Shanghai it's unwise to let people know much about you." Babe arranged the skirt of his long black satin gown over his trousers and crossed his legs.

Ace nodded in agreement.

"As for the Soames, it is Madame who caused the trouble. She's evil. He's no better, either. We Chinese have a name for such a man—*wang pa*, someone who forgets the eight cardinal virtues of uprightness, faithfulness, propriety, moderation, filial piety, modesty, and brotherly love."

"I'll buy that." Ace stroked his chin. "But why don't you forget about them? You can do what you like now. I'll help."

Babe recrossed his legs. "I can't go back to Yates Road. And since you're a square guy, I'll stay with you. Do you need a chauffeur or valet?"

"Wait a minute now. I don't go for servants if I can help it. I don't need a driver, either. I can take care of myself just fine, thanks. Look kid, I'm what you call a loner. I like it better that way. I don't like anyone shadowing me."

"Although I am 15, I'm what you call a 'smart cookie.' I can be useful. Do you speak Mandarin, or Shanghai dialect?"

Ace shook his head.

"In Shanghai, doors are open to me that are closed to you, and vice versa. I can be your eyes and ears, especially in the Chinese underworld. Remember, I grew up on Yates Road. Think it over. I can help you."

"Maybe you've got something there, kid." Ace reached for a pack of cigarettes on a coffee table and lit one. "Okay, we just might be able to work something out temporarily, but I'll pay you. None of that slave business. Right now, I'm in a tight spot. I've got a little problem on my hands that you can help me with. Afterwards, though, you'll have to move on to something else."

"Sounds fine by me."

"Know anything about the Japanese? Not the shopkeepers—I mean the military. Ever heard of Colonel Togawa?"

Babe looked puzzled. "Not especially, he is called the Black Eel and feared."

"Good going, so far. We'll talk over the rest later. Why don't you go clean up? The bathroom's through that door." Ace pointed. "Get out of those clothes while you're at it. You won't go very far dressed like that. I'll have some Western clothes sent right over."

"As you like. By the way, your name is Ace, isn't it?"

"Yep," said Ace, fetching the telephone and lifting its handset.

"I thought I'd seen you once before at the Soames house. The servants there think you're okay, and so do the workers at Asian Aviation. By the way, Mr. Soames won't like it when he finds out that I'm with you."

"I wouldn't worry about that." Ace pressed the handset close to his chest. "I'm all washed up at Asian Aviation. Now run along."

He dialed 12847 for The Trustworthy Department Store.

"Operator, please connect me with Men's Clothes. Is this the Men's Clothes Department? Fine. I need a week's worth of clothes, everything inside and out, in a small size for someone about five feet, four inches tall. You'd better throw in some evening clothes, too. Yeah, that's right. Put it on my account. Jack Jordan. I'm at the Cathay Hotel now, 4th Floor, Suite 444. Send it over right away. I'll be waiting."

Ace remembered the sable wrap for Idina. He called The Siberian Fur Store and made arrangements. Then, he took a drag on the cigarette and walked out to the terrace. He needed Chicago Charlie's help.

The taupe-colored Packard Eight barreled down Nanking Road toward the Bund. The long-nosed sedan veered to the Cathay Hotel's back entrance for Chinese employees and guests. It slid to a stop—sending rickshaw men running for their lives.

Thwack! Splinters of bamboo from what had been a pedicab exploded against the sedan's grill. Three Green Gang enforcers, with ammunition belts crisscrossing the fronts of their tunics, jumped off the running boards of the Packard Eight. They removed Tommy guns slung over their shoulders and fingered the triggers while waiting for One-eyed Wong to alight.

The Cathay Hotel's back door was vacant, yet, a hushed crowd of Shanghainese gathered opposite on Nanking Road where sounds of exclamation arose as the short, bulbous body of notorious One-eyed Wong emerged from the back of the sedan. His head, with drooping earlobes, was shiny and shaven clean. He wore a long pink satin gown stretched tightly over his fat belly. Two 9-m.m. Luger Parabellum automatic pistols were tucked inside a wide leather belt around his waist. Waddling past the Green Gang enforcers, who fell in behind him, he chose the back entrance because it provided a speedy ascent to the 4th floor.

The French hotel manager in the front lobby might try to impede his progress, but the Chinese in the back wouldn't dream of doing such a thing to Pockmarked Fang's infamous henchman.

With a grunt, One-eyed Wong shoved the revolving door, passed into the Cathay, and trotted along a hallway.

A few yards before him, a pair of doors marked "Ladies Water Closet" swung open. Out came three Shanghainese courtesans wearing heavy makeup and proudly displaying American handbags. Catching sight of the Green Gang enforcers with guns leveled strutting toward them, the courtesans ducked into the bathroom.

One-eyed Wong slapped an elevator button. The carriage rattled to the ground floor. Doors parted, revealing an elevator operator, who yelped as he recognized One-eyed Wong and the Green Gang.

Falling to the floor and kowtowing, he pleaded, "Save life! May you become rich! May you become a general! Save life!"

One of the enforcers shoved the elevator boy out of the way.

"On your feet, you turtle egg!" ordered One-eyed Wong. "Fourth floor. Take us there quickly, or I myself shall kill you!"

The elevator operator knelt, raised a shaky arm, and pressed a brass button. The gangsters laughed as the carriage chugged upwards.

When it opened, One-eyed Wong and the enforcers stepped into a deserted hallway and proceeded to Suite 444 at the end.

"You two guard the door. The other comes inside with me. We'll have no trouble from this white ghost," One-eyed Wong, stepping aside, said loudly.

Slinging their Tommy guns over their shoulders, two gangsters threw their weight against the door forcing it to crash open.

In the bedroom, Ace and Babe, who had changed into evening dress of white tails and black slacks, were adjusting their black bow-ties in a dresser mirror.

"What the heck was that?" exclaimed Ace, dashing to the front door. Babe followed, tripping over his black patent-leather shoes, whose toes were stuffed with handkerchiefs since Ace had forgotten to order a pair for the boy.

Reaching the sitting room, they abruptly stopped when faced with a fat man in a shocking-pink Chinese gown. His lone eye bulged like a Pekinese dog. Babe recoiled. The fat man's eye socket was caved in. It glistened from a thick coating of lizard balm.

"What's the big idea busting in here?" Ace demanded.

One-eyed Wong waddled around the room as if inspecting it. The other gangster pointed his gun barrel at Ace.

"Are you deaf, you big tub of mush? What do you think you're doing here? Beat it! Get out!"

One-eyed Wong picked up Ace's pack of cigarettes from a table. He removed one and ran it under his nose.

Peering behind Ace's back, Babe whispered, "Watch out! He's One-eyed Wong, the biggest man in the Green Gang besides Pockmarked Fang. Whatever you do, don't give him any trouble."

Ace ignored the warning.

"What do you want, fatso? You're getting on my nerves. Why don't you say what's on your mind and get out of here?"

One-eyed Wong lazily smelled the tobacco under his nose.

"American cigarettes," he hissed in Shanghainese dialect to the other gangster. Without warning, One-eyed Wong snapped the cigarette in half and hurled it to the floor. "Come, it's time to go."

The Green Gang enforcer strolled up to Ace and shoved the machine-gun barrel in his gut.

One-eyed Wong addressed Babe in Shanghainese. "Lift up your hands, boy. You're coming, too."

Ace and Babe both raised their arms.

"Okay, alright, keep you're shirt on, fat boy," Ace muttered.

The enforcer jammed the steel barrel further into his stomach.

"Okay, don't get hot under the collar. We'll come along nice and easy. We don't mind a ride. We were thinking of going for a spin before you came. The kid here has never eaten an ice cream sundae. I was planning to stop off at The Chocolate Shop. You want to try a sundae?"

One-eyed Wong spat in Ace's face. The glob descended across Ace's cheek; he couldn't wipe it away because the gun barrel jabbed him again.

The gangsters led them to the elevator. Its carriage was empty and waiting. However, One-eyed Wong motioned for them to follow him down a staircase. He removed the Luger pistols from his gun belt as a precaution.

Although certain the French managers and hotel detectives knew of the Green Gang's presence, Ace thought it unlikely they'd interfere. Since the Americans had no police of their own, they relied on the British law enforcement. And the Brits were unlikely to meddle with Pockmarked Fang's affairs.

One-eyed Wong paused before a large window in the stairway. The last rays of sun shimmered on the murky, yellow waters of the Whangpoo River. The group prepared to return to Pockmarked Fang's estate in the Old Walled City under the cover of a dark, moonlit sky.

A palatial home in Shanghai.

An ink-blue sky hovered over the Soames residence. Chief Inspector Haymes followed a string of pearl-like, white gauze lanterns radiating above a walkway leading to the red-brick house. He grabbed the brass ring from a griffin's nose and slammed it against the door knocker. A bolt grated from behind the door.

"Yes?" Ling poked his head out.

"Chief Inspector Haymes, Special Branch. I'm here to see Mr. Soames."

"Come, please." Ling stepped back, opening the door. Their footsteps fell against a brick floor in a wide hallway decorated with red-and-white-striped wallpaper. Hanging on the walls were carved Florentine mirrors and oil paintings of fox hunts in an English countryside. Ling stopped outside a teak door. "Please wait. I fetch *Hsien-sheng*," said Ling, turning the door knob with his white-gloved hand.

Entering the drawing room, Chief Inspector admired its splendor—teak wall panels, zebra-skin rugs, and mahogany furniture upholstered in ruby fabric similar in color to vintage 1919 port. On the mantle was a bust of Arthur Wellesley, the first Duke of Wellington.

"Good evening, Chief Inspector," said Maxwell, clad in a hunter-green smoking jacket. "Won't you sit down? It's awfully good of you to come here to give your condolences to my dear wife. I'm most impressed by your thoughtfulness."

"Sorry to trouble you, Soames, but I'm here for a different reason." Haymes chose an overstuffed chair. "There is something that won't wait."

"Oh, really?" Maxwell moved to a low table topped with crystal decanters and glasses. He picked up a pair of silver tongs. "My wife will be along presently. I'm sure you'll forgive her if she appears a trifle out of sorts; she's trying to pull herself together. No doubt you can understand her shock."

"Yes—quite right," Haymes replied sympathetically. "It must have been a grave shock indeed."

"Yes, and here we are." Maxwell dropped ice cubes into two highball glasses. "Would you care for something? I'm having a whisky and soda."

"Make mine the same."

Maxwell prepared the highballs and handed one to the older man. "I made them on the strong side for obvious reasons. They'll do us some good. As I was saying to Idina today, this is a lesson to us all. Sometimes

I think we too quickly forget about the Boxer Rebellion. It wasn't so long ago, either. I'll make that point without any hesitation whatsoever at the Inquest."

The Chief Inspector sipped his drink and studied Maxwell, who drained the glass and smacked his lips.

The door flung open; Idina sauntered in. Ignoring them, she tottered to the liquor table. She still wore her white Canton crêpe dress, but its ruffled layers were creased and flattened. "Good evening Chief Inspector—whoever you are, if you can call it a good evening." Her disheveled platinum hair fell over her forehead, hiding her eyes as she groped for a crystal decanter containing her beloved absinthe. Her fingers caressed the bottle filled with a gray-green liquid. She carefully filled a glass and raised it to the light. Her eyes were puffy from crying. She emptied the glass, sighed, and wiped her mouth with the back of her hand. Red lipstick smeared across her hand and face.

"Do forgive me, Chief Inspector, if I'm not at my best," she slurred. "I've had one horrific day." She swayed over a couch. Absinthe spilled everywhere. "Nuts!" she muttered, bending to examine the mess. Noticing red lipstick smeared across her hand, she panicked. "There's blood here. I've got blood on my hand!" She savagely wiped her hand against her dress.

Maxwell rushed to her side. "Steady dear," he said soothingly. "Idina, my darling, take no notice of the mess dearest." He wrapped his arm around her and motioned to the couch. Turning to the Chief Inspector, he continued: "Oh, do leave us in peace, my good man. This ordeal is more than she can stand. Can't you see that?"

Haymes offered no reaction.

"Let me go, you fool!" Idina struggled to free herself. "What do you know about how I feel?" Starting to cry, she half-closed her eyelids and slipped into a stupor.

"Poor darling, the rest will do her good." Maxwell carried her to a sofa and placed her down. "She's extremely distraught, as you can see. She doesn't know what she's saying or doing. At the same time, I, too, have been grieving in my own quiet way." He straightened his smoking jacket. "You must excuse me for a moment. This is rather urgent." He strode to a table, lifted a telephone handset, and dialed.

"Hello, this Maxwell Soames speaking. Please fetch Dr. Hanlon to the phone. Yes, I'll wait." He cupped his hand over the mouthpiece. "Idina must be attended to straight away. She cannot possibly go on drowning herself in absinthe." He lifted the handset to his ear. "Yes, I'm here—sorry to keep you waiting on the line Dr. Hanlon. I'm afraid you'll have to come round after all. Idina's condition has worsened since we last spoke."

Maxwell hung up the phone and walked to the doorway. "Idina and I are both grateful for all you've done. We sincerely thank you for your trouble, Chief Inspector, but it's time you were leaving. You'll have to come back another day."

"Murder, Mr. Soames," Haymes said calmly, finishing his drink and placing the glass on a silver coaster. "A ruthless, cold-blooded murder. That's what I've come to see you about—nothing more and nothing less."

"Well, yes, of course. We all know about that," Maxwell replied indignantly. "There's no reason to come calling upon us, particularly at a time like this, merely to discuss it all over again. If you're here to provide gruesome details about your police procedures, I can assure you we're not the least bit interested."

"Details, ah, yes, details. I'm glad you brought that up."

Maxwell's blue eyes grew larger from behind his gold-rimmed spectacles. "What's the point of this entire conversation? I've told you everything already!"

"The paper lanterns, Soames. What do you know about the paper lanterns?"

"Unbelievable, absolutely unbelievable! You come all the way out here to question me about those blue lanterns?" Amused, Maxwell scratched his bald crown and smiled. "Is this really so important?"

"You'd best answer my questions here." Chief Inspector Haymes lowered his voice for emphasis. "Unless, of course, you'd rather talk at Special Branch headquarters. My driver is waiting outside; he would be only too glad to take you to Foochow Road."

"Oh alright, we may as well clear it up straight away. You shall have your details about those blasted lanterns!" Maxwell took a seat. "In the hunt, the lanterns were hung from the mulberry trees, as usual. We were all following the course marked by the blue lanterns when tragedy struck. They race ended. There's really nothing more to it."

Although Idina stirred, no one paid attention. Her heavy eyelids strained to open. She heard voices talking, but couldn't make out all the words.

The Chief Inspector leaned forward.

"I'm afraid you're wrong, Soames. There is indeed more to the lanterns. They were moved by the murderer."

"Surely you don't believe that, do you?" Maxwell gulped. "What on earth could that boatman possibly hope to gain by moving the lanterns? Why, it doesn't make sense at all."

"Nonetheless, facts are facts. Apparently in the killer's haste, he left two lanterns out of sequence. Also, I found a trap, with rope strung between two trees, at the right height to knock a rider off a pony, not far from where Roddy was murdered. The killer forgot about that, as well."

"You're quite sure?"

Haymes nodded.

"Honestly, my dear fellow, I don't quite know what to make of your assessment," stammered Maxwell, with a puzzled expression. "Why would that native go to all the trouble?"

"The killer couldn't have been that Chinese man. No native would bother moving the lanterns and setting up a rope to break the neck of any old English rider who happened to take a wrong turn. A native wouldn't put some lanterns back in place, jump in a boat, and sail away. There's no point to it."

"I know what I heard and saw." Maxwell rose and poured himself another whiskey and soda. He took a swig. "Surely you believe me? Don't you, Chief Inspector?"

"Erskine didn't drown—his neck was broken. Marks are now showing round his neck. He was a sturdy lad. No Shanghainese could've gotten close enough to harm him that way; Roddy would've gotten the best of him. No, Soames, this murder was the work of a brazen killer acting with premeditation. Perhaps, the killer was someone Roddy knew and didn't fear."

"What? Do you mean to say that Roddy wasn't killed by that wretch?"

"Precisely, Soames. Now, suppose you tell me again all about what you saw and heard."

Maxwell frowned and took another drink. His mind reeled off several possible ways to extricate himself. Suddenly he found an answer!

"I say, Chief Inspector, I think I may have made a terrible mistake. Confound it all!"

Tightly gripping the highball, he rushed to the chair beside Haymes.

"You know I did hear a terrific row taking place in the distance before I came upon poor Roddy. I assumed it was with that dreadful native I saw sailing down the creek. But by Jove, it could've been an argument with someone else, and I have a good idea who that scoundrel may have been."

"You interest me, Soames, do go on."

"Ace Jordan, the American aviator."

Maxwell's eyes sparkled.

"Why, that shameless rogue had the audacity to chase me after I'd finished speaking with you this afternoon as I was going to my motorcar. There were plenty of people about. I'm sure you'll have no trouble finding witnesses."

"What?"

"It all makes sense to me now."

Maxwell drank more then resumed.

"I was so shaken at the time due to poor Roddy, I didn't reflect properly on what Ace told me. Threatening it was, come to think of it! He warned that I'd better vouch for him about some photographs. When I told him I hadn't the foggiest notion what he referring to, he acted like a madman. He threw me against my car. He advised me that what happened to Roddy could happen to me if I wasn't careful."

"You're certain those were exactly his words?"

"Yes, indeed. I didn't understand what he was going on about at the time. I warned if he persisted in his outrageous conduct toward me, I'd send for you and have him arrested for assault at once. That seemed to scare him off."

Haymes clenched his fist.

"Are you prepared to make a signed statement about what you've just told me?"

"Certainly. I'd be happy to do whatever I can to put Roddy's murderer behind bars. But how are you going to apprehend that bloke? Surely, he must know that it's only a matter of time before you'll be onto him?"

"Leave that to me, Soames. I promise I'll personally see to your Mr. Jack Jordan. With pleasure, too, I might add."

The Native Quarter in Shanghai.

Ace sat next to Babe in the Packard Eight sedan. Although unable to see clearly out the window because the Green Gang enforcers stood on the sideboards and blocked his view, Ace guessed correctly that they were traveling deep into the Old Walled City in Shanghai's southern district where the Chinese lived. It smelled of sizzling peanut oil in smoking iron woks, salted fish hanging from roof beams in the open air, and human excrement from open-door public bathrooms awaiting collection in oil drums by night-soil vendors. The sedan blasted its horn at stray dogs, ragged children, peddlers, and bicyclists as it traveled slowly down a labyrinth of narrow, cobbled streets.

Eventually, the car rounded a corner and stopped on Dragon of the Black Pool Road. Its headlights shone on a semi-circular barricade blocking the entrance to Pockmarked Fang's estate. Machine guns, propped atop sandbags, followed the movements of car's occupants as they disembarked. One-eyed Wong waddled to the barricade. Ace and Babe followed with their hands raised high. Ace tried to see through the darkness. Two red objects glowed ahead. A gun barrel, jamming against his spine, urged him onward. Beyond the guards at the barricade stood a weathered wooden gate surrounded by high walls. Rolled barbed wire topped the slate-gray walls. The gate itself had curved eaves covered with jade-green tiles projecting outward. Suspended overhead were giant, five-clawed dragon lanterns glowing in the black night. Made of red glass joined with brass, each whiskered dragon lantern had been fashioned with the Nine Likenesses—a skull like a camel, horns of a deer, eyes akin to a rabbit's, ears identical to an ox, a neck of a snake, a stomach like a frog, scales similar to those of a carp, claws resembling an eagle's, and footpads of a tiger. According to myth, these particular dragons came from the sky species called the *lung*—a hairless animal possessing the greatest virtues after man—who held the second-highest rank in the Chinese kingdom of five animals.

Underneath the dragon lanterns was a large brass gong. One-eyed Wong struck the gong and waited for a sentry to open the gate. Babe's arms ached. He glanced at pair of white marble statues flanking the gate. One depicted a fierce soldier in the ancient military garb of the Yin dynasty. Babe recognized it immediately as the Blue Dragon, one of the famous Star Spirits. Before being canonized into the ethereal realm, the Blue Dragon had been a mortal man known as General Téng Chiu-kung.

Babe stared at the other statue, the White Tiger who, before gaining immortality, once roamed the earth as a distinguished military general named Yin Chêng-Hsiu. Babe considered the two renowned Star Spirits and decided that Pockmarked Fang must be a Taoist. Footsteps fell behind the gate. "One-eyed Wong, here. Be quick, Master awaits us." The gate swayed open. When Babe passed through the gate, he saw an edict plastered to the wall. Black calligraphy, on red paper and bordered in gold, proclaimed:

> *Shut your eyes before you seek truth,*
> *Then, you will find it.*
> *The pearl of Tao shines with exuberance.*
> *Use it during the day and night,*
> *Don't ever discard it,*
> *Otherwise the Ruler of the Netherworld,*
> *Will dispatch his vassals to get you.*

A Green Gang enforcer shoved Babe along. They followed a stone path under a series of triple arches snaking around courtyard gardens, single-story pavilions, and halls. Red lanterns interspersed with flaming torches illuminated the pathway. One-eyed Wong brought everyone to a standstill outside a building called The Pavilion of Frozen Light. He disappeared inside. Cicadas buzzed in trees, and crickets chirped in courtyard gardens. Ace heard muffled voices and laughter inside the pavilion. He looked around and began counting the dark outlines of the sloping, tiled rooftops jutting above the grounds of Pockmarked Fang's estate. In the distance beyond, a Seven-Bends-Eight-Crooks Bridge spanned a rustling brook adjacent to a wall where five large metal cages hung. Ace squinted to get a better look. Torchlights shone on the cages which contained Chinese men.

"The Master is ready," One-eyed Wong called out.

Ace and Babe entered The Pavilion of Frozen Light. Inside the large hall, Pockmarked Fang sat cross-legged in the middle of an elevated rosewood couch with White Orchid and another giggling young *ch'ieh* concubine. Both girls wore embroidered satin dresses. White Orchid had a 100-butterfly design, while the other wore a 100-flower pattern. Their cheeks bore festive *yang zhi* rouge made from wild safflowers grown in

China's western mountains. Bean-oil lamps illuminated the room. In a prominent place, a rectangular altar table leaned against one wall. Incense swirled from three-legged *cloisonné* jars before porcelain figures of The Three Pure Ones—Yü Huang, the Jade Emperor and Master of All Gods; Tao Chün, the Controller of the Balance between the Yin and Yang; and Lao Tzû, the Great Supreme Emperor of the Dark First Cause. *Fei t'ao* peaches sat in a bowl before the trio. On the wall above the altar, an assortment of smoke-stained bamboo tablets bore the names of Pockmarked Fang's ancestors.

One-eyed Wong pushed Ace and Babe toward carved rosewood chairs arranged in sets of twos around the perimeter of the hall. The chair groupings were separated by high, marble-topped tea tables. The elevated rosewood couch, where Pockmarked Fang lounged, occupied the center of the room.

"Be seated," ordered Pockmarked Fang.

Everyone obeyed. White Orchid pleaded with Pockmarked Fang, currently still absorbed in a game of chance with his two wives. "Master, please let me be the keeper of the table?"

"No," he said gruffly, hunching over a small rectangular table supported by two-inch-high legs. "One-eyed Wong, fetch some tea for my guests."

"Yes, Master." The fat man rose with a bow and waddled backwards out the pavilion.

Ace and Babe exchanged glances. Ace thought he detected the sickly sweet odor of opium.

Pockmarked Fang scooped two handfuls of shiny silver coins from a basket at his side. Engrossed in a game of *fan t'an*, he poured the coins on the tabletop and covered the pile with a jade bowl.

"I bet you 30 *liang* there'll be three pieces of cash remaining," laughed White Orchid, tossing her head back and causing Mandarin duck ornaments in her hair to tinkle.

"No, there'll be none left." Pockmarked Fang scratched the frayed edge of his ear.

The other *ch'ieh* concubine lifted a piece of paper, dipped a bamboo-reed brush with fox-hair bristles into an ink pot, and recorded the guess as well as the bet. A beautiful *hua dian* kingfisher feather decoration of gold, silver, and emerald-green paint glistened between her eyebrows.

Reclining woman with bound feet.

Pockmarked Fang removed the upside-down jade bowl. Jewels protruded from his golden mesh fingernail protectors, which clicked against the tabletop as he counted out silver coins in fours and swept them into the basket. White Orchid and the *ch'ieh* concubine watched intently until it became clear that only three pieces of silver remained.

"*Aiyah!*" squealed White Orchid, clapping her hands. The other concubine dabbed her writing brush in ink and added 90 *liang* to White Orchid's winnings.

"Tsai Shên, the God of Wealth, is with you this evening," Pockmarked Fang remarked dryly.

White Orchid spoke in a sweet singsong voice. "My Master, Tsai Shên is luck-giving and here at your door. Your pavilion is happy and merry. Every omen is good. My Master, may you have great wealth and good fortune—and may a very long life be yours."

"That's enough for now," Pockmarked Fang said gruffly. "White Orchid, tomorrow you shall be keeper of the table. Go!"

White Orchid and the other concubine gathered the *fan t'an* game, then bowed to Pockmarked Fang and shuffled backwards out the room. One-eyed Wong entered the hall with a servant boy, who poured steaming jasmine tea into celadon porcelain cups. The boy also set out bowls of betel nuts. Keeping his eyes on Pockmarked Fang, Ace reached for a cup, blew at the jasmine petals floating on top, and sipped while watching the Opium Czar.

Pockmarked Fang clapped his hands twice. His nail protectors clanked like small cymbals. The servant boy, waiting outside the pavilion, ran inside. He placed a platter of dried yellow fruit called *lung yen* before the Master and scurried away. Delicately surveying the platter, Pockmarked Fang selected the largest of the dragon's-eye fruit and popped it into his mouth. Choosing another with fleshy folds, he held it out to Ace. "Devil from over the sea, this fruit, do you know it?"

"No, I'm afraid I don't."

"This dragon's eye will help me live forever—as you have done."

"Oh, about last night," Ace replied. "I was glad to help out. I would've done the same for anyone."

"Silence, barbarian!" Pockmarked Fang tossed the dragon's eye into the platter.

Babe ducked; Ace sat upright in his chair. Only One-eyed Wong seemed unfazed; he licked his index finger and rubbed it around his empty eye socket.

Regaining his composure, Pockmarked Fang spoke again. "Yesterday afternoon not long after I awoke, I went for a walk along Siccawei Creek. As I came to an old ash tree, a copper mist appeared from the base of the trunk. I watched the mist swirl as a fox leapt out. It had a human skull on its forehead and white eyes. The fox gnashed its teeth at me, pointed its nose to the north, and crouched down. Without dropping the skull from its forehead, the fox kowtowed three times to the Star Emperor of the North Pole. Suddenly mist encircled it, and the fox became transformed into a beautiful, raven-haired fairy."

Pockmarked Fang nibbled another dragon's-eye fruit. "The fox fairy spoke to me. 'You will never become an immortal,' she laughed, 'but will become dry bones.' Holding a whisk made from the fur of a *fi-fi* monkey, the enchantress was about to strike at me when a foreign dog rushed over. As the dog began to tear at her silver robe, the fox fairy vanished with the copper mist."

He looked happy, savoring the fruit's sweet taste, and continued while chewing. "This omen foretold events. Barbarian, you are the dog who chased death away from me. Since you were sent to me by The Three Pure Ones to ensure my immortality, I shall adopt you as my son even though you're from over the sea."

Ace drank tea to steady his nerves.

Pockmarked Fang set the platter of *lung yen* on his lap. He started to pick through the fruit when a five-paneled folding screen next to him crashed to the floor. From behind it crawled out a wiry Shanghainese— Eggplant Ho! His elongated face was swollen and bloody. A jute cord bound his hands. He'd been kneeling on chains. One-eyed Wong jumped off his chair, shuffled over to Eggplant Ho, and lifted him up by the hair.

"See to it that his mouth is beaten again with a small bamboo." Pockmarked Fang searched among the fruit. "Bring him back to me when his rat's teeth have fallen out and his lips are soft as stewed jellyfish."

One-eyed Wong dragged Eggplant Ho by the hair across the floor and out the doorway.

Ace cast a sideways glance at Babe, who had long since lost all color in his face. Both stared in disbelief.

Pockmarked Fang grabbed a handful of dragon's eyes, shoved them in his mouth, and belched. "I am tired. You go now." He raised a shriveled hand and motioned to the door. "I will arrange for the adoption ceremony when I'm feeling better, but as of this moment my protection extends over you. This news shall become known in Shanghai. Be gone!"

Babe and Ace sprang from the rosewood chairs.

"Thank you. May you live 10,000 years!" exclaimed Babe, bowing reverently. He motioned for Ace to do the same, but Ace simply lowered his head. "We'd better leave while we still can," Babe whispered.

"Not a minute too soon, either," Ace answered, rushing out the pavilion.

The Packard Eight sedan rolled out of Pockmarked Fang's estate at 7 o'clock that evening. "Take us to Nanking Road. The Saints & Sinners Club," Ace told the Chinese driver. No one talked during the 30-minute drive. When the sedan pulled over on Nanking Road in the front of the nightclub, Ace and Babe jumped out the door and onto the wide street. "Follow me," Ace yelled.

Babe scrambled out of the path of a fast-moving automobile. Darting around rickshaws, three-wheeled pedicabs, wheelbarrows, and European pedestrians dressed for a night on the town, they made their way to the two-story, gray building.

At the entrance of The Saints & Sinners Club, Ace turned to Babe. "For now, let's forget about what just happened. I've got some business in here with a pal of mine."

A Eurasian youth in a monkey cap and double-breasted red silk uniform opened the door for Ace, but tried to block Babe from entering.

"Got a problem, brother?" Ace yelled. "The kid's with me. If you don't get out of his way, you'll get a knuckle sandwich right in the kisser!"

Scowling, the doorman stepped aside.

Babe said, "I don't think this is such a good idea for me to be in this place for Americans."

"Listen kid, you're with me. Just remember that and stick close to me."

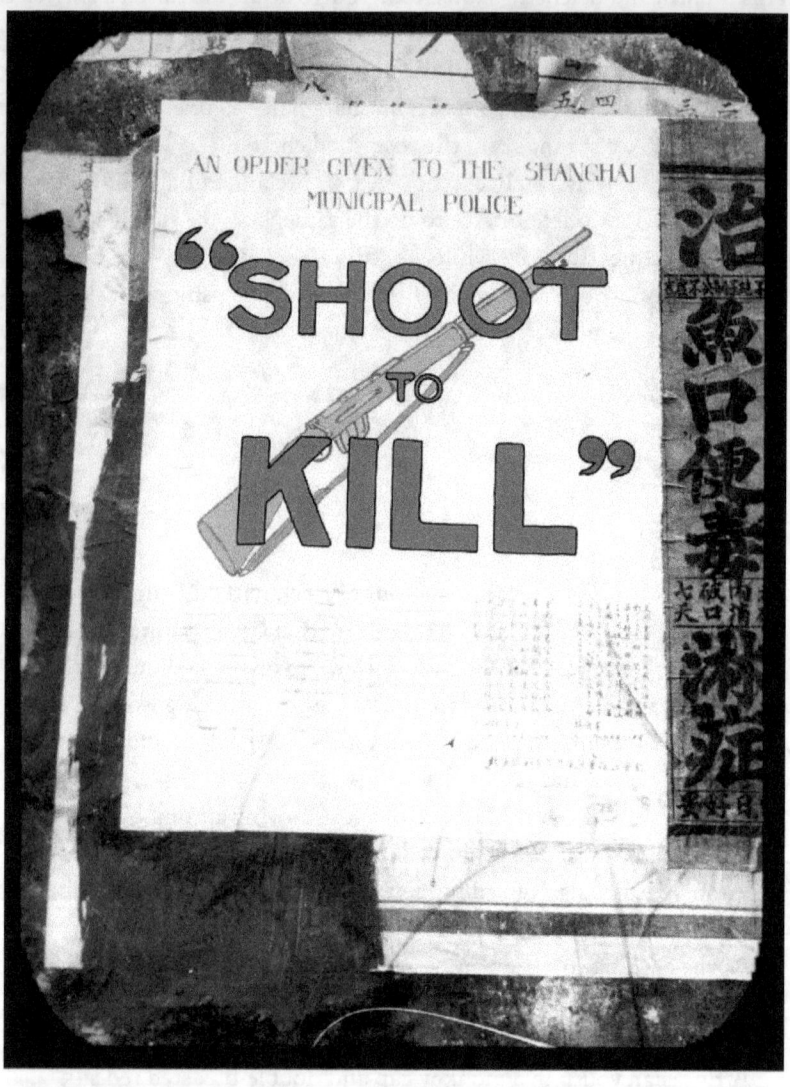

A posted order given to the Shanghai Municipal Police.

They went inside, moving swiftly past potted palm trees, chrome ashtray stands, and mirrors twinkling under amber lights. Trying not to trip over his shoes, Babe took small steps on the plush red carpet. When they reached the split-level dining room, Ace scanned the crowd for Bunny Vance. The lights were low; the air smelled of cigarette smoke. Tables emptied as patrons took to the dance floor. A trombonist in a Black jazz band from Harlem played a haunting, woeful number. Ace spotted Bunny gliding towards him.

"Well hello, flyboy, if it ain't the gent in today's headlines. Why, you've been busy since that little reception the Brits gave you here last night, eh?" Bunny joked. His thin brown moustache curled over the corners of his mouth. A perfumed scent rose from a thick layer of pomade over his brown hair.

"Come on, Bunny, don't get sore about last night. Let it ride, pal."

"Alright, alright." Bunny frowned at Babe standing sheepishly in the background. "Who's your date?"

"Never mind the kid. He's okay. Listen, I'm in one heck of a jam. Someone's trying to put me behind the eight ball. I need to go into a huddle with Chicago Charlie somewhere that's quiet, but this house is packed!"

"How about my office upstairs?"

"That would be swell." Ace grinned. "Thanks, pal."

"Just follow me."

Bunny walked through the dining room to an alcove. Reaching a door-sized mirror on a wall, he pressed a button hidden in the frame. The mirror opened up into a musty-smelling room. A narrow, metal staircase led to an upstairs office. At the top of the landing, Bunny pointed to a chrome door.

"Step right inside, boys. Make yourselves at home. I'll tell Chicago you're here."

"Thanks, pal, I owe you one. Say, would you mind asking Chicago to bring up a couple of cold sandwiches? I could sure use some grub. The kid may want something, too."

"Sure thing, there's plenty of hootch inside. Help yourself."

"Okey-doke, thanks again, pal."

Bunny disappeared downstairs.

Ace and Babe entered the office, decorated with red, tufted-brocade furniture, satin pillows, and beaded dividers. One wall had a two-way, mirrored glass window overlooking the dining area and ballroom.

"Sit down kid. Take a load off your feet."

Ace went to a bar, poured water into a glass, and handed it to Babe. "Here's something to wet your whistle."

Next, he mixed himself a gin and tonic and walked to the window. Down below near the bandshell, Bunny spoke to Chicago Charlie.

Sighing, Ace strolled to a chair and sank into a cushion. He observed a pile of frayed French postcards. The topmost one showed a black-and-white picture of a plump, dimpled woman posing with a fringed parasol and a feathered fan.

When Babe finished the water, he admired his new white tails, black slacks, and shirt studs. Straightening his black bow-tie, he spoke: "As the adopted son of Pockmarked Fang, you can become very rich. He might even find a high place for you somewhere in his businesses…probably in his dealings with foreigners."

"Listen up, kid," Ace interrupted. "I've got plenty of my own money. I don't need any extra family members, either. What's more, I don't want a piece of his racket. I'm not going to be his adopted son, get it?"

Babe scratched his chin.

"It's dangerous to refuse. The foreign powers fear him, even the northern warlords don't try anything with him."

"Yeah, I can believe that, especially after tonight." Ace returned to the two-way glass. "I'll figure something out, though. Maybe I'll get lucky. Maybe that hophead Pockmarked Fang will get charged up on some more opium and have another vision. Who knows? Maybe the fox fairy will tell him this adoption plan is one big mistake."

Chicago Charlie strutted in with a tray of sandwiches.

"Put on your nosebags. Here comes the ham and cheese." He set down the tray and rubbed his hands together.

"Bunny says you're in some kind of a pickle, flyboy. What gives?"

Ace bit into a sandwich. "You know my boss, Maxwell Soames— ex-boss, I should say."

"Yeah, go on." Chicago Charlie went to the bar and poured himself a glass of rye.

Babe watched the little man with wavy yellow hair remove a wax-paper packet from his vest pocket.

Chicago picked up a pink opium pill, dropped it on his tongue, and washed it down with the rye.

"Old Maxwell is doing his best to put the kibosh on me," said Ace, between mouthfuls. "So far, he's done a pretty fair job of framing me. Get a load of this: I'm supposed to be spying for the Japanese!"

"Why that dirty double-crosser! I always thought he wuz a slippery little so-and-so."

Chicago sauntered to a divan and plopped down.

"So that's why the Brits wuz tryin' to muscle in here. Bunny sez they wuz quizzin' yuh about the Nationalists. Do the Brits have anything on yuh?"

"Maybe. I fessed up to taking some photos for Maxwell on those flights he's been sending me on to Hangchow. Claimed he needed shots of the terrain for a railway deal. Now, it seems the pictures were used to blow up arms shipments to the Nationalists. The Japanese, posing as Reds, are supposed to be behind it."

Chicago whistled. "Brother, yuh sure are in a first-class jam."

"No kidding!" Ace went to the bar and refilled his glass. "I'd sure like to take a crack at that Maxwell."

"Well, what are yuh gonna do? Got any ideas?"

Ace paced the floor.

"Yeah, I've got to clear myself, but I need to find out more about what Maxwell's up to. He's working with Colonel Togawa. Know anything about him?"

"Not much. He heads the Japanese military forces in China. I hear they've practically taken over Manchuria. If yuh ask me, I say they're up to something big. Did yuh see their newest gunboat called the *Nippon*? She sure is a beaut!"

Ace jammed a piece of gum in his mouth.

"Look Chicago, here's my plan. You find out as much as you can about Colonel Togawa. The kid here, Babe, will see what he can come up with, too. I'll tail Maxwell. We'll start first thing tomorrow and meet here in the afternoon at 3 o'clock."

"Sure thing, Ace, glad to lend a hand."

Chicago walked up to Ace and playfully socked him in the arm.

"We've been good pals ever since the war. I'm glad to do somethin' for yuh for a change. It's mostly been the other way around. Now, let's go downstairs for some fun."

"Not tonight, another time. We'd better fade." Ace addressed Babe. "Come along, kid, let's scram."

They tramped downstairs.

"Say, flyboy," Chicago spoke up, "have yuh thought 'bout our little chat this morning? I've been tryin' to work out some angles for this Pockmarked Fang deal."

"Don't say another word about that! Do you hear? Not another word."

"Don't get sore." Chicago shrugged his narrow shoulders. "I was only tryin' to look out for yuh. That's all."

They reentered the dining area where Bunny Vance leaned against the wall next to the mirrored door and waited for them.

"Say, Ace, that pip is here—the doll you left here with last night. Boy, oh, boy! She sure is easy on the eye. She's been asking around for you. Says it's important. Wanna see her?"

"Sure, send her right over. There's something I'd like to say to that dizzy dame about that article she wrote."

Bunny disappeared into the crowd and returned less than a minute later with the strawberry blonde on his arm.

Helen rushed to Ace.

"Look, you've got to get out of here, fast!" She tugged his hand.

"What are you talking about?"

"I can't explain it alright now. Listen, my father is Dr. Hanlon. He came home upset tonight. He told me that the man I wrote about, meaning you, is about to be arrested for murder. Special Branch is looking for you now. They think you're a spy, too."

Ace pulled her closer.

"What? Murder? Who the heck am I supposed to have killed?"

"Roddy Erskine, a relative of Mr. and Mrs. Maxwell Soames. My father is a good friend of theirs. Anyway, tonight he was called to help Mrs. Soames. She's in a terrible state. Mr. Soames wasn't supposed to tell my father about the killer, but he did anyway. That's how I found out. I can't explain why—maybe it's a gut instinct or something—but I don't think you're a killer. Now, since I've just done you a favor, how about helping me out? I need a break for my career."

"What?"

"Look, I don't know what you're going to do, but whatever it is, I want to write the story. I need an exclusive. In exchange, I'll do what I can."

"Okey-doke, you've got yourself a deal."

Ace reached for a cigarette. His fingers trembled as he lit it. Blowing smoke through his nose, he spoke. "I was on my way back to the hotel, but that's no good now. I've got to find somewhere to lay low."

"We've got a houseboat in the countryside. You can stay there."

"That's no good either. It's too far away. I've got to be in Shanghai."

He took a drag from the cigarette.

"A junk—I'll rent one! That way I can get around on the waterways. The Brits don't control the waterways. They'd never look for me there."

"Is there anything I can do?" asked Helen.

Ace thought for a moment.

"Yeah, I'll need some money and a change of clothes for me and the kid over there. Can you handle that?"

"Certainly, Mr. Jordan. Don't forget I'm a reporter. I can handle myself."

"Swell. Go the Cathay Hotel. Suite 444."

Ace reached into his pocket and handed her the keys.

"Then meet me in Nantao, next to the Old Walled City. I'll be along the Chinese Bund at the funeral piers. Be there at midnight."

"Okay, you've got yourself a deal. I'll be there, the funeral piers at midnight."

A funeral procession.

CHAPTER THREE

14th Day of the Eighth Moon

Bodies of the dead lay in rows on nine funeral piers that clawed into the Whangpoo River's dark waters. Pairs of gigantic storks made of white paper hovered on bamboo poles 30 feet above each pier. Moonlight illuminated their spread wings and long bodies. The storks served two purposes: spirits of the dead could soar upon their backs to the netherworld, and they also warned passersby on Oue Maloo—a road skirting the Chinese Bund at Nantao, an eastern suburb of the Old Walled City—to avoid unnecessary travel at this junction for departing souls. Two miles from the edge of the piers, a lone *sampan* labored up the Whangpoo in a northerly course past the Native Customs House and a water tower. The sound of the small vessel's chugging engine mingled with splashing water. Rows of lanterns in blue and white colors, symbolizing mourning, glowed ahead in the darkness.

Babe hiked up the collar of his evening shirt over his nose. Muttering to himself, he steered the *sampan* with difficulty around floating coffins of flimsy wood and corpses tied to straw mats or wooden planks twisting in the water. Ace shielded his lower face with a handkerchief like an outlaw and sat next to Babe in the back of the *sampan*. They both cringed each time water droplets sprayed them. Revolted by the stench of rotting flesh in a flotilla of corpses and coffins, Ace had heard of but never before ventured out to this Sea of the Dead. Some bodies had been wrapped like cocoons in coarse white or unbleached cotton. Some wore their best clothing in odd-numbered layers to attract good fortune in the next life. Others wore lucky crimson-colored gowns and scarves tied over their faces. Once people too poor to afford a proper burial, these bobbing corpses were everywhere. Ace recalled hearing that the average Shanghainese died before age 30.

"Hey kid, what are these pieces of paper, tree branches, and buns tied around their arms and hands?"

Babe pointed to a body on the left. "That woman has hard cakes tied around her wrist so she can feed them to the Heavenly Dogs when she tries to pass into Heaven. If the cakes don't appease the Spirit Dogs, she'll have to beat them with that willow stick tied to her other hand."

The *sampan* thudded against a wooden coffin whose sides were rounded like a tree trunk. The impact jolted them off balance, and a putrid stench filled their nostrils as the coffin burst open. "Gee whiz, Babe!" Ace jumped to his feet. "Watch where you're going!" With the coffin seals broken, water seeped over the two-inch-thick walls and began to cover the body of a young man. A red swatch of cloth shrouded his face. He held bamboo sprigs in one hand. Above his head, a small bowl contained uncooked rice grains for him to eat in the afterlife. Underneath his black slippers, packets held paper cutouts of silver and gold ingots, a house, an automobile and a bridge to the afterlife. Water began to cause the ink to bleed on a white paper banner across his chest.

"What does that say?"

Babe looked over. "It's a guide to help his soul reach the Western Heaven. His name was Oong Ming, 24 years old, born in Bao Shan, and died of a lung infection. It says since he was a good man, his soul should be allowed to enter the Western Heaven after it journeys to hell to meet with Ti Tsang, the Ruler of the Dead."

"Let's beat it! This stiff is giving me the heebie-jeebies!" The motor sputtered. Ace walked to the cabin, lowered his head under the thatched roof, and sat on a bench. He held up his wristwatch to a lantern swaying from the roof. A few minutes late to the meeting with Helen. Ace's eyes rested on his gold pinkie ring given to him by the French. It had 25 diamonds shaped like an albatross for each German aeroplane he downed. Removing the handkerchief from his face, he lit a cigarette.

"We've reached the funeral piers," Babe yelled. "Where to?"

Ace left the cabin and pointed. "Over there, the farthest one, next to the street. Take us to the side nearest the shore." When they got there, Ace prepared to disembark.

"Boss," said Babe, holding him back, "you'd better put that handkerchief back over your face before going up there."

"What for?"

"To most Chinese, you're a foreign devil."

"Is that so? Tell me something I don't already know."

Babe squeezed his arm. "If someone should come to put a relative to sea and find a foreign devil, it would be bad luck for the dead! You must hide as much of your face as possible. Please do as I say!"

"Oh, alright." Ace covered his face. "I don't need any more trouble." He scrambled to the pier. Chinese characters covered the lanterns and cloth banners fluttered on bamboo poles stuck in carved holes along the walkway. The banners bore inscriptions citing wonderful deeds of the deceased. Ace crept along the pier. His patent-leather shoes tread over ashes from incense sticks and furled pieces of burnt paper offerings of opium pipes, clothes, servants, furniture, rickshaws, sedan chairs, horses, cooking pots, jewelry, and money—all burnt for the dead so that they could have these possessions in their new "ghost lives." Clattering hooves approached on Oue Maloo. Ace ducked behind a thick bamboo pole supporting a giant white-paper stork. Peering out, he saw a donkey in a white harness pulling a cart covered with coarse, unbleached cloth. A rooster, bouncing on a cloth-draped coffin, had been tied there to frighten away souls of demons. Walking in a line behind the cart, mourners began to wail. Three men proceeded in front, followed by two women and two children; they wore pointed white-paper hats and white sackcloth. One man held a framed scroll mounted on a bamboo pole. It cited his dead mother's good deeds.

Ace observed the funeral procession stop at the next pier. The mourners unloaded the coffin, carried it to the water's edge at the end of the pier, and kowtowed three times before it. One woman lit three incense sticks and placed them in a bronze urn on the pier. Another held a basket, from which she tossed tiny paper images of Chin Shan and Yin Shan, the famed Gold and Silver Mountains. These offerings would buy the benevolence of any stray spirits wandering near the pier. Enthralled, Ace failed to notice Helen's arrival. Still wearing her black evening gown, she dashed up and down the piers searching for him. After distributing the spirit money, the mourners kowtowed and lit firecrackers to ward off demons. A man placed a red-glazed piglet, flanked by joss sticks on a rectangular wooden tray, near the foot of the coffin; then he offered the incense for his dead wife. One son threw rice grains over the coffin, while beseeching the Mountain Dragon to descend over his mother's body and bestow good luck on her and the surviving family. The two sons gathered baskets from the children and burned more paper objects. Their father opened the coffin to search for any pieces of metal that a family enemy could have hidden inside to cause bad luck to their clan. Such a piece of metal near the corpse could trap the woman's ghost on earth to prevent her soul's ascent. Suddenly, the mourners screamed at the sight of Helen.

Ace jumped from behind the bamboo pole. "Helen, over here!" She smiled and waved, but an orange sailed through the air and hit her leg. A volley of other oranges followed.

"Foreign devil, foreign devil!" The mourners hurled firecrackers. A man clutched the bamboo pole with the spirit scroll, held it like a lance, and charged. Helen screamed. Ace ripped the handkerchief from his face and raced down the pier. He grabbed her hand, and they fled to the street.

"This way," said Helen, gasping to catch her breath. "My motorcar is over there."

From afar, One-eyed Wong sat inside the taupe-colored Packard Eight, hidden among the shadows on a side street, while watching them scramble over to the Roamer Roadster. Helen reached into the red two-door convertible and pulled out a large, round hatbox from the floor. "I've got your things in here." She handed him the box.

"Did you have trouble getting into my suite?"

"Not at all. Your key's in the hatbox." Helen laughed. "The hotel boy on your floor was asleep. Don't worry, no one saw anything."

"Anyone from Special Branch there? Were you followed?" Ace opened the hatbox, took out some money, and stuffed the bills in his wallet.

"No one noticed me except for a legless beggar on a wheel cart. He followed me down the sidewalk until I climbed into my motorcar and left. That doesn't count, though. I'm sure his only interest was money, which he didn't get from me!"

Closing the lid, Ace remembered seeing the beggar talking to that gangster on the Bund. "Did that guy have thick white hair, sticking straight up, kind of like bristles on a porcupine?"

Helen leaned against the roadster's door. "I think so. Why?"

"No reason. I just wondered." Ace shrugged. "The little guy has been hanging around the hotel. That's all." He tucked the hatbox under his arm. "I've got to run along now. That was sure swell of you to help me out. A guy could go the distance with a girl like you. Maybe I'll see you around sometime. I've got to go now."

"This looks like the finish. I know a first-class brush-off when I see one!" Helen shoved her hands on her hips. "Trying to pull a fast one on me? After all I've done for you!"

"Don't get into a flap. I'm grateful to you, but I'm in a jam, and I've got business that doesn't involve you."

"I hear what you're saying, brother!" She stomped. "Just my luck to get mixed up with a stinker like you."

"Look, Helen, you come across as a pretty smart girl. You know the kind of mugs I've got to mix with if I'm going to clear myself. Don't hold it against me. I've got nothing against you—on the level."

She glared. "You're right! I *am* a pretty smart girl. And you've just pushed your luck. You owe me. Listen up, because this is how I want to get paid. I'll keep my mouth shut about you, the boat, and anything else, but I get the story when it's all over. Just like I told you before."

"What a kick in the pants! I sure had you pegged wrong." He lit up a cigarette. "I've got to hand it to you. You're quite a girl, Helen, quite a girl."

"Don't give me that load of baloney. Is it a deal or isn't it? This could turn out to be just the kind of scoop I've been waiting for. Who knows? Your story could pack a big wallop. Might even land me a job with the *China Weekly Review*."

"I'm wise to you now, and I know when I'm licked." He jabbed his finger at her. "You'll have your scoop. Just stay out of my way! Get it?"

"Okay, tough guy," snickered Helen, climbing into the roadster.

Ace headed back to the *sampan*. "I'm such a sucker when it comes to women," he muttered, watching her drive away.

Maxwell whistled as he sprung jauntily upstairs to his bedroom. He hadn't bothered to dress before breakfast because he awoke earlier than usual; he had felt ravenous. With his belly now full, he skipped upstairs to the second floor. No need to fear awakening Idina. She was dead to the world thanks to the good Dr. Hanlon. Maxwell rubbed his hands together. Although sunrise was an hour away, he knew it'd be a glorious day. What marvelous luck about young Roddy's demise.

The morning's *North China Daily News* called it "an unfortunate accident." Those Special Branch fellows certainly were discrete! Maxwell congratulated himself for creatively lying about Roddy and Ace to ensure his dealings as a Japanese spy remained secret. Money wasn't his primary reason for betraying England. The Japanese rather *understood* him better than his countrymen, who often dismissed him at first glimpse because of his scrawny stature. If anyone could empathize, the Japanese did, especially in China where they known as "devil dwarfs." Well, well, the Japanese would show the Chinese in the end sooner rather than later, too.

Entering his bedroom, Maxwell walked to a full-length mirror where he admired himself, thinking of someday returning to London as a man of wealth and power. He wondered if Major Fujiwara would pay handsomely for his brilliant maneuver with Roddy that would end Special Branch's snooping into the Hangchow affair. Perhaps the great Colonel Togawa would appreciate how valuable such a clever Englishman as he could be. Time to bathe. Then, off to the Shanghai Club for his morning routine. There, he'd enjoy playing the part of a grieving relative. After an hour or so, he'd leave for an errand. And, what an errand indeed! If they only knew he'd be rendezvousing with Major Fujiwara. Maxwell strode to a nightstand and pressed a buzzer to signal his readiness for a steaming bath.

Cupping icy water from a chipped enameled washbowl, Ace splashed his face. The cold water refreshed him. He hadn't slept well, and the straw mat on the cabin floor of the junk he'd rented the previous night hadn't helped either. Mosquito bites dotted his limbs. Resisting a temptation to scratch a welt on his elbow, he noticed he was alone.

"Babe!"

A heap of evening clothes sat on the floor next the gaping hatbox. Ace searched for his wallet. Leafing through the bills, he noticed only $20 was missing. He reached for a pair of beige silk socks and a matching linen shirt and suit. Except for the black patent-leather evening shoes, his outfit was inconspicuous. Ace grabbed one of the floor mats, scooped up the pile of discarded clothes, and held the bundle away from his body before tossing it overboard.

A haze hung over the yellow Whangpoo River where the junk was anchored among dozens of others near the East Gate of the Old Walled City. It was relatively still aside from the sounds of water lapping and *sampans* chortling back and forth. A conch shell periodically bellowed from a river junk. Donkey carts and bicycles formed the only early morning traffic on the Quai de France, a short thoroughfare parallel to the river that separated the Bund in the International Settlement from Oue Maloo byway in the Old Walled City. Ace walked to the stern, built high above the water level, and saw Babe climb aboard. "Breakfast is here." Babe held up a basket in each hand. "I took some money from you. Here's your change."

"Keep it. You'll probably need it." Ace frowned at the boy's tattered pants, tunic, and straw sandals. "Say, where did you get that outfit?"

"Not bad, eh?" Babe grinned while removing small tins from the baskets. "We'd better eat this while it's still warm." They sat down. Babe laid out a teapot, cups, rice bowls, and chopsticks. The tins contained soft-boiled rice with pickled cabbage and bits of pork, scorched whole yams, and steamed buns glazed with egg yolk.

"You didn't answer my question. What gives with those duds you've on?"

Pouring two cups of green tea, Babe piled his bowl with food. "Today, I'll be a beggar—one who will see, but remain unseen."

"Come again?" asked Ace, stuffing rice into his mouth.

"What better way to learn about the Japanese without arousing suspicion?"

"Go on, I'm all ears."

Babe split the skin of a yam with the blunt ends of his chopsticks, cracked it open, and picked out the soft middle with the chopstick's pointed tips. "Everyone knows that prominent Japanese go to the Hongkew district, north of the International Settlement. I shall start there at Osaka Gardens."

"That makes sense." Ace nodded to himself and sipped tea. "I've never been there, but I've heard that the Japanese big shots like the geishas there."

"I'll ask the beggars about Colonel Togawa."

They finished their meal in silence, while looking at the junk anchorages on the same side of the river. Columns of coolies formed on the piers leading up to 50 or more opium junks as far as the eye could see. The junks had wooden hulls with giant eyes painted on the prows, weathered from numerous voyages 10 miles upstream to the Yangtze and 60 miles further to the place where the mighty river's mouth led to the Eastern Sea and beyond. The coolies, wearing only baggy, faded-blue, short-legged

Laborers boarding a ship.

pants, worked in teams of two up the gangplanks. Each carried a thick bamboo rod slung over his shoulders, weighted down under wooden casks containing 40 pounds of gooey opium balls. The black dirt, as the Chinese called it, had been wrapped in poppy leaves and placed in wax-sealed chests to maintain its freshness during the ocean voyage. However, the buyers didn't know the opium being loaded into cargo holds had been laced with water-buffalo dung, mud, and hemp oil.

A *sampan* a few yards away roused Ace's interest. He rose, shielding his eyes from the sun, and recognized the young Chinese man, with greased hair and a widow's peak, standing in the *sampan*. He wore the same long brown gown and strand of amber beads and jade amulets as the day before. Exercising his fingers around steel balls, the Red Pole enforcer looked directly at Ace with a blank expression as his *sampan* sputtered past.

"For crying out loud! That looks like..." Ace kicked the empty teapot, which rolled across the deck.

Startled, Babe fell backwards. "What's the matter?"

"Nothing!"

Ace took out a cigarette, banged one end on his palm and lit it. He inhaled and expelled smoke from his nose.

"We've got to scram. We'll take this junk upstream and moor it near Pootung. Then we'll switch to the *sampan* and go for a little ride across the river to the Bund. There, we'll part. You find out as much as you can; I'll do likewise." Ace looked at his wristwatch. "We'll meet at the Temple of Heaven at 5 o'clock sharp."

Putting the dishes, chopsticks, and tins into the baskets, Babe spoke without looking up.

"What are you going to do? Do you have any ideas?"

"Yeah, I'm going to the Shanghai Club. That's where Maxwell always starts his day with his pals. I'm sure he'll be at his usual spot in front of the Long Bar, probably spinning a one heck of a yarn about Roddy."

Ace flicked the cigarette butt over the side of the junk and into the water.

"Come on. Let's blow. It's getting late."

Oval clocks lined a row on the north wall in Special Branch's
briefing room at Shanghai Municipal Police Headquarters. Each clock had
black lettering displaying the time in key cities. At 7 o'clock in Shanghai,
it was 8 a.m. in Tokyo, 4:30 a.m. in Delhi, and 11 p.m. of the previous day
in London. Chief Inspector Haymes stood behind an oak podium facing
a roomful of plainclothes detectives all dressed like British colonials with
their white drill trousers, white shirts rolled up at the sleeves, and dark
ties. They all wore black socks and brown pigskin shoes. Some chattered
loudly; others looked in front and squirmed like schoolchildren in their
desks, waiting for morning recess to begin. Haymes cracked a wooden
pointer across the top of a podium. Once satisfied he commanded their
attention, he walked to a yellowed map of China that took up most of the
west wall. "Look sharp, pay attention, and get your pencils ready now, lads,
because I'm only going to say this once. You're not at the Gordon Road
Police Station and Training Depot any longer." The pointing stick slid in a
northerly direction from Shanghai, continued over the Gulf of Pechili, and
rose above the base of Shêngching province.

"As you no doubt know, the Japanese continue to build up commercial
and military forces in the Kuantung area, which they control in
Manchuria." The pointer followed a slatted line marking the South
Manchurian Railway and stopped midway on a black circle around the city
of Mukden. "Yesterday, we received a secret cable from one of our agents in
Mukden. It appears the Japanese are trying to hide the fact they're
constructing a factory there."

The pointer slid south, following the Liao River to Yingk'ou, near the
Gulf of Liaotung. "Also, an Anglican missionary sent word to us that
significant activity is occurring here at the port in Yingk'ou, 20 kilometers
from the mouth of the Liao River. Apparently, numerous berths are being
erected in anticipation of some as-yet unknown shipments."

Haymes turned to the men. "The missionary is unable to learn what
cargoes will be brought it, or taken out for that matter. These two pieces of
intelligence may be related. In any case, Special Branch must know what

the Japanese are up to. His Majesty depends on all of us throughout China to do our part for the Empire. Also, no doubt as some of you may know already, yesterday Admiral Iwasaki sailed into Shanghai aboard the S.S. *Nippon* gunboat." He tapped the pointer against the side of his leg. "And, that brazen heathen had the cheek to moor it in the Whangpoo next to our *War Diadem*!"

The detectives whistled derisively and hissed. "That swine!" exclaimed a deep voice in a Scottish brogue.

"Now settle down lads. I know just how you feel," said Haymes, motioning like a conductor to silence the din. "Be that as it may, Special Branch are determined to get to the bottom of this whole business concerning the Japanese. Although Young Marshal Chang Hsueh-liang raised the national flag earlier this year over his three northeastern provinces, our agents tell us this inexperienced warlord is being wooed by the Japanese."

A young detective in front raised his hand. "Pardon me, Guv."

"Yes, Boyle?"

"Wasn't the Young Marshal's father blown to bits in a railway a few years back by Japanese agents?"

"Right you are, Boyle, however, it appears the Young Marshal and the Japanese Secret Police now are on good terms; they are united to aggressively hunt and capture Chinese, Korean, and Japanese Reds."

He glanced at the clocks. He had an appointment at 8 a.m. with the American consul general to inform him about the inquiries concerning Jack Jordan for possible espionage and murder charges.

"In summary, I want you all to keep your eyes open about anything and everything that has to do with the Japanese. Report anything directly to me." Walking to an empty desk, Haymes sat down wearily on the desktop. He rested the pointer on the empty seat. "Secondly, for those of you who are unaware, one among us is missing today. Detective Roddy Erskine is dead."

Some of the detectives reacted to the announcement with groans, while others gulped or looked blankly at the floor.

"At present, I'm not at liberty to discuss this matter any further, suffice to say we're seeking vital information from an American pilot, Mr. Jack Jordan, commonly known as Ace. He failed to return to his rooms at the Cathay Hotel last night. One of our artists is composing a sketch of him now. You should have that as well as other pertinent information shortly. The mosquito press must know nothing. Is that understood?"

The detectives grunted in affirmation.

Haymes clenched his fists. "Lads, I want him brought in immediately! You'll need all your wits about you because he's clever, ruthless, and dangerous. Watch the Hungjao Aerodrome, the Shanghai North and South Railway stations, and the steamship ticketing offices. He also patronizes The Saints & Sinners Club. I don't care how you go about it, but I want him, preferably alive. Now, clear out."

Maxwell strolled downstairs to the front door wearing a black armband around one sleeve of his white linen suit and matching black-leather gaiters covering the tops of his white shoes. Ling, the butler, darted from the main hallway just in time to open the door.

"If Madame Soames awakes this morning, tell her I've gone to the Shanghai Club."

"Certainly, *Hsien-sheng*." Ling bowed.

"I shall return sometime this afternoon. Is Orloff ready with my motorcar?"

"Yes, *Hsien-sheng*."

Placing a homburg of coarsely woven white straw with a wide black hatband squarely on his small head, Maxwell strode out to the driveway.

Slumped in the driver's seat of the brown and white striped Auburn sedan, Orloff guzzled from a beer bottle that held *kaoliang*, a cheap, 50-proof sorghum whiskey that Europeans used in winter to start their fireplaces. A Czarist exile, Orloff was among the luckiest of the city's 2,500 White Russians who fled the Bolsheviks only to find themselves to be stateless social outcasts in China. Orloff's family had fled to Shanghai from Russia because of his father's service in the Far Eastern White Army. They escaped from their home in Novaya Andronovka, a suburb of Moscow, for a harrowing journey across Siberia to Manchuria. A few months passed before they managed to bribe a ticketing agent from the China Merchants Steam Navigation Co. Ltd. to gain third-class passage in the steerage of the *Kien-Kuo* steamer from Tientsin-to-Chefoo-to-Shanghai. His mother had become a seamstress, his father sweated over a stove at Tachenko's, and his sister worked as a taxi dancer at Del Monte's.

Orloff blinked lazily under a pair of dark sunglasses and took another swig of *kaoliang*. He hoped the *huo chiu*, or fire-water wine, burning its way down his throat would help spark an idea in his mind for a poem he could enter in the local Shang Churayevka literary society's annual contest. However, his concentration was interrupted by the prancing sound of a pair of spats approaching along the pavement. Quickly capping the bottle and shoving it under the seat, Orloff jolted upright, smoothed his long blond hair, parted in the middle, and adjusted his black cap.

"*Dóbraye útra*. Good morning, sir."

"Dash it all, you blithering idiot! Open my door at once!"

Orloff hung his head sheepishly and obeyed.

"The Shanghai Club!" Maxwell ordered from the backseat. "And don't honk that blasted horn so much along the way. You can best prove your driving abilities by using the quickest possible way instead of constantly blaring that horn."

"*Dá*."

The sedan started down the driveway. Maxwell's thin nostrils quivered.

"What is that violently hideous odor in here?"

"*Eta, eta*, cleaning solution," Orloff stammered, thrusting his left heel backwards to ensure the beer bottle remained hidden under the seat. "*Ya bilá* cleaning, I was cleaning here, sir."

With his nose still twitching, Maxwell rolled down his window. "Don't use that rotten brand again! You'd better see to it that this loathsome odor is removed from here whilst I'm at the Club. Otherwise, you'll be in for it when I return. Is that understood?"

"*Dá!*"

Maxwell removed his straw homburg and fanned his face. "I sometimes wonder about you White Russians. I can honestly say, without the slightest degree of prejudice, that you're not like us at all—not in the least. Much more daft and lazy, too. You'll never amount to much, but I suppose that can't be helped."

Orloff's fingers tightened around the steering wheel. During the 20-minute drive to the Shanghai Club, he imagined various punishments he wished to inflict on his employer. Finally, Orloff turned left onto the Bund and joined a long queue of cars in front of the club, a solid structure of white stone interspersed with monstrous Corinthian columns.

Tennis Club in Shanghai.

On the opposite side of the street, Ace sat in rickshaw and held up *The Daily Wager Gazette*, devoted to the ponies at the Race Club, the Far Eastern Race Course, and the International Race Course and Golf Links. Passing over a section on the *jai-alai* matches at the city's stadiums, he looked over the odds for the greyhound races at the Canidrome. Motorcars, bicycles, and rickshaws clogged the street. People scrambled to work at banks, trading companies, hotels, stores, and shipping firms along the Bund. A bell let out a painful clang as a trolley car blocked Ace's view when it stopped. Portuguese trading company clerks, Eurasian stenographers, and Shanghainese office managers poured from the trolley towards the Union Building next to the Shanghai Club.

Ace squirmed on a frilly pink cotton cushion and withdrew his feet from a carpeted footrest. The private rickshaw he rented that morning was parked on the waterfront side among many others. Some rickshaws had miniature foreign flags posted on each side of their shafts to distinguish private carriages and their owners nationalities from public rickshaws. The pullers, forbidden to wait inside rickshaws because their master or missy feared catching lice, squatted together on the Bund. The bell clanged again as a trolley car labored ahead. Ace crunched the newspaper on his lap. Shoving the brim of his newly purchased Panama hat lower on his forehead, he leaned forward, searching frantically among the people outside the Club, to see if Maxwell had arrived.

At the head of the traffic queue, Orloff stepped from the sedan and opened the back door. Maxwell skipped up the granite steps and disappeared behind an enormous set of double teak doors restricting access to the Shanghai Club.

"Well, say it ain't so, if it isn't the little rat himself!" Ace chuckled. "I knew he wouldn't skip his gum-flapping session with those *taipans*."

Ace laughed again. He could imagine the cock-and-bull story Maxwell would tell his pals. Oh well, the little double-crosser might as well enjoy himself while he still had time. Pretty soon, his hash would be settled and the score evened. Ace lit a cigarette and blew smoke towards one of the Egyptian flags hoisted on his rickshaw. What a break finding those flags! No one would pay any attention to his rickshaw. There weren't many Egyptians in town. Ace lifted the newspaper and braced himself for a long wait. The day was shaping up swell.

Foochow Road.

Daylight sent shafts of light piercing through Idina's bedroom—illuminating white mosquito netting over her bed. Half asleep, she stirred beneath ivory-colored satin sheets. Her teeth grated, making a sandpaper sound, and the temples pulsated on her forehead. *Thrump! Thrump!* She envisioned ebony ponies thunder across an open field in the dead of a blue-black night. Their red eyes glared, their mouths spewed golden-red foam, and their hooves gouged holes in the dirt. A bluish-white full moon shot across dark sky above the field. The moon's gleaming orb stopped suddenly in the middle of the sky and loomed, growing bigger and bigger until it was all she could see. Within the moon, hazy blue veins began to swirl, forming the features of Roddy's face. "Murder, murder!" he whispered; his eyes shimmered like stars within the moon's pallor. "Why? Ask Maxwell why!" The moon turned into white stork as its huge wings flapping across the blue-black sky.

Idina screamed. Wide-eyed, she bolted upright and dug her fingers into the sheets. Surrounded by what appeared to be a suffocating white fog, her arms flailed. The mosquito netting ripped from its ceiling hooks and came crashing down. Shrieking again, she wrestled with the netting.

Number One Maid, a humorless old woman with a lined, wooden face, rushed into the room, ran to the bed, gripped the mosquito net, and flung it across the room. Idina, breathing heavily, looked through swollen eyelids. "Fetch me my absinthe."

"Yes, *T'ai-t'ai.*"

"Also, fetch the Master. Tell him I must see him at once."

"Not home. *Hsien-sheng* at Shanghai Club."

Idina rubbed her forehead. How could Maxwell go to the Club on a day like today? Surely arrangements must be made about Roddy. Maxwell would simply have to do that. She very well couldn't. "Never mind about my husband. Bring round the absinthe and a glass. No water. And be quick about it!"

"Yes, *T'ai-t'ai.*"

Idina lowered her head back on the feather pillow. She felt too lousy to cry and didn't want Dr. Hanlon fussing again. Absinthe was all she needed. What was keeping that old cow of a maid? Staring at the ceiling, Idina thought about closing her eyes. No, mustn't do that. Roddy might return in that horrible nightmare. Shivering, she pulled the satin sheets around her neck. Maxwell? What did Roddy mean about Maxwell?

Jinricksha.

Babe bent down and tossed a frayed straw mat on the sidewalk in front of the Osaka Gardens in Hongkew, a Northeastern district of Shanghai. A cloud of fine dust flew up. Coughing and waving his hand to clear the air, he sat down and looked around. Shops bearing signs in Japanese lined the streets.

A few yards away, a wooden stand sold the latest edition of the Japanese newspaper that informed the city's 50,000 Japanese residents congregating in Hongkew. Dwarf barbarians, as most Shanghainese called them, were everywhere. Men in European suits rode in rickshaws toward the Japanese consulate. A group of officers in trim military uniforms sat in a touring car racing to the Japanese Naval Depot. Women in kimonos shuffled in and out of shops.

Babe shook a rounded Three Castle cigarette tin at passersby, but it remained empty. Although he didn't really want any money, he muttered to himself about stingy people.

A door creaked behind him, and Babe turned around. Stepping out of Osaka Gardens was a Japanese man, clad in a dark-blue cotton kimono, and a Shinto priest wearing a flowing white robe with sleeves down to the knees of his wide-legged trousers.

The restaurant was a two-story structure of angular blond wood. Bamboo shades masked the windows. The man turned over a wooden sign with Japanese writing proclaiming the restaurant had opened for the day. He spoke softly with the white-haired priest. They bowed to each other. The man in the kimono returned to the restaurant, while the priest approached Babe.

"Give money, give!" Babe called out.

The priest smiled again beneath his large cone-shaped black hat. He reached in his sleeve and tossed some coppers in the tobacco tin before heading to the Shinto temple.

Babe peered into the tin—50 coppers! Enough to buy three full meals of boiled noodles, plus fried bean curd.

Wheelbarrow travel in Shanghai.

Clank. Clank. A pair of battered wooden dumbbells slammed against the sidewalk. The noise grew louder. Four rusted wheels skidded to a stop. Babe lowered the tobacco tin and looked into a weathered brown face of a beggar whose torso was bound with leather straps to a small platform cart of aged bamboo. "You haven't been here before," said the face, lumpy with sores.

Babe scooted back on the mat. "Is this your territory?"

The beggar inched forward. "Yes," he lied, setting the dumbbells on the platform. A tiny bug fell from the white tips of his bristled black hair and landed at Babe's feet.

"I can go to another place."

"Why you here?"

"I think I'll move across the street." Babe stood up.

The beggar quickly reached for Babe's leg. Wide-eyed, Babe felt a grip around his calf as the beggar pulled him. "Wait a moment." The beggar released Babe, who had fallen backwards on the mat. "We'll stay here together. We should help each other."

"Sure," Babe said hoarsely.

"Why you here?"

Babe gulped. His Adam's apple seem to protrude more than normal. "The devil dwarfs. I hear they're very rich."

"That's so?"

A rickshaw coolie, panting heavily, ran to the south side of Osaka Gardens. A bell inside the carriage rang loudly. The beggar turned from Babe to the street as the rickshaw pulled up in front of them. The coolie laid down the shafts bearing flags of the Rising Sun. He stepped around to open the carriage door and wiped his hand at perspiration streaming down his forehead. His bare back glistened with sweat, which soaked a dirty rag tied around his neck. Babe glanced at the beggar as two Japanese businessmen stepped from the carriage. Thrusting out the tin, Babe waited. When the businessmen were a few feet away, he threw the can as hard as he could at the beggar's head.

"*Aiyah!*" the beggar screamed.

Babe sprang to his feet, knocking over one of the businessmen, and bolted across the street, dodging past rickshaws, cars, wheelbarrows, and bicycles. In the distance, the dumbbells clanged along the pavement, but Babe disappeared near the riverfront where his *sampan* waited.

A view from Shanghai's city wall into the French Concession.

Chicago Charlie lingered on the lawn at 57 Mohawk Road outside The Scratch, one of the International Settlement's 700 brothels. Stepping back, he squinted up at the brick building. "Which room's hers?"

Counting the windows on the 3rd floor, he wished someone would answer the door since he didn't like making mistakes. His blue eyes darted between the 5th and 6th windows. "Criminy, which one is it? Only one thing to do." Shrugging his shoulders, he took a Mexican dollar out of his pocket. "Heads sez it's the 5th, tails sez it's the other."

The coin fluttered up, then twirled to the grass. Tails. Chicago Charlie retrieved the coin. He wound his arm around and pitched it at the window. A pane shattered.

"Doggone!" he yelled, jumping back to avoid falling glass.

A woman, with a floral scarf wound in a headband around her auburn hair, shoved up the window, and thrust her head out. Leaning out the window, she clasped the neckline of her green robe and scowled down at the little man with wavy blond hair and a hawk nose.

"Hey! What's the big idea, you two-bit hunk of nothin'? What duh yuh think you're doin'?"

"Sorry, sister! I'm lookin' for Lulu."

"Beat it, half-pint! Come on, beat it, I said!"

"Pipe down, sister! I know you're sore, but it wuz an accident. I'll make good. Now, be a good girl and get Lulu for me."

"Oh, yeah, sez who?"

"Chicago Charlie."

"Beat it, sucker! I'm not in the mood to jaw with yuh. Why, you're face could stop a clock! I'm goin' back to bed. I need my beauty rest."

The woman pulled her robe around tighter and leaned back into the room.

"Listen up, sister!" Chicago Charlie shook his fist at her. "If yuh don't get Lulu but quick, I'm gonna come in as soon as this cathouse opens and sock yuh right in the kisser!"

"So, ya think you're a tough nut, eh?" she scoffed. "Why, ya don't look like ya could even knock the skin off rice puddin'."

A window next to her slid open. A brunette popped her head out. Black pencil lines smeared around a pair of cat eyes. "What's this ruckus about?"

"Hey, Lulu, let me in! There's somethin' I gotta see yuh 'bout, pronto!"

A Shanghai barbed-wire entanglement barricade.

"Chicago?"

"Yeah, open up!"

"Alright." Lulu yawned. "I'll tell Cook to let you in. Wait for me in the kitchen. It'll take me a little tiny minute to freshen up."

"Hey thanks, Lulu. That's swell." He glared at the auburn-haired woman who stood at the window with her hands on her hips.

Outside the Shanghai Club, Ace pulled out another cigarette from the pack. He looked at the pile of butts on the ground near the rickshaw carriage and decided he would smoke slowly to make it last longer. As he bent back the edge of *The Daily Wager Gazette*, he saw Maxwell leave the Shanghai Club, look in both directions at the street traffic, and jauntily descend the steps.

"Hey, boy!" Ace crumpled the newspaper on his lap and beckoned the coolie, intently playing cards with the other rickshaw pullers on the sidewalk, who muttered to his colleagues, threw his cards down, picked up a shirt from the ground and tied it around his waist before scrambling to the rickshaw. Ace pointed across the street to Maxwell, who was adjusting his homburg and walking briskly on the south side of the Bund. "Look-see," he explained in pidgin English. "Follow man in white hatee there. *Chop-chop!*"

The rickshaw coolie nodded his shaven head and grabbed the shafts. Ace fell backwards into the carriage as the rickshaw moved around a tourer sporting French flags and a flatbed American truck piled with sacks of cotton. When the rickshaw coolie reached the inside lane where the Bund and Foochow Road intersected, he started to backtrack in the middle of traffic. A whistle shrilled. Ace, who'd been keeping an eye on Maxwell, turned around to see a Sikh policeman lean over from his post on a circular pedestal and crack the rickshaw coolie's back with a riding crop. The coolie screamed in pain and dropped the rickshaw.

"What do you think you're doing? Leave him alone!" yelled Ace, peering from the window. Lowering his khaki turban, the Sikh stared at Ace for a few seconds while the coolie cowered.

"Don't touch him again!"

Undaunted by the revolver in the Sikh's holster, Ace held up his fist. "Now, we're going to pass, see? And you're not going to stop us."

Carrying cotton.

The Sikh, curling his lips, looked from the coolie to Ace. He slowly raised the riding crop. It hovered in mid-air. Studying Ace, the Sikh brought the riding crop to his chin, where he scratched his thick black beard curled up in a hair net under his chin. "Off with you!" shouted the Sikh, deciding to avoid fighting with a Westerner. Then, the Sikh blew a whistle and cleared traffic, allowing the rickshaw to change direction. Ace exhaled with relief even though he had counted on the Sikh backing down.

The rickshaw driver thundered ahead while Ace spotted Maxwell, whose straw hat with a wide black hatband moved in front of the French Embassy. Maxwell flagged down a pedicab and climbed into the tricycle's turquoise-colored metal passenger compartment.

"Boy! Look at the blue pedicab."

The coolie, panting loudly, bobbed his head. Blue veins bulged on his neck and sweat raced down a long, red gash on his back. He trailed the pedicab by a few yards. The pedicab turned right on Avenue Edward VII, a wide tree-lined thoroughfare marking the International Settlement's southern boundary and the French Concession's northern section. Instead of passing through barbed-wire barricades into French territory, the pedicab wheeled in a parallel course for two blocks and passed the French Municipal Offices and Police Station. Watching the pedicab turn right on Honan Road, Ace wondered where Maxwell was going. Why wasn't he using his motorcar? The pedicab crisscrossed from one road to another in a northeasterly course through the streets of the International Settlement. It looped around Shantung Road Cemetery, turned right after clearing the Chinese Telephone Co. building, rolled behind a Japanese Bank, zipped by the YWCA, and spun above Soochow Creek on Garden Bridge on the way to Hongkew where Japanese storefronts appeared.

"Boy, slow down, slow!" said Ace, removing the Egyptian flags from the rickshaw. He didn't want to take any chances. The pedicab passed the Shanghai Lusitano Club and traveled deeper into Hongkew. It breezed by the Japanese Club and the Ritz Theatre before stopping outside The Tiger's Tail Restaurant, a two-story building tiled in rows of black and yellow. The rickshaw coolie parked near the Ritz Theatre.

Maxwell hopped out of the passenger compartment and waved his hand to shoo away the driver before sauntering over to The Tiger's Tail, which took its name from a strip of the Liaotung peninsula reaching into the harbor of Riojun, formerly known as Port Arthur before the victorious

Japanese renamed the naval base in 1905 following the Russo-Japanese War. The furnishings inside were black lacquer. A giant painting of a growling golden tiger greeted patrons.

"Rest here," Ace told the coolie and left the carriage.

He wondered how to proceed. Noticing a tobacco stand next to the Ritz Theatre, he bought three packs of cigarettes and opened a package. He lit up, turning to a poster plastered outside the Theatre. It showed a girl in a snug red cap peering from a white-feathered collar. Fear-struck, she clutched the shoulder of an ashen-faced man. His mouth was grim. Red ink blasted across the top of the poster:

UNDERWORLD GANGSTERS.

Lowering his brim, he looked to the sidewalk while approaching the restaurant. According to the Shanghainese, The Tiger's Tail was built in violation of the laws of nature since it had one floor higher than the roof of the travel office on its left side. The Japanese builders unknowingly created a "white tiger" that dominated the "green dragon" of the travel office. Death or disaster could stem from such bad *fêng shui*.

Ace stepped inside. The air smelled of cigarettes and raw fish. A fat Japanese waiter in a black silk *haori* coat hanging down to his calves sat behind a bamboo desk blocking the curtained entrance to the dining area. Ace walked up and grabbed a menu. Raising it in front of his face, he looked around. Hanging at eye-level over the doorway, the black curtain with yellow Japanese writing shielded patrons from view. Only the floor was visible. Pairs of shoes lined a wall. Maxwell's black and white spats stood out as did his European hat with the black hatband on the rack. A hand with dimpled fingers grabbed the side of Ace's menu. He let the cigarette drop from his lower lip down to the black and gold-checkered floor.

"Take it." Ace shoved the menu into the waiter's gut. "It's all yours."

Ace ground his cigarette with his shoe into the tile, kicked away the butt, and exited. The street was filling as lunchtime approached. Ace walked casually around an alley alongside the restaurant. A series of large octagonal windows, covered with shades of fine bamboo reeds, were set inside the walls. Ace leaned against the wall and listened at the first open window. Only the tinkling of porcelain dishes could be heard. He moved to another. A group of men chattered in Japanese. At the next window, a haunting lute-like melody strummed from a *samisen*. Only one more window remained. The mosquito bites on Ace's arm itched, and his shirt stuck to his back. What if Maxwell wasn't there? It'd be impossible to learn what was going on in there. Creeping to the window's edge, Ace waited. Lacquered trays grated across a tabletop.

"I've always admired the way you chaps use warm, scented towels to cleanse your face and hands before meals," Maxwell purred. "Such a jolly good custom. So civilized!"

Ace listened closer. Maxwell reclined in front of a square two-foot-high red-lacquered table. A dignified Japanese man in a pinstriped gray suit sat across the table on a *tatami* mat. His gray hair was parted down the middle and cropped short. A monocle dangled from one eye. "Maxwell-san, I have taken the liberty of ordering our meal. It is traditional in Japan for this time of year and in honor of our Tsukimi Festival for the Moon."

"Splendid! What'll we have?" asked Maxwell, rubbing his hands with delight.

"*Akadashi* soup, steamed abalone and cucumber, broiled trout, fern fronds, bamboo shoots, rice, bean curd, shrimp, eel, and an egg."

"Sounds marvelous, simply marvelous."

"To drink, would you like *saké*, or beer, perhaps?"

"Oh, Major Fujiwara, thank you, no," Maxwell answered. "Some of your fine Japanese lemonade will do nicely. I make a point of never imbibing alcohol during the day. I find it can clutter the mind."

Major Fujiwara squinted through the monocle at Maxwell for a few seconds before turning to a serving maid in a yellow kimono. She knelt next to Maxwell. "Bring my guest a bottle of lemonade." He turned to his own serving girl and ordered *saké*. The girls scurried off leaving the men alone.

Smiling, Maxwell glanced about. A tiger skin adorned a wall. In front of another, a red wooden shrine hung over a three-foot-tall ceramic statue of a fat bearded man with a menacing blackened face and flowing blue cloak. He rode a snarling black tiger and held a pearl in his hand.

"I say," Maxwell pointed to the shrine. "That bloke on the wall looks dreadful. Isn't it Chinese? What's it doing here in a Japanese restaurant?"

Major Fujiwara looked at the idol, standing in front of a money tree whose branches were strings of golden coins that bore golden fruit ingots. "He is Hsüan Tan, the God of Wealth. He rides a tiger. The Chinese believe the tiger, or *lao hu*, helps destroy evil spirits."

"Surely, a gentlemen such as yourself doesn't believe that rot!" Maxwell chuckled. "These Chinese are full of superstitious nonsense!"

Major Fujiwara's small, dark eyes flashed. "We Japanese respect the Chinese culture. In some ways, it's similar to ours. When possible, we try to abide by their culture and use it to our advantage."

Looking sheepishly, Maxwell cleared his throat. "I see your point."

"Furthermore, the Chinese have a maxim: 'You cannot catch the cub of the tiger without first going into his den.' A most appropriate sentiment for what we both are doing, don't you agree?"

"Yes, quite," he said dryly.

The serving maids reappeared at the table with the drinks. No one spoke. A tiny green porcelain cup and bottle of warm *saké* were placed before Major Fujiwara. An empty glass and chilled bottle of lemonade appeared in front of Maxwell. Lifting up the brown bottle of lemonade, Maxwell noticed the label hailed it as a "Purveyor to the Japanese Imperial Household." The Major poured *saké* into the tiny cup. "Maxwell-san, after you rang me last night, I informed Colonel Togawa-sama about how you solved the problem with the Special Branch regarding your unfortunate brother-in-law. He trusts the matter is settled with the American pilot blamed. Togawa-sama was most pleased at your resourcefulness and quick actions. Shall we toast to your past and future success?"

"Splendid!"

Major Fujiwara stretched his thin lips in a tight smile. "To your bright future!"

"And yours as well, Major!" The *saké* cup clinked against the lemonade glass. Both men sipped. "Today, I wanted to see you Maxwell-san, about the matter of the banquet. You still will be in attendance tonight at The Catherine the Great restaurant? Yes?"

"Of course. It'll be a bit tricky leaving my wife alone—she's had a great shock, you know. But I'll manage."

"And, the English, French, and German gentlemen exporters of antimony, each of them will attend?"

"Yes, us four. Everything is arranged. They confirmed the arrangements with me at the Club this morning."

Fujiwara set down the cup. Reaching into a vest pocket, he produced a slim manila packet and placed it on the table. "Here's the substance. You know what to do."

Ace pressed his face to the windowpane, but couldn't see anything.

Maxwell grabbed the packet and ran his fingers over a soft lump inside. "Have you done your part to make it look like the Green Gang is involved?" The Major nodded and removed his monocle. "The letters were posted yesterday." He breathed on the lens and polished it with a napkin. "They should arrive this morning. You'll receive one, as well."

"Splendid," he noted before placing it in his waistcoat pocket. "Now the rest is up to me. If I may be so bold as to say, you fellows will never have any cause for regret with myself in the picture."

Fujiwara answered with a grim smile. He picked up a small, rolled towel from a lacquered tray and wiped his hands. "Ah, Maxwell-san, it's time for our *akadashi* soup. We shall speak no more of business."

Realizing there was nothing more to be gained, Ace trudged back to the rickshaw. Major Fujiwara? He must be Maxwell's link to Colonel Togawa. Better wait in the carriage to get a good look at him. What did they mean about the banquet—and antimony?

Chicago Charlie pushed away an empty plate, leaned back in a chair, and rubbed his stomach. Lulu's cook was something else. What a class act! Footsteps came down the hall.

"Hi-de-hi!" Lulu beamed.

"A hi-de-ho back at yuh!"

Admiring the yellow ribbon in her coifed, short brown hair and her snug coral-colored dress, Chicago Charlie let out a wolf whistle.

She laughed. "I see Cook has got you all fixed up."

A skinny Chinese chef stood in front of the stove. Pulling up a chair next to Chicago, she sat down, crossed her legs elegantly, and hiked up her flared hem. Chicago Charlie shoved a stack of bills on the table at her. "Here's some dough to make up for the window."

"No sweat." Lulu glanced at the money, but didn't touch it.

Cook carried a coffee pot to the table. He poured Lulu a cup of steaming coffee and refilled Chicago Charlie's mug.

"Thanks Cookie," teased Lulu, dropping five cubes of sugar into the mug. Raising her pinkie, she stirred the sugar around and around. "What gives, pal?" Chicago felt his throat burn. "Just a sec." Sniffing, he wiped tears welling in his eyes. "I gotta have some 'O' first." Digging into a pocket in his pants, he retrieved a roll of pink opium pills and plopped two onto his tongue. "Want some?"

Lulu shook her head. "Too early, for me, the java will do me just fine." She sipped her coffee. He wiped his nose, popped another pill, and shoved the roll into his pocket. "Whadda yuh know about the Japanese? Any of 'em been 'round here lately?"

The mug slammed down on the table. Coffee spilled on the lace tablecloth. From a low stool in the corner of the kitchen, Cook watched them. He was accustomed to quarrels at The Scratch and knew better than to interfere. "You've got your nerve! You must be dead from the neck up. Asking me a question like that. Why, me and my girls wouldn't have any of them for all the rice in China!"

"Gee, baby! Simmer down!" Chicago mopped up the spill with his napkin. "I didn't mean nothin' by it. I wuz only looking for news, that's all." She crossed her arms over her chest. "Come on, Lulu. We're pals. Remember? Ever since we met comin' out here on the *American Mail Line*. We've sure had a lot of laughs since then."

Lulu's cat eyes softened. "Yeah, I know, but don't go talkin' to me like I'm some square head from Kalamazoo!"

Chicago relaxed. "I hear yuh."

Lulu, turning to Cook, tapped the tabletop with a jeweled index finger. "Get you're caboose off that stool and come clean this up! Bring us some fresh coffee while you're at it, will yuh?" Chicago Charlie burst out laughing. The opium was making him feel giddy. "Let's start over," he said, holding back laughter and wiping away tears. "Heard anythin' 'bout a Colonel Togawa?" She shook her head.

"Know anythin' 'bout what his bunch have been up to lately? Anythin' at all?"

"Well, let's see," her voiced trailed off. Lines appeared on her forehead as she thought for a moment. "Twyla Delight!" She jumped in her chair. "We were havin' new permanent waves put in our hair a couple weeks ago at the Majestic Hotel. A White Russian gal has a beauty shop there. Her name is Madame Petrovna. Ever hear of her? They say she used to be a countess, but times ain't treated her so good."

"Let's talk 'bout Miss Delight, okay?"

Lulu shrugged her shoulders and sipped coffee. "Well, Twyla Delight runs a flophouse on the Avenue Joffre. She wuz showin' off a five-strand dog collar made of these big pearls, said this captain gave it to her." She raised her black-penciled eyebrows for emphasis. "He's a Japanese, just come over from *Tok-eeyo*. Been here waitin' for some kind of cargo line to start from Hangchow to, to...wait a sec, just you wait a sec, I'll remember." She paused. "I got it! Port Arthur or Dairen—one of those places up north in Manchuria!" Pleased, she batted her eyelashes. "How's that? Not bad, huh?"

"Swell, Lulu. That's real swell." Chicago smiled feebly. "Maybe that'll help. I ain't exactly sure how yet, but maybe it's of some use." His eyes were glassy. She noticed his sallow skin appeared more jaundiced than usual.

"Thanks a million, Lulu. You're a real pal," said Chicago, yawning loudly. "This 'O' is makin' me want to catch a little shuteye." He lumbered to his feet and patted her on the shoulder. "I'll be seein' yuh soon, real soon. Thanks again, kid!"

Lulu watched him wobble out the kitchen. "That's swell Chicago. Come 'round anytime."

Idina lay on the floral chintz couch in the sitting room. Her platinum hair flowed across stuffed pillows. A white brocaded robe of iron-loom silk was tied loosely over her pajamas. Staring at the ceiling, she clutched an invitation, a white card embossed with flourishing gilt type. Tomorrow night Count Panozzo, the Italian Consul General, requested her presence:

Signor e Signora Soames
10 o'clock, Temple of Heaven
Masquerade ball celebrating
15th Day of the Eighth Moon, Mid-Autumn Moon Festival Party
Required: black masks, white dominos, and black shoes

Forcing herself to shut out thoughts of Roddy, she imagined having fun at the fancy-dress ball. A sumptuous banquet spread out behind the marble terraces of the Temple of Heaven—amid glowing moon lanterns and champagne, not to mention handsome young Count Panozzo dancing in hooded robes to an orchestra under the light of a full moon. Leaning over a low Chinese peel table next to the couch, she dropped the invitation for an open bottle of absinthe. A bitter licorice flavor filled her mouth.

The Chief Inspector's deep voice jarred her memory. Roddy didn't drown—his neck was broken…The killer couldn't have been the Chinese… No, Soames, this murder was the work of a brazen killer…someone Roddy knew and didn't fear.

Idina nearly jumped out of her skin. Was that a dream? She remembered stirring in her sleep as Haymes spoke to her husband the evening of Roddy's murder. She started crying as she recalled Roddy whisper to her something about asking Maxwell. They say people can communicate with a loved one after death. Roddy could've been giving her a message. Besides, who else could've done it? Maxwell was on the hunt, and Ace had been with her that very afternoon. Come to think of it, Maxwell had been acting none too sorry about her brother's fate. Maybe Maxwell did it, she told herself, surprised at how easily it came out and how calmly she reacted. That scoundrel would pay with his life. But how to do it? The telephone rang a few times before she answered.

"Idina, darling. I'm so glad you're up and about. I've been so worried about you."

She exhaled loudly.

"Idina?" Maxwell's voice became flustered. "Idina? Are you there, darling?"

"Yes," she answered sharply.

"Do forgive me for leaving you alone today. I had business to attend to that simply wouldn't wait."

Maxwell paused. "Idina? Are you well?"

She didn't reply.

"Should I send for Dr. Hanlon?"

"No-oo."

"Are you quite sure you're alright?"

"Quite."

"I'm calling to let you know I'll be home soon. However, I shan't be able to stay very long. Remember that beastly banquet I'm hosting at that White Russian place—The Catherine the Great? Well, I'm afraid it's tonight, darling. I cannot possibly cancel now, not at the last minute. That wouldn't do, not after all the preparation, despite the, er, circumstances of yesterday. I do hope you understand, dearest." He paused. "Idina, darling, you do see, don't you?"

She coiled the telephone cord around her fingers. "Yes, Maxwell. I see everything now."

"What? What's that you're saying?"

"Nothing. You go to your banquet tonight. I shan't mind being alone. I can take care of myself."

"That's a good girl. I'll see you soon. Bye now."

Idina dangled the handset by the cord, twirling it in a circle while her mind raced.

Pressing a telephone receiver against his ear, Ace dialed 11490. "*North China Daily News?* Hello? Miss Helen Hanlon, please." He stood in a telephone booth inside the Imperial Oriental Hotel's lobby in Hongkew. Pushing up his hat brim, he scratched a mosquito bite on his forehead. "No, I don't want to leave a message. Can you try to find her? I've got a scoop. It's important. No, she's the only one I'll talk to...Okay, I'll hang on." Seated on a wooden stool in the phone booth, he wasn't worried about Special Branch finding him in Hongkew even though this district contained seven of 20 police stations within the International Settlement and French Concession. With the exception of the large Dixwell Road Police Station at the northern part near the Japanese Naval Depot and other scattered substations, the British police confined themselves to the eastern portion—a four-square-block area holding the Police Hospital, Wayside Police Station, Police Living Quarters, and Ward Road Gaol. In any event, everyone knew Special Branch's real interest in Hongkew focused on hunting down Chinese communists and interrogating prisoners in Ward Road Gaol's cork-paneled, suicide-proof cells. The Japanese were left to themselves.

Ace turned toward the door and looked through glass panels into the main lobby. A walkway led to a registration counter flanked by life-sized, bronze statues of prancing horses, which honored the valiant steeds slain during the Russo-Japanese War. Bronze busts of Marshal Oyama and Admiral Togo, with battlefield tributes, dominated each side of the concierge's teak desk. A German-Jewish family from Europe lugged their belongings and pointed to a sign overhead.

IMPERIAL ORIENTAL HOTEL ACCOMMODATIONS

JAPANESE PLAN: EUROPEAN PLAN:

3 YEN AND UP -- SINGLE 10 YEN AND UP -- SINGLE

8 YEN AND UP -- DOUBLE 22 YEN AND UP -- DOUBLE

(MOTORBUS MEETS ALL TRAINS & STEAMERS!!!)

Hearing a sound on the line, Ace shifted his attention.

"Miss Hanlon, here. Who's calling?"

"It's me, Ace."

"Where are you?" She caught her breath and spoke excitedly. "Are you ready yet? Do you have the goods?"

"Listen, things are moving fast, very fast. The picture could be changing, getting bigger, so I need a couple of favors, right away! Otherwise you can kiss our deal goodbye."

"Oh, really?" Helen asked suspiciously. "What's up?"

"I can't say now. I'm still trying to fit the pieces together. Right now I need your help, or it's no dice."

"No dice, huh?" Her voice flattened. "First, tell me what you have in mind, then I'll see if I feel like doing you any favors."

"Maxwell Soames is going to a banquet tonight. I've got to know when and where. Get a hold of Chicago Charlie. Tell him to meet me at the Temple of Heaven at 5 o'clock sharp. Be there, too, with the info. Get it?"

"What's in it for me?"

"You don't have a choice, Helen, if you want that scoop, and I think you want it pretty badly. You'll be there. Remember, it's all or nothing. Think about it, but don't take too long."

Ace hung up, lowered the brim of his hat, and exited the phone booth. A wiry bellhop struggled to load the Jewish immigrants' trunks on a metal cart. Ace walked briskly out of the lobby to his rickshaw. Climbing inside, he leaned back as the coolie tilted the rickshaw and trotted through the busy streets. The midday sun beat down. Two days earlier, before he'd flown back to Shanghai, a soothsayer in Hangchow had spoken to him about bad luck and this hot, dry Autumn Tiger weather. She had quoted an ancient saying: "Rivers and oceans wash, and the Sun god sends the Autumn Tiger to dry."

Worrying about his predicament, Ace glanced at the albatross ring on his finger—25 diamonds, one for each victory. The stench of Fokien Market caught his attention with its overpowering fishy smell. Slimy, dark liquid ran down the gutters around the open market where Shanghainese crowded the stalls. Vendors wore stained aprons and rubber boots. Many yanked live pigs, geese, chickens, and ducks from cylindrical baskets.

A few blocks later, Ace pressed a copper wall button inside the carriage. A bell chimed. The coolie halted in front of a square, two-story white brick building streaked with soot. He left the rickshaw and walked up stone steps to the Chinese General Chamber of Commerce. Still in Hongkew where he was safer, he hoped to find the information. His options were few. To reach Aurora University, he would've had to travel through the International Settlement and into the French Concession. Aurora University was too close to the Shanghai Special Area District Court. Moreover, St. John's University, founded by Episcopalian missionaries from America, was too far away for a rickshaw.

Inside along the foyer's walls sat tarnished brass spittoons on a hardwood floor. A massive, full-length mirror in a rosewood stand blocked the direct path to the main room, thereby warding off evil which the Chinese believed traveled in straight lines into buildings. In the main area, clusters of Shanghainese compradores and foreign businessmen sat on stiff-backed settees arranged in rectangular sections. They sipped tea and held discussions. Bright exterior sunlight was muted by windows covered with white paper and lattice patterned in geometric bats (known as wing-concealers, night swallows, or sky mice) that symbolized good fortune. A finely polished blackwood counter ran the length of the back wall. Behind it, Chinese clerks handled transactions under a lattice railing of bats.

A sign, hanging from the railing at the far end of the counter, said in scrawled both in English and Chinese characters stated: *Inquiries Here.*

Ace approached the counter. A dignified, white-haired Shanghainese gentleman in a long gray silk gown bent over a glossy purple gourd on the countertop. He spoke in Chinese to the eggplant-shaped gourd and wiggled his finger through one of the holes in the lid.

"Pardon me."

Removing his finger from the gourd, the old gentleman straightened his back and gave Ace an inquisitive look.

"My name is Jordan," said Ace, craning to see the gourd's contents. "Mr. Jack Jordan."

"Good afternoon," replied the gentleman, clasping the gourd to his chest. "How may I be of service, Mr. Jordan?"

"I'm from America and thinking about investments."

"Ah!" The gentleman unveiled a top row of long, yellowed teeth. "Textiles? Paper? Fur? Tobacco? Jute?"

"Well, not exactly. You see, I'm interested in something entirely different. Antimony."

Studying Ace, the gentleman shifted the gourd to his left hand and stroked a wispy white beard.

"Antimony, you say? Umm."

"Yes." Ace chuckled nervously. "You see, I've been told there are tremendous financial opportunities in the antimony trade."

"You've been misinformed, Mr. Jordan. You have no chance to invest in Chinese antimony trade because the market is controlled by the Hua Chang Antimony Refining Company of Changsha. It enjoys a monopoly in Honan province and only deals with three exporters—English, French, and German. No one else. Everyone wants antimony these days for manufacturing shrapnel."

"So you're telling me I don't stand a chance? Is that it?"

"Correct. Not even the Japanese, with their vast resources and operations in Manchuria, can get their hands on it," the gentleman replied.

Uncertain what to say next, Ace shifted his weight. "What's that you've got there?"

"A cricket." The gentleman protectively hugged the gourd.

"No kidding! What are you going to do with it? Turn it loose?"

The gentleman laughed. "No, he's a *chu chieh hsü*—a bamboo-joint whiskers. Still a youngster, but soon he'll be a great fighter."

"Well, if that doesn't beat all!" Ace whistled. "A bamboo-joint whiskers, too."

"Yes, his nature is one of conquest, but after his 10th month, when he can no longer fight, he'll have the sound of *shang*."

"My, my, that cricket sounds like a beaut! No wonder you're taking such good care of him. Mind if I take a look?"

"That is not possible." The gentleman frowned. "He has never seen a foreigner. No, the sight of you may upset him."

"Gee, that's too bad! I haven't had any luck at all today."

Ace reached for his wallet and pulled out a Shanghai Bank of Communications $20 bill, woven with red, the color of good luck.

"Here's something to bet on that cricket of yours for his first fight. Maybe you've got a real winner on your hands."

Ace tipped his hat to the gentleman and left.

Idina, lazily fanning herself, reclined on white wicker divan in a garden on the east side of the Soames estate. Large white roses sprung from tall rambling bushes covered with strong, hooked thorns. A pleasant fragrance from the roses permeated the air. The blossoms were named after Lord Macartney, a British envoy known less for his success in impressing the Manchu court in 1792 than for refusing to kowtow to the Son of Heaven unless a Chinese of equal rank did so before a portrait of King George III.

In the garden's center, a huge Chinese umbrella with clouds painted on oiled brown paper shielded Idina's fair skin from the sun. She had changed into a creamy, ruffled pantsuit and applied a heavy coating of makeup on her face. Her stomach no longer felt queasy from the absinthe. She had forced herself to drink four prairie oyster hangover concoctions, made with raw eggs and a pungent sauce.

Number One Maid arranged the table with Earl Grey tea, scones, and cucumber sandwiches.

Ignoring the refreshments, Idina stared from behind her through round tortoise-shell sunglasses in the direction of a low green hedge.

Orloff, in his dark chauffeur's uniform, polished the Auburn sedan's chrome grill. His blond hair swayed against his chin as he bobbed up and down, wiping away dust from the day's journey into the city.

The maid filled a teacup. Hesitating, she held it out on a saucer. "*T'ai-t'ai?*"

Idina snatched the cup and saucer. "Leave me and don't come out here again. When Mr. Soames is finished bathing, tell him I'm resting and don't wish to be disturbed. Off with you now!"

Amusements at a Shanghai park.

Madame Soames returned the cup and saucer to the table. Orloff's every move held her undivided attention. She felt like a cat waiting to pounce on an unsuspecting sparrow. She knew exactly what to do, and Orloff was essential. In the past, he had responded favorably to her casual flirtations; now, she was certain he'd do as she asked, especially after hearing her proposition. Idina closed her sandalwood fan with a quick jerk of the wrist. She dropped it on her lap, scooped up a silk scarf draped across the chair's armrest, and waved the scarf. "You-who? Oh, Orloff? You-who?"

He stood up, wiped the sweat from his brow with his sleeve, and saw her beckoning.

"Orloff!" She smiled prettily. "Oh, do come over here, please."

He wound the polishing cloth in a ball, set it on the hood, and walked across the driveway. His long legs easily cleared the top of the hedge as he moved to the table. Idina released the scarf, letting it drop to the grass. A red fingernail pointed to a rattan chair.

"*Dóbriy dyen*, Madame."

"Please sit down. I must have a word with you."

He did so. His long face betrayed no emotion, but his blue eyes looked her up and down.

"Orloff, there are some things I must ask you. How are you getting on? Are you quite satisfied here with things as they are? I'm sorry my husband treats you so dreadfully. Don't deny it. I know he does because I've seen it for myself. Disgraceful if you ask me."

He unfastened his collar buttons. "Madame?"

"Just today I was thinking, wouldn't it be grand to get away from here? Not merely this place." She picked up the fan by its bone handle, motioning with the blunt end. "But Shanghai. Don't you ever think of leaving this dreadful place?" She batted her eyelashes. "I know I do."

"*Prastítye?* Madame, I don't follow."

"No, I suppose you don't." She stroked her cheek with the tip of the fan. "I'd forgotten you're an exile—a White Russian with no passport, no money to buy your way out, no future. Such a frightful pity. You're such a sweet boy, too." She paused to dazzle him with her smile. "Well, here we are. I was wondering if there is something you'd like to do in your life, if you could? Never mind your present situation. I mean, if you were truly free to do what you really wanted?"

"Of course, Madame *dá*. There are many things, many things, I'd like to do."

Idina flicked open the fan and lazily waved it in front of her face. Orloff breathed in sweet whiffs of sandalwood.

"My dear boy, I may as well get to the point straight away. No sense beating around the bush. I have a proposition for you and you alone. It's my very particular secret. It could be yours, as well, if you're interested in clearing out of this filthy rotten country once and for all. Tell me, does that interest you?"

"Please continue, Madame." Orloff leaned forward. He had longed to live a poet's life in Paris, but never thought it remotely possible.

"I have a plan, you see. It concerns my husband. I'd rather like to be free, too." Idina grabbed his hand. "Oh, Orloff! Haven't we the right to be happy? Don't we owe it to ourselves to seize an opportunity to give us that right? Can't you see things my way?" She toyed with his cuff. "I'll pay you enough money to buy a passport and your way out of here. No doubt, I may show you my gratitude in other ways as well. All I ask in return is for you to do a neat job for me. Naturally, I've worked out all the details. You'll get through it all with no risk to yourself, but you must promise me you'll say nothing of this to anybody."

Orloff freed himself of her grasp.

"Well? Speak up dear boy! What do you have to say? I'm not at liberty to reveal anything more until you assure me you'll do as I ask!"

"Madame, I've longed to leave Shanghai for some time. I'm most interested in your proposition. Please continue, *pazhálsta*."

Idina fluttered her fan. "I should be grateful if you would poison my husband."

"*Shto? Ya nye panimáyu!* What?" he asked with a shocked expression.

"You heard me right! I'm asking you to poison my husband."

"Madame," Orloff said with a throaty laugh. "*Eta*, this thing you ask. It is most difficult."

"Not in the least. I have the poison right here." She pointed to a packet on her lap. "I got it from the gardening shed. I hear it works wonders with rats. You know for yourself from living here that we don't have many rats about. It should work marvelously with a rat as large as my husband! With this strychnine, I know you'll make short work of the job. Providing, of course, you don't lose your nerve."

"I need more than you offer." He started to rise, but she caught his arm. "Papa, Mama, *syestrá*, and my sister," he continued, "all must have passports also."

"That's quite alright. Whatever you wish. Do we have an agreement?"

"*Dá!*"

"Good. It's all settled. Now, you must do as I say because I have my own fussy ways of doing things. It'll be tonight. You'll accompany my husband to a banquet. I'll arrange it all. Take this packet with you now."

Orloff began to lift up the flap to peer inside.

"Oh, do put that away at once! You'll ruin everything! We can't very well have someone look out from the window and see you with that!"

Orloff nodded in agreement as he folded the packet and tucked it under the crown of his chauffeur's cap.

"My husband will order liquor after his meal. It's a habit of his, you know. In any case, you must find a discreet way to put a pinch or two of the powder into his glass."

He frowned.

"Don't look so puzzled. You're a smart boy! I'm confident you'll manage splendidly. Leave the rest to me. I assure you there'll be no trouble. I'll fix it up with my husband so you'll accompany him to the banquet and act as his bodyguard, shall we say." She threw her head back in laughter. "Can you believe it? You'll be his bodyguard! Well, that's that. Come to me tomorrow morning. I'll make arrangements for your money. You'd better get along now."

"*Kharashó!* Very good Madame." He jumped to his feet. "I await your summons. Until tomorrow. *Dasvidánya!*" As he crossed the lawn to the motorcar, Orloff looked up to the clear blue sky. The moon was rising above the horizon.

Also noticing the gleaming moon, Chief Inspector Haymes leaned against a stone-crenelated tower on the second floor veranda at Special Branch headquarters. He stirred tobacco in the bowl of his wooden pipe and lit it. The only time he smoked was when he worried. His detectives had failed to turn up Ace. Where the deuce had that blasted Yank gone? What was he up to? Was he still in Shanghai hiding among the city's 3 million? Even so, Westerners attracted attention because there were so few of them compared to the Chinese. The good news, though, was that the American and French police had begun cooperating in the manhunt. Perhaps it was time to bring in the Green Gang. Pockmarked Fang performed such deeds from time to time to store up favors. If anyone could turn up Ace, the Opium Czar surely could. His secret society had members everywhere. Beggars, thieves, peasants, money changers, pimps, and kidnappers belonged to the Green Gang's lower order. Shopkeepers, factory owners, civil servants, and military officers occupied the middle echelon. The highest rank were politicians, *taipans*, and bankers. Yes, it was time to call on Pockmarked Fang.

The pipe emitted bursts of bluish-white smoke, which parted into rolling strands wafting upward to the sky. Gazing at the smoke, Haymes thought of Roddy. Poor chap hadn't even begun to live. Such a shame! Erskine might have been his son's age, but the old man had no one since his wife, Antonia, died suddenly after the onset of pleurisy. After that, he'd left for the Orient to start a new life. He journeyed for six weeks at sea to Shanghai aboard the *Kashgar* liner. The P&O vessel called on the ports of Columbo, Penang, Singapore, and Hong Kong before arriving in Shanghai. Haymes didn't mind the isolation in Shanghai, or even that most Europeans thought policemen their social inferiors. The job was all that mattered.

The Duesenberg sedan crept so slowly along Lantern Market Street in the Old Walled City that its miniature Union Jack flags sagged from their mounts on each side of the long, black hood. Shanghainese jostled everywhere. Lantern Market Street choked from shoppers preparing for the Mid-Autumn Moon Festival. From the thick leather padding in the back seat, Chief Inspector Haymes lurched forward and barked at the driver.

"Confound it, man! What on earth do you think you're doing? We're not curb crawling. There's business to attend to! If you wait patiently for them to clear off, we'll be here for hours. Now, honk your horn!"

The driver complied, but it didn't help.

The bicyclists, rickshaw coolies, pushcart pullers, street urchins, and pedestrians ignored the horn blasts.

"Sorry Guv, it's a bit tricky here. I'm doing the best I can, but I don't want to hit anyone."

"Oh, this cursed hole!"

Haymes wrestled with the window handle, rolled the window halfway, and grabbed his pipe. Through puffs of smoke rising from the pipe, the old man glared at bluish-gray brick buildings outside.

Wooden boards written in black, red, or gold square Chinese characters dangled above shops selling silk, embroidery, porcelain, bamboo pipes, cookware, and bronzes. The busiest places were stationary shops selling lanterns, paper spirit money, clay figurines of rabbits, three-legged toads, incense sticks, and paper images of gods and goddesses. In front of the stationery shops stood eight-foot-tall paper effigies of T`ai Yin Hsing Chü, the Goddess of the Moon, looming over the street. Her hair was piled high over a delicate oval face, and her robes swirled among cloud spirals. She sat cross-legged above the round Palace of the Moon. Inside the moon, a cassia tree for long life flanked the Jade Rabbit, T`u-er Yeh. Dressed in a skullcap and gown, he clutched a pestle in his hand and stood on his hind legs pounding out a golden elixir of immortality in a mortar.

Chief Inspector Haymes' eyes rose to the brilliantly painted effigies. At each of the top corners, a pennant of red, yellow, or blue rippled. The horn screamed as the Duesenberg edged forward.

A throng of Shanghainese spilled into the street outside the Peace and Virtue Bakery. They carried full-moon cakes in red cardboard boxes suspended by thick gold-ribbon handles supporting the weight of the cakes two feet in diameter. The cakes held with such delicacies as melon seeds, almonds, orange peels, and cassia blossoms. The tops of the *t'uan yüan ping* were covered with paper images of the Moon Goddess, the Gentleman Rabbit, or the white, three-legged toad, who also was said to reside on the moon.

Haymes shook his head in disgust and refilled his pipe. He disliked Chinese holidays. Fortunately, it would soon be a left turn to Dragon of the Black Pool Road and Pockmarked Fang's mansion.

The home of a wealthy Chinese.

One-eyed Wong bent over a jade mortar and pestle situated on a tall, honey-colored wooden tea table in the Chamber of Good Fortune. He listened to Pockmarked Fang wheeze out a chuckle as a roly-poly, 10-year-old boy unfurled a gold-leaf scroll made from ground cinnabar, mercury sulfide, and perfumed oil and decorated with vermilion calligraphy. Pockmarked Fang slouched in a corner of a peach-wood throne carved with dragons. A purple damask robe shrouded his atrophied body.

"Father, here is a poem of Lü Tung Pin. I have made it for you." The boy smiled, revealing dimples in his rosy cheeks.

With sluggish movements, Pockmarked Fang stretched out the scroll. His metal fingernail protectors rasped against the gilt paper. Struggling to raise grayish-yellow eyelids, he directed his deadened pupils to rows of vertical lines written in free-flowing, *hing-shu* brush strokes of the running-hand style: *Elixir of 10,000 Years.*

"Very good." Pockmarked Fang grunted to Number Eight Son. "You are learning well, and I am pleased. Now you may return to Wan Teacher."

"Yes, father." The boy stood on his tiptoes next to his father's dais, reached up to the throne, and retrieved the scroll.

One-eyed Wong, listening to the rustle of the paper scroll being rewound and the cloth soles of the boy's slippers slap against the stone floor, concocted the Dragon-Tiger Elixir of Immortality. He pinched clumps of powder and shriveled flakes from small mounds on a bronze tray and dropped them into the jade mortar. First came bits of chrysanthemum petals, tree fungus, ground pearls, and bat skin—ingredients for longevity. Next came the Three Plenties for long life, many sons, and good luck—dried pieces of wild peach and pomegranate, and a fresh *fuh-shao* orange, known for its five finger-like stumps that grew from a Buddha's Hand citron. One-eyed Wong removed a dagger from a rhinoceros-horn scabbard, which was hidden inside a horseshoe cuff of his long gown, scraped the orange rind. A sweet fragrance filled his flat nostrils. A dash of *shaohing chiu* fermented rice wine completed the recipe.

Pockmarked Fang turned vapid eyes toward One-eyed Wong, pouring the elixir into a miniature golden teapot and fastening its lid with a chain. The head of the Green Gang had awoken 30 minutes earlier with itchy dryness burning in his throat. Thus, he quelled by inhaling from the smoking pistol. His mouth now had an oily, sugary taste left by the opium. He licked his thin lips as they took on the same grayish-yellow hue as his eyelids. Easing himself forward, he guzzled all the elixir from the teapot's spout. Upon finishing, he closed his eyes. His upper body swayed haltingly in a circle as he put himself in a trance. In his mind, he summoned the mystical powers of Chang Tao Ling to descend from heaven and fill his being. He saw the Taoist immortal's mystical satin robes of reddish-brown jasper drift from the skies then float over his head and cloak his body. A cloud of silver swirled around his right hand. Radiant sparkles materialized into a two-edged, crescent-shaped sword. Cocking his ragged ear to a thunderous roar from above, Pockmarked Fang beheld a 15-foot Manchurian tiger descend from heaven. Black patterned stripes on its forehead formed the character for king. The beast bestowed the divine power to destroy demons as well as the gifts of courageousness, ferocity, nobility, and severity. Pockmarked Fang mounted the tiger. His left hand dug into its long, woolly coat as he grabbed the folds of skin on the tiger's neck. Clutching the hilt with his free hand, he brandished Chang Tao Ling's magical sword just as the Five Poisonous Creatures that Threaten Mankind appeared. They spat and hissed. The crescent-shaped sword swooped down. One by one, heads rolled from a lizard, snake, spider, and toad.

"Master, master!"

Pockmarked Fang cracked his eyelids. The apparition vanished. A servant boy froze prostrate on the veined, oxblood-marble floor at his feet.

"Master, an ocean man has come."

"Where is he?" demanded Pockmarked Fang. He hurled a silk cushion in anger due to the interruption and inability to obtain victory over the centipede in his celestial vision.

"In the Garden of Great Enjoyment."

"One-eyed Wong, tell him I'll be there in a little while!"

"Yes, Master!" bowed One-eyed Wong, whose nozzles of the two Luger pistols slung on a wide leather belt across his fat middle jostled as he left the chamber.

Outside Chief Inspector Haymes strolled, with his hands clasped behind his back, in the Garden of Great Enjoyment.

It was paved and shaped in a quadrangle surrounded on all four sides by detached buildings raised on low plinths. A gang of coolies, standing on a wooden platform in the middle of the courtyard, argued about how best to affix a colossal *yüeh kuang ma-er* effigy of the Goddess of the Moon topped by yellow pennant flags on top. Potted flowering shrubs lined walkways punctuated with chrysanthemums in ceramic jars on three-legged wooden stands. Other coolies struggled to carry over two five-foot-tall clay statues of a gaping three-legged toad as well as a rabbit dressed in a helmet and armor who bore a general's banner flags.

"How do you do, Mr. Wong?" Chief Inspector Haymes doffed his white-straw fedora as he eyed a short, bald man with long Buddha-like earlobes waddled over in a long gown of fuchsia satin that tightly held One-eyed Wong's bulbous torso.

"Chief Inspector," murmured One-eyed Wong, clasping his hands together and nodding his head. "Please wait for Master in this pavilion."

The square pavilion was painted crimson and crowned with a double set of sloping, tiled eaves projecting from a four-sided roof. Along its base, green bristled stems from dragon's beard bamboo formed a low hedge.

"Very well. I'm grateful Mr. Fang could receive me on such short notice this afternoon."

One-eyed Wong said nothing as they approached a narrow, arched bridge spanning a pond near the front of the pavilion. A long, snake-like creature jutted its head from the murky waters before submerging.

"What was that? It looked like a snake."

"Eels. This is a dragon pond!"

"You don't say? I'd never have guessed it. I'm not that clever."

Pockmarked Fang drifted across the garden, leaving terrified coolies prone in his wake. A purple damask robe, woven with dragon medallions, hid his feet. He stooped occasionally to admire the chrysanthemum buds ready to bloom. He liked this year's variety: Blue Mist at the Break of Day, Precious Monastery of the Spring Dawn, Peach Blossom with a Human Face, White Crane Sleeping in the Snow, Oblique Light of the Evening Sun, and Immortal's Palms.

One-eyed Wong slid into the background when Pockmarked Fang arrived.

"Good afternoon, Mr. Fang. Nice to see you again. I do hope your health is well."

"Yes, thank you." With hands tucked inside his cuffs, Pockmarked Fang cordially inclined his head. "I am quite fit, despite the unfortunate shooting—a situation that has since been resolved to my satisfaction."

Haymes continued, "If it suits you, I'll get right to the point."

"Please continue, Chief Inspector. I've always found it beneficial to be frank with one another."

"I've come to you on a rather urgent matter. Actually, I'm hoping you can be of service to Special Branch."

Haymes toyed with the brim of his hat.

"There is an American fellow we'd like nab, but he has eluded us. Perhaps your people could help? What do you say?"

"I'm curious, Chief Inspector, about your proposal."

Pockmarked Fang eased himself onto a circular ceramic stool carved in double-coin symbols for financial prosperity.

"What do you offer? You must want this foreigner very badly to come to me with this request."

"I'm offering you a square deal. Be as quick as you can about finding this chap, and you can name your price—within reason, of course. The Americans, as far as I can judge, are helping in the search, and they're content to leave the matter up to Special Branch after he's apprehended. We do indeed want him rather badly."

"Who is it you seek?"

"A Mr. Jack Jordan, who also goes by the nickname 'Ace.'"

One-eyed Wong cast a furtive look at his chieftain.

"Mr. Fang, I'm not at liberty to disclose the reasons why we must find that fellow. All I can tell you is that he's involved in a matter of great consequence and was found out. I'm confident, though, that with your help, we'll make short work of catching him if he's still in Shanghai."

Pockmarked Fang closed his eyes and replied: "When the moon is high, I'll take my cane for a walk. When the wind is cold, I'll put on some clothes. My heart is hidden in thick bamboo groves. I come home alone, leading the white clouds."

"Hello? How do you mean? What's that you're trying to tell me?"

Pockmarked Fang opened his topaz eyes.

"When the rabbits are dead, the hounds that tracked them will be cooked."

Haymes sifted uncomfortably. "Very well then, I'll find out for myself. I can tell by your answer that you won't assist us." He rose. "I shan't give up Mr. Fang. I thank you so much for your time. No harm done, I hope. We'll let the whole thing go. Now, if you'll excuse me, I'd better get along now."

"My dear Chief Inspector, do walk slowly."

"I'll see myself out. Cheerio to you both."

Haymes walked briskly out through the garden. Something queer was afoot with Pockmarked Fang's answer he puzzled as he ventured over to The Catherine the Great Restaurant where that fool Maxwell insisted on hosting that blasted banquet. Tonight of all nights, too!

Maxwell stared at a white envelope, with crude lettering etched by a black fountain pen that lay on an ornate silver tray. He wondered whether he should read the letter again. After all, he was alone in his study. What did it matter? Both the envelope and letter were addressed to him. As planned, Ling, the butler, witnessed Maxwell collapse on a chair after the dramatic first reading the letter. He pulled his pocket watch from his white waistcoat. A few minutes after 4 o'clock, enough time for another look before setting off for the restaurant. He reached for the letter, an example of the Black Eel's genius. Tomorrow morning, it would be handed over to Special Branch as evidence against the Green Gang. His bottom lip quivered. It was all so thrilling! What a chancer he'd become. No one would ever suspect the treachery and murders planned for tonight! Replacing the letter on the tray, he grabbed his white buck gloves. Time for Idina.

He bounded upstairs and rapped loudly on Idina's bedroom door. A booming trombone from inside the room vibrated against the wooden door. His tongue clucked against his teeth. She had moved the Gramophone up from the sitting room. He raised his fist to knock harder, but decided it won't do any good. She couldn't hear. He straightened the lapels of his black, single-breasted tailcoat and adjusted his white, wing collar and bow-tie before entering.

Idina stood at the end of the room a few feet from the wide moon doorway overlooking the veranda. She hadn't heard him. In one hand, she held an absinthe cocktail and in the other a recording. Slurping from the glass, she pondered over the next musical selection. The needle slid to the end of the disc—emitting a scratching noise as it went round and round.

"Darling, pardon this intrusion. I'm frightfully sorry to bust in like this, but I understood you wanted to see me before I run along."

"Hello there!" Idina flashed a smile and mumbled unevenly. "You're all dogged-up. Why, you look like a film player—a regular Valentino!"

Maxwell beamed. Forgetting about the needle grating on the Gramophone, he fingered his rose *boutonnière* and adjusted the points of his silk handkerchief.

She started to replace the disk on the turntable.

"You're just in time for another hot number!"

"You might turn that off for a little while, will you?"

"You win!" She raised the cocktail glass and drained it. Satisfied, she set it down gingerly and teetered across the bedroom toward the divan. The feather trim on her alabaster *crêpe de Chine* dressing gown fluttered as a pair of feathered mules with three-inch heels clapped an irregular beat against the parquet floor. She stopped in front of Maxwell. Her red fingernail lingered against his lapel.

"I had to see you because there's something I must discuss before you leave."

His nostrils arched at an overpowering licorice smell on her breath. He shoved his gold-rimmed spectacles over the bridge of his nose. "Idina darling, please don't think me disagreeable, but I think perhaps you'd better sit down."

"Don't be silly now! I assure you I'm feeling quite alright. Tip-top! I was just listening to a little music before I turn in."

His brow furrowed. "Although you do seem to be coping much better than I thought possible, you still must rest. I insist!"

"Yes, indeed," she replied, trying to keep her temper in check. "Yes, of course!"

He clutched her by the elbow and seated her. "Darling, I know you'll manage this evening, but I hate to leave you just the same," he said, pausing to study her expression. "About the banquet, I realize the timing is most unfortunate, yet I must be there because I'm the host. I do have to show the flag."

Idina motioned for Maxwell to sit beside her. He did. "I'm very alarmed about the banquet," she blurted, her words rising. "I don't like you dashing about with that American on the loose. He's a tough customer and liable to try to get nasty with you." She sniffled. "Oh Maxwell, I'm afraid for your safety!"

"Ace was found out, you know." Maxwell patted her hand. "It's only a matter of time before he is captured. Everything's going to be quite alright. The police shall put a stop to him. You needn't worry about me."

She shoved his hand away. "You men are all such fools! The only difference among you idiots are your neckties!"

He protested, "We cannot live in fear. We must go on with our lives. It's the only sensible thing to do. I have a right to do what I think best. And I shan't stay put! I'm going tonight, and you needn't try to change my mind, do you hear?"

"Don't be cross," Idina whimpered.

Sighing, Maxwell said, "There, there, I'm sorry dear. I'm ashamed of myself for becoming angry. Please realize I don't want to cause you the least bit of unhappiness."

"Would you at least let Orloff be your bodyguard tonight? I would feel so much more at ease."

"Well," he pondered, "I suppose no harm could come of it."

"He must be with you at all times! Inside the restaurant, not outside. Mind you, I won't have it any other way! I shudder at the thought of losing you, too!"

"Righto!" He petted her head. "Well, that's that. I must attend to it before I clear out. If Orloff is to be my bodyguard, his uniform won't do at all there."

"Oh, thank you Maxwell!" Idina hugged him, while rolling her eyes behind his back.

He stood up and smoothed his tailcoat. "Now, don't get into any mischief while I'm away."

"I won't," she laughed. "Soon it'll be beddy-bye for me."

"Good night, darling."

"Goodbye," Idina answered definitively. She sank into the pillows without watching Maxwell leave. Instead she wobbled to the Gramophone and chose a record. The needle brought the music to life. Jaunty trumpets resounded as the orchestra joined in.

A tenor warbled, "*You're for me, doll. I'm for you, Sue. Let's we, two, have a honeymoon…*"

Tapping her toes, Idina grabbed a nearby bottle of absinthe, took a swig, and danced the Charleston. The heel of one mule landed on the open toe of the other. "Yeow!" she shrieked. Trying to untangle her feet, Idina lost her balance and landed squarely on the wooden floor with a thump. Tousled curls clouded her face. The feathered trim on her dressing gown was wet and matted. She threw her head back, roaring with laughter.

A Shanghai temple.

Ace made his way on foot to the Temple of Heaven. His rickshaw tire had blown out. On the main street leading up to the temple only one car could pass at a time along the narrow thoroughfare. Sidewalks overflowed with Shanghainese. By the looks of it, he'd be late. The Mid-Autumn Moon Festival was but one night away. Every Shanghainese around the stalls and tables was frantically buying essentials: rolled clusters of fiery-red cockscomb flowers to signify the Eighth Month, bowls of juicy yellow beans to entice the jade rabbit T'u-er Yeh to leave the moon for a nibble, and lucky nine-jointed lotus roots to offer first in sacrifice as a symbol of purity and then to eat later to cleanse their bodies of all evil. At last, Ace reached a high red wall enclosing the Temple of Heaven compound. Shoppers had given way to diseased beggars, who hoped for alms from temple patrons disposed to please the gods with acts of charity. The temple had a three-layered tiled roof of imperial yellow indicating that a Son of Heaven, one of China's emperors, had blessed the temple, which looked down from a hill to the street below with a personal appearance.

Commanding a more spectacular view was a nine-tiered pagoda behind the temple. It loomed 50 feet above the ground from its octagonal granite base. The afternoon sun glinted on red, yellow, green, and white porcelain tiers as well as on the pagoda's projecting green rooftops that seemed to shrink with each ascent up the spire. Unlike other pagodas with from three to 13 odd-numbered tiers, this pagoda was special. Not only was it a *hua t'a*, or a flowery pagoda esteemed for its brightly glazed, porcelain exterior, but it was a tribute to geomancy. Represented both within the pagoda and the temple were the sun, moon, and stars (the Three Lights of Illumination), Buddha, the law, and priesthood (the Three Treasures), and heaven, earth, and man (the Three Powers of Nature). All elements combined to make the number "nine" reign as befitted heaven.

Ace passed through a turreted red gate at the entrance with posts engraved in gold characters.

One beseeched: *"May Heaven Send Down Happiness."* The other commanded: *"Ask and You Shall Receive."*

Paying homage before ancestral tablets.

He proceeded up an inclined granite walkway through venerable magnolia, cedar, and pine trees.

Resting on his haunches against a massive archway at the first of three elevated terraces, Babe munched nervously on a grass stalk. He spat it out at the sight of his friend approaching.

Ace called out, "Brother, am I glad to see you! Where are the others? Are they here?"

"Hi, boss. I didn't turn up anything at Osaka Gardens. The American woman is inside waiting. Your friend, Chicago Charlie, he has not yet arrived."

Ace took out a cigarette, rapped it against the archway, and lit it. "Let's find a place to talk where we can see Chicago if he shows."

They hurried along through the next archway with its nine steps leading to the next elevation. Paths sprung from the main walkway to the abbot's and monks' living quarters in the back. At the third arch, Ace stopped at a life-sized statue of a burly god armed with a sword and fan. The statue's thick hair, swirling past its shoulders, blended in with its moustache and beard.

"That's a pip! Who is it?" He ran his fingers along a cluster of peaches of immortality dangling from one end of the statue's black, bat-winged hat.

"He's Chung K'uei, the Great Spiritual Chaser of Demons for the Whole Empire." Babe kowtowed to the idol.

"He gives me the willies. I've never seen such mean-looking eyes!" Ace tossed the cigarette aside and whistled. "I'd hate to come across him on a dark night!"

Babe read an inscription on the sword. "Like the fan and sword, his face, too, is a weapon against demons. That's why he is called the Protector Against Evil Spirits."

"What does it say?" Ace examined the statue's sword.

"The letters are of an ancient style. I believe it says, 'Lead on Happiness and Restore the Heavens."

"Sounds swell to me. We'd better get going. Let's blow and find Helen."

They bounded up white marble slabs that formed ringed patterns of nine concentric circles outside the temple. A sapphire building, unlike the commonplace red-painted temples, loomed before them. An unusual crest of an enormous full moon, as white and lustrous as a pearl, and figures of a

A wall dragon.

dragon and a phoenix sprang from eaves on the blue building's massive triple roof. Rows of clouds and stars arose on a roof curving up to the sky. This temple gave an impression of elegant simplicity and grace. Next to the entrance, an abbot fussed with a movable lattice screen. Instead of wearing a traditional Buddhist saffron-yellow robe, he had on a deep-blue gown in a color chosen in deference to the sky. Stooping to the ground and picking up a mallet with a long handle, the abbot disappeared inside the temple.

Ace and Babe followed through the front opening that faced south in reference to life. Immediately inside the main hall, they saw two identical golden screens towering nine feet above the marble floor. Growling golden dragons writhing among spinning, silver-flecked clouds, warding off evil spirits, adorned the screens.

"Come on, let's step over this way," Ace said.

The sun's final rays slipped through the lattice windows. In the roof's center was an opening for a smoke tower. Candles glared as darkness descended on the main hall and adjoining chambers. Fragrant smoke from three sandalwood incense urns, placed in a semi-circle behind the double screens, wafted through the air. Looming on altars, white porcelain temple gods and goddesses reflected a ghastly aura. A dozen Shanghainese men and women offered joss sticks and bowed in front of altars. Some worshipers dipped ladles into large porcelain vases to retrieve water sanctified by the deities to brew in tea or blend with medicine.

"Hey, Helen is nowhere to be seen. Babe, are you sure she's here?" When no response came, Ace searched among the Chinese and found the youth mesmerized along the south wall in front of a shrine of the 10 Kings of the Courts of Hell. It portrayed P'an Kuan, Keeper of the Register of the Living and Dead, reading a long scroll near the center row of gods. Below, figures with the heads of horses and cows prodded tridents at sinners agonizing in accordance to their misdeeds in 16 pits. Dogs tore at a merchant. Fire burned a peasant woman's mouth. Oil boiled around a magistrate in a cauldron. Two stones ground at a farmer pressed in the middle. Sabers pierced a courtesan who had slipped onto Sword Mountain.

"Babe, come on." Ace tugged at his tattered sleeve. "Snap out of it, will you? Is Helen here or not? I don't see her anywhere. Come on, let's find her."

"What's that you said, boss?"

"Are you sure she came in here?"

Babe turned to Ace, but his eyes remained fixed on the shrine. "I'm sure."

Ace stepped in front of the altar to block his view. "If you look at that any longer, you're going to go screwy! Now, shake a leg! I'm on the run, and I've got a big night ahead." *Bong, bong!* They jumped at the deafening sound. The abbot slammed the wooden mallet against a notched side of a nine-foot bell suspended in a wooden frame. The bell had been cast with an open square at the top of its dome to prevent fracturing. Placing the mallet on the floor, the abbot walked a few paces away and lit three joss sticks in front of a reclining statue of the Goddess Mercy.

"What's the idea? Is the temple closing?"

"No," Babe replied. "It's time for the abbot's evening prayers."

"Okay, then," Ace pointed to the Western chambers. "You go that way, and I'll take the other side."

Ace moved away; his eyes had adjusted to the interior dimness. The ceiling timbers, walls, and pillars were the same sapphire-blue as the outside, except for the wooden pillars supporting the roof etched in The Five Colors—black, white, red, green, and yellow. Some pillar's inscriptions bore a double *Fu* character for good luck in lettering painted in two different colors symbolizing the fundamental principles of good and evil. Other pillars bore the painting of an axe cleaving a head to signify dual powers of administering justice and punishment.

As Ace walked across an open court to the northeastern section, he saw Helen with two monks standing next to a shrine of T'ien Hou, the Goddess of Heaven, whose image was flanked by two attendants, Thousand League Eyes along with Favoring Wind Ears. One monk whisked a duster of bamboo twigs over golden incense burners shaped like dragons and phoenixes. Near the back of the statues, Helen spoke to a tall monk hugging a basket of beans, tea leaves, pebbles, and straw. Seeing Ace, she muttered to the monk and hurried over. "Here you are. Oh, I've just had the most amazing conversation! I think it could lead to good story. Maybe even a piece for the Mid-Autumn Moon Festival."

Ace pulled her aside. "I don't give a hoot about any article! Tell me what you've found out!"

Helen's mind worked over the angles. "This could be a nice sidebar. How does this grab you? 'While the Chinese offer moon cake sacrifices, their gods feast on beans, straw, and rocks.' Sounds pretty good?"

"Not now, Helen. I'm not interested in any of that," he snapped.

"Don't get into a flap! Just listen. How does this sound? 'Everyone knows people can't live without their heart and other organs, but what about Chinese gods? Well, the Temple of Heaven monks make sure the idols aren't left out. Statues have holes stuffed with beans for the heart and brains, and straw for intestines.' Doesn't that sound like a swell article?"

"Sure, it sounds swell, Helen. First things first, though. Did you get a hold of Chicago Charlie like I asked?"

"Yeah, don't sweat. You know, this oddball story could make Page One at the bottom of the fold if it has a bang up headline."

Ace put his arm around Helen's shoulder and steered her away from the Goddess of Heaven. "Let's go find Babe and look for Chicago. Maybe he's here by now."

Babe ran up. "Any sign yet of Chicago?"

Ace shook his head. "Let's go outside and talk this thing over while we wait for him."

"Sure thing," Helen answered, coolly lifting his arm from her shoulders. The trio left for the top of the triple terraces with its vantage point where they could see Chicago Charlie. Babe sat on a marble bench underneath an old magnolia tree, thick vine curled around its trunk. Ace stood looking down the pathway.

"Helen," he said, "you go first."

"Nah uh," she shook her head and sat next to Babe. "I'm no dumb Dora! I'm not going to do all the talking and then have a mug like you tell me to blow. You're not going to hold out on me. No siree! I go last, do you hear?"

"Yeah, I hear." Ace lit a cigarette. "Say, I bet you think you're a pretty smart Jane."

"You better believe it, brother. Helen's the name. Don't start getting fresh with me!"

Ace was about to answer when Chicago Charlie bounded up. Hidden nearby among a cluster of pine trees, the Red Pole enforcer crouched on the dirt watching them from afar.

"Hi yuh, flyboy! How goes it, kid? What's up, coppernob?" Chicago plopped down on the bench. "Hey, I didn't mean to make you folks cool your heels, but I had to lay low for a little while. A couple of lightweights tried to tail me. Sooner or later, I knew those Brits would try to pull some monkey business on me. I ducked 'em though. Piece a cake!"

"That's okay, pal. You didn't miss much. Jane, I mean Miss Hanlon and me were ironing out something before we all get started. Isn't that right?"

"Yeah? What of it?"

Chicago leaned forward. "Take it easy, sister! This ain't the time to roughhouse! Ace here is being made the fall guy. We're all tryin' to clear him."

"Speak for yourself!"

"Aw, now don't go gettin' hot under the collar," Chicago whined. "How'd you like it if someone was tryin' to pin somethin' on yuh? Give him half a chance."

"Oh, alright."

"Gee, that's swell!" Chicago winked at Ace. "Well flyboy, the gang's all here. It's your jamboree."

Tossing the cigarette on the ground and rubbing it out with the sole of his shoe, Ace turned to Babe. "Okay kid, suppose you tell us how you made out today."

Avoiding eye contact, the youth shrugged his shoulders. "Not much to tell, I'm afraid. All I saw at Osaka Gardens was Japanese businessmen before a hooligan chased me away."

"A hooligan?"

"Oh yeah?" Chicago Charlie asked. "What's that supposed to mean? What kind of bird are you talkin' 'bout?"

"A beggar." Babe squirmed on the bench. "He had no legs, but was very cunning and fierce! I had to flee. I'm sorry I was no help!"

Ace dropped down on his haunches and looked into the boy's eyes. "Was he in a basket strapped to a platform? With a wooden dumbbell in each hand?"

"Yes."

"What gives, old buddy? Do you know that panhandler he's talkin' about?"

"I've seen him around lately. I don't know who he is, or what he's up to, but 'Torso Man' sure gets around town on that little cart of his."

Chicago turned to the terrace and spat over the edge. "Aw, don't give that bird another thought. He sounds harmless enough. What can a guy with no legs do to anyway? Besides, if yuh don't mind my sayin' so, you've got more important troubles."

Helen removed a pair of gauntlet gloves and placed them on the lap of her matching green sweater and pleated skirt. Reaching for her envelope-shaped pocketbook, she pulled out a compact. "Let's get this show on the road and call it quits. I've got things to do." She looked into the mirror's reflection and fluffed her bangs from beneath a matching felt béret. "Chicago, why don't you put in your two cent's worth now? I want to get out of here."

"Suits me just fine." He replied with a sniffle, an indication of his need for opium. Pulling a roll of pills from the pocket of his lavender vest, he unfurled the wrapper and put two tablets on his tongue. "I called on a good pal of mine. Lulu's the name. She's on the level. A real bundle of laughs, too! She runs The Scratch over on Mohawk."

Helen stopped preening and shut the compact with a loud snap. "Surely you're joking? You don't mean to say you went to that place!" She laughed. " 'Come to The Scratch and see our Yankee-doodle dolls. It's a cinch you'll find a match if you've got an itch that needs a scratch.' Isn't that how the radio jingle goes?" She dabbed at the tears in her eyes with a perfumed hanky. "With an important job to do, you go to that flophouse for help!"

"Clam up, Lady Jane."

"I bet your lady friend is a real lulu, too!"

"I'm warnin' yuh, it ain't polite to talk like that 'bout a friend of mine!"

"Are her nails as long as a cat's…get it, a cat—cathouse!"

His knuckles whitened. "I don't go for takin' a sock at no dames, but if any dame ever wuz askin' for it, you're the one!"

Ace grabbed his fist. "Simmer down! No rough stuff here. If you want to get tough with her, wait until I'm in the clear. Then you can have my blessing!" Releasing his friend, he jabbed his finger at her. "Why don't you get wise to yourself and stop shooting off your mouth! I've got my back up against the wall. I don't need any grief right now from you!"

"Sorry for losin' my temper, pal." Chicago glared at Helen, who stuck her tongue out at him. "As I was startin' to say when she horned in, yuh see, it's like this. Lulu don't know nothin' 'bout no Colonel Togawa, but there's a Japanese captain who's gonna be movin' some cargo on a new shipping line from Hangchow to somewheres in Manchuria. My apologies, flyboy. Looks like I drew a blank. See, those boys of the Rising Sun ain't no suckers. They know how to keep the cap on the bottle."

"That's alright. You did fine." Ace removed his hat and ran his fingers through his thick black hair. "Look's like it's your turn, sister."

"Not so fast! I'm last! Remember?"

"Alright," Ace said, twirling his straw hat around his fingers. "I tailed Maxwell to Hongkew. He had lunch with a Major Fujiwara. They were hashing out the finishing touches for a banquet tonight. Sounded like some sort of business scheme. That's the long and short of it. Looks to me like this day has gone to nothing unless you've turned up something good, Helen."

She leaned over. "Is this the straight dope? This afternoon you said the picture was getting bigger."

Ace rested the hat on his knee. "It was just a hunch. I'm still trying to put the pieces together. Until I do, I'm not about to jump to conclusions with any half-baked ideas. That is, not as long as my neck is on the line."

"You sure you're not holding out on me? Because if what I've been hearing is the whole shebang, brother, they're going to throw you in the can! You don't stand a chance of clearing yourself. You're through!"

"Listen, I'm giving it to you straight. I'm fed up with being pushed around. You may think I'm snowed under, but I'll make out alright in the end. I always do. Isn't that so, Chicago?"

"Yeah, that's so. Yuh got that albatross ring on your pinkie to prove it, too! Twenty-five Hun flying machines down in smoke! Boy, them were the days!"

"Alright, alright!" Helen said brusquely, stretching the chamois gloves over her hands. "Maxwell Soames is supposed to be putting on a banquet tonight at The Catherine the Great's. Some business affair. As far as I could find out it doesn't have anything to do with the Japanese or their military officers. From what you say, if the Japanese are involved, they're probably in it for the money, as usual." She clutched her pocketbook and rose. "I'd better be getting along. It's almost dark out here, and I'm going to be late. Give me a ring if and when you do have that big scoop for me, otherwise, I'll plan on writing your obit."

"Hey, what time is that banquet?"

Haughtily glancing over her shoulder, she answered: "Seven o'clock."

Chicago spat over the terrace. "That skirt is somethin' else! She sure gets under my skin! Did yuh see the way she high-hatted me 'bout Lulu?"

"Let it ride. Babe, where's that *sampan?*"

The boy stopped pulling a loose thread on his tattered sleeve. "Soochow Creek."

"Well son, that's a mighty long creek. Where exactly do you mean?"

"Ten minutes' walk from here. A boatman is minding it for us," Babe sprang to his feet. "Shall I take you there?"

"Let's shove off." Ace put on his hat. "Chicago, I've got a job for you."

"Gee flyboy, I'm all wet. Just now, I wuz wishin' we'd go back to the junk and sit tight 'til we think this through. It'll do yuh some good." Chicago Charlie cocked his chin toward the street below. "Come on, Ace, let's blow. You're better off layin' low out on the water for a while where you're safe. It's no use doin' anythin' in the city tonight."

"Sorry pal, but I'm off to Catherine the Great for a date with a louse by the name of Maxwell. But first, you're going to buy me some glad rags so I won't arouse suspicion when I walk through the front door."

"Nuthin' doin', pal. I ain't leavin' yuh in the lurch. Say? What do yuh take me for? I ain't yella, and I ain't the nervous type neither! Why, I'm loaded for bear!"

"Snap out of it. I know you're a regular guy so ease up, will you? I'm playing my cards close to my chest. I'm not about to lug you and the kid around. Get it?"

"Don't be a sap! I don't know 'bout the kid, but you ain't got a chance in there without me. It's run by the White Russians. They're pals of mine. Besides, I know the whole layout. I can be the lookout, see?"

Rubbing his chin, Ace replied, "Okey-doke, you're in. The kid can come along too, but he stays outside. Now, let's quit yammering and high-tail it over to the *sampan*. You've got to buy us some evening clothes. It's getting late."

As the trio left the temple, a pair of bats fluttering by in a zigzag formation from the pagoda's lower roofs passed over their heads and blended into the night sky. Ace and Chicago followed closely behind Babe, who spearheaded a path on North Honan Road to Soochow Creek. Chinese pimps in European suits leaned against lampposts next to parked rickshaws. Money changers called attention to their trade by jingling coins in their pockets. Food sellers stirred frying meatballs in woks. Up ahead, Ace saw lanterns glowing from a myriad of riverboats and rafts jammed in

A ferry ride.

the middle of Soochow Creek where they were moored along its banks. This was called "The Water Slum." Thousands of creek people lived on, bathed in, and dumped waste into the muddy fetid waters that rose 77 miles away at Tai Lake and emptied into the Whangpoo River. Babe led them to the *sampan*.

"Climb aboard while I pay the boatman."

Ace and Chicago Charlie did so as Babe ducked into an adjacent hooded slipper boat.

"I gotta hand it to yuh, flyboy, yuh sure know how to show a fella a good time. This place is a real cosmic phenomenon, if yuh get my drift."

"Pipe down!" Ace removed a cigarette from his depleting pack.

"Do me with one, too. Maybe the smoke will take the edge off this stinkin' trough."

Smoke drifted from underneath the rattan roof. Babe's muffled voice argued in Chinese with the boatman.

"Say Ace, I heard somethin' screwy today from Ch'in, the head dishwasher at The Saints & Sinners."

"Oh, yeah?" Ace flicked cigarette ash.

"Yeah. Old Ch'in sez you've got a new daddy. The granddaddy of all daddies—old Pockmarked Fang. Any truth to it?"

Ace exhaled a stream of cigarette smoke directly at his friend.

Wincing as the smoke stung his eyes, Chicago sputtered: "Hey, what's the idea?" They both teetered as Babe climbed aboard the *sampan*.

Ace spoke to the boy. "What took so long?"

"Sorry boss, but the boatman wanted more money when he saw foreigners. I had to bargain with him."

"Okay," Ace called out. "Let's shove off."

"Sure thing, boss." Babe brought the motor to life. "Where to?"

Looking from the rattan roof, Ace yelled above the sputtering motor. "Take the canals to St. Peter's Church. Down the street is a men's ready-to-wear store next to the Carlton Theatre. We'll get lost among the White Russians there, and no one will bother us."

Babe replied silently by making an "okay" sign with his fingers. Chicago flicked his cigarette into the water and turned to Ace, who sat on the bench toying with his pinkie ring. "Come on, pal, quit stallin'. Sing to your buddy boy here! Is the word on the street on the up and up? Yes or no? If it's yes, then you're on the gravy train."

"Knock it off, buster!"

"Oh, don't get sore! I wuz just tryin' to make some conversation. That's all." When he ascertained that Ace wasn't looking, Chicago went over to the boy. "Say, Babe, is it true that our pal, Ace, has been adopted by Pockmarked Fang?"

The boy nodded.

"So," Chicago commented, "Mr. Jordan 'the Gallant' has finally hit the big time with his good deeds. Boy, oh boy, that sure is swell." He elbowed Babe. "That's mighty grand, don't yuh think?"

"Perhaps not. Trouble is more likely to result from their relationship. Pockmarked Fang is not a man to trifle with. I don't think he'd like being turned down if he knew the Boss doesn't want to be his adopted son."

Chicago Charlie chuckled. "Yeah, I'd like to get a load of those two together in the same room. The saint and the sinner. Just like the moniker of the joint where I sling the amber nectar, the fizz, and the rye."

Babe snorted. "You may think the situation is funny, but I don't. Since the gods spared Pockmarked Fang's life, he must adopt the Boss. And the Boss must be obedient as a son with filial piety, otherwise he will lose his life."

"Yuh got a point there kid. Maybe I can get him to see the light after this whole thing with Special Branch blows over." Chicago Charlie gazed at the checkered patterns inside skyscraper windows across Soochow Creek.

Waiters in silver satin liveries trimmed with sable moved among large tables inside The Catherine the Great Restaurant. In the center, crystal pendants shaped like teardrops radiated from three chandeliers suspended above an orchestra section where a violinist in a white sash and high-collared Cossack tunic of scarlet satin performed a brooding solo. Maxwell sat with three men at a table along the back wall. They nibbled smoked eel, sipped chicken consommé, and spooned Beluga caviar from cut-glass pots onto small pieces of toasted white bread. A waiter set before them dishes of crayfish soufflé.

From a side table near the entrance, Chief Inspector Haymes watched Maxwell chat effortlessly. Old Soames acts as if nothing has happened, he thought. I know he's here on business, but he's behaving without a care in the world! Never mind about himself being targeted by that Yank. What about young Roddy, who is barely cold? Soames should behave better in the interest of decency! Haymes turned to his table's centerpiece—a dwarf tree laden with plums in a silver planter on the table. A waiter replaced it with a brass samovar. A porcelain teapot nestled in a holder above the urn's draft chimney. Reaching for a tea glass in a filigreed silver holder, the inspector stopped at the sound of shuffling feet and bantering in Japanese from a group of men entering the restaurant. His eyes scanned the delegation. Checking in their white kid gloves and hats, they all looked alike in black top hats and tailcoats except for Admiral Iwasaki, who wore a plumed cap and a much-decorated naval uniform with gold braid. One of them had a bushy, gray moustache set below wild, ink-black eyebrows and short, wavy black hair. That man smiled as he passed Haymes.

Colonel Togawa—why, it if isn't the Black Eel himself! Chief Inspector Haymes told himself. Look at him, making an appearance and looking as elegant at King George V. What the deuce he is up to? Haymes winked at a plainclothes detective in formal dinner dress who leaned against a wall in the corner and nodded toward the Japanese delegation. So help me, the Inspector promised himself, one of these days I'm going to catch that Black Eel. He's not going to slither away so easily! Reaching for the teapot and filling his glass, he turned the samovar's spigot, unleashing boiling water into a pungent concentrate of tea. He added a dash of milk and three cubes of sugar, stirred the tea, and took a sip while looking at Maxwell's table.

A tall man, with blond Dutch boy hair, clad in ill-fitting evening clothes hovered in the background. Every now and then, the blond man spoke with the Russian waiters and slunk to a secluded spot where he took a nip of vodka. Haymes recognized him to be Orloff, Maxwell's chauffeur.

Four waiters slid plates of steaming asparagus *au gratin* before Maxwell and his companions. Two waiters struggled under the weight of a platter transporting a giant roasted swan to the table. Peering through gold-rimmed spectacles at the skinned bird sitting with its neck held high and reshaped on a bed of rice, Maxwell exclaimed, "I say, look at the size of that swan!" He rose from the table, turned to each of his companions, and smiled broadly. "My dear friends. Herr Schroeder, Monsieur Devereux, and my fellow countryman, Mr. Selwyn-Smyth, it's with great pleasure that I've invited you to dine with me this evening. Tonight, we celebrate Asian Aviation Corps' new chartered service to the Hua Chang Antimony Refining Company in Honan province." Maxwell lifted a glass of champagne. "Let's all raise our glasses and, at the same time, recall to mind this ancient Chinese witticism: 'Good wine reddens the face, while riches excite the mind.'" His dinner companions responded.

"Bravo, my good man!"

"*A votre santè!*"

"Here, here!"

Chuckling heartily, Maxwell clinked his glass against the others'. "Before we partake any further of this sumptuous feast let us remember yet another pearl of wisdom from old Cathay. It goes something like this: 'The mouth is an unlimited measure.'"

The English, French, and German exporters of antimony all roared with laughter.

Maxwell lifted the champagne to his lips. From over the top of the glass, his blue eyes darted momentarily across the room to the Japanese.

Chief Inspector Haymes grunted in disgust at Maxwell's decadent behavior. He left the table and tread across dark-brown *moquette* carpet to the young plainclothes detective in the corner.

"Yes, Guv?"

"McCooper, I want you to keep watch from my table. See to it that Wingate takes your place here. I'm going to wander outside for a bit while Soames and his cronies enjoy their swan repast. That should keep them busy for a while. Send round for Hamilton. I want him to listen in as close to the Japanese as possible."

"Very good, Guv."

"Off with you then, lad. I'm going outside for a smoke."

Meanwhile, hurrying along an alley facing The Catherine the Great Restaurant, Ace charged ahead of Chicago Charlie and Babe. In the distance, the restaurant's golden neon sign glowed in Cyrillic lettering. The night was dark except for a cloud masking light of the rising moon.

"Come on," Ace yelled back. "Shake a leg!"

"Gee whiz! Take it easy pal!" complained Chicago, whose toe caught an uneven slab of cobblestone, causing him to trip and fall. Following too closely to stop, Babe tumbled head first over Chicago as an alley cat yelped and ran from the commotion.

Ace hurried back to them. Groping about in the darkness, he rasped: "This cinches it! You're no better than a Laurel and Hardy comic opera! If you two don't stop with the funny business right now, I'm on my own. Do you hear me?"

Chicago brushed off his clothes. "Sure, I hear yuh, flyboy. Don't get into a flap. We ain't tryin' to gum up the works for yuh."

"Yes Boss, be reasonable! I'm scared stiff, but I'm here to help."

"Hear that, pal? We ain't against yuh. We's here to be of service!"

"Oh, alright!" Ace pulled out a cigarette. His face tensed against the glow of the match. "Listen up boys, this is how we'll play it. Babe, we'll wait here while you go first and case the outside of the joint. No one will pay any attention to a beggar."

"Fine, Boss. Anything you say."

"Chicago, when he comes back with the 'all clear', you go inside and size up the layout. Babe will be begging near the entrance. Come out and toss him some dough if Maxwell's inside. I'll be watching Babe from this alley. Then wait for me in the foyer, and I'll come in straightaway."

"Boss, what if Maxwell isn't there?"

"We'll head for the *sampan* and go back to the junk so I can think about another plan. But we'll worry about that later. You'd better run along, Babe, time's a wasting."

Babe rushed to the end of the alley. When he reached the crowded street, he hunched his back as if plagued by a spinal ailment and hobbled around slow-moving rickshaws, pedicabs, and automobiles. Most shops along the street sat in darkness. Babe noticed the entrance to Catherine the Great's was cordoned off by brass posts supporting velvet ropes. Under a crimson canopy, two White Russian doormen, with daggers tucked under the waistbands of their Cossack uniforms, leaned against the wall and clutched the handles of their carbines. Seeking to avoid being manhandled by the Cossacks, Babe went next door in front of the Ukrainian Bakery where other beggars had gathered. The aroma of black bread and braided twists taking shape in the bakery's ovens filled the air. The other beggars glanced suspiciously at Babe while guarding their tattered straw mats.

A congregation of beggars.

Moments later, a maroon sedan eased to a stop in front of the restaurant. A red-haired woman wearing a full-length, white-velvet evening wrap with a white, fox fur collar alighted from a door opened by a chauffeur. She grasped the arm of her male companion, in a black top hat and tails, and passed Haymes standing underneath the canopy. Loosening his stiff white collar, he looked about the street. Nothing seemed amiss. He reached into a pocket for his pipe in a movement that caused the beggars to screech out and hold out their hands at him. Ignoring their pleas, he strolled past, rapping the pipe's bowl against his palm.

Although Babe watched puffs of smoke rise above the Inspector's back, he didn't recognize the man to be the head of Special Branch who was on the lookout for Ace. The old man meandering down the street signaled no alarm in the boy's mind so he crossed the street to the alley back where Ace and Chicago Charlie waited.

"No trouble over there, Boss."

"Okay fellas. It's my turn to skedaddle. Leave it up to old Chicago here. Don't yuh worry none, flyboy, I won't fall down on yuh. A better gate-crasher there never wuz!"

"Hang on a sec," Ace replied. "Do you remember what Maxwell looks like?"

"That crumb? Sure I knows what 'four-eyes' looks like! I could recognize that lightweight anywheres!"

"Alright then, if you notice anything suspicious, hightail it back here."

Babe and Ace hid in the shadows and watched Chicago cross the street. Ace nudged Babe.

"Okay kid, it's your turn. Sit tight once you get there; I'll wait until Chicago comes outside the restaurant. If he tosses you some money, that's the all-clear signal, and I follow. If not, you get back here as fast as you can, okey-doke?"

Ace looked to the sky. Cloud wisps formed a glowing veil of gauze over the moon. This white shroud reminded him of a trail of smoke streaming from an Albatross before he had attacked it a second time at close range above Dunkirk. All four wings had splintered to pieces; and the Albatross had dropped from the sky like a lead ball crashing to the ground.

His mind drifted from the past and returned to the present just as a 1920 Cleveland Roadster backfired as it passed the restaurant where Babe hid among a throng of beggars.

A Cossack stepped aside, allowing Chicago Charlie to saunter out the front door.

Chicago dug into his pockets and tossed a handful of change at the beggars, who squealed and dove for the money. At the signal, Ace strolled briskly to meet Chicago halfway.

"No Special Branch gorillas anywheres," Chicago said. "My buddy Serge is checkin' hats tonight. He sez there's nothin' doin' inside but a bunch of stuffed shirts puttin' on the nosebag and gettin' blotto."

"What about Maxwell?" Ace asked as they stepped under the canopy and out into the foyer.

"I spotted that clay pigeon. He's in the back whoopin' it up with three meatballs."

"That's swell. Let's check in our hats and go to the bar. We'll play it from there."

They walked a few steps to the hatcheck. Chicago winked at Serge who took their top hats.

Shielding his face, Ace walked steadily along a dark corridor that led to a bar at the right-hand corner of the restaurant and passed the back of the plainclothes detective, who was seated at Chief Inspector Haymes' table. The bar was surrounded by Roman pillars and low tables overlooking the dining area and center orchestra section. Ace chose a side table. From there, he spied Maxwell across the room sipping champagne.

Chief Inspector Haymes strolled over the dark-brown *moquette* carpet to his table and slid into a chair next to McCooper.

The lights dimmed. A spotlight flared on a sultry brunette in a yellow flowing peasant blouse and skirt with a scarf over her forehead. Strumming a balalaika, she crooned a doleful Russian folk song.

Waiting for darkness at the singer's solo, Orloff stood next to the kitchen thinking about the money Idina promised. His hands cradled a tray with four glasses of lemon-flavored vodka to accompany dessert. The glass with the biggest lemon wedge contained a deadly dose of the bitter-tasting rat poison. He knew the end of Maxwell's banquet neared.

Also taking advantage of the darkness, Ace left the bar and slunk closer to Maxwell's table. He stood opposite Orloff along the wall; a kitchen door separated them. Neither man recognized the other in the dimness.

Toting a silver tray topped with four cut-glass cups of frozen cream, a waiter scurried out the kitchen and rested the tray before Maxwell.

"Stop right there, my good man!" Maxwell ordered, arching his eyebrows haughtily at the cups. The French, German, and English guests turned to the waiter. Maxwell continued, "How could you ever dream of bringing these things out in such a dreadful state? This rubbish is not at all what I ordered!"

"*Prastitye?*" the waiter asked. "Sorry?"

"There are supposed to be raspberries on top! Raspberries, do you hear? I demand you fetch them at once!"

"*Ya panyatna,*" the waiter apologized, and began to remove the tray.

Maxwell grabbed his elbow. "Leave it here you simpering fool! Just bring me the blasted raspberries. I'll darn well serve my guests by myself. Off with you now!"

The waiter scrambled over to the kitchen.

Ace noticed something odd. Maxwell produced four cigars. Passing one to each guest and keeping one for himself. Maxwell never smoked. Not even an occasional cigarette, much less a cigar.

"Gentlemen, let us not allow that rather frightful waiter to dampen our spirits," said Maxwell, rising to his feet. "Tonight we shall smoke, drink, and be merry! After all, we've got a grand future ahead."

The guests grunted approvingly. Maxwell went over to each man and lit their cigars using a cigarette lighter from his vest pocket. Red tips glowed. Then, Maxwell slipped out a matchbox from his sleeve and into his curled palm before returning to his seat. Clenching a cigar between his teeth, he smiled broadly at his companions. He rolled the matchbox around in his left palm and waited. When the men became captivated again by the beautiful White Russian singer, Maxwell leaned over the dessert tray and raised his elbows as if also listening intently, but instead he opened the matchbox and poured fine, white crystalline powder onto three frozen cream desserts. Within seconds, the matchbox closed beneath his fingers. Herr Schroeder, Monsieur Devereux, and Selwyn-Smyth contentedly puffed their cigars and watched the singer. Placing his cigar in an ashtray, Maxwell eased into his chair.

The waiter reappeared with a bowl of raspberries. "*Mozhna?* Will these do?" The waiter offered a pair of silver pincers.

"Yes, these raspberries are lovely."

"*Spasiba.*" The waiter bowed and disappeared.

Maxwell nonchalantly deposited the empty matchbox on the tray. Next, he topped the desserts with berries.

Orloff approached the table after Maxwell served the desserts.

"Sir, your vodka is ready."

Maxwell's nostrils quivered at Orloff's stale breath laced with alcohol. "Oh, you!" he hissed. "Set the glasses down and make yourself scarce. I'll attend to you later—you drunken scoundrel!"

Orloff cast a contemptuous sideways glance and distributed the glasses of lemon-flavored vodka before receding into the dark corridor.

Standing erectly, Maxwell puffed out his chest.

"Gentlemen, gentlemen! May I have your attention, please! Our festivities here are coming to a glorious conclusion. In the eloquent words of the Chinese: 'The Earth has no feasts which do not break up.' Still, the night is yet young, and the White Swan Cabaret awaits us. Let us hasten to finish up because we mustn't keep Madame Rambova waiting!"

All four men laughed.

"*Oui!* Madame Rambova!" Monsieur Devereux gleefully rubbed his hands together. "*Très bien—très bien!*"

Herr Schroeder stomped his feet in agreement.

Mr. Selwyn-Smyth yelled across the table: "My compliments to you, Mr. Soames. The White Swan sounds perfectly delightful! I've heard Madame Rambova is a quite a looker, too!"

Patting his stomach as if too full, Maxwell pushed aside his dessert cup and lifted his glass. "My dear friends, you must partake of both the dessert and the vodka, otherwise I shall be ever so disappointed."

At once, his guests drained their glasses and dug into their raspberry desserts with gusto.

Maxwell felt elated. Victory was at hand! To celebrate, he downed the vodka.

Ace—too busy watching Maxwell—failed to notice the singer conclude her last number by raising her balalaika and curtseying. When he heard the wild applause, he realized its implication. Lights snapped on. Ace instinctively looked across the dining room.

Meeting his gaze from the opposite room, McCooper muttered, "Well, blow me down with a feather! I may be mistaken, but I'm almost certain that's our man. Guv, there's your Yank, Mr. Jack Jordan!"

"What?" Inspector Haymes sputtered. "He couldn't possibly have gained entrance in here!"

"I assure you, Guv, it's him!" McCooper pointed. "There, moving quickly along the back the wall! Looks like he's leaving the Soames' table and heading to the bar."

The Inspector's dark eyes flashed. "Why, that fellow must be mad! Go after him. Don't let him escape through the kitchen!"

McCooper leapt from his chair and knocked it backwards.

"Look, he's onto us. He's reversing direction!"

McCooper dashed around the tables, upsetting a waiter carrying a samovar, which crashed down to the floor. Music from the orchestra skidded to a halt. A woman shrieked.

Chicago Charlie, who had been popping opium pills to steady his nerves, jumped at the sight of Special Branch. Cupping his hands around his mouth, he shouted, "Ace, they've got the front covered. Make a break for it out back or you're done for!"

Orloff, leaning against the wall near the kitchen door, had been making mental plans about getting tickets out of Shanghai for himself and his family.

Aware that Ace was nearby trying to escape from Special Branch, Maxwell signed a chit for the bill. He wondered why the poison wasn't acting sooner on his guests. With the three exporters dead, China's enormous antimony supply would fall into the hands of the Japanese. He'd be paid handsomely and given another assignment. The Green Gang would be blamed, and the Japanese could manufacture as much shrapnel as they pleased for their conquests. The fate of that wretched American pilot was of no consequence whatsoever.

Hamilton, another Special Branch detective, left his table near the Japanese delegation to join the pursuit along the corridor towards Orloff.

"You there," Hamilton cried out to the chauffeur. "Don't just stand there. Stop him! I'll arrest you if you don't seize that man at once!"

Fearing a Chinese jail, Orloff sprang into action after Ace.

McCooper vaulted over a toppled chair as a woman scrambled away. Pans and dishes crashed in the kitchen.

Maxwell gazed at his guests cowering around at the end of the table.

"Gentlemen, gentlemen, remain where you are for the time being. This situation will be resolved shortly, and we can set out for the White Swan Cabaret. There's no need to fear. See for yourselves gentlemen."

Along comes our good Chief Inspector Haymes."

Maxwell stood up and beckoned the Inspector. Suddenly, he felt his muscles stiffen. A worried expression passed over his face. He glanced at his arms and legs.

"Yes, Soames?" Haymes replied.

Maxwell's face and arms began to twitch violently. Convulsions seized his entire body, and he dropped to the floor.

"Mr. Soames!" shouted the Chief Inspector. "Soames! What's wrong, man?" He bent over Maxwell, whose muscles writhed in spastic contractions as he tried to breathe. The Inspector yelled to a waiter. "Quick! Call a doctor!" Turning to Maxwell, whose face and lips began to turn indigo, Haymes grabbed Maxwell's arm, which swung wildly, and felt a pulse beating strongly, but slowly.

A frying pan flew out the kitchen and landed near the Chief Inspector, who knelt beside Maxwell.

"Confound you!" Haymes roared at the kitchen.

More commotion followed, indicating the struggle Ace was putting up. At first, Haymes heard faint wheezing, which turned into loud snorting sounds. He turned toward the grotesque chorus to see Maxwell's dinner companions jerking awkwardly like marionettes.

Herr Schroeder fell backwards onto the next table and hit a platter of golden chicken Kiev nestled among peas.

Selwyn-Smyth toppled over a chair that cracked under his weight.

Monsieur Devereux spun in an out-of-control pirouette.

Although startled at this scene, Chief Inspector Haymes knew they were dead. He'd seen the Green Gang's handiwork before. The few remaining waiters, orchestra members, and patrons gathered around. Haymes rose unsteadily to find out why Ace hadn't been apprehended yet.

Pots, pans, and cutlery lay strewn across the floor in the kitchen. McCooper, Hamilton, and other Special Branch detectives waded in their shoes through the remnants of cabbage, beets, and green vegetable soup. Siberian meat dumplings stuck to McCooper's hair. Mocha frosting from a chocolate-almond torte stained Hamilton's white shirt and waistcoat. The detectives fanned out in a semi-circle closing in on Ace, cornered next to the back door, which had been braced shut from the outside by chefs and other police. Ace held wooden handles of long metal *shashlyk* skewers menacing at the advancing detectives.

"You'd better mind your manners Jordan, or else I'll be only too happy to see you get what's coming to you," bellowed Chief Inspector Haymes, treading over a pile of sturgeon on the floor.

Noticing a wooden barrel a few feet away, Ace realized it was his only means of escape. He jumped on the barrel and began working his way along the top of the counter to the kitchen doorway—unaware Orloff was crawling on the floor towards him.

"Jordan, I'm warning you! Stay where you are!" Haymes barked. "It's a pity, Jordan, I didn't know you'd be with us tonight. Otherwise, I'd have brought along a revolver. At this moment, I'd love nothing better than to shoot you on the spot and finish the job once and for all! Tell me now, why did you have to poison all those other poor chaps? Why were you not content to kill Maxwell alone?"

"Come again?" asked Ace. "What did you say?"

"Is it cowardice perhaps, or brazen malice that fills your black heart?"

"You're off your rocker! I don't know what you're talking about. I haven't done anything to Maxwell."

Two hands gripped his ankles, and he struggled to free himself. Loosing his balance, he dropped the skewers and fell sideways as Orloff tugged with all his might.

Ace plummeted to the counter; his head cracked against a cast-iron frying pan, knocking him out cold.

Orloff slipped off Ace's diamond ring and shoved it into his pocket just before McCooper arrived.

"Guv, it's alright. He's quite harmless now. Out like a light!"

"Leave him to me," Chief Inspector Haymes replied. "I'll see he's deposited in Ward Road Gaol. I'll want to have a word with the commander there."

"Shall I send for a physician?"

"No need. I expect one should be here out front by now. Hamilton, call for a black paddy wagon. I want this one transported under heavy security to the Ward Road Gaol. He's killed five so far, and I don't want to take any chances."

Chinese National Army maneuvers.

CHAPTER FOUR

15th Day of the Eighth Moon

A low, white haze spun into Section 8 of the Whangpoo River at the outskirts of Shanghai. The vapor spread a mist scented with seaweed over the Old Ningpo Wharf, property of the Shanghai & Hongkew Wharf Co. Ltd. It advanced beyond clapboard sheds housing electric tramway cars, rolled across Studley Park's bowling lawns, engulfed the Japanese Naval Club's garden, and rippled above steps leading to the Telephone Exchange before undulating past sandbag and barbed-wire fortifications outside Ward Road Gaol. In a concrete checkpoint at the Gaol's main entrance, a New Zealander guard sipped coffee. Glad that the dawn's arrival meant the end of his watch, he adjusted a Vickers .303 light machine gun, slung over his shoulder. He gazed out a window facing East Seward Road and watched a trash collector guide a mule cart heaped with rags and paper towards a municipal incinerator three blocks away. An old Shanghainese woman lifted a twig broom and stepped aside, allowing the mule cart to rumble past into the fog before she resumed sweeping garbage from the gutters.

At length, the rattle of approaching motors signaled the arrival of a convoy of three open-bed trucks filled with soldiers. The middle one transported Chinese executioners and suspected Communists. Out jumped a firing squad in gray-green Army uniforms. Clutching rifles affixed with bayonets, they were followed by professional stranglers distinguished by loose, blue-cotton shirts and pants, and swordsmen, experts in beheading, who wore ankle-length black robes topped with sleeveless black vests.

The New Zealander left the checkpoint to meet a Kuo-min Tang officer. The KMT officer handed over orders for inspection. Returning them, the New Zealander saluted. "Proceed with the first transfer of Communist prisoners." The KMT officer climbed into the lead truck's cab. A pair of metal gates swung open, and the convoy charged through to the Annex where Ace was.

On a floor mattress, Ace slept in his black tailcoat from the night before. Mercurochrome-tinged bandages formed a turban around his head. Dried blood streaked his white shirt and single-breasted waistcoat. The cell was dark. He dreamt it was Thursday, Sept. 12, 1918. His ears reverberated from a thunderous drone surrounding his two-seater, reconnaissance fighter. Soaring through the haze, Ace's aeroplane numbered among 1,481 Allied planes in World War I's largest air armada of American, French, and British aviators—America's first such operation in the Great War. Ace wondered if he'd survive the day.

The objective was in France: St. Mihiel, 44 miles south of the Belgian border in the heart of Germany's Mézières-Sedan-Metz railroad system that linked Paris to the east and ore deposits in the Briey Iron Basin on the Western Front. Ace looked from the cockpit below to the cool waters of the river Meuse that cut through the 40-mile battlefront and the Argonne forest ahead. The Germans had been dug in the sector since 1914. In preparation for the offensive the day before, 600,000 Allies took battlefield positions under the cover of darkness. Four hours had passed slowly since the dawn attack. Artillery shells exploded beneath Ace's plane. Infantrymen in four divisions of the First Army Corps pushed forward from the south. Tanks, accompanying three divisions of the 4th Army Corps, advanced west to Mont Sec.

Turning fitfully, he rolled off the mattress in his cell and smacked his head against the cold cement floor. Ace awoke at the pain surging from his head. Pulling himself upright, he felt bandages wrapped around his head and peered about the room. Daylight streamed inside the cell, which reeked of disinfectant. A heavy metal door without a handle, the bars on the window, and a rusted bucket in the corner told him that he was in jail. The cork wall panels meant Ward Road Gaol—infamous for its suicide-proof cells. Struggling to his feet, he noticed turned out pockets on his black tailcoat and pants. Laces had been removed from his patent-leather shoes to stop him from making a noose. Vaguely remembering being captured, Ace knew he was in trouble.

Footsteps outside. A hatch opened at the metal door's base, and a rice bowl slide inside. Ace clutched his forehead and stumbled to the window where he peered between bars. Outside mostly young Chinese male prisoners in manacles and shackles formed lines before open-bed trucks. They wore Western suits like some university students. A few older men wore traditional aristocratic robes, gowns, and satin slippers. All displayed a wooden sign hung around their necks. Unable to read Chinese, Ace surmised that the signs proclaimed them guilty of Communism. Executioners accompanied the prisoners, whose death sentences would carried out in public squares for all to see, especially the Shanghainese in the Old Walled City. Decapitations were often followed by the carrying of the prisoners' heads on platters through streets or being impaled on gateposts. As Ace turned from the window, he noticed that his gold pinkie ring, with the black onyx and albatross-shaped diamonds, was missing.

In red satin lady's pajamas trimmed with brown monkey fur, Babe slept on the floor curled on a soft pillar carpet of scrolling red and blue flowers inside The Scratch, where he and Chicago Charlie had taken refuge after Ace's capture. Leaving an adjacent bathroom, Chicago dabbed McNeals Antiseptic Solution on a shaving cut on his chin. Deciding to awaken the kid, he tugged on the teen's leg.

"Hey?" Babe muttered, pulling himself upright and yawning. "What's the big idea?"

Chicago Charlie smoothed his wiry bond hair. His black evening pants and white dress shirt showed creases. He put on his black tailcoat and adjusted a white bow-tie. "Well, I figure flyboy has landed in the Ward Road pokey. I'd bet my bottom dollar on that!"

"Yes," agreed Babe. "I believe you're right."

"It's a wicked business. We ain't got a snowball's chance. It's no dice. There's no way we can bust him outta there. We gotta think of somethin' else, but I'm stumped! Yuh got any bright ideas, kid? If so, don't be shy, let 'em roll."

Babe inhaled the bedroom's lilac perfume and rubbed his nose with his sleeve. Briefly pausing, he replied, "Perhaps I have a thought of interest to you."

"Quit stallin'. This ain't no fun and games here. Ace is in a jam! Yuh better start talkin' turkey before I kicks yuh square in them pretty red pants!"

Babe snapped his fingers and blurted out, "Pockmarked Fang!"

"Hello? What's the idea? Are yuh tryin' to make a monkey outta me?"

Shaking his head, Babe answered, "No, not at all! He'll help. He can free Ace. *Nobody* in Shanghai—no Chinese or foreigner—will oppose Pockmarked Fang."

"Hmm," Chicago Charlie frowned. "Maybe I had yuh pegged all wrong. After all, Ace is sittin' mighty pretty with Pockmarked Fang as his daddy. Kid, I think you're on to somethin'. I really do!"

"Yes, I hope so."

"Let's go chase up some grub in the kitchen and figure out how we're gonna talk to old Pockmarked Fang."

Idina pressed her ear against the cool mahogany door inside her bedroom. The outer hallway yielded no sound, not that she expected it to, but she took precautions just the same. After last night's news from Dr. Hanlon and young Detective McCooper about Maxwell's "mysterious" death, she'd given the servants leave. Dr. Hanlon readily supported her need for solace. If he only knew her real intentions. She stepped from the door, smoothed the folds of her beige jodhpurs, fastened the buttons of her gray, whipcord coat, and pulled the brim of her *écru* hat to hover rakishly over her eye. She gave a last look at her jeweled boudoir clock: half-past seven. Her gloved fingers turned the door handle. Carrying an ivory-handled riding crop, she stepped into the hallway. It was dark and quiet. Turning towards Maxwell's closed bedroom door, she smiled and proceeded. Her black riding boots skipped down the stairs and through the house to the servants' quarters out back. She paused to feel a drinking glass inside her pocket. Freedom was at hand! Her rouged lips snickered.

Rosebushes lined a walkway leading to a cluster of single-story, red brick buildings. Just beyond, a high wall separated the grounds from the causeway where burial tumults jutted from dirt banks along a forsaken canal. Walking jauntily along, Idina struck a yellow rose with her riding crop. Petals burst, trickling to the grass below. Soon no one would stand in her way; she could go where she pleased and do as she liked. The first dwelling was larger than the others. After all, White Russian chauffeurs weren't expected to reside in one-room living quarters like the Shanghainese servants. Orloff's curtains were drawn and his front door unlocked as mandated. Turning the doorknob, Idina nudged the door forward, stepped inside, and silently shut it behind her. Fountain pens, dried ink pots, empty vodka bottles, sheets of crumbled writing paper, and dirty clothes littered the main living area. Piles of Russian books and copies of the city's two Russian newspapers, the *Shanghai Zaria* and the *Slovo*, covered a rattan table. Her nostrils quivered at the smell of dust and stale liquor. Orloff lay facing sideways on a green blanket on the bed with his stocking feet hanging over the mattress. One arm cradled a half-empty vodka bottle. Picking through the clutter, Idina placed the riding crop on the rattan table. Something gold gleamed near the handle. She scooped up a ring with diamond chips glistening in an outline of a bird, spreading its wings over a black onyx square. Rolling Ace's ring around in her fingers, she wondered how Orloff had obtained such a prized possession. She slipped the ring into her coat pocket and stepped up to the bed. Unconcerned about waking Orloff, who snored in a deep slumber, Idina wanted to finish the job as quickly as possible. Towering over him, Idina gazed at a pillow on the floor. She grabbed it by its white and blue pinstripe ticking and leaned over Orloff.

With his white drill waistcoat slung over his shoulder, McCooper bounded down the second-floor veranda of the Shanghai Municipal Police Station to Chief Inspector Haymes' office. The early morning fog had rolled away, and the temperature seemed remarkably cooler than the previous day. McCooper's cork sun hat rested on his baby-fine brown hair. Hurrying along, he scanned the top of a stack of papers he held.

"I say, McCooper! Mind where you're going!"

McCooper looked up and nearly collided with a fellow detective wearing a similar thin dark tie, white shirt, and white trousers. "Sorry, Pryce, I was engrossed with the Soames affair. I'm just on my way to brief the Guv now."

"Best of luck with the old man." Pryce leaned over and whispered. "I've just left him. He's been up til all hours. In a frightful temper and completely disagreeable. That's a fact! He's got a visitor now."

"Righto, I'll surely be on my best behavior. Thanks for the warning.

Cheerio!"

"Abyssinia!"

McCooper slowed his gait. No one wanted to be near the old bulldog when he'd been without a good night's rest. McCooper heard a gravelly voice thunder from an open transom above the closed door.

"Get knotted! I've nothing further to say, young lady!"

"Hey, you can't push me around! I've got my rights! And one of them to is know what's going on!" yelled a woman with an American accent. "I don't believe a single word you've said!"

McCooper rapped loudly on the door.

"Come in," Haymes barked.

When McCooper stepped inside he saw a woman with yellow béret over strawberry-blonde bobbed hair. She stood defiantly pointing her finger at the Chief Inspector, who was hunched over his desk equally as defiant. The skin on his sagging jowls looked sallow against his rumpled, white drill jacket. They both turned to McCooper, who cleared his throat nervously.

"Morning, Guv."

The woman in the tailored suit of canary yellow, topped by a blue and yellow polka-dotted scarf tied loosely around her shoulders, appeared to be in her early twenties.

"Don't you say another word til this dreadful young woman clears out. Wait in that chair. Miss Hanlon is leaving. This interview is at an end, isn't that right, Miss Hanlon?"

"Not so fast, not so fast! The readers of the *North China Daily News* have a right to know what really happened last night at The Catherine the Great. Is the Green Gang connected? The word on the street says it was poison! If so, the Green Gang could be in cahoots with Ace Jordan. What do you say?"

Haymes flushed with rage. "Young woman, I'll say it once more, but slowly this time in the event you're a bit thick, which I suspect you are. It was smallpox, my child, smallpox. Certainly not rat poison!"

"Humph!" Helen shoved her hands on her hips. "Imagine that! Smallpox instantly killing four healthy men—all at the same time, at the same banquet. Just like that!"

"Wait and see. Smallpox will be listed as the cause of death at the Inquest. Now, I bid you good-day."

"I see it's no use wasting my time here anymore." She folded her arms. "If that's the word from Special Branch, there's nothing else I can print." She stomped to the door and spun around. "Smallpox! That's a big lie if I ever heard one!"

With that, she slammed the door behind her.

"I resent that!" Haymes shouted at her.

McCooper crossed his leg and rested the stack of papers on his lap. "Here are the preliminary reports you've sent for, Guv," he said cheerfully. "Where shall I begin?"

"Confound it! You can begin by waiting til I'm ready Detective McCooper, and I'm not ready."

"Sorry, sir!"

Haymes tried to open a side desk drawer, but it refused to budge. "Rubbish, that's what this cronky desk is—absolute rubbish." He grabbed the handle and heaved with all his might. The metal drawer squeaked open. "About time," he grumbled, rummaging around until producing a tin of Finch & Arabella's Ladies' Afternoon Tea Biscuits, a jar of M.C.M. Sheep Tongues, a bottle-cap opener, and a bottle of Browne's Orange Crush. "Alright now, lad, you may begin." McCooper watched him unscrew the lid off the jar of sheep tongues. Haymes then fumbled in his trouser pocket for a pocketknife. "Speak up," ordered Haymes, spearing the meat with the blade. "Don't mind my breakfast. How have the lads been getting on? What evidence are they turning up?"

"At the moment, I daresay the poison is the most important of the lot. From the death agony, there's no doubt about it. Strychnine. Rather a neat job of it, too. The chemist is testing the food taken from the Soames table." McCooper's eyes wandered across the room to a wall map of Shanghai with red pins sticking out to signify police stations.

"Yes, just as I suspected." The old man licked his fingers. "A nasty business that strychnine. That's why the triads favor it so for settling scores…especially extortion, you know. When someone refuses to pay for so-called protection and the like."

"There's something queer Guv," said McCooper, who became momentarily distracted by rolling up his sleeve to examine the small pockets of water forming near his elbow. His case of prickly heat was common during hot months because of his constantly leaning over desks. Rubbing the red pimples to relieve the itching, he continued, "Last night, I found an odd letter in the Soames study. It contained a rather crude demand for 5,000 gold units. It was unsigned, written in black pen and ink, and sent by post."

Haymes stopped chewing.

"What do you make of it Guv?" McCooper loosened his tie.

"Well, well." Haymes thought back to Pockmarked Fang's evasive behavior during their meeting. No doubt he's behind this. Rather queer, the way he refused to cooperate, but why should he be involved with that Yank and the Japanese?

"If you'll pardon me, Guv? You don't suppose the Green Gang is involved, do you? I can't very well see how. I rather think it was the American. Unless I'm very much mistaken, he's the only person with a motive about young Roddy and Soames. I daresay the other gentlemen simply got in the way. As for the Green Gang, there's no proof, you know."

Haymes wiped his mouth. "Look here, McCooper, you'd better put someone on it at once. Find out if any of the dinner companions received similar demand letters. Send word the minute you have any news."

"Righto Guv!"

"Hang on, before you shove off, do tell me about Madame Soames. How did she take the news? Did Dr. Hanlon sedate her?"

McCooper laughed. "No need. By the looks of it, she'd been doing a fair amount of that herself before we arrived. Nipping a good deal from the old bottle, I'd say."

"How did that poor woman react? She must've been beside herself with such tragedy in so short a time."

Putting on his hat, McCooper answered, "She seemed to hold up pretty well, considering the circumstances, you know. I broke it to her gently, exactly as you ordered. I said Soames had been killed in an accident. I didn't mention the others as you instructed. She fainted straight away. So, there we are."

"Yes, poor woman. I expect I'll have to check on her today to ensure she's alright."

"Mind if I clear out? I'd like to start finding out if any letters were posted to the other poisoned gentlemen."

"Right you are. That'll do for now, Detective."

When he was alone, Haymes picked up the telephone and dialed a five-digit number. "American Consul? Yes, good morning, Special Branch here. Chief Inspector Haymes speaking. Kindly put me through to the Consul General." A blast of static caused him to pull the handset from his ear.

"Yes, it's Special Branch!" His voice rose. "I'm trying to get hold of the Consul General! You shall have to speak up. Speak up, I say! I can't hear a word you're saying. Yes, I'll hold the line." He muttered, "These hopeless telephone lines! There aren't enough to go round. Um, good morning, sir. Yes, it's Haymes here. Sorry to trouble you, but I have important news. There's a possibility that your Mr. Jack Jordan…Yes, that's right, the aviator is involved with the Green Gang. If that's true, the Green Gang could have a new arrangement with the Japanese. Yes, that would be dreadful!"

Settling back in his chair, Haymes continued, "Yes, he's still in Ward Road Gaol. No need to worry. I've got the extradition papers right in front of me. One of your runners brought them by hand scarcely an hour ago." Switching the telephone headset between his hands, Haymes dropped the pocketknife inside his jacket's front pocket. "Yes sir, I quite understand. My Consul General feels much the same as you do about the need for secrecy. You needn't fear. If Mr. Jordan refuses to cooperate, I'm prepared to extradite him to the KMT and Chinese jurisdiction for espionage. No one will be the wiser. I'll soon be over to interrogate him. Yes, I'll keep you informed. Cheerio."

Haymes slid the handset into the cradle and glanced at the wall clock. The black hands ticked at 45 minutes past 9 in the morning.

All eight guest villas run in Shanghai by the Japanese Secret Police had a second floor hidden behind tile roofs in what appeared to be single-story structures. Alone inside one, Colonel Togawa leaned against the back of a circular wooden tub able to hold a dozen bathers. Steaming water lapped around his barrel chest. His short, wavy black hair frizzed above the warm mist. Wondering where Major Fujiwara was, he closed his eyelids and inhaled a pine-oil scent rising from hot vapors. Footsteps approached along a ground floor corridor. Colonel Togawa opened his eyes. Reaching his right arm over the edge of the tub, he grabbed a Browning automatic pistol, held it above the water, and slipped deeper in up to his bushy gray moustache. Realizing it probably was Major Fujiwara causing the creaking on the nightingale floor, whose boards were designed

Japanese Army officers.

to squeak a warning at the slightest pressure, Togawa told himself he couldn't be too careful. He heard a cord being pulled down on a ceiling panel to a concealed stairway to the second floor's bathing chamber. Soles of rubber slippers, squishing against wooden steps, ascended. At the top of the landing a semi-transparent paper door slid aside. Colonel Togawa saw a blurred image of a slender, gray-haired man in a gray robe through the glazed glass. Major Fujiwara had arrived. He needed a good scare.

Sliding the glass wall, Major Fujiwara stepped inside and hesitated. Squinting through his monocle, he scanned the room. On one side, the dressing cubicles stood vacant. Rows of long, white towels hung from racks with none amiss. The wooden floor had no wet footprints. Stepping forward, he peered into small, wooden rinsing buckets scattered about the floor underneath cold-water spigots. No signs of use. He tightened the sash around his knee-length, beige cotton robe. In the room's center, steam rose above the tub, making it impossible to see whether it held an occupant. Chuckling to himself, Togawa bolted from the water.

"*Keto-jin!*" he screamed, leveling the Browning Automatic Pistol at his subordinate.

Major Fujiwara shrieked in surprise at being called a hairy foreigner. Seeing the pistol, he stepped back in horror. The monocle popped from his eye and dangled by a gold chain. "I'm Fujiwara. Fu-ji-wara!"

Colonel Togawa let out a guttural laugh and lowered the pistol onto the bathtub ledge as he slunk into the water. "Oh, Fujiwara-san, you've kept me waiting. In my apprehension, I could have shot you so easily!"

"I'm sorry, very sorry."

"Come inside!"

"Yes, Colonel," the Major replied breathlessly. He marched to a dressing cubicle and shed his robe, monocle, and rubber slippers before climbing into the wooden tub.

Colonel Togawa eyed the older man who lowered himself into the steaming water. "I await your report."

"Yes, Colonel. We cannot definitely ascertain who eliminated Maxwell-san."

"It is doubtful the foolish *keto-jin* poisoned himself. Maxwell-san was not so stupid."

"I agree. This morning our spies reported that the English Special

A roadway past Shanghai's cotton mills.

Branch believes the American aviator, Jack Jordan, is the culprit. He was arrested at the restaurant after our departure. He is in Ward Road Gaol awaiting extradition to the Chinese Municipal Police."

Colonel Togawa grunted in satisfaction. "Good, very good! Anything else?"

"Yes, I was late this morning because Lieutenant Saito cabled from the Yamato Hotel in Dairen. He arrived an hour ago on the South Manchurian Railway. He awaits your instructions before sailing to Changsha."

Leaning forward, the Black Eel cupped his hands and dipped them into the boiling water, silently watching it fill his palms. He splashed the pine-scented liquid on his face, shook free the droplets, and reclined against the tub's wall. "Tell me, Fujiwara-san, what kept Lieutenant Saito? He was to arrive at 7 o'clock yesterday evening. Why was he delayed?"

"The Koreans again. A riot in the city Chosen. How shall I respond to Saito-san? He awaits your orders."

"Book me railway passage to Shantung on the Kiaochow-Tsinan rail line. I leave tomorrow morning for Tsingtau. I must look over our occupation forces there."

"And Saito-san?"

"He is to sail tomorrow aboard the *S.S. Sakaki Maru* to Tsingtau. I will meet him there. In the meantime, he will prepare the necessary papers to establish the Nippon Antimony Export Co. Everything awaits him at the Manchurian Enterprise Co.—new identity papers and financial guarantees. Everything must be ready for us to quickly open an office in Changsha. There must be no further delay in obtaining the raw materials for our munitions!"

"Yes, Colonel. I shall cable Saito-san."

Both men left the tub for the wooden buckets to rinse their bodies in cool water.

Helen Hanlon stepped on the gas pedal of her red Roamer Roadster, spurring it along an open stretch of Boundary Road opposite Ward Road Gaol. Streaming past the hood of the convertible, fresh air cooled her flushed cheeks. Her hands clenched the wooden steering wheel. If that old buzzard Haymes thought he'd put a stop to her investigation with that

A bridge over Soochow Creek.

brush off, he was dead wrong. She slowed down as the street turned into Singmin Road in Chapei, an oak-leaf-shaped district north of the International Settlement, to avoid traffic near the Shanghai Nanking Railway Station.

Three miles later the roadster turned left on a bridge over Soochow Creek, marking an exit from the district of poor European and Shanghainese laborers and entrance into a playground of rich foreigners in the International Settlement. The roadster crawled to a halt on top of the bridge behind dozens of vehicles seeking entry past a Settlement Police checkpoint. Helen glanced below to the creek, glutted with fishing boats, rafts, flat-bottom skiffs, and riverboats. Sun glinted across the waterway against the silver metal of the Sinza Water Tower next to the Foo Sing Flour Mill where its coolies loaded sacks aboard large vessels. In the next block over on Chengtu Road stood the Number One Mill of the King Chen Paper Mill Ltd. Hanging at intervals on the sides of the mill between the second-floor windows were white cloth banners bearing one of China's most famous trademarks: a shaggy, black bear raising his right paw in mid-step and turning his face with a stern expression.

A horn blared behind Helen's roadster as a heavily armed Sikh, in a red turban and khaki uniform, tried to wave her through to Myburgh Road. Helen accelerated and drove into the International Settlement past the Sinza Police and Fire Station. Continuing south, she cruised by the Jewish Cemetery and the Union Jack Club until the road narrowed five blocks later and became Mohawk Road. Ahead, a green carpet of grass unfolded at the entrance to the Shanghai Race Club. Her destination approached. Chinese grooms exercised Mongolian ponies there amid dust clouds along the dirt racecourse. Helen lifted her foot from the gas pedal so the Roamer Roadster could coast along the street. European pedestrians averted their eyes from occasional beggars on the sidewalks. Further down opposite the pristine Shanghai Race Club grounds was a section of mostly three-story buildings and neon signs.

"Number 57," Helen said aloud, scanning the addresses. She cringed at the thought of having to venture into this district. If she hadn't been so keen for a big scoop, she'd never think about crossing the threshold of a nasty place like The Scratch! Spotting an American flag hoisted above a huge bronze plaque outside a building, she exclaimed, "That must be it!" Helen parked the roadster and alighted. She tugged her berét tightly over her head and cut across the lawn to the door. Catching sight of her gloved fingers while pressing a buzzer, she felt comforted by the protection against disease that her gloves afforded. She jammed the buzzer down. The door opened wide. A dark-skinned Chinese cook appeared. His eyes swept over the intruder, dressed in the smart, yellow suit with a polka-dot scarf draped over her shoulders. "Missy?" he asked, with a smirk.

She demanded, "I'm looking for Chicago Charlie."

"Missy go 'way! Scram, I say."

Brushing him aside, she stomped into a red Victorian-style entertainment parlor. "Chicago Charlie, are you here?"

Helplessly following, the cook screamed, "Missy, you better scram. Go away!"

Footsteps hammered the stairs. "Oh nuts!" a woman shrilled. "Can't a girl get any shuteye 'round here?" A brunette, with a long, orange robe thrown over her, glared over the banister. Black eye makeup smeared the corners of her green cat eyes. "Cookie, what gives?"

Removing his chef's hat, he shrugged his shoulders.

"Who's the dame? What's she tryin' to pull by muscling in here?"

Helen froze in her tracks and shot back a challenging look.

"You've got some nerve bustin' in here, sister! I'm Lulu, and this here's my joint. I say beat it. Come on, scram, vamoose, get goin'!"

"Why don't you go mind your own business and take a bath. You can start, too, by washing your face." Tossing her head high, Helen resumed her search. "Chicago?"

"I get it!" Lulu removed her high-heeled slippers and held one in each hand. "So yuh want to play tough, do yuh?" A gold slipper spun over the top of the stairs and clipped Helen in the back of the head, sending the yellow berét soaring.

"Ouch!" Helen recoiled.

Lulu raised the second slipper. First taking aim, she swung her right arm back like a baseball pitcher. Chicago Charlie raced over to Lulu and grabbed her wrist. "Knock it off, Lu!"

Spinning around, Lulu screamed, "Get your dirty paws off me. I'm gonna kick the stuffin' out of that dog-faced, fat-headed dame!"

Helen scooped up her yellow cap. Still holding Lulu's wrist, Chicago spoke sympathetically. "I don't blame yuh one bit. I felt like doin' the same many times. Why don't yuh leave her to me?"

"What's it to yuh, anyways? Why don't yuh go lay an egg! She's got some nerve bustin' in my joint and mouthin' off to me! I don't give a hoot if that sister's a pal of yours, or not. Now, let go of me."

Turning to Helen, Chicago yelled, "See what yuh gone and done, Lady Jane? Yuh made Lulu sore, and it ain't smart, see? I'm gonna turn her loose, but before I do, yuh got a chance to say your sorry and play nice. Otherwise, her mitts is gonna yank some of that red hair of yours. Yuh might even get a shiner out of it, too."

"Alright, Chicago, I see your point." Helen walked towards the open front door. Chicago Charlie released Lulu's wrist. Helen called out sweetly, "Oh, Lulu?"

"Yeah?"

"Don't hold your breath. Never in a million years would I apologize to a chiseling, flatback alley cat like you."

"Why you, dirty little...!" screamed Lulu, hurling her high-heeled gold slipper at Helen. It crashed against the wall and fell to the floor.

Helen called, "Chicago, I've got news about Ace. My car's outside."

Ace sat on the mattress and stared at a tin cup on the floor at the opening of a hatch at the steel door's base. Despite his thirst, he hadn't touched the water because he didn't want to get sick if it hadn't been boiled. He wriggled his fingers underneath the bandages around his head and pulled them off. "That's just dandy," he thought, feeling the smooth scalp where his hair had been shaven. Wincing as his traced a six-inch track of stitches, Ace knew what he was about to do would be painful, but he had to make sure he'd be taken to the Infirmary. It was his only way out. His fingernails tore at the stitches. Smearing blood over his head and face, he heard the door hatch creak open.

A hand reached inside, groping for the cup.

Crouching at the door, Ace yelled, "Hey you! I've got to see a doctor. My head's not so swell."

"Sorry, mate," answered a man with an Australian accent.

"Look, I've got to see a doctor right away! My head is really bleeding, and I feel like I'm going to faint."

The cup disappeared through the opening. "Listen, mate, you're two pence short of a bob if you think I'm going to believe that jiggery-pokery. You'll be leaving here soon enough. Chief Inspector Haymes is waiting to have a word with you."

A short while later, Ace found himself seated in an interrogation room. Fetters restricted his feet; handcuffs bound his wrists.

"Fancy meeting you here, Jordan." Chief Inspector Haymes sneered. "Tisk, tisk, Jordan, by the looks of you, I daresay you've removed your bandages. After we patched you up so nicely, too."

Ace's gray eyes faced the older man, who sat next to a younger one holding a note pad. "Yeah, the pleasure's all mine! If you want to chat with me, you'd better ask that gorilla by the door take off these handcuffs. I'm not much for bracelets. I could use a cigarette, too, if you don't mind."

"Certainly." Chief Inspector Haymes nodded to the guard. Slinging his Lee-Enfield rifle around his shoulder, the guard came over and unlocked the handcuffs.

Ace rubbed his wrists. The young detective handed him a pack of cigarettes and a book of matches. "These English ones aren't bad, but I prefer American smokes."

Haymes frowned. "My dear fellow, I strongly suggest you put your Yank pride in your pocket and adapt yourself to the situation at hand. I'm here to discuss a most serious matter. After all, what's done is done. Therefore, you really owe it to yourself to confess. It's the only respectable way to go."

Ace blew smoke rings.

"That sort of thing won't help," exclaimed the Inspector. "You've been found out. You're under arrest for five murders. It may interest you to know your own U.S. government won't help you. I have your extradition papers right here in my pocket! Unless you cooperate, you'll be turned over to Chinese authorities. They'll ensure you'll be quite forgotten and soon dead. Do I make myself perfectly clear? Now, will you answer my questions? Yes or no?"

Ace acted as if he had no cares in the world.

Haymes leaned forward. "Whilst you're making up your mind, Jordan, I'll tell you about the Kuo-min Tang 'aeroplane.' You're an aviator. Ever heard of it?"

"Sorry to disappoint you, but I can't say I have."

"It's not at all the sort you fly. It's a beam, really, or rather a man suspended from a beam. His hands are tied behind his back by a rope cast over the beam. His head hangs low, and his chest becomes extremely taut. You can imagine the rest, can't you, Jordan?"

"I get the point. Get on with it. What do you want to know?"

"Now take your time, Mr. Jordan. If you answer truthfully no harm will come to you. If you lie, I can't answer for the future."

"I'm on the level. I'll tell you what I know. You see, I'd like to live to a ripe old age."

"Very well then, I'm glad you've come to your senses." Chief Inspector Haymes relaxed. Reaching into the pocket of his white drill jacket, he produced his pocketknife and proceeded to trim his cuticles with a blade. "You know, I'm most interested in the Japanese. You've profited nothing by your association with them, so you may as well tell us all about it. Your crimes were no ordinary ones. Hence, we can only surmise that the Japanese had a very good reason behind the murders."

Ace mashed the cigarette into an ashtray on the desk. "Let's get this straight. I didn't murder anyone! I don't know what five murders you're talking about! If you're referring to what happened to Roddy, Maxwell is your man. He's trying to frame me. If anyone is in cahoots with the Japanese, it's him!"

"Won't you kindly, how do you Yanks say, stop trying to pull our legs? Soames is dead, as you well know. You poisoned the poor chap and his three dinner companions last night at The Catherine the Great Restaurant."

Ace leaned over. "I'm not holding out on you! I'm on the up and up."

Concentrating on his cuticles, the Chief Inspector sighed. "Calm yourself, my dear fellow. It's really no use going on with that gibberish. If you imagine for one moment I believe you are innocent, you're much mistaken. However, cold-blooded criminals such as yourself often are reluctant to tell the truth straight away. Do go on, just as you wish, but I expect to have the truth shortly."

Deciding he had to get that knife, Ace sunk in his chair and spoke calmly, "It goes like this." He hesitated as the young detective put the pencil to the notepad. "I didn't murder anyone, just like I said before. Maxwell killed Roddy. Why, I don't know. I wanted to clear myself, so I followed Maxwell yesterday to a restaurant in Hongkew. He met a Japanese guy there. First they got a laugh over me being framed; then they talked about the banquet and the antimony."

"Antimony?"

"Yeah, well no, not exactly. The main Japanese fellow asked Maxwell about the antimony exporters. Maxwell assured him they'd be at the banquet. The Japanese said something about the Green Gang, but I couldn't make out what he meant. Later, he gave Maxwell something. Maybe the poison. Who knows? Afterwards, they didn't say much else, just small talk. I didn't bother tailing them when they left. I decided to find out about antimony since I didn't know what it was. I learned it's used for making shrapnel and bullets. If anybody poisoned Maxwell and his pals last night, it must have been the Japanese. I'd bet they'd sure find a use for antimony. Look what they're doing in Manchuria!"

"Oh, come now, Jordan. Your theory sounds very interesting indeed! However, you fail to take into account your presence at the Russian restaurant and at the Blue Lantern Hunt. Surely no mere coincidence?"

The fetters clanged around Ace's ankles as he stomped his feet. "I'm getting fed up with you and your wisecracks! I've told you all I know." Wincing in pain, Ace clasped his head. "Look tough guy, I don't feel so swell. I'm sure you'd like to chew the fat some more right now, but I can't. My head's coming apart. I need a doc."

"My dear fellow, I shouldn't count on that for a second if I were you! A doctor won't be necessary. Whatever suffering you are experiencing was coming to you." Placing the pocketknife in front of him, Haymes paused to fetch his meerschaum pipe from his trouser pocket. "War hero or not, you've become a menace, and I'll have no such foolishness about your medical condition interfering with this line of questioning. Your crimes are more serious than you can possibly realize. Be quick now! Tell us all about Major Togawa. It's your only chance! You do see that, don't you?"

Ace turned to the window as if mulling it over. He didn't stand a chance pulling the knife on anyone in the room. They'd either shoot him, or toss him back into the cell. Getting past the door was impossible; it was blocked by the guard armed with the rifle and a .455 Webley-Fosberg revolver. The Infirmary remained his only escape. What could he do with the pocketknife? His mind flashed back to the Great War. Once a German prisoner got hold of a knife and failed to kill himself because he slashed his wrists the wrong way. Ace didn't relish such a move, yet it would get him into the Infirmary where he could attempt an escape.

"One thing more," said Chief Inspector Haymes, packing tobacco inside the pipe bowl. "Tell us about your involvement with the Green Gang. It has come to my attention that you've been adopted by Pock-marked Fang. You're supposed to be his son, or some such rot! What's his role in this whole affair? Has he thrown in his lot with the Japanese?"

Ace needed a distraction to throw them off. "There is something I'd like to bring up. Where's my ring? The one with a diamond outline of an albatross."

Chief Inspector Haymes raised his eyebrows. "How do you mean?"

Ace leapt from his chair and shouted. "Who stole it? It was on my finger when I got the kibosh last night. It's not here now. I want it back! The French gave it to me at the end of the war, and I want it back!"

"Oh come, now, Mr. Jordan, that'll do. I haven't the faintest idea what you're carrying on about. The very idea that we'd steal your ring is ridiculous!" Haymes thrust his pipe towards Ace as the young detective scribbled away. "Be seated and calm yourself at once, otherwise, you'll have this nasty guard to deal with instead of me."

In a swift motion, Ace snatched the pocketknife and ran the blade across his wrist.

"You fool!" Haymes shouted.

Before Ace could slash his other wrist, Chief Inspector Haymes dropped his pipe and punched him in the face. The butt of the guard's Lee-Enfield rifle crashed against his head.

"He's out cold Guv," the guard replied. "His wrist is bleedin' like a pig."

"That imbecile," muttered Haymes, nudging his foot into Ace's stomach. "Confound that man! Better get him round to the Infirmary straight away. Ring me once he comes to. I'll be at my office."

Helen Hanlon tossed her head and laughed. Chicago Charlie hung his forearm out the car window and watched the brown-brick Clock Tower of the Shanghai Race Club disappear from view. Babe, wearing a cook's uniform minus the hat, sat between them in the roadster with his arms pressed against his sides. "That stunt yuh pulled back there with Lulu ain't so funny," Chicago said dryly. "So what's the lowdown on Ace?"

The Willow Tea House in the Native City of Shanghai.

"He's in Ward Road Gaol."

"Some keyhole peeper! I couldda told yuh that! Where else would Johnny Bull put him? Them Brits is probably workin' him over right now. Poor mug! He's sure goin' into a nosedive."

"If you don't snap out of it Chicago, I might start bawling and ask you for a hankie," Helen snickered. "Let's get serious. It's my guess you'd like to help Ace. As for me, I'd like a scoop for my newspaper."

"Keep goin' sister, I'm all ears."

The roadster swung left onto Weihaiwei Road. "Alright then, it's settled." Helen leaned on the horn, shoving a rickshaw aside. "I'm taking us to a little place just around the corner. We can have a quiet chat there without any prying eyes."

A block later, the car nosed its way into an opening in front of a one-story green building: Human Harmony Tea House. Its exterior walls were covered by gilt wooden panels carved with Chinese characters for the Five Eternal Ideals: humanity, uprightness, propriety, insightfulness, and faithfulness. The trio left the red convertible. Five coolies, only wearing loose folded shorts, squatted in a circle on the pavement. They hollered over a roll of six dice in a game of Kan Mien Yang, or Chasing Sheep. Leaning near the moon-door entrance, a young KMT Blue Shirt dangled a cigarette from his lip while chatting up a waif-like Shanghainese prostitute.

Helen went inside, followed by the others. Dismissing a hostess, she strode to a table far from clattering dishes and singsong girls trilling as nymphs and fairies in a lovelorn Chinese Opera called "Donating a Pearl on Rainbow Bridge." Chicago's nostrils tingled. He recognized the smell of opium-laced cigarettes. Digging into his pocket, he retrieved a roll of opium pills and stuffed some in his mouth. "Well, here we are," Helen said. "Let's not waste time. I've got a party tonight."

Toting a bamboo tray, a waitress appeared with a pot of steaming tea and porcelain cups. She wore a turquoise silk jacket embroidered with butterflies, black trousers reaching below the knees, white stockings and turquoise cloth shoes. She frowned at Babe's kitchen attire. He admired her stylish "weeping-willow bangs," shorn in a semi-circle to resemble fringed branches on each side of her face. The waitress poured green tea of a variety called Sore Crab's Eyes and set down a bowl of dried watermelon seeds before departing.

"This morning a buddy at the American Consulate gave me the goods on Ace. He's not going on trial in front of an American prosecutor here at the U.S. Court for China. It's all been worked out and is on the hush-hush. Unless Ace tells Special Branch what they want to hear, he's being extradited to the Chinese for murder and spying. He won't be exempt anymore from their laws. And we all know what that means!"

"Whew," said Chicago, running his finger under his chin like an executioner. "That means them KMT hatchet men. If he's lucky, they might toss him in a cross-bar hotel and throw away the key, otherwise, it's a cement kimono and bye-bye! Either way, they'd just as soon torture him as look at him!"

Babe's hand trembled as he picked up watermelon seeds, and he nervously stuffed them into his mouth.

"Keep your shirt on!" Helen hunched over the table. "Remember, it's being handled on the 'q.t.' Now here's where I come in. Special Branch says those mugs died of smallpox last night. That's the official word, but my dad heard it was poison. Everyone knows the Green Gang loves to use poison to settle its scores. Now, supposing you tell me why Ace rubbed out those guys. Then, I'll have my scoop; it'll be a dandy, too! Big enough to splash across the front page and possibly save Ace from a firing squad. What do you say?"

"Ace didn't kill nobody! Not in China, anyways. He ain't that kinda mug." Chicago Charlie slammed the teacup on the table. "I should know cause we go back 12 years. We was pals in the Great War. Believe me, yuh sure get to know what makes a fella tick when he's on the wrong end of a bullet. Besides, my eyes wuz on him the whole time last night. He never got close enough to those mugs to lay a finger on 'em!"

"Well big boy, if he didn't do it, then who may I ask did it? The same mystery person who's supposedly framing him?"

"Listen up, Lady Jane. Somebody put the whisper on my pal. When I find out who, I'll give 'em the third degree, too, if Ace don't beat me to it. I ain't gonna play ball with yuh! If yuh don't like it, amscray! Get it? Me and the kid here got work to do. We is gonna see if we can help spring old flyboy from the slammer. Thanks for the extradition dope. Come along, kid. Let's blow. We got places to go and people to see, like Pockmarked Fang!"

Babe jumped to his feet.

"Hold on! Wait a minute, just wait a minute!" Helen motioned for them to remain seated. "Let's talk this thing through. Maybe you are right. Maybe there is another angle to this story. Just maybe I can help you boys out. My newspaper credentials give me an edge and besides I've got a car. Be reasonable fellas!"

Chicago's blue eyes began to glaze over. The opium made him feel light-headed and giddy. He elbowed Babe in the stomach.

"She's got a point there kid. Maybe she can tag along. We might need some razzle-dazzle from a dame. We can sure use her buggy, too."

"Swell! It's all settled then." Helen flashed a smile. "What next?"

Chicago cocked his head towards the exit. "Let's scram. There's a gent we gotta see. I'll tell yuh 'bout it on the drive over."

Helen opened her purse and dropped a few copper coins on the table.

Idina stood under the wide moon doorway on the veranda in her upstairs bedroom. A white, hooded robe draped her body. Rising beyond the second floor through the opening, a warm breeze ruffled the folds of her robe. Silk tassels swayed from white lanterns made to look like silken pearls hanging below the arched doorway. She faced the burial mounds along the causeway bordering the Hungjao Aerodrome's runways. Her red fingernails nervously twirled around Ace's albatross ring suspended by a gold chain around her neck. A motorcar engine rumbled in the distance. Idina ran to the edge of the veranda and looked out. A Duesenberg sedan turned from the Street of One Hundred Blossoms, passed through the estate's double wrought-iron gate, and snaked up the driveway. She narrowed her eyes to identify the flags mounted on the hood. As it neared, she made out the main red cross of St. George, the white cross of St. Andrew, and the red of St. Patrick all against the Union Jack's blue background. Idina looked down at her robe. No time to change. No servants to waylay intruders. She flew downstairs just as Chief Inspector Haymes swung open the front door.

"I beg your pardon! Look here, I'm not the least bit interested in who you are and why you've come. Would you be so kind as to run along now?"

The Chief Inspector cleared his throat. "Madame Soames, it's perfectly obvious from your, how shall I say, lack of suitable attire that you're suffering from the strain of a great shock. However, I'd be grateful for a few minutes of your time. No doubt you're unable to recall our first meeting two nights ago. I'm Chief Inspector Haymes, Special Branch. If you please, I've come to see how you're getting on and ask a question or two."

"How do you mean? Questions? Is this necessary? I'm terribly sorry, but I'm afraid I really don't know what to think. First my dear brother, and now my husband. I'm in a dreadful state. It's all such a muddle."

"Wouldn't you rather we chat inside?"

"Quite the contrary. I'd rather not," she answered curtly, before regaining her composure. "Do forgive me. I'd like to get this over with quickly. Look here Chief Inspector, as you can tell from my appearance, I'm unprepared for visitors. In fact, I've given the servants leave today."

"Very well. Whatever you think is best. I'll be as quick as I can. Madame, first I'd like to tell you a bit about our investigation into your husband's accident."

"Very decent of you, Chief Inspector. I'm most grateful. I've heard little since the initial word last night."

"Yes, well, he was poisoned." Haymes waited for her reaction.

Pulling the collar of her robe tighter, Idina swayed. He steadied her elbow. "Please don't bother about me," she said feebly. "I shall be alright shortly."

"Don't you worry, Madame Soames, we've got the matter in hand. That American aviator who worked for your husband is behind bars."

"Hang on a minute! Are you referring to that horrible Mr. Jack Jordan?"

Haymes nodded.

"Why he's the most insolent man I've ever known! That brazen creature had the cheek to try to get chummy with me! Can you imagine that? Don't tell me that scoundrel is responsible for my husband's death?"

"I'm afraid so...and young Roddy, as well. Furthermore, we've reason to believe he may have been conspiring with the Green Gang to murder your husband along with his three gentlemen guests."

"Hello? Please, I'm not that clever. Repeat that last part again. Whatever do you mean by 'three gentlemen guests?'"

"Jordan also poisoned your husband's dinner guests."

"Oh, he did, did he? What's the point of it all?"

"I'm sorry. This is all I can say until our investigation concludes. In the meantime, I should be grateful if you can recall to mind any mention of the Green Gang made by your husband."

Idina's tousled bob swung to and fro.

"You're quite sure, Madame?"

"Yes, quite. Nothing comes to mind."

"Well, that's the end of that. I'm quite finished now, my dear. If you'll excuse me, I'd best be going. Thank you for your trouble."

"Very well." Idina watched him walk away.

"Oh, by the way," he said, turning towards her, "you needn't worry about Mr. Jordan or the Green Gang. I'm certain they've no quarrel with you."

"Thank you ever so much, Chief Inspector." Idina stepped back inside the entry way and carefully closed the door. Leaning against it, she took a deep breath.

Seated alongside Chicago Charlie, Helen rested her chin on top of the steering wheel inside the red roadster, which was parked on the shoulder of Dragon of the Black Pool Road facing a sandbag barricade. They watched Babe from afar gesticulating to three Chinese hoods, whose sweat-stained straw fedoras swiveled behind machine guns mounted on the barricade.

"Gee whilikers! Seems like that kid's been keepin' us waitin' for a dog's age!" lamented Chicago, resting his head in the crook of his arm on the window frame.

"Don't be a sorehead. Did you expect those guards to roll out the red carpet for some kid who comes knocking in a cook's uniform? He looks ridiculous."

Although they heard Babe's outpourings in Shanghainese, neither had a clue what he said. Chicago mopped his brow with a handkerchief and murmured, "This sun'll be the end of me."

Minutes later, Babe ran over to them and jumped on the running board.

"Whaddya say, kid? Is them gorillas gonna let us beat the gums with the King of Shang, or not?"

"Hard to say, Chicago," Babe answered, looking over his shoulder.

One of the toughs left the sandbag embankment and disappeared behind the main wooden gate, the only opening in the gray plaster walls topped with rolling barbed wire.

"Well, that's a good sign," Helen remarked. "There's nothing we can do at the moment but sit tight." She turned her attention to an aged Chinese woman pushing a cart down the cobblestone street. Selling brown roots, the peddler called out in a haunting tone.

"Say, Babe, what's that old lady flogging?"

"Nine-sectioned lotus roots, formed that way because nine is a lucky number. Tonight, the roots will be offered to the Moon."

Further up the street, a professional letter-writer stopped in the middle of the sidewalk. He was a middle-aged man dressed in a scholarly, long tan gown and black skullcap. He sat and unloaded a stack of papers, an ink stone, and brush from a cloth satchel. The letter-writer's voice crackled in a song. His words exalted a T'ang Dynasty poem about the forfeiture of a slave-girl.

A round of gun blasts shattered the air behind the roadster. Babe, Helen, and Chicago Charlie jolted in surprise and looked to Pockmarked Fang's walled estate where the sounds originated. A short man, whose stomach strained the mid-section of a long, pink satin gown, stood before the gate. Flesh drooped from his Buddha-like ears. An eye squinted at the threesome; the other was greased shut. Grinning, he beckoned the trio by waving the barrel of a Luger Parabellum automatic pistol. Its mate rested in a side holster on a wide leather belt slung around the bald man's waist.

"He don't look too palsy-walsy to me," Chicago commented. "I don't like the way that double-gutted palooka's swingin' that gat around."

"Ah, Tubs looks kind of cute to me, especially with that suede head of his. It's as bald as a baby."

"Hey, Buttercup, put a lid on that sauce. It's time to scram. We ain't got all day! Let's get them dogs movin' over there just like he sez. It won't do us no good to be on the wrong side of that goon, even though he looks like a painted tulip in that cherry rag."

"His appearance is of no importance," said Babe, "for he is One-eyed Wong."

Helen sucked in her breath.

Chicago Charlie whistled. "No kiddin'? One-eyed Wong in the flesh! Wait til I tell Bunny and the rest of the fellas at The Saints & Sinners. Not too many Westerners ever seen either him or Pockmarked Fang and lived to tell."

The afternoon sun shone on two gigantic dragon lanterns made of ruby glass. They swayed from curving eaves above each side of the entrance. Walking ahead past a large brass gong, One-eyed Wong pointed his Luger to the ground and waddled into a courtyard. Trailing, Babe noticed a pair of gray marble general statues of Taoist star gods flanking the gate: the Spirit of the White Tiger and the Spirit of the Blue Dragon.

Beyond a narrow strip of grass were parallel rows of tall shade trees covering the perimeter wall. These Trees of Heaven bore leaves that were small and fanned out in dense clusters. One-eyed Wong motioned the group to cylindrical porcelain stools under a tree. Lifting his gown's skirt and straddling over the seat in his black satin trousers, One-eyed Wong put his automatic pistol in the holster, crossed his arms in front of his chest, and slipped his hands inside horseshoe cuffs at the end of his long sleeves.

"Howdy do! Chicago Charlie's my name." Chicago extended his right hand. When it became clear no handshake was forthcoming, he withdrew his arm and chuckled foolishly. "Like the kid said out front, me and my pals is here about a mutual friend of Pockmarked Fang. His moniker is Jack Jordan, but he goes by Ace. Seein' how he's in one heck of a jam, we wuz thinkin' if anybody could bust him outta Ward Road Gaol, it's Pockmarked Fang. Ain't that so, kids?"

Babe gulped, but Helen spoke up. "Yes, that's right. Special Branch believes he poisoned a group of men last night. Do you know if someone's trying to frame Ace? Could we please speak with Mr. Fang? Maybe he could shed some light on this. Special Branch may believe your Green Gang has something to do with the poisoning."

One-eyed Wong closed his good eye for a few moments and remained still.

With puzzled expressions on their faces, Helen and Chicago shrugged their shoulders.

One-eyed Wong spoke, "Tonight, men will not bow to the Goddess of the Moon, nor in the 12th month will women sacrifice to the God of the Kitchen."

"Try me again?" Helen asked.

Babe spoke up from his place near the foot of a Tree of Heaven. "I'm sorry Miss Hanlon, but I'm afraid it's no use. You're a woman. He's just stated a proverb to show he refuses to discuss this matter with you."

"Why, of all the low-down…"

"Shush," Chicago interrupted.

One-eyed Wong addressed him. "The Master is resting now. When he awakes, I'll tell him of your request." He inclined his shaven head. "Good afternoon." One-eyed Wong disappeared into the inner grounds.

"Gee thanks," Chicago jumped up and called out. "Oh, by the way, tell Pockmarked Fang we'll be waitin' outside the jail in this dame's heap so Ace can scram with us after yuh boys bust him out. If that's what yuh decide to do."

An acrid odor from Dreaking's solution permeated the patient area, partitioned by white curtains on the Infirmary's ground floor. Seated there, a police guard drooled over blonde starlets in *Pictureplay* magazine as Ace gradually regained consciousness nearby. Ace resisted the temptation to open his eyes. Instead, he listened to footsteps against tile floors and glass bottles tinkle on trays. Despite a pain in his wrist and head, he was in the Infirmary and wondering about his next move. Hearing magazine pages being turned, he realized he wasn't alone. The guard thumbed to advertisements in the back and paused at one for Fancy Lady's Miracle Cream, which declared its ability fill in womanly charm in rounded figures and firm skin into youthful tissue.

Ace's left eye cracked open from underneath bandages around his forehead. A bayonet-tipped Lee-Enfield rifle rested across the guard's lap. Ace closed his eye. Groaning, he rolled off the bed to land face down on the floor.

"What the blazes are you doing?" The guard tossed the magazine aside, grabbed the rifle, and sprung to his feet. "Up with you now!" The guard kicked him.

Grunting again, Ace rolled over, quickly yanking the guard's leg out from under him. The Englishman tumbled to the floor. Ace jumped up and knocked him unconscious with the rifle butt. Ace ripped off the bandages, switched clothes with the guard, and covered him with a blanket on the bed. Pushing the guard's cap on his head, Ace walked into the hallway. Nurses and doctors gathered around a tea cart at the far end. Ace turned opposite and quickly strode out a back door into an alley where a male beggar passed by. The beggar held dumbbells, and his torso was strapped to a rickety cart.

A red Roamer convertible sat quietly parked a distance from Ward Road Gaol along East Seward Road. Babe dozed in the backseat. Chicago slouched in the front next to Helen, who glared into her compact and dabbed powder above her upper lip. "Say, what's the use? Let's get wise to ourselves," she complained. "It feels like it's 100 degrees out here."

"Aw, pipe down. I've got a lot on my mind right now, see. It's plenty hot without yuh being a pain in the neck."

"Listen, you crumb," she said, tilting the mirror. Its reflection showed a Shanghainese man in a long brown gown. Twirling two metal spheres around in his palm, he leaned against a shade tree along the sidewalk and leered at her. A cigarette dangled from his lip. Scowling, she snapped the compact shut and continued. "Don't talk to me like that! Where's Pockmarked Fang's strong arm fatso? Where's his busload of boys? If they haven't shown up by now there won't be any big jail break."

"Figure it out anyways yuh want sugar, but yuh threw in with us. I'm runnin' the show, and I sez we're stayin' put, so sit tight and put a lid on it, will yuh?"

Helen yanked the key from the ignition. "I don't care about you and that kid snoozing back there. This has the makings of the biggest newspaper story that ever happened to me, and I'm not about to stick around here cooling my heels and gawking out into the street like you, Mack. Nothing doing! I like to be right at ringside. I'm going inside to see my pal, Haymes." Adjusting the polka-dot scarf over her canary-yellow jacket, she stepped out.

"Anything yuh say, doll face," Chicago yawned. "Me and the kid are gonna sit tight in this swell car of yours. Besides, this heat is makin' me feel like a nap."

Helen called back. "I'm going to find out what gives. Chicago, are you coming with me, or not? Babe stays here."

"Some other time, honey, run along. Don't let us keep yuh. I bet yuh dollars to dog biscuits they'll throw yuh out on your ear. And when they do, don't come cryin' to us."

"Why, you weak-sided louse! I'll do it by myself then. I've got my press pass, you know."

Chicago turned to Babe. "Hey kid, ain't she a pip? A regular girl with hair on her chest!"

"Oh, you think you're plenty smart! Just you wait. We'll soon see just how smart you are!" Helen stomped off.

Chicago sunk back in the red-leather upholstery and watched her walk away. "Get a load of that dame! She sure thinks she's the Queen of Hearts in the flesh. Why, those Brits are liable to climb all over her. Who duz she think she is tryin' to bust in there? I bet yuh she'll squeal like a rat if those birds get rough with her!"

Ace crept down the alley to an ambulance; an attendant whistled in the back while wiping it down. Sneaking up unnoticed, Ace decked the attendant out cold and placed him out of sight behind a stack of empty boxes in the alley. Ace slipped off his guard jacket, put on the attendant's white coat, and hopped behind the wheel. The ambulance lurched forward to the entrance. A line of military vehicles began to form on both sides of the checkpoint. The ambulance halted behind a convoy truck and a jeep. Amid the rumble of engines, a woman shrieked. A motorcycle with a sidecar skidded to a stop next to the ambulance.

"What the deuce is going on?" barked the lieutenant from his sidecar. "Sergeant, get cracking and help that blithering idiot over there turn out that poisonous woman who's making such a row!"

"Very good sir."

"Off with you now. I must be at the Club at 4:30 pip emma."

The Lieutenant's gaze followed the officer as he sprinted to the checkpoint. A few minutes later, vehicles began passing through the gates, and the motorcycle with the Lieutenant sped off. Ace sighed with relief as he was waved quickly through. Turning left onto East Seward Road, he noticed Helen walking away and guessed she had been the one making the fuss at the gate. He drove past. Further down the road, Chicago Charlie sat smoking a cigarette on the red Roadster's hood. Ace pulled alongside.

"Say, what gives?"

Chicago frowned at the unknown intruder. "Whoever yuh is in there, I don't want no funny business, get me? Scram before I get tough with yuh. I ain't in the mood."

Ace stuck his head out the window and grinned. "Salutations, pal."

"Me oh my, it's flyboy! Sorry pal, I didn't recognize yuh. Boy, yuh sure take a lot of punishment by the looks of that blood across your head."

"You can say that again."

Helen raced up. "What gives, you mug?" she demanded. "Chicago, are you on the make again?"

Chicago pointed his thumb over his shoulder at her. "This dame, who does she think she is? Always givin' me the third degree! Small wonder she ain't never been hitched. Who'd want to tie the knot with such a cock-eyed..."

"You've got some nerve talking to me that way!"

"Pipe down, you two. Helen, get in the car and start her up. Hold tight, while I ditch this jalopy." Ace left the ambulance down a side street before climbing into the back seat next to Babe.

"Say, where's Pockmarked Fang's boys? Ain't they with yuh?"

"Nope. Did it solo. No time to explain. We've got to scram but quick. They're probably on to me by now. Don't mind if I crouch down back here."

"Anything you say," Chicago answered. "Step on it, copper-nob, or we is all gonna find ourselves in a pickle."

The roadster jerked to the left, narrowly missing a Shanghainese youth propelling a wheelbarrow piled with rabbit-shaped paper lanterns for the Moon Festival. They zoomed past the Telephone Exchange's white pillars flanked by magnolia trees. As they approached Wayside Market, rickshaws, bicycles, carts, and pedestrians clogged the road. Helen leaned on the horn.

"Gee whiz, you're a regular speed merchant! Slow down and lay off that horn. We don't want to attract no attention with flyboy bein' on the lam and Wayside Police Station bein' around the corner, sister."

"Listen up, Helen," Ace said. "Pull over on Yuenfong Road; let's pull the top up on this car plenty fast. I don't want no cops seein' me and drillin' us before I have a chance to square away with a certain dame called Idina."

Pockmarked Fang leaned forward in his red-lacquered throne and clutched a small teapot. His three-inch nail protectors clinked against the porcelain. Shoving the spout in his mouth, he gulped the musty-tasting Dragon-Tiger Elixir of Immortality while One-eyed Wong stood nearby smearing lizard balm over his sunken eyelid.

"Master, may long-eyebrowed longevity be yours."

Pockmarked Fang smacked his lips and belched. "Go, I must rest."

"But, Master, the foreign devil, Mr. Jordan?"

Pockmarked Fang smiled faintly and dozed. Before long, he saw himself on the ground staring into green grass. Turning sideways, he noticed four black hooves less than a foot away. Nearly piercing his eardrums, a high-pitched metallic voice shrilled, "Heaven hears, and Heaven sees!"

His skeletal arms trembled beneath the sleeves of his tea-brown gown. His eyes gaze rose from the hooves up to the legs of a black unicorn. He realized they were inside the first garden of the Golden Door Palace on Jade Mountain. Lei Tsu, the God of Lightning and Great Ancestor of Thunder, was nowhere in sight. Relaxing, Pockmarked Fang approached the unicorn and chuckled at the thought of a talking beast. Yet, in the First Heaven, it was entirely possible for a Yü Ch`ing to speak. Without warning, the unicorn screamed and reared. Pockmarked Fang froze. A violet ball of mist, with three red spots in the center, shot across the tops of the Three-Colored Lotus flowers. A fiery orb and four balls of smoke followed, tumbling over the red, blue, and white flower petals. Pockmarked Fang watched in horror as they surrounded him swirling into a blur.

"Heaven hears!" the same voice screeched. "Heaven sees as you mortals do! Heaven hears, and Heaven sees!"

Pockmarked Fang covered his ears. Suddenly, all was still. He cowered for a few minutes, but the whirring smoke had disappeared. Only the lotus garden lay before him. Then someone tapped his shoulder.

"Pity me! Save life!" he yelped, falling backwards on the grass.

Clad in bronze a fox-faced helmet and fish-scale armor, the Celestial Regulator of the Universe towered over Pockmarked Fang, who shivered near the creature's black-leather boots. At Lei Tsu's side were four maidens dressed identically in white gowns, their long sleeves flowing like waves of water. Silver Curling-Cloud Crowns topped their black hair shaped in

Flying, Swallow-Tail Buns. They swayed to and fro while holding hands.

Crawling away, Pockmarked Fang gasped as he recognized Tien Mu, the Goddess of Lightning and Instrument of Punishment for Evil. Her gown shimmered of blue, green, red, and white. Golden threads glittered in the fabric. Strands of pearls and emeralds, twinkling like stars and planets, draped from gold hairpins across her Alerted Swan Bun. A brilliant light flashed from Lei Tsu's third eye onto Pockmarked Fang, who wilted under the beam, and moved slowly to Tien Mu. She glided toward Pockmarked Fang. Her eyes hardened. They were framed by blue-black eyebrows curving in the Tender Willow-Branch style. Between the brows, specks of gold, silver, and emerald-green dust formed the shape of a kingfisher's tail feather.

Pockmarked Fang scrambled away on his hands and feet. The maiden sisters turned into white spiders, and their robes became webs. Encircling him, they flung their webs over his body.

He shrieked, "Tien Mu, Celestial Mistress of Lightning, have mercy!"

She reached for her magical mirror dangling from a copper waistband. He knew that her mirror's reflection transformed invisible thunderbolts into lightning directed from above at the wicked below.

"No," he pleaded, "save life!"

Her black lips parted to reveal the same shrill voice he'd heard before. "Heaven shines blessings and pours forth horrors. Men can shine blessings, but some will only meet with dread."

Tien Mu raised her oval mirror. *Crash!*

Wincing at a sharp pain in his left knee, Pockmarked Fang opened his eyes. He found himself sideways on the brick floor of his bed chamber. One-eyed Wong extended a dimpled hand to help the Master to the throne.

Pockmarked Fang ran his fingers over his shaven head. His voice trembled. "One hundred coffins for the poor! No—no, buy 1,000 coffins!"

One-eyed Wong bowed. "Master, Mr. Jordan, the devil from over the sea, is with two foreigners and the Chinese boy."

"What?" Pockmarked Fang looked up. His topaz-colored eyes narrowed. "When did this happen?"

"This afternoon, he escaped from Ward Road Gaol. Now, they appear to be driving to Hungjao."

"Keep watching him."

The polished, wooden door opened silently. With Helen and Babe at his heels, Chicago Charlie stuffed a wad of opium pills into his mouth. Ace stepped inside. Idina's bedroom reeked of licorice. Half-full cocktail glasses with gray-green absinthe littered tabletops. Ace paused at her bed. Its white mosquito-netting curtains were crumpled and pushed aside. He removed an empty glass and sat down.

"It's no use. I had my chance and muffed it. Ain't that just sweet. Come on in here, kids, we won't find anything. She's ducked out."

"No kidding," Chicago Charlie sat next to Ace. "Alright, flyboy, let's have it; no need to stall with us no more. What's the gag?"

Helen stood before Idina's dresser prowling among the contents on top. She lifted a red leather lipstick case and whistled approvingly.

"Not bad. She's even got her name etched on this case. He's right, Ace, enough with the merry-go-round. What are we doing here? I've put my neck on the line for you."

"Keep your sticky-fingers out of there!" Chicago yelled at Helen. Then he turned to Ace.

"What do yuh say, can I give her the works? She's been askin' for it all day! I got some brass knuckles and a sap right here, see. Shall I slap it outta her?"

"Shower down!" Ace snapped.

The lipstick tube sailed across the room, smacking Chicago in the stomach. "Serves you right, you crawling louse!" Helen laughed.

"That did it!"

"Stay right where you are." Ace grabbed his arm. "Don't fly off the handle! Let her alone, will you? I said let her alone."

Helen snickered.

"Oh, alright! Just give it to me straight, will yuh? Spit it out."

"Pretty simple pal. It's a frame up, and I'm the fall guy. The Japanese are up to something with Chinese antimony. It's used for making munitions. No doubt they plan to use it in Manchuria. The way I've got it figured, old Maxwell and Idina were spying for the Japanese. When it looked like things were going to catch up with them, they bumped off her kid brother Roddy. Then Maxwell got himself bumped off. Looks like Idina has set herself up pretty swell."

"Take a bow flyboy. Those ideas are plenty smart, but they ain't soundin' good enough to clear yuh."

"Don't I know it! But I've got to get my hands on Idina because she's in the know and is the only one who can clear me. She's a first-class rat, but somehow I've got to make her talk and hand her over to the cops. We've got to find her while I'm still on the run."

Helen walked over to the white-brocaded divan. Scooping up an open dress box, she examined the tissue lining printed with flowery black writing bearing the name *Madame Garnet*. She held up a sheet of the pink tissue paper and waved it coyly.

"Well Ace, this is your lucky day. Nothing like a woman when it comes to doing a man's job, as I always say. I'm fairly certain I know where you'll find Idina Soames tonight. According to this paper and dress box, she's hotfooting it across town to the Temple of Heaven. You'll find her there at Count Panozzo's Mid-Autumn Moon Festival bash. It's the hottest show in town."

Chicago rolled backwards on the mattress and giggled.

"Get a load of that dame. I tell yuh! Why, I never heard such a cock-and-bull story."

"Give your face a rest, ning-nong," Ace replied. "Okey-doke, Helen, I'm all ears. How do you mean at the Temple of Heaven tonight?"

"A headliner costume ball. Madame Garnet is the official seamstress for tonight's party. It's the first social event of the season. Anyone who's anyone will be there. I've got an invitation myself and am going, too. As a matter of fact, boys, here's the pay dirt. My costume happens to be inside the trunk of my car."

"No kiddin', Jane! That's plenty hot."

"Yeah, Helen, you're plenty smart alright."

Babe, who had wandered away, burst in. "Boss! Orloff, the chauffeur!"

"Yeah, the White Russian. Orloff, the boozehound. So what?"

"He's dead in his bungalow."

"So, he kicked the bucket. That's kind of a raw deal," Chicago commented.

Temple entrance.

Ace frowned. "You're sure he's dead? Any sign of violence, a struggle, any blood around?"

Babe shook his head. "I don't think so. His room smells of liquor." The boy shuddered.

"Okay, get a grip on yourself, kid. Everything's going to be alright. He probably drunk himself to death. All the same, it's a shame you had to see that." Ace turned to Chicago.

"Let's all go to Maxwell's room to find some monkey suits for us gents. Maxwell won't need them anymore. Helen, go get your costume. Babe, duck in the servant's rooms and see if you can't trade for that cook's uniform for something spiffier. Looks like we're all going to a party tonight."

Chief Inspector Haymes leaned against the door inside the Duesenberg and propped his elbow on the window frame. Every so often, he winced at his headache, intensified by the thought of Ace slipping out of reach. Now his neck was on the line. And the Black Eel may be free to have his way in Shanghai. If so, Haymes could be pushed from pillar to post in China's vast hinterland—maybe even Tibet! The Consul General as much as promised not 10 minutes hence. He cringed and shouted out, "Blast it!

As the sedan crawled in front of the Bund, he noticed boatmen fastening lanterns to the masts of fishing boats docked along the Nanking Road Jetty. The Moon Festival gave him the jitters. Dash it all! Instead of leading the charge to capture that murderous Yank, he'd been reassigned to protecting Madame Soames. Imagine, playing nursemaid for that half-crazed girl who must've taken complete leave of her senses to attend this fool party. What madness!

The Duesenberg rolled past luxury convertibles parked along the narrow street where a red wall enclosed the Temple of Heaven compound and came to a halt in the front of a red turreted gate.

Detective McCooper opened the door and extended his hand to help Haymes out of the sedan. "Good evening, Guv."

"I'll be hanged! I don't approve of this ridiculous waste of time," barked Haymes, brushing him aside and walking through the gate.

The Great Pagoda in Soochow.

The younger man followed with a sigh. Stomping up the inclined granite walkway, they passed the three stone archways. At the third elevated terrace, Haymes paused midway and thrust his hands on his hips. "I say, I've never seen such a display of insanity!" As if honoring a Hollywood premiere, two klieg lights cast alternating spotlights on the Temple of Heaven's blue walls and its three-layered yellow tiled roof. Beyond the temple, white oval lanterns glowed like miniature moons dangling from each of the octagonal pagoda's nine roofs.

"Beg your pardon, Guv, but I think it's pretty marvelous, actually—a wonderful sight."

Both watched the spotlights illuminate the guests, whose faces were hidden behind black face masks. They wore white dominos with black slippers.

"Awful-looking creatures, the whole lot of them," Haymes remarked. "Feeble-minded people! Why, they look like a pack of ghosts floating about in there. Don't you find this utterly absurd?"

Mesmerized, McCooper answered, "Very curious. Don't you think they look like phantoms? Why, I can't think of a pleasanter experience."

"Oh, come now! Don't be a such fool."

A bandleader in a white dinner jacket and black trousers reached for the microphone. "Good evening, ladies and gents! I'm Snooky Knight. This here is my orchestra. Our first number is a jag-time melody straight from the jazz parlors in New York City. Hit it, boys."

The robed figures drifted in and around the temple. Some milled about the back where it faced the pagoda. Haymes and McCooper kept a distance. A cymbal crashed, raucous trombones kicked in, violins wailed, and the band members yowled like alley cats and sang: *"She's like a cat in Tin Pan Alley. She just won't scat and that is that…"*

"That's the end of this nonsense!" Haymes turned away. "No use hanging about these weak-willed morons. We'd better have a look round. I'll want more detectives posted in case that Yank shows his face here."

He strode off to survey the grounds and barked orders to plainclothes detectives conspicuous in their white drill suits. At length, he settled at a table replete with delicacies. "Rather disheartening posting us out here on a lark. It's this tedious hanging about that really gets me! No telling where that Yank is or what he's up to."

McCooper watched him swallow a boiled prawn. "Nothing is going to happen here tonight of interest to Special Branch. In any event, it looks as though we're here to stay until this party finishes and we escort Madame Soames home. With all those costumes, it's difficult to tell which one is her." Haymes, pointing to platters of cold asparagus and roast beef between blocks of ice with frozen roses inside, answered, "Lad, you may as well make the most of it and have something to eat."

Moonlight illuminated Ace's white robe as he hurried from the roadster parked outside the Temple of Heaven. A black mask covered his forehead, nose, and eyes. Chicago Charlie, Babe, and Helen followed in the shadows on the opposite side of the street. Ace hastened his pace despite seeing the Special Branch Duesenberg sitting at the entrance. A dozen plainclothes detectives in white suits and Panama hats were posted along the street. This is your last chance, pal, Ace reminded himself. Throwing his shoulders back, he walked purposefully past the detectives. He felt their gaze. As he started up the path to the temple, one of the detectives called out.

"Having a good evening, are you, sir?"

"*Was sagen Sie?*" Ace answered in German. "*Sprechen Sie langsamer!*"

"Blasted Boche!" said the detective, spitting on the pavement and turning away.

Ace continued up the steep path to the Temple of Heaven. The panorama of Shanghai's lights glittered below. The temple's squat three-layered roof provided a muted backdrop against the slender pagoda in the back. Round white lanterns ringed each of the pagoda's roofs. Ace neared the court at the base of the temple. Its roof was edged with ceramic birds and fish. Saxophones screeched close by. Ace followed the sound around the temple's octagonal base. Low walls divided the grounds from court-yards and gardens. The monks lived in clustered quarters a respectful distance away amidst their departed brethren, whose cremated ashes rested in a nearby burial ground.

A few feet away some guests in hooded white capes drank champagne in front of a goldfish tank along one wall. Gazing at them through the mask, Ace wondered how he'd ever find Idina. She could be anywhere. Everyone looked almost exactly alike. He knew one thing for certain. Chief Inspector Haymes was in his midst. It would be best to get lost among the dancers.

Pockmarked Fang stood in the Garden of Great Enjoyment with his arms folded and his hands tucked inside the cuffs of his long gown. He looked at the 18-foot-tall effigy of the Goddess of the Moon, whose bodhisattva base rose above an oval painting of the Palace of the Moon. His wives hovered around an altar table illuminated in the darkness by torchlight. The women arranged nine-sectioned lotus roots, lotus-petal watermelons, and "full moon" cakes two feet in diameter. Some clutched incense burners, joss sticks, and paper spirit money. Turning to One-eyed Wong, he spoke, "Get the car and bodyguards ready at once. We leave for the Temple of Heaven."

At that time, Chicago hoisted Helen and Babe over the wall in an out-of-the-way section of the temple. Perching on top of the wall, Babe reached down and pulled Chicago up. Then they jumped onto the grass and looked at the party in the distance. Chicago lit a cigarette and blew smoke rings. "I don't like the looks of it one bit. Not one bit!"

Jamming a cigarette in her mouth, Helen clenched her teeth and struck a match. "What are you shooting your mouth off about? Don't tell me you're turning yellow on us?"

"Fat chance!" Chicago crushed a smoke ring. "On the level, sister, I gotta hunch. It ain't a good one neither. Why, just look at all 'em over there. How are we ever gonna know who is Ace, or who is Idina, or who is anyone else? Even if we could figure all that out, how are we gonna get in the middle of all that when we stick out like a sore thumb because our duds don't match those masks and hooded capes?"

Babe looked down at his embroidered emerald gown, pilfered from one of the Soames' menservants to pass himself off as one of the ceremonially dressed moon worshippers. "Yes, I see what you mean."

"For crying out loud! Why don't we use our heads? Why don't we sneak over there to catch someone leaving? We can ask for their costumes before they go. All we need is three people to leave. That's not so hard!"

"Alright, Jane, why don't yuh lead the way and do the askin'? You've got more class than either of us, and you'll be able to pull it off better. Babe and me will follow."

"Fine by me," Helen replied. "Let's get moving."

Drifting away from his partner as the tempo slowed for the next number, Ace paused near the corner of the bandstand. He reached into the hood and lowered the strap on the mask cutting across the back of his hair. He'd had enough dancing. No sign of Idina anywhere. He couldn't say that for Special Branch though. Chief Inspector Haymes periodically strolled around the outskirts and perimeter of the bandstand. The old bulldog was back at the food table again. Thunder droned overhead as a clarinet proclaimed the next song. Wondering what he'd do if he failed to find Idina, Ace started to slip away to think. Just then, a masked woman grabbed his hand and pulled him back for a dance. The band struck up a love song. The woman hugged Ace tightly and began to whisper the lyrics into his ear. Ace froze. He recognized Idina's voice. And they were dancing together. His mind raced. He had to get her away from the others so he could make her talk. He pulled her closer and guided her off the dance floor.

Idina purred in his ear. "Are you looking for a chance to get chummy with me, or am I mistaken?"

Ace kissed her hand and shook his head for "no."

"Oh, you are making this a lovely party," she squealed. "Let's go somewhere quiet and do it properly. Let's not fight it, rather, let's give in to it."

He nodded, leading her to the pagoda in the back of the grounds.

Without any trouble, Helen had acquired a costume herself, but not any for Babe and Chicago. She mingled about on the dance floor trying to locate Ace, while her companions remained on the third tier of the pagoda surveying the party scene down below. From the 4th floor of the pagoda,

Pockmarked Fang and One-eyed Wong peered through the lanterns watching the goings on below.

"Well here we are, kid, cooling our heels. I wish Ace would've blown town today. Instead Acre is riskin' his neck tryin' to get that dirty, double-crossin' dame to fess up."

"Don't worry Chicago, she'll get what she deserves. We Chinese have a saying, 'Good and evil do not wrongly befall men, but Heaven sends down misery or happiness according to their conduct.' "

"Hush, someone's coming inside the pagoda. I hear voices over there."

On the ground floor, Ace pulled Idina into the center of the principal hall where an idol of the Mood Goddess Chang E was enshrined and illuminated only by candles in front. An immense golden rabbit glistened on the red marble altar. "Awaiting the Moon," was written in square characters above. Two huge wooden demonic figures guarded the Moon Goddess.

Idina looked up as a bat flew overhead. She frowned at the spider webs, blackened by the smoke of rising incense, that hung from beams above. "You haven't a cigarette, have you?" she asked Ace.

He nodded and handed one to her.

"Look's like you're the silent type tonight. That quite alright my dear, as long as you can raise me up to paradise. This party was a dreadful bore until you came along."

Smiling, Ace nodded his head in agreement. He eyed the strand of enormous white pearls she wore around her neck as he struck a match.

Her cigarette moved to the flame. Glancing into his gray eyes, she coughed and stepped backwards. "You must excuse me," she said, her voice trembling. She dropped her cigarette and backed away. "I think we'd better let the whole thing go. No need to see me out. I'll be on my way. Thank you for your trouble."

"Not at all. I like trouble," said Ace, reaching out and grabbing her wrist. "And I'm plenty glad to see you, too."

"I beg your pardon," she answered. "Unhand me at once or I'll scream."

"I wouldn't try that if I were you, Idina. I'm liable to slug your pretty face for what you've done. You're going to clear me with the cops if it's the last thing you do."

"That's it, flyboy, tell her like it is!" hollered Chicago Charlie, who blocked one doorway on the ground floor while Babe stood guard at another. "Sugar, don't yuh be playin' possum. Better do as he sez, or were gonna help him make yuh squeal like a yella rat!"

Knocked off guard by Chicago's intrusion, Ace slackened his grip for a second—just enough time for Idina to break away and dart past Babe up a flight of stairs. The boy gave chase, and the others followed.

Idina rushed along the first tier, knocking the lanterns aside. Two fell onto the floor. Flames began to spread.

Babe hurriedly tried to stamp out the fire as he raced past, but the wooden wall started burning. Closing in, Babe lunged and grabbed her by the hem of her long white cape.

She twisted and punched the boy, knocking him against the carved wooden rail overlooking the main hall.

"This is what you get for trying to stand in my way," she shouted, trying to shove him backwards over the edge. There was a sharp crack as the centuries-old rail began to split.

"Idina!" yelled Ace, rushing up to her and tearing her away from Babe. "Leave him alone!"

She bent down, took off her high-heeled shoe, and slammed its point against Ace's head wound. Blood burst from his stitches as he stumbled, clutching his head.

"Looks like that's the end of it, Mr. Jordan. I'll be on my way to find Inspector Haymes. No doubt he's seen the smoke by now. I daresay we'll probably run into each other, and the Inspector will be ever so glad to take you back to jail where you belong."

Thick smoke rose. Chicago yelled through the haze. "Hey, this place is burnin' up! We'd better scram or we'll go with it."

Coughing, Babe tugged at Ace. "Boss, are you okay? Let's get out of here!"

Idina shrieked with laughter and smacked her heeled shoe against Ace's head again. This time, he fell against her, knocking her backwards against the rail. The wood snapped. Idina teetered precariously on the edge as the carved barrier behind her broke, clattering to the floor below. Flailing her arms, she took a rocking step forward with her high-heeled foot and narrowly regained her balance.

Ace wiped away blood dripping into his eyes and reached out his hand toward Idina.

She glared at the red smear on his hand; a flash of blurred memories and dreams came back to her about the death of her brother Roddy. Predominant among them were the smell of absinthe and a horror of blood.

"Come on!" Ace yelled, still offering his hand.

In an outburst of rage, Idina swooped up her shoe to strike Ace again.

Suddenly, there was a dull whistling noise followed by several sharp thuds. Idina shrieked and let the shoe fall from her hand. She reeled forward, revealing a cluster of arrows sticking out from her back. Then she lost her balance and fell backwards.

The last Ace saw was a swirl of white cape vanishing past the broken rail. From the balustrade directly across from them, Pockmarked Fang lowered the bow and handed it to One-Eyed Wong. His slanted topaz eyes met Ace's before he turned away and disappeared into the smoke. Soon the pagoda became engulfed in flames. Partygoers screamed as chaos broke out. Ace fled, only stopping once he was out of danger.

Chief Inspector Haymes ran toward him at the same time as Chicago Charlie met up. "Well, looks like my head is split open again, but that's not the worst of it. With Idina dead, who's going to vouch for me?"

"Don't worry flyboy, we'll figure something out."

Smoke curled upwards from the charred spire of the pagoda wafting across the black night sky. Thanks to the intervention of Special Branch, local authorities arrived quickly to put out the flames. However, it had taken some time to completely extinguish the blaze; what remained of the pagoda's wooden interior smouldered. The air was thick with the odor of burnt wood. The dull exchanges of policemen mingled with the chatter of bystanders, the cries of distraught Chinese pilgrims, and the laments of resident monks. Although Special Branch cordoned off both the pagoda and temple, a crowd continued to clamor from the main gate downhill.

Chief Inspector Haymes stood at a distance from the yellow-roofed temple. In front of him, a massive archway loomed over the hillside, its nine granite steps leading down to the topmost of the triple terraces. Haymes wasn't interested in the view; he wanted to be left alone. Madame Soames hadn't been seen since the onset of the fire. The Chief Inspector had more than a sneaking suspicion she'd been dragged inside the pagoda and killed by that abominable Mr. Jordan, who had probably started the fire to cover up his 6th murder. She'd have been better off staying at home, the daft creature! He shoved his hands into his coat pockets.

Capering about in a mask and cloak like a confounded pantomime, with a killer on the loose… Once the Consul General gets wind of this….

Detective McCooper approached him from behind. "Beg your pardon, Guv."

"Blast!" Haymes spun around and glared at him. "Well, what is it? Have you found that body yet, or is it just another of your disintegrated beam poles? And that venomous redheaded woman reporter—have you managed to get rid of her, or is she still lurking about the monks' quarters?"

McCooper brushed traces of ash from his sleeves.

"Not to worry, Guv. Peake's just escorted her from the premises."

"Peake? Who the?"

"Your driver, sir. I daresay her tantrums didn't go very far with him. The man ought to be decorated."

"Never mind that. Has any trace been found of Madame Soames?"

A grim expression came over the young detective's face.

"That's what I came to tell you about, Guv. One of our men discovered something in the debris not five minutes ago…"

"Very well, lead on," said Haymes gruffly tramping off towards the pagoda.

While the two policemen conversed above, Ace sat in the middle of the nine granite steps leading down to the third terrace with his hands cuffed behind his back.

Detective Hamilton stood guard slowly puffing a cigarette.

Ace shifted his patent leather dress shoes against the gravelly stone.

"Getting restless are we, Jordan?"

Hamilton's hand drifted toward the lapel of his suit jacket.

"The Guv wants to see the KMT have their way with you, but I'm not so picky. Try any more antics and I'll give it to you right in the head."

"Yeah, keep your shirt on. My head's had enough grief from your type."

Ace nodded to indicate the makeshift bandages on his scalp.

"Anyway, I'm not interested in any trouble."

"That's rather amusing coming from you," Hamilton sneered with the cigarette between his teeth.

Ace threw the detective a dirty look over his shoulder.

"Aw, why don't you shut your trap and grab yourself some sense?" He stared back down the pathway. "They'll clear me in the end. You'll see."

Hamilton shook his head disdainfully and blew out a stream of smoke.

Suddenly, a stout, dark figure stepped out from the shadows of the archway at the base of the steps and began ascending towards them. The silver moonlight illuminated the bright pink hue of the man's long Chinese gown and glinted off what seemed to be a pair of pistols he wore belted around his bulging waist.

Ace recognized One-Eyed Wong.

"Stop where you are!" snapped Hamilton.

He stepped forward menacingly as the Chinese man ignored him and continued to approach. Then suddenly the detective hesitated.

"Oh, Wong."

Hamilton stepped back again.

"I'm sorry, but this area is off-limits. Unless—did you have something to say to the Inspector?"

One-Eyed Wong nodded at Ace.

"My Master wishes to speak to the American."

Hamilton and Ace looked at each other.

"Very well, I see no harm in it," the detective said reluctantly after looking back over his shoulder and finding Haymes nowhere in sight. "He can't possibly get away again."

Latching one pudgy hand onto Ace's shoulder, One-Eyed Wong led him down the flight of steps and out onto the second terrace. They walked a short distance, turned to the left, and approached a twisted magnolia tree. Underneath the tree was a weathered stone bench where the slim, blue-robed figure of Pockmarked Fang sat waiting.

"Greetings, Mr. Jordan."

"Hello," Ace replied as One-Eyed Wong released him. He plopped down beside Pockmarked Fang on the bench without being asked.

"What a pity about Madame Soames," the gangster remarked dryly. He regarded Ace with cold topaz eyes. "On such a night as this, I am reminded of a poem called 'Autumn Moon' by Li T`ai-Po. 'The jade staircase weeps with dew. It wets her silken shoes, as she climbs slowly to the pavilion. She too weeps. Letting down a curtain of crystal beads like a tinkling waterfall, she sits staring through it at the Autumn Moon.' It is fitting that this evening's events happened on the Mid-Autumn Moon Festival."

"Yeah, I guess it fits alright," said Ace sourly. "Maybe you're like the archer, too, who shoots at the Moon Goddess."

"It is unwise to jest about such things, Mr. Jordan. I want to let you know that you are my adopted son no longer—I am free of this burden."

"That suits me fine. No hard feelings on my part, even though you just killed the only person who could clear me. Thanks anyhow for saving my skin."

Ace glanced sideways and noticed the tips of Pockmarked Fang's gilded fingernail protectors gleaming in the moonlight where they peered out from the cuffs of his dark sleeves.

"I'd shake your hand on it, but you can see I can't manage at the moment."

"Quite alright, Mr. Jordan."

Pockmarked Fang clicked the claw-like protectors together as he brushed out a crease from his blue silk gown. With a movement of his sleeve, a broken strand of large, white pearls appeared in his hand. One pearl fell to the ground and rolled against Ace's shoe.

"Say, I recognize those." Ace looked down grimly. "Idina was wearing them."

"Yes," replied Pockmarked Fang. He motioned aside to One-Eyed Wong, who dutifully took the pearls from his master. Then, pulling Ace to his feet, One-Eyed Wong shoved the broken necklace into the pocket of Ace's suit jacket.

"Hey! What's the idea?"

"Silence!" Pockmarked Fang hissed.

He nodded at One-Eyed Wong, who promptly pushed Ace back down onto the bench again.

"With this, I repay my debt to you."

"Look here, brother, I'm grateful for your help but..."

The opium czar folded his arms and looked away airily. "The pearls will speak for themselves. You may say as much to the Chief Inspector, if he should ask you about them."

"Alright, fine. But now it's my turn to ask you a question." Ace suddenly became aware of One-Eyed Wong hovering in the shadows behind him. "If you don't mind, that is?"

"Ask."

"How did you know what my plans were, or that I was coming here tonight? Did Babe or Chicago spill it to one of your boys?"

Pockmarked Fang continued to sit there with his arms crossed. He threw a sideways glance at Ace.

"The city of Shanghai belongs to me. Within it, I have 1,000 eyes and ears. They see and hear everything for me—without the assistance of devils from over the ocean."

"Oh, so you were having me snooped on. I guess that explains the Red Pole enforcer and the beggar with the dumbbells."

Pockmarked Fang rose from the bench.

"I have given my answer," he replied. "The rest is not my concern."

With his hands clasped behind his back, he stepped silently out into the moonlight followed by One-Eyed Wong. They turned past the bench and began to step towards the shadow of the wall behind the magnolia tree.

"Well, thanks anyway," Ace called out after them, trying in vain to glimpse where they moved. "So long to you both!"

Pockmarked Fang pivoted and regarded Ace for the last time.

"Farewell, Mr. Jordan," he said curtly.

Then he and One-Eyed Wong vanished into the darkness.

Ace stared after them as Detective Hamilton reappeared at the base of the stone steps. He walked towards Ace with squared shoulders.

"Alright, Jordan. Come along. And do let's be civil about it. The Chief Inspector wishes to speak with you, and he's in no temper to be trifled with."

Chicago Charlie and Babe waited on the first terrace. Standing beneath the massive statue of the demon-warding deity Chung K'uei, they watched the policemen talking in low tones amid the glow of the lanterns hanging on the archway. Chicago turned and looked up casually at the burly stone figure behind him.

The flickering light illuminated the sword in the statue's hand and cast an eerie glow into its fierce face; shadows highlighted the wild-looking beard and bushy, swirling hair.

Chicago shifted his eyes away and nervously popped a wad of opium pills into his mouth.

Babe stood with his arms crossed tightly and his hands tucked in the cuffs of the sleeves of his embroidered green gown, silently observing everything that went on. His right cheekbone was marked with a red bruise where Idina had punched him.

"Well, kid, got any smart ideas?" Chicago muttered. He peered at the policemen. "I don't know 'bout you, but I'm quittin' this burg just as soon as them coppers give us the breeze. Things is gettin' too hot around here for a mug like me, yuh get my drift?"

Babe remained quiet as if he didn't hear.

Just then, Chief Inspector Haymes came stalking up towards them. Detective McCooper trailed in his wake.

"Well, well, if it ain't the big noise himself. You gonna free us from this dump yet?"

Haymes came to a halt in front of Chicago and glared.

"Perhaps you'd prefer the inside of a Black Maria."

"Aw, quit kiddin'. Me and the kid here's just a couple of regular bystanders. No buzzard is gonna put the cuffs on us."

"We'll see," growled Haymes. He motioned to Detective McCooper, who quickly produced a notebook and pencil.

"I've just got through speaking with your friend, Mr. 'Ace' Jordan. He'll be spending the few days left to him in Ward Road Gaol before he's extradited to Chinese jurisdiction. You might be paying him a visit there if I find you had anything to do with tonight's catastrophe, but I'm giving you a chance now to merit some lenience. Tell me, what were the lot of you doing inside the pagoda in the company of Madame Soames?"

"Pardon? In company of who?"

"You know very who, you lying scoundrel! Now let's get straight to the point, and don't try to deny anything—I myself witnessed you and this native here come dashing out of the pagoda behind Jordan. Why do you suppose you were apprehended? Do you think I would waste my time interviewing a petty opium peddler without any solid reason? Now, answer my question!"

"Keep your temperature down brother, or else somebody might mistake yuh for Confucius over here," said Chicago, jerking his thumb over his shoulder at the ferocious-looking statue of Chung K'uei.

Haymes glanced at the statue. His face flushed. "Why, of all the…"

"Listen, pops, yuh got all the angles figured backwards," Chicago cut in. "It's the Moon Festival, and there was a big shindig, weren't there? With all them big shots hobnobbing around in drapes and monkey suits, what smart guy wouldn't poke around and give the joint a once over? Besides, one of the monks here's an old pal of mine. He had a wise idea he wanted to cut me in on, see?"

"A charming story. I suppose you'll be telling me next that this Chinese here is one of your relations."

"Aw, cut with the cracks, Chief. It ain't polite."

"I've heard quite enough from you!" Haymes spun to face Babe.

"Well, what's your hand in this matter? You're one of Pockmarked Fang's underlings, I assume, sent to help Jordan. I don't suppose you wish to shed any light on the Green Gang's role in this affair? Well, speak up!"

The boy regarded him with crossed arms and a perfectly calm expression.

"Shootin' the works, ain't yuh pop?"

Haymes whirled back to Chicago again.

"Very well then, you've made yourself quite clear. If I can't get the truth out of you, then the KMT will get it from Jordan."

He looked at the detective standing next to him. "McCooper, show these 'persons' away!"

Chinese gunboat on the Yangtze River in Shanghai.

CHAPTER FIVE

16th Day of the Eighth Moon

Clutching a small brown parcel in his hand, Detective McCooper hurried along the second-floor veranda of the Shanghai Municipal Police Station towards Chief Inspector Haymes' office. It was somewhat cold that morning; a blanket of thin fog draped over the city. McCooper hardly noticed. He swept over to the door and, after a quick rapping knock, strode inside. "Morning, Guv."

Chief Inspector Haymes stooped over his desk poring over a stack of papers. "Well?" He glanced over his shoulder at the detective.

"Some rather unexpected evidence has surfaced, sir."

McCooper set the brown parcel on the desk and sat down stiffly in an empty chair.

"As you're aware, the Soames estate is now being disassembled given that all parties named as beneficiaries in the will are now deceased. In sorting through the Soames' effects, sir…well, to make a long story short, sir, we've discovered some paraphernalia at the estate that vindicates Mr. Jordan."

Haymes stood slowly and leaned over his desk with a menacing expression.

"Mr. Jordan innocent? What the blazes do you mean?"

"You recall the large strand of pearls we found on Jordan shortly after his arrest?"

"Certainly. They've been identified as the property of the late Madame Soames. Property which, I might venture to point out, was apparently pilfered from her remains by Mr. Jordan himself in a most despicable and felonious fashion."

"With all due respect, Guv, our own Detective Hamilton has sworn the pearls were absent from Jordan's person until his farewell chat with Pockmarked Fang."

"Nonetheless, they belonged to Madame Soames!"

"Indeed they did, sir." McCooper shifted nervously in his chair. "The point I am trying to make, Guv, is that these pearls of the late Madame Soames have been positively identified as genuine Dong-chow pearls."

A railroad train in Shanghai.

Haymes snorted. "Indeed? What of it?"

"Those variety of pearls are only to be found in Manchuria, sir...which, as we all know, has been cordoned off by the Japanese. The region's being evacuated, and no one has had access to the area for quite some while. We had considered, sir, that perhaps the pearls had somehow been purchased prior to the occupation, but, when the Soames estate was liquidated, we discovered a certain piece of evidence that is—if you'll pardon the expression, sir—nothing less than damning."

The Chief Inspector furrowed his thick eyebrows. Following McCooper's glance to the brown parcel, he seized the package and tore it open. An oblong, embroidered necklace box dropped from the rustling paper and fell with a light thud onto the desk.

Haymes snatched it. As he flipped open the soft lid, his keen eyes fell immediately to a small emblem of gold-stitched Japanese lettering in the top inside corner.

"The brand of the Iwata Corporation in Dairen," announced McCooper, scratching the back of his head. "A Japanese-owned pearl manufacturing company. It used to be run by the Chinese, of course, but the Japanese seized it as soon as they could get their hands on it. Iwata Corps is known for the quality of its Dong-chow pearl necklaces."

He dug into his jacket pocket and set a small metal object down on the table. "Also, we appear to have found Mr. Jordan's stolen ring."

The Duesenberg wedged into a parking space in front of the Shanghai-Woosung Railway. McCooper stepped out and opened the rear passenger door. Chief Inspector Haymes exited followed by Ace and Babe.

"This way, my good man," said Haymes, guiding Ace by the elbow past the ticket counter to an area for departures near the tracks. "We've made arrangements for your trip to Tientsin. I hope you'll get ample rest and speed up your recovery during your holiday."

"Thanks, Inspector, I appreciate all you've done for me and the kid. No hard feelings, right?"

"None whatever." Haymes turned to McCooper. "Take his bags to that porter over there. The train's preparing to leave."

The detective turned over three pigskin suitcases to the porter. The train whistled. Passengers bid their farewells to friends and relatives.

"Thanks again, Inspector. That sure was swell of you to give us a ride over and see us off."

"Not at all. I'm glad to be of service especially given the misunderstanding. Why if it hadn't been for those pearls, there's really no telling where you'd be today."

"No kidding." Ace shook the older man's hand. "Thanks for getting back my ring, too."

"All in the line of justice sir. Have a splendid trip."

Haymes watched Ace and Babe board the train. They disappeared through the doorway, but soon reappeared seated inside at a window a few feet across the way. Haymes, however, had already turned around. He had become distracted by a gaunt Chinese man in a long European jacket and top hat covering what looked like a mismatched, waist-length pigtail—a fading symbol of the fallen Ch'ing Dynasty. Haymes watched the curious gentleman enter the train and come into view again opposite Ace in the same carriage. Something odd about that chap, he mused.

Railway station.

Reflecting on the events over the last five days amid what should have been the normal gaiety of lanterns under the Moon Festival, Chief Inspector Haymes turned to McCooper.

"I'm suddenly reminded of my wife's favorite Bible proverb. Solomon 13-9, if I'm not mistaken. It goes something like this: 'The light of the just shines gaily, but the lamp of the wicked goes out.' Funny how things pop into your head when you least expect them."

Puffs of white steam spewed out as the train left the railway station. Ace and Babe waved goodbye as the bizarre elderly Chinese gentleman leaned forward in front of them and pulled down the shade in their carriage to block out the light.

THE END

List of Photographs

Page 2: The Shanghai Club and the Canadian Pacific Ocean Services Ltd. building. Photo courtesy of the Library of Congress (LOC). The Shanghai Club, an English men's club, was aptly described by a traveling British magician as a daily gathering spot for businessmen and merchants. "It is a small Stock Exchange where everybody seems to combine business with a desire to drink the greatest number of cocktails in the shortest possible time. Indeed it is the most hospitable place I have every found!"

• Charles Bertram, *A Magician in Many Lands*, (London: George Routledge & Sons Ltd., 1911), p. 160.

The six-story building was designed in an English Renaissance style. Its hallmarks included two billiard rooms, card rooms, a library for 20,000 books, a reading room, an oyster bar, a barber's shop, a bicycle stand, a bowling alley, and 40 bedrooms for members and visitors. The Shanghai Club was operated by European stewards and 135 Chinese staff. Nearly half of its 1,300 members lived in Shanghai, and 75 percent were British,

• Arnold Wright and H.A. Cartwright, editors, *Twentieth Century Impressions of Hongkong, Shanghai, and Other Treaty Ports in China: Their History, People, Commerce, Industries and Resources*, (London, Hong Kong, Shanghai: Lloyd's Greater Britain Publishing Co. Ltd., 1908), p. 388.

The Canadian Pacific Ocean Services Ltd. operated a fleet of 74 steamboats and 15 ocean liners operating across the Atlantic and Pacific oceans; boasted 16 hotels; carried mail under an Imperial contact between Liverpool and Hong Kong; and operated its own express, telegraph and news service.

• Moodys Manual of Railroads and Corporation Securities Issue of 1917, *Moody Manual Co.*, p. 120.

Page 4: The so-called "king" of a beggar's guild in Loong Wah near Shanghai. Photo, circa 1900, LOC. Documenting a trip to China, James Ricalton met the head of Loong Wah's beggar's guild, who "marched directly into our presence" asking for alms. "We were at once struck by his extraordinary manner as well as by his extraordinary appearance; the first thing unusual in his manner was his smiling face and cheerful willingness to stand before the camera." As in other provinces of China back then, Loong Wah had a beggar's guild composed of fee-paying members as well as leaders known as "Kings," who were respected authorities and even street watchmen under a magistrate's protection.

• James Ricalton, *China through the Stereoscope—A Journey through the Dragon Empire at the Time of the Boxer Uprising*, (N.Y. and London: Underwood & Underwood, 1901), pp. 114-118.

Page 8: A band of four men with traditional Chinese instruments. LOC.

Page 10: Removing silk from reels for drying. LOC. An honorary member of the Agriculture-Horticulture Society of India described a visit to the silk district north of Shanghai. He entered a feeding area for "millions" of silkworms in hundreds of round sieves stacked above each in open frameworks. "In one large hall I observed the floor completely covered with worms. I shall never forget the peculiar sound which fell upon my ear as I opened the door of this hall. It was early in the morning, the worms had been just fed, and were at the time eagerly devouring the fresh leaves of the mulberry. Hundreds of thousands of little mouths were munching the leaves, and in the stillness around this sound was very striking and peculiar."
◆ Robert Fortune, " Fortune's Residence among the Chinese," in *Littell's Living Age*, Vol. 54, July-September, (Boston: Littell, Son and Co., 1857), p. 343.

Page 12: Terraced fields. LOC, LC-DIG-ppmsca-07414.

Page 16: Nanking Road in Shanghai. LOC. Among its evaluation of various Asia ports, a British publication contained typical sentiment from that era in describing Nanking Road as "worthy of special note" for being a road flanked by businesses near the Bund that widened to take on grander edifices such as the Town Hall, Hotel Metropole, and Library before becoming a tree-lined avenue called Bubbling Well Road leading to grand mansions. "Shanghai is the finest city in the East for a European. ...The foreigner has pleasure resorts which are forbidden to the Chinese, and the Chinese have resorts never desecrated by a foreign foot. Shanghai is the city of contrasts. You may see the dainty, clean occidental maiden buying flowers within a yard of a pox-stricken, pest-ridden filthy oriental hag. You may see flour ground by the finest machinery man has devised, and within a stone's throw you may see it pounded in a hollow stone by methods antedating Adam. Some of Shanghai's buildings are worthy of any city on earth. Some of the native hovels (beyond municipal limits) would be unworthy homes for swine. Perhaps in no other city could such contrasts be found."
◆ Allister Macmillan, Seaports of the Far East—Historical and Descriptive Commercial and Industrial Facts, Figures & Resources, (London: W.H.& L. Collinbridge, 1907), pp. 94–95.

Page 18: Protesters amid a crowd. Photo courtesy of Regents of the University of Minnesota from the Kautz Family YMCA Archives Collection; used with permission of the Metropolitan Design Center, ymca084-p1031. A resurgence in nationalism and anti-imperialism protests, particularly among Chinese students, was sparked in Shanghai in 1925 in what became known as the May 30 Movement. On that day, 12 people were killed by police commanded by British officers in protests arising from Chinese workers who died at the hands of Japanese factory managers. Protests spread throughout China as student political activism increased.

✦ David Strand, *Rickshaw Beijing—City People and Politics in the 1920s,* (California: University of California Press, 1993), pp. 182–183.

Page 26: American goods for sale (warehouse in Hankow). LOC. Because "only 216 strictly American" firms were conducting business as of 1921 in China, the American Chambers of Commerce hoped to promote Sino-U.S. trade in six key markets: Hankow, Shanghai, Tientsin, Changsha, Harbin, and Peking.

✦ Cyril H. Tribe, "Approach and Development of Chinese Markets in China Review," *China Trade Bureau,* August 1921, p. 377.

Page 34: Busy waterway traffic on Soochow Creek near Garden Bridge. Photo courtesy of Special Collections and University Archives, University of Oregon Libraries, Gertrude Bass Warner Collection, PH014_53-09. The Garden Bridge was built of steel to support the introduction of tramways in Shanghai.

✦ Wright and Cartwright, editors, *Twentieth Century Impressions of Hongkong, Shanghai, and Other Treaty Ports in China,* pp. 375–376.

Page 38: A busy section of the Bund in Shanghai. LOC. "A broad and beautifully kept boulevard, called, of course, The Bund, runs round the river, with a row of well-grown trees and broad grass plat at the water's edge, and this Bund is lined on the other side, from one end to the other, with mercantile buildings second to none of their kind it [sic] the world. At the upper end of the Bund a large patch of green shows the Public Garden, where the band plays on summer evenings."

✦ Henry Norman, "The World Over—A Series of Pen Pictures, Shanghai Surprises" in *Current Opinion* from *Current Literature: A Magazine of Record and Review,* Vol. III, July–December 1889, p. 237.

Page 40: British warship alongside Shanghai waterfront. LOC. In 1927, following struggles among Chinese factions for control of the country, heightened hostilities against the British combined with a Chinese mob's seizure of a British Concession in Hankow, foreigners from Yangtze cities fled to Shanghai for refuge. Britain responded. "With the increasing danger of the great international settlement at Shanghai the

British Government at length announced that an expeditionary force of 16,000 men, in addition to the volunteer guards of the settlement and the detachments of the warships in the river, would be concentrated at Shanghai as soon as possible, the greater part of the troops being brought from England, to protect British life and property from a possible reoccurrence of the mob action at Hankow and to restrain the fighting armies from entering the soil of the international settlement."
◆ Frank Moore Colby and George Sandeman, editors, *Nelson's Encyclopedia, Vol. III*, (N.Y.: Thomas Nelson & Sons, 1907), looseleaf March 1927, p. 98.

Page 46: Weeding the lawn of a rich foreign house in Shanghai. LOC. An American missionary's wife compiled her letters from a two-year stay in Asia into a book. "The number of servants necessary to moderate-sized family of medium style in Shanghai would terrify a New England housewife, who prefers to do her own work, rather than have one Irish girl to look after. First in the list is 'the boy.' He would feel insulted to be called anything else. ...Next in position is the cook. He must have a scullion to wait on him and two table-boys who do the work of chamber-maids, ...at least one inside coolie for the menial work about the house, and one or more outside coolies who work a few hours each day in bringing water from the river. ...there is a child's nurse or lady's maid...In wealthy families this number would be increased, and a man of still higher position than 'a boy' added, a comparadore, to deal with the Chinese in buying or selling, to go to the bank or carry valuable parcels. He would receive a good salary and expect his squeeze out of every bargain or commission."
◆ Lucy Seaman Bainbridge, *Round the World Letters*, (N.Y.: C.R. Blackall and Co., 1882), p. 116.

Page 48: Feeding a prisoner in a cangue. Photo, circa 1902. LOC. An article in the *Shanghai Mercury* newspaper described this form of castigation. "It is a very common mode of punishing a thief to place him in the vicinity of the place where he committed the theft; he will have to stand there all day, for he is chained so that he cannot sit down without strangling himself, and a native emissary of the police force will keep an eye on him and bring a supply of 'chow-chow' rice to him. Thieves are often chained up this way in the settlements or in the outskirts, and have to remain at their post as a terror to evil-doers for 8 or 10 hours a day, being taken home to the police stations at night."
◆ J.D. Clark, "The Cangue and the Chain-Gang" in *Sketches in and Around Shanghai, etc.*, (Shanghai: Shanghai Mercury and Celestial Empire, 1894), p. 97.

Page 54: A bridge over Soochow canal. LOC. "Soochow is considered by the Chinese one of the foremost cities in the empire. The gates are mostly built at an

angle or 'L,' double or triple. This is owing to a belief that spirits always travel in a
straight line. When a spirit enters the first gate, it strikes the angle wall, becomes
confused, and does not get by the second gate. Still, I should think that any evil
spirit in a fair state of preservation could easily sail over the whole business."
• James H. Worman and Ben J. Worman, editors, "Lenz's World Tour Awheel, from
Shanghai to Tanyang'" in *Outing—an Illustrated Monthly Magazine of Sport, Travel and
Recreation*, Vol. 23, October 1893–March 1894, p. 430.

Page 60: A Manchu horseman. LOC. A famed British authority on horses, Capt.
M. Horace Hayes, who served in Colonial India, described the passion among
Shanghai's foreign elite for horse racing in his book chronicling his worldwide
teachings. "Our experience of the Shanghai folk, during our month's stay among
them, was that they were the most hospitable and charming people we ever met.
They all own ponies, and nearly all race. Their Mongolian ponies are reared under
very rough conditions, in their native steppes, having frequently, during the long
winter of that Siberian climate, to scrape away the snow with their feet in order to
get a mouthful of grass. Like Himalayan and Tibet ponies, they show they are wild
and not domestic animals, by, when first brought down, their habit of shying."
• Matthew Horace Hayes, *Among Men and Horses*, (N.Y.: Dodd, Mead & Co., 1894), p. 160.

Page 72: A palatial home in Shanghai. LOC. A U.S. Marine Corp member of the Asiatic
Squadron penned a book of his travels and described the view in front of Shanghai's
British Concession. "It presents an imposing front of large, elegant mansions, many of
them having beautiful yards in front, and over which fly the flags of several different
nations, showing them to be the residences of consuls. At intervals can be seen fine, broad
streets, leading back from the Bund, lined on either hand by stately buildings."
• James B. Lawrence, *China and Japan, and a Voyage Thither: an Account of a Cruise in the Waters
of the East Indies, China, and Japan*, (Conn.: Press of Case, Lockwood & Brainard, 1870), p. 175.

Page 78: The Native Quarter in Shanghai. LOC. Leaving New York City in 1909
for a round-the-world trip in a motorcar, Trenton, N.J. society maven Harriet
White Fisher encountered much during her travels. She detailed her excursion
into Shanghai's Native Quarter. "This is about the only trip where it is necessary
to take with you a private detective or guide from the hotel. We were informed
that we would not be allowed to enter this place without a guide, although we
felt no fear; but they told us that many Western visitors who had gone in there
were never heard of afterward. It gives the government a great deal of trouble

and anxiety. Our guide advised us to buy 500 coins to throw out to the people and prevent them from touching us. We were also advised to wear raincoats or provide ourselves with a covering of some kind, and to wear short skirts, as otherwise we might carry back some disease; but we were out for sightseeing, and after passing through so many experiences, this seemed a trivial affair to us."

♦ Harriet White Fisher, *A Woman's World Tour in a Motor*, (Philadelphia & London: J.B. Lippincott Co. at the Washington Square Press, 1911), pp. 229-230.

Page 82: Reclining woman with bound feet. LOC. A news review by the Equitable Life Assurance Society of the U.S. noted, "The rich Shanghai officials have started a Tien Tsu Hui girls' school for the girls of good family who have either not bound their feet or have unbound them, with the hope that the girls there educated may eventually become teachers. Although only just started, 80 young ladies are already boarding at this school, and when it finished its first term the place was packed, chiefly with Chinese gentlemen, to see the results. Thus the unbinding of the feet of the girls of China is gradually developing into a movement for their higher education."

♦ "Side-Lights on Current Events," in *The Search-Light: A Condensed Weekly of the News and Progress of the World*, Vol. III, No. 1, Jan. 6, 1906, p. 104.

Page 86: A posted order given to the Shanghai Municipal Police. Photo, circa 1925, courtesy of Regents of the University of Minnesota from the Kautz Family YMCA Archives Collection; used with permission of the Metropolitan Design Center, ymca10841-p1037. Posted in Chinese cities after the Shanghai Incident, the sign said under the command: "Do not shoot unless absolutely necessary—but if you shoot, shoot to kill". A newspaper overview of Shanghai's Mixed Court (for foreign plaintiffs and Chinese defendants) praised the Municipal Police (who also acted as court prosecutors) for their efficiency in investigations and closing cases involving foreigners and Chinese under the jurisdiction of the International Settlement. "The greatest part of the work of the police in investigating any case is to disprove all the lies told by the natives who are implicated. ...The police here have a wonderful power which could not be exercised over people at home. If they can't get hold of a man they want, it will help them greatly to take his brother, or his father, or any of his relations into custody; if any of these relations of the 'wanted' individual have a *jinricsha* or wheelbarrow, or anything that can be got hold of, the police will retain that, and tell the owner he won't get it back till he assists the native detective in finding out where the relative has gone."

♦ Clark, *Sketches in and Around Shanghai, etc.*, p. 112.

Page 92: Funeral procession. Photo courtesy of Special Collections and University Archives, University of Oregon Libraries, Gertrude Bass Warner Collection, PH014_49-26.

Page 100: Laborers boarding a ship. LOC. "It is amazing with what rapidity a heavily laden ship can have all her cargo taken out, be reloaded, coaled, and sent away outward bound. This work is done by coolies, whose whole time being occupied in it are well qualified by experience to do it thoroughly and expeditiously. The moment a ship arrives, and the hatches are thrown open, a stream of poorly dressed but sinewy men invade her at every open gangway. They are noisy but good-tempered, and every man with his bamboo and rope has business stamped on his face. ...The merchants know nothing of coolies. They have compradors, or headmen, who contract to load and unload a ship for so much. The coolies, therefore, are the servants of these men... for the coolies are underpaid and have to do all the hard work whilst their masters pocket the gains."
• Rev. John Macgowan, *Pictures of Southern China*, (London: The Religious Tract Society, 1897), pp. 23-24.

Page 106: Tennis Club in Shanghai. LOC. "Tennis is exceeding popular among Americans and British, as well as French, Germans and other continentals who reside in Shanghai. Tennis is played from the first of May until November. The clubs include the Shanghai Country Club, the Shanghai Cricket Club, the German Country Club, the Cercle Sportif Francais, the Club de Balin, St. John's University and Nanyang University. Besides these, many private residences have from one to five courts attached. The Chinese rarely play, but the native markers at the various clubs have developed great skill, and these and the students at one or two of the local foreign colleges play some very creditable matches."
• "Lawn Tennis Notes," in *Wright & Ditson's Official Lawn Tennis Guide*, 1913, p. 229.

Page 108: Foochow Road. LOC. A news account stated: "It is but natural that Foochow Road should be chosen by the bulk of Celestial *chevaliers d'industrie* for their headquarters. The light-fingered fraternity usually pitch their tents in this vicinity, where they seldom experience any difficultly duping strangers from the outlying rural districts whom they happen to come across. Charlatans, such as quacks, conjurers, fortune-tellers, and mountebanks of every imaginable description, make this street their temporary home."
• Clark, *Sketches in and Around Shanghai, etc.*, p. 53.

Page 110: *Jinrikisha*. **LOC.** A collection of personal observations jotted down "to while away some of the idle hours which hang so heavily on the hands of many

lady residents in the East" was published in a British wife's account of her time in Asia. It relates the misfortunes of a rickshaw driver and injustice. "I know there are amongst the wretched *jinriksha* coolies of Shanghai many of the outcasts of society, gamblers, cheats, opium-smokers; I know, too, that drunken sailors are sometimes imposed upon, and, I suspect, even robbed by these men. But to the most superficial observer the other side of the picture is constantly proved to be only too true, and I will venture to assert that for one honest tar who gets led astray or injured by the *jinriksha* men, 50 of the latter are cruelly beaten by sailors, and are thankful if they receive any reward from their inhuman employers."
◆ Mrs. Thomas Francis Hughes, *Among the Sons of Han: Notes of Six Years' Residence in Various Parts of China and Formosa*, (London: Tinsley Brothers, 1881), p. 287.

Page 112: Wheelbarrow travel in Shanghai. LOC. An American journalist observed: "The first thing that arrests a traveler's attention on landing is the novel mode of conveyance peculiar to Shanghai. The popular carriage is a wheelbarrow. The streets of the old city are narrow and rough, and so much broken up by bridges that this vehicle can not be used; but in the foreign settlement you find the Chinese men and women everywhere riding on wheelbarrows."
◆ Edward Dorr Griffin Prime, *Shanghai to Hong Kong, Around the World: Sketches of Travel through Many Lands and Over Many Seas*, (N.Y.: Harper & Brothers Publishers, 1874), p. 135.

Page 114: A view from Shanghai's city wall into the French Concession. LOC. Special jurisdictional powers made the French Concession a place of intrigue. Once two Japanese, wanted for espionage, fled from Chinese authorities seeking safe haven with the French. "There was evidence that they were spies, and not students, as they pretended to be, in the fact that they wore Chinese clothing and were older men than students usually are, and direct incriminating evidence was found, when they were searched at the French consulate, consisting of numerous dispatches that had been sent to the Japanese Government, and in drawings of Chinese fortifications sewed in the lining of the jacket of one of them." Turned over to a Chinese viceroy, the spies were tortured and decapitated in Nanking.
◆ *Appleton's Annual Cyclopaedia and Register of Important Events of the Year 1894*, New Series, Vol. *XIX*, (N.Y.: D. Appleton and Co., 1895), p. 134.

Page 116: A Shanghai barbed-wire entanglement barricade. LOC. Such barriers were used in the International Settlement.

Page 118: Carrying cotton. LOC.

Page 132: Amusements at a Shanghai park. LOC. Retiring from public life following a noteworthy career which including being N.Y.governor, a U.S. Senator, and Secretary of State under Abe Lincoln, William Seward documented a 14-month worldwide trip involving time in Shanghai. "Our lady-friends at home will be interested in knowing that all China furnishes not one mantua-maker or milliner. The dresses for the ladies come on orders from Paris, London, or New York. Native women have no need of European costumes. The work here of the seamstress and tailor is done exclusively by men. They come to your house and execute your commands quickly, patiently, and cheaply, and in doing so they faithfully copy every pattern you give them, and omit nothing. We are inclined to think that the story of the American merchant who ordered a dozen pairs of yellow nankeen pantaloons, and, sending as a pattern a pair which had been torn and patched, received 12 pairs similarly patched in execution of his order, is not altogether an invention. "
• Olive Risley Seward, editor, *William H. Seward's Travels around the World*, (N.Y.: D. Appleton and Co., 1873), p. 110.

Page 138: The home of a wealthy Chinese. LOC. A 6-month stay by an American missionary included chronicling women's issues in China. "In Shanghai the sight of wealthy Chinese driving through the streets in handsome carriages, with gorgeously apparelled coachman and footman in attendance, is so frequent as to excite little attention except from newcomers. ...Handsome houses, of foreign architecture, are quite likely to belong to Chinese. Even in houses built in purely Chinese style, I have sat on an American sofa, partaking of refreshments in the shape of tea and Huntley & Palmer's wafers, listening to a stirring Sousa march issuing from the mouth of a Victor phonograph."
• Margaret Ernestine Burton, *The Education of Women in China*, (N.Y., Chicago, London, Toronto and Edinburgh: Fleming H. Revell Co., 1911), pp. 185-186.
Page 146: Shanghai temple. Photo courtesy of Special Collections and University Archives, University of Oregon Libraries, Gertrude Bass Warner Collection, PH014_33-17.

Page 148: Paying homage before ancestral tablets. LOC. "In China boys are considered more valuable than girls, because they continue the family name and are needed to discharge what are considered important duties, in connection with worship at the graves and before the tablets of their dead parents and other ancestors. These ancestral tablets are usually small rectangular pieces of wood... with characters written on them, such as *ling wei*, 'seat of the soul,' together with

the name and office of the departed. The tablet itself is not looked upon either as supernatural or sacred, and it is only during the time of worship that it is supposed to be occupied by the spirit of the departed one who is being worshipped."
• "The Church of Scotland Home and Foreign Mission Record," in *Publication Offices of the Church of Scotland*, January 1887, pp. 537-538.

Page 150: A wall dragon. LOC. Missionaries in China often wrote books and magazine articles. "A few weeks ago, close to our English 'model settlement' of Shanghai, such superstition was illustrated by a ceremony, the most grotesque: before commencing the work of a new road beside the river, the dragon guardian of the [Whangpoo], as well as the earth god, must be propitiated; according on the breaking of the first sod, Whang-Tao-Tai, chief magistrate of the native city, with his subordinates, offered sacrificial worship to the divinities in question on a temporary altar beside the river. Furthermore, a public apology was read to the dragon for the invasion of his hitherto peaceful retreat, while his spirits were besought not to drag the workmen into the water in revenge for such turbulence of his domain; the document was then solemnly burnt, and its ashes cast into the current."
• Howard B. Grose, editor, "The 'Gods' of China," in *Missions: An International Magazine*, The American Baptist Home Mission Society, January 1910, pp. 632-633.

Page 158: A ferry ride. LOC.

Page 164: A congregation of beggars. LOC. "I was sorry to see that the foreign policemen in the streets of Shanghai ill-treated the poor low-class Chinese, or coolies, as they are everywhere called. There were several instances of uncalled for kicking and rough pushing when the 'coppers' hustled the poor natives out of the way. In all these cases a word would have been promptly obeyed. It is said that harsh treatment is necessary when dealing with the Chinese, but I fail to see how Europeans can expect anything else but bitter hatred in return for such a policy. Of course, the Chinese hate all whites or foreigners, as they have good reason to do."
• Worman and Worman, "Lenz's World Tour Awheel," p. 427.

Page 172: Chinese National Army maneuvers. LOC. "Until 1895 China had no regular troops in the modern sense. Military forces consisted of the eight Banners (composed of Manchus, Mongols, and Chinese, these Chinese being the descendants of those who aided the Manchus in the conquest of China) and the Green Flag or provincial troops. In the eight Banners were enrolled

all descendants of the Manchu forces that had overthrown the Ming dynasty; originally these were a fine body of medieval soldiery, but they have degenerated into a worthless rabble, living on government rations. As modern soldiers they were entirely useless....Careful regulations now govern enlistments, and opium smokers and other undesirables are not accepted. Military service is now looked upon with favor as an honorable profession, whereas in past years the soldier was ranked among the lowest in Chinese life—in fact, was treated with contempt."
‣ *The New International Encyclopaedia*, 2nd Ed., Vol. V, (N.Y.: Dodd, Mead and Co., 1914), p. 217.

Page 182: Japanese Army officers (in Peking). LOC. A popular historian wrote: "A high opinion was entertained of the Japanese army. Up to the time of the Franco-German war the instructors of this army were Frenchmen. The result of the war was sufficient, in Japanese opinion, to make a change desirable, and the French instructors were changed for English, German and Italian. Few of these remain, as the Japanese now think they know enough about the art of war to prosecute it without foreign assistance. The Japanese army is equipped according to the most modern ideas, and is of considerable size....The Japanese are not only well drilled and well armed, but they are brave and competent."
‣ Henry Davenport Northrop, *The Flowery Kingdom and the Land of the Mikado or China, Japan and Corea*, (Philadelphia and Chicago: International Publishing Co., 1894), p. 525.

Page 184: A roadway past Shanghai's cotton mills. LOC. The founding father of modern China, Sun Yat-sen shared his views on national socialism and called for abolishing the prevailing "spheres of influence" in a book that contained discussions of various industries. "Cotton is a foreign product which was introduced into China centuries ago. It became a very important Chinese industry during the hand-loom age. But after the import of foreign cotton goods into China, the native handicraft industry was gradually killed by the foreign trade. ...However a few cotton mills have been started recently in the treaty ports which have made enormous profits. It is reported that during the last two or three years most of the Shanghai cotton mills declared a dividend of 100% and some even 200%!"
‣ Sun Yat-sen, *The International Development of China*, (New York and London: G.P. Putnam's Sons, The Knickerbocker Press, 1922), p. 209.

Page 186: A bridge over Soochow Creek. LOC.

Page 194: The Willow Tea House in the Native City of Shanghai. LOC. "Perhaps the object of greatest interest to the visitor is the willow pattern tea-house which

is said to be the original of the willow pattern ware so popular in England. It is a two-storeyed wooden building of octagon shape standing in the centre of a small weed-covered lake and approached by a zig-zag bridge, which is supposed to offer an insuperable barrier to the passage of evil spirits. A delightful contrast to its congested surroundings is afforded by the mandarin tea-house and garden."
• Wright and Cartwright, *Twentieth Century Impressions of Hongkong, Shanghai, and Other Treaty Ports in China*, p. 383.

Page 210: Temple entrance. LOC.

Page 212: The Great Pagoda in Soochow. LOC. An American doctor reflected: "One of the best pagodas of China is in Soochow and from it a fine view is obtained of the city with its so-called dragon street, probably named from its winding course, though many believe that a dragon lives under it. Another noted street is called dog-bite alley, so narrow that it would be no doubt be hard to escape from an excited dog. As in all the large cities, there are public execution grounds with a stand for the magistrate to witness the beheading. The prisoner is usually summoned from jail and is at first uncertain whether it means freedom or death, but as soon as he finds a chair in waiting he needs no further notice for the prisoner is always taken to the place of execution in a chair."
• Irving Ludlow, "Observations on the Medical Progress in the Orient," in *The Cleveland Medical Journal, Supplement, January 1909*, Vol. VII, p. 561.

Page 226: Chinese gunboat on the Yangtze River in Shanghai. LOC. "The Chinese Navy in 1912 consisted of two squadrons: the Cruising Squadron of five cruisers, one destroyer, one gunboat and eight torpedo boats; and the Yangtze Squadron of 12 gunboats for river purposes. A third squadron, the Training Squadron, to consist of two cruisers, then under construction, and 10 gunboats, was in the process of formation, and a scheme of naval reorganisation was occupying attention."
• Hugh Chishhom, editor, *The Britannica Year-Book*, (London and New York, The Encycolopaedia Britannica Co., 1913), p. 978.

Page 228: Railroad train in Shanghai. LOC. A North Carolina farming advocate and editor commented about China at the end of its dynastic rule. "Until very recently, however, the Chinese have not wanted railways. Coming from Hankow to Shanghai I passed in sight of the site of the old Woosung-Shanghai Railway, the first one built in China; but before it got well started the people tore it up and threw it into the river."

· Clarence Hamilton Poe, *Where Half the World Is Waking Up*—The Old and the New in Japan, China, the Philippines, and India, Reported with Especial Reference to American Conditions, (N.Y.: Doubleday, Page & Co., 1911), p. 139.

Page 230: Railway station. LOC. An American reporter described a train trip. "Of course no self-respecting white man in Shanghai—not even the most brazenly democratic of the American colony there—would have had the fortitude to get on board a third-class passenger car. ...There were in that car evidences of the most abject poverty, of squalor, of bitter toil—a dozen examples of the hopelessness of betterment that marks untold millions in China; yet there could be laughter from the midst of it at a trivial jest. Laughter is stronger, nearer to the surface, than tears in this people."
· Carroll Michener, "Traveling Third-Class with the Chinese," in *Travel*, Vols. 26-27, (N.Y.: Robert M. McBride & Co. Publishers, 1915), pp. 26–27.

More Books from Fletcher & Co.

FLETCHER & CO.
PUBLISHERS
Every book is a journey

Every book is a journey. Fletcher & Co. Publishers is an independent, art-house publishing company. We use new media and graphic design techniques to transport you into the world of the novel. Our books aren't just written words. They're experiences: international cultures, art, suspense, history, and adventure. Watch our video trailers on our YouTube channel to preview each book, see interesting images, and learn more about our newest releases. Visit us on Facebook to find out about our latest news.

Coming Soon!

Erwin Rommel: Photographer, Vol. 1: A Survey
by Erwin Rommel & Zita Steele

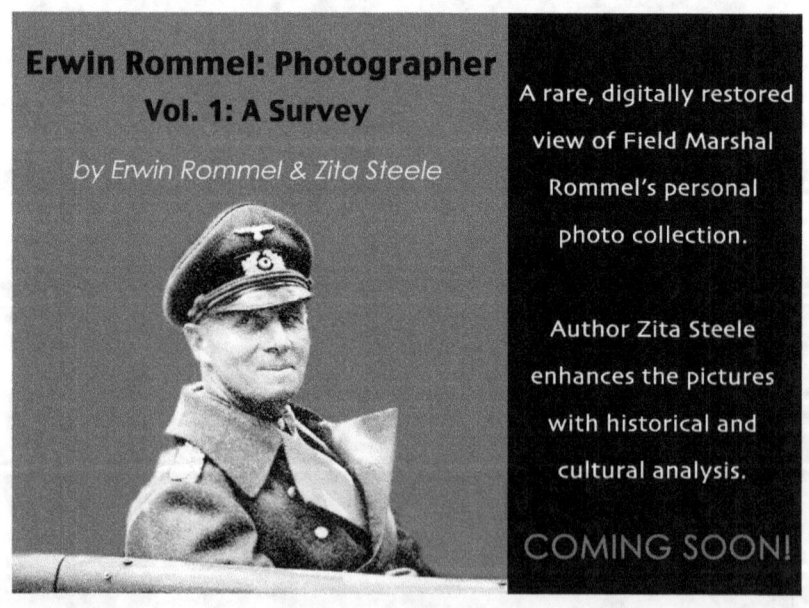

Erwin Rommel: Photographer
Vol. 1: A Survey

by Erwin Rommel & Zita Steele

A rare, digitally restored view of Field Marshal Rommel's personal photo collection.

Author Zita Steele enhances the pictures with historical and cultural analysis.

COMING SOON!

The Strange Side of War

by Sarah Macnaughtan & Noël Fletcher

THE STRANGE SIDE
of WAR

A Woman's WWI Diary

By Sarah Macnaughtan
Introduced & Edited by Noël Fletcher

Take a journey across the dangerous battlefields of a world at war.

Accompany Scottish novelist Sarah Macnaughtan as she volunteers alongside British humanitarian groups to alleviate the suffering in war-torn lands. A daring and spirited woman, Sarah encounters many people caught up in the mayhem – thrillseekers, aristocrats, refugees, diplomats, royalty and ordinary citizens.

Her many adventures tell unique stories of tragedy and triumph, taking readers on an unforgettable journey from the trenches of Belgium to the distant frontiers of Persia and tsarist Russia.

Author/editor Noël Fletcher provides new historical context that brings Sarah's story to life and helps readers to remember the bravery and sacrifice of those who died.

Illustrated with 130+ rare photos and propaganda posters from World War I, this important work features historical insights about the people and places involved in the conflict.

River of My Ancestors: The Rio Grande in Pictures *by Noël Fletcher*

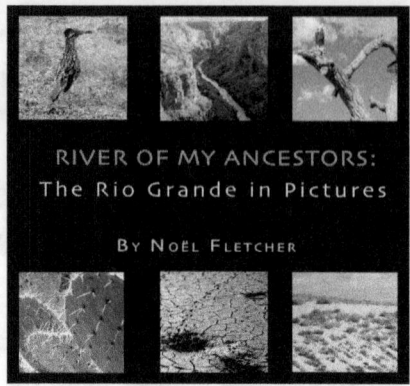

Take a journey along the wild and rugged Rio Grande. Beautiful pictures capture the essence of the famous river and its importance in the arid Southwest. Native New Mexican author and photographer Noël Fletcher provides family stories and insights about frontier life.

Follow the Rio Grande through deserts, wetlands, and rocky cliffs. Experience natural wonders, including volcanic lands and river rapids, and encounter wildlife such as snakes, wolves, cranes, and bighorn sheep. With 180+ striking color photos, This captivating book combines vivid photos and the written word to tell a living history of the famous Rio Grande and the beautiful desert land of New Mexico.

Two Years in the Forbidden City *by Princess Der Ling*

This true story was the first eyewitness account of the Imperial Court written by a Chinese aristocrat for Western readers. It provides an up-close personal view of the notorious Dowager Empress Tzu-hsi in the final years of her reign. Illustrated with 100+ historical photographs, illustrations, and paintings from the late 1800s to early 1900s.

The Spy *by James Fenimore Cooper*

Take a journey into the intrigue and excitement of the American Revolution. During the dark days of the Revolutionary War, America struggles for nationhood. In the shadows, a spy is trading secrets of vital importance to the cause - but for whose side? This edition of America's first spy novel features 30+ illustrations and other material to give you a front-seat experience.

Envoy: Rule of Silence *by Zita Steele*

Take a journey into a thrilling world of secrets and lies in modern-day Europe. Polish ex-secret policeman Michal Krynski is tired of working as a double agent for France's security bureau. His last mission - to track down a runaway DJ. As he travels to the strange island of Malta, Krynski plots revenge against the system that ruined his life. Will he catch the DJ or kill him? Zita Steele is a novelist and artist. She writes with an expertise in criminology, cybercrime, and international relations. She creates her own illustrations.

The Yellow Room *by Gaston Leroux*

News of a strange crime spreads like wildfire in Paris. Someone has attempted to murder the daughter of a brilliant scientist. But nobody can explain how the murderer got in and out of the locked room of her isolated country home. Only Joseph Rouletabille, an impatient young journalist, has the genius to solve this crime. But can he match wits with a seemingly supernatural killer?

New Mexico Ghosts & Haunting Images *by Ariela Desolina*

Take a journey to the untamed Southwestern wilderness of New Mexico. Let explorer-photographer Ariela Desolina spirit you away to New Mexico, where haunting ruins - some with ghostly inhabitants - will capture your imagination. With photos from the St. James Hotel, a notorious hangout of Western outlaws and gamblers, and other mysterious locations.